“Every day i

Praise for *Makoto*

“Oriental eroticism and thunderbolts of violence.”
— John Farris

“Wilde’s prose style fits the story perfectly—it’s as sharp and polished as a samurai sword, and just as dangerous.”
— Rick Hautala, author of *Winter Wake*

“A remarkable novel, full of subtleties and compelling force.”
— Lisa W. Cantrell, author of *The Manse*

Praise for Kelley Wilde’s award-winning first novel, *The Suiting*

“Wilde handles [his] ideas with wit and energy. A skilled writer has produced an engaging novel.”
— *Publishers Weekly*

“Highly readable, with both laughs and chills. An excellent choice.”
— *Library Journal*

“[A] tasty bit of modern horror with just the right touch of madness. A writer to watch.”
— Dean R. Lambe in *The Buffalo News*

TOR BOOKS BY KELLEY WILDE

Makoto
The Suiting

MAKOTO

KELLEY WILDE

TOR
A TOM DOHERTY ASSOCIATES BOOK
NEW YORK

This is a work of fiction. All the characters and events portrayed in this book are fictitious, and any resemblance to real people or events is purely coincidental.

MAKOTO

A Tor Book
Published by Tom Doherty Associates, Inc.
49 West 24th Street
New York, N.Y. 10010

Cover art by Paul Stinson

ISBN: 0-812-50036-9

First edition: September 1990
First mass market printing: April 1991

Printed in the United States of America

0 9 8 7 6 5 4 3 2 1

For anyone who has been to New York
and lived to tell about it.

ACKNOWLEDGMENTS

Warm thanks to Melissa Ann Singer, editor of genius and guardian angel at Tor. Melissa said yes to the outline . . . then counseled and encouraged and baby-sat and questioned and suggested and was *there* for the three years that it took. She guided the book through the blocks at the pass and horsewhipped it through a long, messy divorce. She worried over paragraphs, debated single words. In the end, the book became a true collaboration. And for that, I thank her. And hope someday we are partners again.

Thanks also to Graham Weinroth for showing, dramatically, why A Woman Needs Her Exercise.

To Yasuko Iwatani for the calligraphy.

And to Lou Myles, Disegnatore—whose style inspired a novel that went on to win an award.

PREFACE

To the Japanese, *Nihongo* is the simplest, most logical language on earth. English, on the other hand, is a nightmare of maddening reversals—with verbs stuck in the middle of sentences instead of where they belong, at the end . . . with words made of *letters* no civilized soul can pronounce, instead of syllables spelled out with mere brush strokes . . . and so on and so on—or *nado,* as they say with a sigh in Japan.

This story does contain a fair amount of Japanese. But, of all things in it, that should scare the reader least. The Japanese has been, by and large, translated as the story goes. In isolated instances, footnotes have been provided.

There are, however, a few words the reader should know from the start.

MAKOTO

Sincerity, Japanese-style.

> When modern Japanese have attempted to make some one moral virtue supreme over all . . . they have usually selected "sincerity" . . . *Makoto* does not mean what sincerity does in English usage. It means both far less and far more.
>
> —Ruth Benedict

> Sincerity, that is, not-deceiving, means "putting forth one's whole being," technically known as "the whole being in action" . . . in which nothing is kept in reserve, nothing is expressed under disguise, nothing goes into waste.
>
> —D. T. Suzuki

HYAKU MONOGATARI

An ancient ghost-story game, related to the *hyakki yako,* Night Parade of One Hundred Demons. To play the game, a group of people would assemble soon after sunset and light one hundred candles. They would then take turns telling their scariest tales, extinguishing one candle for every story told.

ONII

The Japanese word for brother. Very short. Very simple.

BUT . . .

The reader should be warned: There is, in Japanese, another word quite like it. And when that second word is spoken, all hell will break loose.

PROLOGUE

JAPAN: MAY 1971

No one had ever scared the girl like her brother Matsuo. And when she saw his shadow centered in the doorway, wielding the family sword, she thought: the glory days are back again. He'd returned to save her from this stretch of dreary days . . . or to help her forget—for an hour, no more—with one of his fabulous stories . . .

In the small town of Shizumi his *kaidan* were legendary, with nightmares guaranteed for weeks. Tales of vengeful *yurei,* malevolent *oni,* and other bloodcurdling demons and ghosts. No one ever got into a tale the same way as her brother.

And when he was really inside—*abunai*! His voice would change from a howl to a whisper . . . his eyes would bulge and roll and leer . . . he would circle the young girl's futon like a wolf and pounce on the edge with a scream . . .

She could not remember when brother had told her the first one. But that first year after mother died, when they landed at the Grand Hotel—ah, those were the very best. *Natsukashii,* dear glory days, the two of them against them all!

The shadow stepped into the room, swinging the sword in a slow lazy arc.

The girl whispered his name. It came out as a croak.

And brother, though he rarely smiled, seemed to as he answered. *"Kaeru-chan . . ."*

Little froggy . . . Some things never changed . . . At five the downslide had begun toward her life's deep *haji*—that special shame, her voice. The girl, just twelve, now realized that it was lower than brother's.

"Okite! Get up, we'll be late."

The morning sun, now streaming through her bedroom window, set him in a frame of light. A picture of power and grace. She'd never seen *onii-san* in uniform before. Or in, for that matter, a sling. The same shade of yellow-brown as his army uniform, the sling had at first escaped her attention. She wondered how he'd earned it and regarded it with envy; a trophy, she suspected, from some secret kendo match, with multiple casts for his partner. And though she cared nothing for soldiers or guards—and although brother was neither—her heart began to race. Towering above her, this morning he looked like a god.

With a swift and feathery movement, *onii-san* sheathed the sword—then knelt on the tatami mat at the foot of her futon, taking the quilt in his hand.

"Ichi," brother said. *That's one . . .*

The girl's eyes widened; her jaw dropped. Since mother's death the two of them had been almost *ittai,* one flesh. But, *ittai* or otherwise, brother was nineteen now, and since the last time he'd seen her she'd—

"Ni!" He gave the quilt a little tug. Instinctively, absurdly, she clutched the cloth to her throat. *Onii-san* knew that she never wore—

"San!" His arm recoiled, quilt in tow.

The girl's hands fluttered stupidly, unable to decide which part they should cover. The two budding *chichi*—their *chibusa* pink and stiff with May's morning coolness—or the fluff of black *immo* where his eyes seemed to have settled. Seemed. A little lower, actually. On the bright red droplets that stained the fresh white sheet. A wave of shame engulfed the girl and common sense was lost at sea; so she just lay there before him, drifting aimlessly inside herself.

Onii-san watched her quietly, the quilt in a heap at his side. Her eyes fluttered, as her hands had, searching for somewhere to focus. In the end, they settled on his jacket's second button. She might study it for hours.

"Look at me, *kaeru-chan.*"

"Hai," she answered. And she raised her glance to the button above, a flash of brass gleaming in the cherry blossom sun.

"Look," he commanded. "Who am I?"

"Onii-san."

"Then look in my eyes."

The girl did, though the journey was painful and slow. To her surprise, she found no laughter there. If they reflected anything, it was a special tenderness he'd never shown before. For that, the girl felt grateful.

And when he whispered, "Come, let me see you," how could she deny him? Who knew her better than brother? Had there ever been secrets between them? . . . *Saa* . . . Never in the glory days—but yes, perhaps there had been now . . . Brother had been *different* since his first year in Tokyo: sounding more and more like grandpa in his gloomy cryptic letters . . . She'd come to read between the lines, above and around all the samurai twaddle (Ah, see, he misses me although he doesn't say so! Oh, the pressure's gotten to him and he's really feeling lonely!) . . . In the end, no matter how much he had changed, they couldn't take him from her. For underneath it all they truly were *ittai*. And if it felt strange, being with him like this, her whole life had consisted of crossings from the known to the unknown.

She sailed the length of the futon.

Brother watched her as if in a trance. And when she stood before him he continued staring, her *immō* even with his eyes, black cotton candy all sprinkled with blood. She could not guess how long he stared; he did not appear to be breathing, but when he moved it was perfectly fluid and the movement had no place in time as he leaned to lick a droplet from her burning bush.

"Onii-san," the girl murmured. All of her life had been crossings, but this . . .

Slowly, and still staring, brother tugged the sling over his head, then slipped it off his arm.

The girl had a vision of perfect synchronicity as their four hands moved at once, as one: her fingers interlocking behind *onii-san*'s handsome cap, his hands—all scars and calluses—resting on her hips. The pain of moving his left arm had made brother wince, and when he looked up there were tears in his eyes. Surely, though, those tears were for her too, because her eyes were burning with tears of joy for brother.

"Aa," he murmured, "*sō desu ka*? Look, you are a woman now."

"Hai." If she could have chosen any one moment to treasure and keep, surely it would have been this. The glory days were back again, more beautiful than ever. And if the moment could not

last, she was grateful to have known it—ready, even willing, for whatever crossing came.

Brother rose, quite slowly, through the circle of her arms. On the way he paused to pray at a small number of shrines. The button on her belly was a revelation: when he kissed it she stiffened as if she'd been cut and she whispered, *"Kimochi ga ii"* . . . That feels good . . . She repeated those three words again and again as brother continued to pray, moving north, then suddenly—most wonderfully—to the east and west. When he was finished she swooned and he caught her, his lips three inches from her own. I shouldn't be so tall, she thought, I don't know when I grew like this, *onii-san* mustn't like it. But his grip was stronger than she'd remembered and through his uniform she felt brother's powerful arms. And her voice didn't matter, her size didn't matter, brother was glad that she wasn't a geisha and whatever crossing followed now she wanted to travel it with him.

"A woman . . . You're a woman now . . ." *Onii-san* kissed her eyes.

"Hai." This time the croak came out almost a whisper.

"Do you love me, *aka-chan*?"

Little baby girl . . . Brother hadn't called her that since she was four and mother died. And now she shook with tears of memory and gratitude. *Aka-chan* . . . Oh, glory days . . .

"Hai!" she answered. "I really do." And she wanted him to kiss her now and start the crossing with her. She cocked her head, parting her lips.

And the bush, burning minutes before, suddenly erupted.

"Will you always love me, though—no matter what I do?"

"Hai."

"Promise me."

"I promise."

"Say 'I hope to die, *onii-san,* if I do not love you.'"

"I hope to die, *onii-san,* if I do not love you."

"Say 'I hope to die a most terrible death.'"

"I—I *hope—Onii-san—*"

"Say it!"

"I hope to die—a most terrible death."

Onii-san nodded solemnly. He held her eyes for a long moment. Then he kissed her, hard and wet, and her world was spinning—and burning as it spun—with fear and love and desire. This broke all the rules. But when had the rules made her happy? No matter what happened, this way, *onii-san* was the first . . .

Quite suddenly, the spinning stopped. He pulled away, his breathing almost as wild as hers. For a moment, just a moment, the girl thought he looked almost crazy. But in a flash the look vanished and brother was himself again.

"Aka-chan"—he slapped her butt—"let's go before we wake them."

"Where?"

"You want to hear a story?"

"Hai!"

"The scariest story in all of the world?"

"*Hai, hai, hai,* you know I do!"

"I'll tell you then the story of The Hapless Number Five."

Onii-san insisted she wear a kimono: her ceremonial best, all in white. And, though "mother" would kill her, the girl did not care.

The glory days were back again—the two of them against the world!

Brother stared across the lake. Beneath the mustard jacket his massive shoulders scrunched. From behind him, where she knelt, she felt the tension travel from his shoulders to her heartbeat along an invisible wire. And when she thought she heard him sob, she knew that this morning was special. A tale that pulled out all the stops.

Until this morning she'd never imagined the lengths that he'd go to, to set up the mood.

From his dramatic appearance . . . to his perfect, perfect silence on the walk to this, their secret spot ("*Onii-san,* where are we going?") . . . through resort Shizumi's sleeping streets ("Isn't that a uniform from the Tatenokai*?") . . . past the fork in the road at the edge of the town ("But the Tatenokai no longer exists!") . . . across the bridge beneath which carp waited to outwit the town's still-sleeping fishermen ("*Onii-san,* you never told me: were you in the Tatenokai?") . . . and on along the white sand beach to the cherry blossom grotto that overlooked the lake ("*Onii-san,* what are the swords for? Will you teach me some more kendo, then—new tricks you learned in Tokyo?") . . . every step of the way had been perfect—so sinister, mysterious . . . Yes, today's tale would be the best ever, for sure!

The girl resettled her weight on her heels, a square red cloth between the earth and her white kimono. The faintest breeze had just started to stir, rustling the petals strewn on the grotto's floor. In a few more days cherry blossom time would be a distant memory. But today these too were props, the air both sweet and bittersweet with blossoms and decay.

Brother's shoulders eased into place. He took a few good long deep breaths. And then he turned to face her.

"It was a magnificent morning . . ." he said.

---

*The private army formed by novelist Yukio Mishima (1925–1970) in 1968. Disbanded after his death.

* * *

It was a curious story.

He had taken her out of Shizumi to the military base in the heart of Tokyo. May in Shizumi no longer existed. Now it was November, a sunny day with a north wind blowing, the last day in Mishima's life.

Helicopters whirred and whirled while soldiers scurried through hundreds of hecklers and stunned Japanese. Above them on the balcony brother stood, hands on hips, reciting Mishima's last rantings.

"It is a wretched affair," he cried, "to have to speak to soldiers in circumstances such as these . . ."

The girl fidgeted from knee to knee, ill at ease in a new kind of way. The only thing she wanted now was for *onii-san* to stop. She liked his stories better when he pulled them straight out of the air. Murder, plunder, madness, torture: anything would do—so long as there was nothing to it. What she missed this morning was the element of play.

Or maybe what she missed was the certainty of play. Or a tone to get a grip on. Brother seemed to have crossed an invisible line between play and not-play.

And then, before she could locate the line, he crossed it again to purr, "Relax. Whatever happens, it's only a story."

"*Hai* . . . Whatever happens . . ."

"Good." Brother held her eyes, then winked. And the girl settled back with a sigh.

"It was as if I'd tapped into the sun. I felt the truth, plain and simple, filling me with strength and light. And the truth was, quite simply, that I'd really do it. There was no doubt, I was going to die!"

Maa, there he went again . . . The voice that told her this was flat and cool and disembodied. It came from somewhere further out, perhaps within the lake. With a shiver, she whispered, "It's only a story . . ."

"*Aa* . . . Good girl . . . That's the spirit . . . Anyway, where were we? . . . *Sō* . . . Yes, it was all very simple. The time had come to teach Japan a thing or two about honor. So I raised my right arm to the sun. 'I salute the emperor! *Tennō heika banzai!*' Then, without another look below, I sprang back from the parapet and entered the room in a couple of strides."

The grotto now became the barricaded office. General Mashita sat motionless, tied to his chair, surrounded by four Tatenokai . . .

Brother marched straight to the fourth—and set down the long sword before her: three feet of razored steel with a double-handed hilt, inlaid with black and white diamonds. *Onii-san*'s eyes were burning.

" '*Aka-chan,*' I told him—"

What?

" '—don't leave me in agony too long.' "

It's only a story . . . only a story . . .

But how could she remember that when *onii-san* himself kept forgetting?

His features had settled into a mask of deadly concentration. As he spoke, *onii-san:*

—undid the brass buttons of the Tatenokai jacket . . .

—stripped briskly to the waist . . .

—unlaced his boots, then tossed them aside . . .

—and knelt, placing his watch beside the dagger at his knee . . .

"Mite," *onii-san* commanded. "Look. Do you see how simple everything is? Logical, easy, and neatly arranged. The watch goes here, the knife

goes here . . . like pieces in a puzzle. Mishima Sensei took a breath—how sweet the air tasted!—and then . . ."

Brother loosened the clasp of his trousers, sliding the waist to his knees . . .

—eased down the white *fundoshi* thickly coiled about his loins . . .

—massaged a small spot on his belly . . .

—slipped the foot-long *yoroidoshi* from its ancient sheath . . .

"And I motioned for Morita to take his place behind me."

With his hair cropped short, almost to the skull . . . with splendid muscles pumped and rippling under a layer of sweat . . . and with that mad, eerie look in his eyes: brother *was* Mishima now.

"*Onii-san,* stop, you're scaring me!"

"The great sword lay between them, its blade a bridge between the two. And a love that could not be. Mishima looked at *aka-chan.* You took up the sword . . ."

"Brother, I don't like this story!"

"*Makoto!* I tell you, you took up the sword!"

Makoto, makoto, makoto! That one word, the difference between them . . . The reason why she was a child—and he would always be *onii-san* . . . *Makoto:* going the distance, no matter what, to the end . . . even if just in a story . . .

Gingerly, she touched the sword, her palms already slippery. She tightened her grip as *onii-san* had shown her—almost as if one were wringing a towel.

"It's only a story . . . only a story . . ."

Onii-san held the dagger at the small spot on his belly. He capped his right hand with his left, grimacing as the arm started to shake. Brother looked at his arm and again the girl saw a certain something in his eyes. For a moment it seemed possible—

"Will you ruin my story, then?"

She advanced, two tiny steps. He shook his head. She took a third and then a fourth.

"*Onii-san,* let's go now."

Brother laughed, the old laugh, the old look in his eyes again. "So you think *onii-san* has truly lost his mind?"

"*Iie.*"

"You think I'll ever forgive you if you ruin the ending like this?"

"*Iie.*"

"Morita, that brave soldier, took his place behind me."

Slowly and despondently, the girl followed brother's instructions.

"Morita raised the mighty sword."

Brother's shoulders rose and fell in a series of deep, measured breaths. The muscles in his back bunched into powerful clusters. Then, when the sun threw the sword's shadow over him, his whole body seemed to relax. For a long time brother did not stir and the girl thought the tale might have ended. Before she could ask him, though, he turned his head a quarter. Not enough to meet her eyes, but enough for her to see that he was smiling. Finally. Really and completely.

"*Oshiete.* Tell me. Did you really think I'd kill myself?"

"*Iie!* Never, not for a second!"

Brother turned his eyes back to the lake. "*Totemo ii* . . . Very good . . . But there's just one thing missing . . . Hey, what's a good story without one?

"*SURPRISE!!!*"

The cry flew through the grotto like some savage, crazy bird. And before she could be certain of just what was happening, he had plunged the dagger in.

Or had he? . . . No, he was always tricking her, with twists and turns and horrible faces . . . And the jolts and spasms she saw now . . . the rattle that came from the back of his throat . . . these were just more of his special effects . . . Brother, dear brother, always the clown . . .

Suddenly, *onii-san* screamed as the dagger flew out of his belly . . . or seemed to . . . his right hand dripping bright red. He moaned and moaned and screamed again, a pale echo of the first "*Tenno . . . heika . . . banzai!*," driving the dagger back in. A part of her mind still clung to the hope that it was still a story . . . that brother had outdone himself with the spasms and rattles and splatter . . . And as she scurried around him, she thought, They do have movie knives, the sort with the blade that springs in when you stab . . . And, of course, there's movie blood and—

"*Ten-nō . . . heika . . . ban-zai . . .*"

Brother jammed the blade in a third time. And it was here that she started to scream, waving her sword in the air like a wand. His face was already as white as a corpse's; his eyes, empty yet focused on keeping the blade in his gut. His right arm, though powerful, lacked the strength alone. Entrails and muscles united in a desperate alliance as brother once again encapped the right hand with the left.

"*Onii-san!*" the girl wailed.

But brother was beyond her now, in the center of the Void. In his eyes appeared a look of almost inhuman resolve. Suddenly his left arm rippled and flexed into life as both hands hammered home the dagger and started cutting sideways.

The girl paced and looked and averted her eyes

and muttered and cried to herself and at brother, the great sword shaking in her hands.

By the time the dagger made its way across his belly, the blade was cutting shallowly again. *Onii-san* studied the tip, slippery with blood and grease, before the knife slipped through his fingers. For a second the bleeding appeared to have stopped and the girl thought that brother might still be all right. Much too much blood had been lost, she knew, and the cut was too long and too deep and too cruel. But brother was stronger than most men and maybe—

Brother was full of surprises, he'd—

Suddenly, *onii-san* began to vomit fiercely and his belly opened, screaming, like a mouth. And with this final, silent scream, blood splashed and entrails flew. The girl felt something like a slap as the scream sounded red on white silk.

She called his name over and over again, pacing doubletime. Brother sat, soaked to his knees, on his heels with one hand on the ground. At his side, the left arm jerked in quiet little spasms. In books he had shown her she'd seen pictures of ghosts with eyes like his right now. And haunt her he would if she failed to . . . She had to . . .

The girl tightened her grip . . . like wringing a towel . . . just as *onii-san* had shown her . . .

"Isoide," he whispered.

Hurry . . .

She shuffled around to his side, where she stopped. Brother's head, too heavy now, had lowered, exposing the neck.

One good cut . . . He'd shown her how, with thousands of test cuts at melons and ropes . . .

"Makoto . . ." he begged her, *"ma-ko-to . . ."*

There was no decision now . . . It was brother's will . . .

To die, begging on his knees, would be complete dishonor . . .

The girl steadied the sword, bracing her feet in a solid front stance. If she failed to do this single thing . . .

The sword started, almost without her, and just might have made it.

If only he hadn't kissed her like that . . .

"Onii-san," she cried, "*dekinai!* I can't!"

A raw smell filled the air—pungent, overpowering—followed by another smell as brother's bowels burst.

For the rest of her life, she knew, she'd remember the last look in his eyes.

And the awful word he spoke.

The short word that sounded, a *little,* like "brother."

A SUMMER'S END FORETOLD

NEW YORK CITY: JULY 1985

Saa . . .

So close and yet so pathetically far.

So very close to the window . . . Shackled, though, so artfully that the distance, six feet, might as well have been miles. The lengths of chain that bound her to the vast four-poster bed had been tested and retested time and again. She could shift her position a little and rest half on either side. But her wrists had grown raw from her struggles to reach the gag he kept stuffed in her mouth. On her neck she wore a collar studded with faux pearls. And through a ring attached to it he'd rigged another length of chain. This allowed sufficient slack for her to view his marks: the burns and punctures on her breasts—from his interrogations. And, at first, she had looked, till revulsion outpowered the last of her hopes that this could not be happening.

So close to the window. So close to the light.

The light of understanding, too. Looking in his haunted eyes, or hearing his mad accusations, she could not help but think: What a natural ending . . . Guilty as charged . . . A bad wife . . . A traitor . . . And ready to die . . .

But the end was as close, and as far, as the light.

She heard his footsteps on the stairs.

And knew he wasn't finished yet.

PART ONE

PASSIVIST

MAY 1985

ONE

Shadow images of pink and white creamed against the sunlight melting on her half-closed lids. There were moments, sometimes hours, when Motoko half imagined that she'd never left Japan. Two Sundays in particular, in late May each spring, New York seemed almost worth the list of everything she hated: graffiti-splattered subway cars . . . young toughs with ghetto blasters . . . garbage blown down filthy streets and from the mouths of cabbies . . .

And if the cherry blossoms here were only a pale imitation, still they carried her home in a powerful rush that lingered for months in her mind. A mist that swept in and swept out like the tides, washing over the filth of the city, bringing her back to Shizumi. Back to the grotto. Back safely before—

She closed her eyes completely, the lids light as butterfly wings. No pressure now. No tension.

That's it, easy, *yasashii.* No wishing, no guilt, no regretting.

The mist was back and working now and taking the city away. She was home again, back in Shizumi before—

before brother and—

Mishima and—

before—

before—

before—

"Hey, miss?"

Motoko felt the mist begin to slip away again. The city was like that. Relentless and tricky. Waiting ever patiently for cherished illusions to pass. When you opened your eyes, there it was, as it was. In the rough and proud of it.

Noo Yawk . . .

But Motoko had her Exercise—infinitely varied—and if nothing else her patience might rival the city's. In time, with luck and cunning, the mist might be evoked at will. And variations—mixed just-so—might succeed in holding it close until the worst had passed.

Special Exercise, Variations 3 through 6. By degrees, her rocking grew more pronounced, until either way Motoko teetered on the brink of falling. The porcelain geisha as bean-bottom doll. But the mist had left her now and even through closed lids the city lights were coarse and brutal. Motoko stood still and felt forlorn, wondering what to do.

She felt a tugging at her sleeve and heard the voice again, "Yo, miss!"

Two black boys loomed before her. One, in studs, spiked gloves, and chains, shouldered a wall-sized boombox. The second had a boxer's face, with flattened nose and scarry eyes beneath a steel-gray, jailhouse toque. But the smile, shattered by two missing teeth, was tenuous and shy.

"O-hi-yo?" the boy said to her. *"O-hi-yo . . . zymahz . . ."*

Motoko bowed deeply, wanting to leave. She'd seen that look too many times in the years since *Shōgun*. But what she was was in her blood and so she murmured throatily, *"Ohayō gozaimasu."*

"We was wondering if you was okay, miss. You rockin' like a rockin' chair."

"I'm fine," Motoko managed. "Fine."

"You not lost or nothin'?"

Motoko nodded, instantly perceiving her mistake. "The Chink is lost," the first boy said.

"You dumb nigger, watch your mouth—can't you see she's Japanese?"

"Japanese . . . Chinese . . . Where you goin', babycakes?"

"Don't call her babycakes, that's rude. You call these ladies Nee-hon-jeans!"

Motoko cursed her foolishness and wondered once again if she would ever master this impossibly intricate tongue. Americans enjoyed their jokes about "backward" countries—the British drove on the wrong side of the road, Asians wrote from right to left—but what could be more backward than saying yes when one meant no? In *Nihongo* things couldn't be simpler. *Aren't I going to the store? Yes, I'm not . . . No, I am . . .*

Motoko shook her head, erasing her reversal. "Not lost. I'm not. Really." This last word came out "Rearry" despite hundreds of hours of practice and she felt her cheeks turn scarlet.

The two boys exchanged a look, then gave her another.

"She all right," the first boy growled.

"Foxy," said the second. "You sure you gonna be okay?"

Motoko nodded, loosening the muscles in her

neck with a once-over psychic massage. Special Exercise, Variation 27-B.

"I know the way," she answered. "I am in New York now."

The first boy chuckled darkly. "Huhhhhh! Baby, you in Brooklyn."

"I hear that," the second said.

Motoko bowed and slipped straight into *Shōgun*, with an almost bell-like croak. *"Dōmo, arigatō gozaimashita."* Thank you for all you have done . . . Such a difficult gift to repay . . .

The second boy said, "Yeah . . . Oh yeah . . . *Dōmo ring-a-toe,* man."

Motoko knew the way, in fact. The Double R train was an old, retarded, and disfigured friend whom she could not abandon. Even though it shamed her, it scared her much less than the others. Undoubtedly the dirtiest, and arguably the slowest, train in all of New York City, it rattled and creaked from south Brooklyn, in a varicose vein through Manhattan, under the East River, and onward to the pits of Queens: Astoria, her *uchi* . . . Home . . .

There were faster ways to travel. Motoko had figured them out on the map. On paper they were child's play compared to Tokyo's underground maze. But the transfer points were perilous, with endless halls, confusing signs, trains marked poorly if at all. Even *onii-san* might have been beaten by Times Square at eight in the morning and crushed at any time of day by the filth and the stink in the trains.

In time, she guessed, she'd graduate. But for now the Double R, revolting but reliable, made all the stops she needed for the limited map of her life.

At Fifty-seventh, the train curved right, putting

more rail between it and the Upper West Side. Motoko approved. It was too far to walk, despite its fabled attractions and Michael's disapproval. ("Pseudo-funky-artsy chic!")

Fifth Avenue . . . Fifth Avenue! . . . Fifth Avenue by taxicab and limousine and buggy . . . With Michael . . . Always with Michael . . . To Cartier's . . . Saks . . . St. Patrick's Cathedral . . .

Lexington . . . The last stop in Manhattan: only steps from Bloomingdale's . . . from their penthouse and nights at Lutèce . . .

"Watch the doors!"

Motoko did.

The overhead speaker repeated with crackling intensity, "I said watch the doors!"

Motoko watched them harder.

"Hey, you turkey, watch the doors!"

Motoko watched fiercely. When the doors finally closed, she settled back, relieved of her memories of Michael.

The Double R, packed firmly now, burrowed under the river to Queens. The lights flickered, failed, brightened to half, flickered, darkness washing over the sorely splattered walls. Most of the markings were nonsense, she knew. She had seen two vandals once, wielding their spray cans like pistols. When they opened fire—on glass and metal, seats and floor—the look in their eyes had been gleeful. And when they left, no one could doubt that their aim had been right on the mark.

Motoko lowered her eyes, New York–style, and studied the still life of shoes on the floor. No high heels or wingtips here. They'd left those behind in Manhattan. To right and left the floor was filled with canvas shoes and sneakers, work boots and synthetic pumps. Her new Reeboks stood out in comic relief, like two yuppies slumming in Woolworth's.

The Double R ricketed into the light, then stretched into Queensboro Plaza, where it emptied by half in a shuffle of shoes that unveiled the faces.

She'd come to know these portraits well: the waiters and students and doormen and maids drawn to affordable rents.

Across the aisle, a little Greek boy regarded her intensely. She tried to meet his eyes but failed, her gaze falling back to her Reeboks and the pleated navy dress with two thousand cherries on it.

Special Exercise: the Pure State: total concentration. Motoko willed her eyes to rise. Slowly, by degrees, they did, from the boy's black sneakers . . . to his corduroy pants . . . to the yellow jersey striped with pink and splotched with ice cream chocolate . . . to the cute—oh, *kawairashii!*—small mouth that started to smile and then—stuck its long pink tongue out.

His mother knuckle-rapped his skull.

And Motoko—Special Exercise—*would not, would not, would not* cry.

Grand Avenue never failed her: from Thirty-first to Twenty-first was her private street of dreams. A thoroughfare of donut shops and realtors and fruitstands, many with names she could never pronounce, not one of them not badly needing new paint or fumigation from the smoke that packs of Greek men left behind.

Mother might have liked this place: pronounced it, even, *yasashii:* simple like she was and gentle and warm, though grandfather and grandmother—and, of course, *oya-san*—that "stepmother-person"—would never have set foot here. This was not the Old Japan.

At Twenty-third, the shops gave way to rows of finely kept houses—duplexes of dark red brick with white trim and gold awnings. All with gardens and trees in the front. Exuding warmth, security, and the glowing sense of home.

At Twenty-first, the feeling grew. Approached from this perspective, rather than from the next station, with its platform elevated over fifteen lanes of traffic, her apartment seemed to share some of the glow, to seem less remote, less in exile.

Twenty-first was wide and plain, a far cry from her street of dreams. But it had been available and, like the dreary old Double R, it would have to do for now.

Astoria Boulevard . . . *Maa, maa* . . . Special Exercise: Variations 35 and 36 . . . Motoko rotated her hands at the wrist and shook them briskly at her sides until the blood was humming. The intersection had cracked Michael up the first time he'd driven her out here.

("Fishbein's Variety Store? . . . *Fish*bein's? . . . Oh look: a Greek pizzeria! . . . And the Papadoupuolopalis Coffee-Donut Shop . . . How nice . . . You're really stepping up in the world . . . Have to write your mama-san, sorry, *second mother* . . . What's that? . . . Oh right, *oya-san* . . . Lookie, lookie, check that out!" He'd cleared the intersection and pulled over to the right, where half a fenced-in city block had grown waist-high with weeds. "Oh yeahhh, that's really mahhh-velous. Way to go, Motoko." Michael eased the red Mercedes on to watch a crew of fattened Greeks tearing up the walk. "Number fifty-three . . . We're getting warm . . . I can hardly wait . . . These people all look so—you know? . . . Forty-nine . . . Forty-three . . . Thirty-seven . . . Oh, no! Let me guess! . . . Mo, Mo, say it ain't so, how could you be so *droll?*" Michael's inner calculator had been right on the mark. And when he stopped, his grin was triumphant and slick. His laughing eyes shifted from 25-B to the lot across the street. The cemetery with some hundred-odd headstones.)

"You get used to it," a deep voice said.

Motoko looked over her shoulder, then turned, smiling and, yes, bowing, deeply and reflexively, one year in America and still bowing everywhere she turned. Still bowing like a chambermaid in the Grand Hotel.

"You get used to most things," Ben Shacklette continued, the light breeze moving through his long white mane like fingers. He stroked his beard and gave Motoko a lingering glance that seemed at once thoughtful and mournful. "Hell, some days at my age it seems almost inviting. If you know what I mean."

Motoko nodded solemnly, murmuring "Yes" and "*Sō* . . . I see."

Her neighbor, who towered above her even with his stoop, leaned in a little to equalize their statures. The mournful look had left his eyes. His nose, a few inches from hers now (Americans! Americans!), curled, somehow boyishly, up at the tip. His skin, too, was smooth as a boy's; around the eyes, unwrinkled. And Motoko realized how changed—and charmed—life might have been if grandpa had been—more like this . . .

Ben tilted his head to the right, toward Motoko's ground-floor apartment. "'Course, getting used to some things doesn't always work, you know. Take the couple who lived there before you, at number 25-B. The Alvarezes, I believe. Nicest couple, Mexicans, you'd ever want to meet. They were crazy about the apartment, you know, but—" Ben glanced quickly to the left, as if to ensure he was not being watched. Then he turned back to Motoko and blinked.

"One night Mrs. Alvarez—did I mention that

she was a smoker?—I guess it wouldn't matter much if this wasn't the story I'm telling you. But one night Mrs. Alvarez—who was, in fact, a smoker—had some trouble sleeping. Their bedroom was this front room here—same one you use, I'd imagine—right behind those curtains. And Mrs. Alvarez was lying right beside her husband Mister. It was three A.M. Maybe four. It's a little hard to say. But Mrs. A.—that's Alvarez—was tossing and turning a storm. When suddenly, quite suddenly, she felt overtaken by the most curious, compelling sensation."

Ben Shacklette paused dramatically. The theatrical touch wasn't wasted. Motoko's heartbeat quickened. Her eyes opened and stayed open wide. One or two of the twistier sentences had lost her in the middle, yes. And Motoko couldn't fathom, really, "tossing and turning a storm." But Ben's voice was majestic.

And she understood enough to know: this might be, with a little luck, a radical, major *kaidan*.

"Where was I?" he asked her.

"Sensation!"

"Ah yes." Ben Shacklette straightened his stoop a good inch and threw a sly look at the window. "She was overtaken by the strangest and strongest sensation. Too weird for words. Too far out to believe. And yet too wild to resist. While her husband snored and slept, she swung her legs over the side of the bed and eased into her tasseled pink slippers.

"She slipped on her flowered blue robe and padded to the window. She tapped out a cigarette from a fresh pack of Camels. She flicked her Bic . . . lit her thumb . . . and smoked it half to the knuckle, smoke rings blowing from her ears. In her bones she knew the terrifying scene that would greet her eyes behind the purple curtains . . . Yet her poor hands were powerless, even with the smoking thumb, against the queer gravitational suck—oh, dear Lord, where was I? That last sentence lost me completely."

Motoko redirected Ben, repeating softly, "Queer suck."

"Right. Well, supposing we say 'pull,' then? The queer—the strange—gravitational force that pulled her hands to the curtain.

"The poor dear hesitated, frozen like—a statue, her fingers curled around the hem. She thought she'd caught a moaning sound—like a whisper—from across the street. Like this . . ."

Ben rolled his eyes while rotating his head and keening very softly, the pitch at low A on the Japanese flute.

Motoko nodded, spellbound, inhaling the mist to her Reeboks. *"Sō . . ."*

Ben's eyes stopped rolling and locked into place like berries in a slot machine. His head settled into a medium loll. And his body sank into the pits of his stoop as if the bones above his waist had clattered to his feet.

"Just then," the old man murmured, "something very strange occurred. Of all the strange things that had happened so far, this was certainly the strangest. The world stopped outside her window. What I mean, of course, is it seemed to. That is, if you know what I mean."

A moving van roared by with an angry blast of horn. And a cab, left behind in the cinders and dust, howled its hurt obscenely.

Special Exercise: the Pure State: Subvariation 2. Motoko closed her eyes and heard the bubbling of Shizumi streams. And suddenly even Ben's voice sounded stooped, though he raised it attempting to reach her.

"Excuse me . . . Miss? . . . Motoko?"

She nodded, just barely moving her head.

"I'm fine," she whisper-croaked. "Okay. Please to contin— Please continue."

"Can you hear me okay?"

Motoko nodded serenely.

"You sure?"

"*Hai.* But more lower is better, I think."

"I see. You mean like this?"

"Oh yes!"

"All right, nice and easy then. But you should open your eyes for the next part."

"I'm fine."

"Oh, you really should, though. The end is always better when you see it coming."

Subvariation 2-A. Eyes shut with eyes open.

"That's better. Now, where were we?" Ben's blue eyes were twinkling.

"World stopped," said Motoko.

"Ah . . . Yes, the world certainly did. Mrs. Martinez—"

"Alvarez-san."

"Why, yes, of course. Of course she was. Frozen right there at the window, the left one—"

"*Migi,*" said Motoko.

"Eh?"

"Right window," she corrected him.

"Why, so it was, but on our left. Behind the purple curtain. With her hands, I might add, still attached to the hem and her thumb still smoking. Suddenly, quite suddenly, the world started up with a vengeance—with wave upon wave of those terrible moans. 'Ohhhhhhhh . . . Ohhhhhhhh . . . Ohhhhhhhh!'"

Ben Shacklette rose a good eighth of an inch with each otherworldly moan.

"At first, she thought she'd heard a solitary moaning. Which is spooky enough, if you know what I mean, at two o'clock in the morning."

"Three."

"That's exactly right. Daylight Savings Time. Now then—just a second—"

"Ohhhhhhhh!" A low moan escaped her that brought a smile to Ben's lips.

"Yes, that's it, exactly. That's exactly what she heard. Only now it was so powerful it sounded like a choir: "OHHHHHHHH!"

If Ben hadn't straightened completely by now, Motoko couldn't picture how much further he would go. At the moment he looked like a very young man made up to look like an old one.

He raised his hands before him, twisted so the palms were out and holding the hems of the curtains. "A lightning bolt lit up the sky like a Roman candle. Thunder followed, a low rumble that grew like the gods playing bass drums. And then the damn sky cracked and *roarrrrrred* with a cosmic and deafening *BOOOOOOOOMMMMM!*"

Ben's eyes lit up as if fired by a sudden blast of lightning.

Just then he might have straightened out to six feet two or three.

Motoko looked up, thrilled to the soul, as Mrs. A. whipped open the pair of purple curtains—

"—and the damn sky cracked again, this time cracked right open, rain by the oceans proceeding to fall. And from the tiny cemetery wave upon wave of the terrible 'Ohhhhhhhh's'—"

"Ohhhhhhhh!"

"Ohhhhhhhh!"

"Ohhhhhhhh!"

"—came at her in procession. When suddenly—believe me now—faster than she can believe to this day—an 'Ohhhhhhhh!'—"

"Ohhhhhhhh!"

"—very much like the others turned into a shattering *'EEEEEEEE!'*"

Across the street a Pinto piled into the rear of a Dodge.

"And in another bolt of lightning, Mrs. A. saw the hands reaching out from the graves—"

"Wonderful! That's wonderful!" Motoko clapped and bobbed her head and bubbled like a schoolgirl. The Variations and all Subs, beyond her imagining.

Ben Shacklette froze, arms outstretched, and looked at her with wounded eyes.

"That's not exactly the effect that I had in mind."

Motoko giggled nervously, uncertain what to say.

"Then again, I suppose, an old man should be thankful if anyone'll listen."

Poor Ben . . . *Kawaisō* . . . Only five six now . . . a few inches taller than she was . . . Old Ben in gray jogging sweats, the maple cane hooked in his pocket . . .

"It was wonderful," Motoko said. "You are plo—professional."

"Only problem was," Ben said, "it didn't *start* to scare you."

Motoko took a moment to consider her reply. Finally, she ventured, "Different things . . . maybe . . . scare the Japanese."

"Like what?"

"*Wakaranai,*" Motoko said. "I honestry—I rear—"

"Honey," Ben Shacklette told her. "Relax. I don't know the first thing about you, but this is New York City. And you don't apologize to *anyone* for who you are or how you talk. You just be yourself, okay?"

"Thank you," she said. "*Really.*"

"You all right?"

"I felt a rit—a little chill."

"You'd better get inside then. May weather still gets a bit tricky."

Motoko bowed. Half thankfully, half to steal a moment to stop the tears from starting.

"Child, when you bow like that you make me feel like dancin'."

Motoko giggled nervously and followed with a half bow.

Ben matched it, mock arthritically.

"The world needs more Japanese women," he said. "Hell, *I* need more Japanese women!"

"Thank you . . . Thank you . . ." *Dōmo* . . . This difficult thing to repay . . .

"You take care. And if you ever need a friend, or just someone to talk to, my door is always open."

Motoko's ears pricked up at that and she made a mental note. *My door is always open . . . My door is always open . . .*

Motoko said thank you and bowed and was gone.

The front door had been crafted of brick-thick finely detailed oak. Motoko locked it behind her.

The hallway, roughly three by six, was lightly papered, freshly cleaned, and lit around the clock. Within this inner sanctum, Motoko felt inviolable.

For, at least, six days a week.

From above, she heard the start of the familiar soundtrack: the drunken Sunday rumblings of her neighbor, Cotter Sloan.

Only Sundays. But all Sunday long.

"What?" he screamed. "Oh, really? Well, isn't that *wonnnnn*-derful, you fucking bitch?" A glass shattered, pinkering in a spray down the steps to the door.

She slipped her key in the lock, in a funk. She had met Cotter Sloan several times in the hall. On Sundays, as it happened. And she couldn't recall meeting any New Yorker who frightened her more. There was something, just something about him. More than his size—he looked smaller than Ben. But, ramrod straight and wild-eyed—as if his spine were welded to a burning iron cross—he seemed, not just taller, but like a rocket about to be launched. When he spoke, he looked down on her, literally. And Motoko would think, in succession, of a cobra poised and ready to strike and a drunken marine on the rip. And the things he would say when he pinned her with those sullen, Mitchum eyes.

("Well, look what we've got here. Why, it's a little geisha girl come all the way here from Japan to tame the big bad city with her sexy and civilized ways." That was the first time he'd caught her. The second time, as if in direct continuation: "Then again, you never know. Maybe the big bad city will do the taming instead." And last week he'd been swinging a huge, bloody rat by the tail. It had jumped him, he said, in the cellar, and he held up a badly chewed hand. "It's us against them and they're winning. Or, should I say us against *you?*")

Motoko's key had stuck. She fiddled some and twisted it as Cotter took the stairs in a drunken tumble, crashing hard into the door.

The key caught, miraculously, and Motoko slipped safely inside before he lumbered out into the hall.

She heard the cool click of locked tumblers; the cocky jingle of his keys. Then footsteps—light, deliberate—as he softshoed to her door. Finally, she heard—and felt—the doorknob twisting in her hand . . . her heartbeat pumping, thumping . . . and the low, menacing chuckle.

"Don't forget to lock it."

Motoko did. And Cotter Sloan began to laugh

delightedly. He laughed all the way out the door, to the street.

Motoko scurried the length of the hall, not forgetting to slip off her Reeboks, and rounded the corner in a soft rush to the bedroom window.

The purple curtains were long gone.

Motoko had covered the windows with more affordable rolled shades: light beige flecked with nubby white. She lifted one edge with one finger to see Cotter Sloan still laughing and watching on the walk. Wild eyes. Black devil-beard. He made a deep, ironic bow and walked off, laughing and shaking his head.

Well, what of it?

Let him go. New York was filled with surly men who bullied and looked down their noses.

Size was nothing. *Onii-san* had taught her.

Motoko had her Exercise.

And with luck and patience . . .

One day she would perfect it.

One day she would find peace.

For now, the doors were closed and locked and all the shades were drawn.

Except . . .

In the living room Motoko turned—with her first apprehension that things were not right.

The couch was positioned correctly . . . But—No!

She raced to the bedroom.

The kitchen. The den.

And then she sat in her cherry-tree dress and wondered for the longest time how she would not, would not, cry.

She considered Variations of the Special Exercise that she hadn't attempted for years. The magic spell was broken, though, the only unfailing thing in her life—her constant faith in this one thing—had been taken from her. And of all the other changes that she saw about her, this one truly broke her heart.

To the left, through the screen, regular as heartbeats, Motoko heard a steady sound of *Swoosh, swish! Swoosh, swish!* Above the high thicket of weeds of her yard, she saw the rising, falling swings of old Ben Shacklette's scythe. Caught a flash of a scent of pure heaven and home.

And then the tears that would not start threatened not to end.

"Ben!" she cried. "Oh Ben! Prease!"

TWO

Lucky she hadn't been there, Ben explained.

As it was, the police took an hour to come.

And when they arrived, she soon wished they were gone.

Ben greeted the team at the door. Officer Nesbitt was lost in his thirties, with a linebacker's shoulders, a beer drinker's gut, and a shaggy, brown walrus moustache. The woman, Davies, was younger but tough, with no-nonsense eyes and a hard-talking mouth. Motoko placed her accent as either Bronx or Brooklyn, and thanked God she had Ben to interpret.

"Yuh wanna taykus troo, please, miz?"

On their belts black radios crackled. Motoko imagined revolving red lights, distant sirens, a crowd at her door. (She was Japanese, you know . . . What happened? . . . Don't you know? . . . Poor thing . . . Robbed in broad daylight, can you believe it, right here in Astoria . . .)

Officer Davies looked over at Ben, who took Motoko by the arm.

"Come on, hon, let's start in front."

The front bedroom was large, fifteen feet by eighteen, with a two-chandelier twelve-foot ceiling. Her Tokyo apartment had been smaller than this room.

"Diz diz way diz mornin', miz?"

Ben led her eyes with a sweep of his own to the window on the left.

"*Was* it open this morning?" he asked her.

Motoko tried to answer, anticipating, in a flash, all of their ensuing questions. It was foolish, of course—looking back, she could see—Michael must have been waiting for months. How thoroughly like him, to wait with such cunning—knowing that she had to go . . . in cherry blossom time . . .

Motoko answered, "Making air," suddenly sick in her soul.

(She was Japanese, you know . . . What happened? . . . Don't you know? . . . Poor thing . . . One year in the country and she slipped right back to baby talk—making air, ga-ga goo—before they took her away . . .)

In the living room Officer Nesbitt parted the curtains and stared. The Bronx Babe scribbled a note on her pad, murmuring "Maykin' more ayuh. Yuh wanna ged zum bahs for duh winnuhs, miz."

Motoko turned again to Ben, the sense of supplication sweet. Someone, one someone, to turn to at last.

"She's right," the old man said kindly. "You should get some bars for the windows. I'll have a word with that landlord of yours. For all the good it'll probably do. That Daez is one smooth-talking son of a bitch."

Motoko noticed something in the policeman's eyes. He cocked his head to the left and asked her, "What's that door over there?"

Kitty-corner to the bathroom, the door in question suddenly loomed with unspoken menace.

Motoko hastened to the door, her light footsteps echoing through the sparsely furnished and high-ceilinged room.

"Security door," she informed them.

She twisted and pulled at the gleaming brass knob. Her landlord alone had the key. She slid the bolts above and below it back and forth so all could see. She couldn't get through to the basement. And no one could get in.

Security . . . Security . . .

Officer Nesbitt curled his moustache, something very much like sadness showing in his eyes. "You're new here, aren't you, miss?"

Motoko nodded once again, the sickness growing in her soul. Special Exercise . . . Forget it . . . Already half-forgotten . . .

The policeman walked off to the kitchen, its cheery mint-green papered walls fallen under an air of suspicion and gloom.

Ben followed and she heard him say, "Look, this girl's in shock, all right?"—when another, immediate voice overrode.

Something about ". . . foinuhjuh?"

Motoko stayed calm, very calm, and said "Sorry," stalling for translation time.

Officer Davies repeated, "Dey didden taykno foinuhjuh, huh?"

Foinuhjuh . . . Foi-nuh . . . Special Exer—

Iie! . . . Foi . . . Fah . . . Foo . . . Fuh . . . Fah-nuh . . . Fuh-nuh . . . Fuh-nuh-juh . . . Fuhnuh-chuh!

Motoko nodded—shook her head! Didn't . . . No, they didn't!

"Japanese-style," she answered, with a small flip of her hand. The single gesture said at once *I'm sorry* and *Please, no more questions.* Nine times out of ten it worked.

The woman looked almost impressed by the slim pickings around her: the tiny fold-up foam futon that doubled as a sofa . . . the oak end table, veteran of who-knew-how-many garage sales . . . the twelve-inch black-and-white TV atop a collapsible stand . . .

"So *dadz* Jappuhniece-tile."

Motoko nodded, thinking, No, it's what I can afford.

And I'm sorry and Please no more questions.

"Budt . . . Yuh know, idz fahnny—say, c'n I asgk yuh sumpin'?"

"Sal? Miss—er, Mrs. Leigh?"

Officer Nesbitt flagged them into the kitchen.

"Window," he said to his partner, who scribbled and muttered, "More ayuh."

"This another *security* door, miss?"

"Oh, for heaven's sake!" Ben cried.

The Stop-sign hand that silenced him signaled Police Business.

"Miss?"

Motoko regarded the door with a mixture of deep embarrassment and growing apprehension. So friendly and warm and inviting: nine minipanes of dime-store glass, the ninth pane mere inches from the twist-me-open lock.

"Whatcha wanna do's cuddem weeeeds bag dair, miz."

Motoko followed her eyes to the yard, too suddenly seeing the obvious point.

"The lady's landlord," Ben said, "is a real sack of shit. I'll take care of the damn weeds myself, soon's my back lets up a bit. They're getting close to tree size."

"Tank yuh, zir, dat'd be nize."

"Sal." Officer Nesbitt pinkied his ear and made, as if pained, small circles with his hand. He handed the Bronx Babe a small metal case. "Would you do the honors?"

The woman balked, stepping back. "Awww, c'monnnn, y'always—"

"Sal." Officer Nesbitt may have been smiling somewhere on the inside. But his voice and eyes were not. "Would you do the dusting, please?"

Motoko's inner computer often worked on Scan, singling out essential words and filling in the blanks. In this case, one word started blinking, dead center on the screen. *Dusting* . . . Her apartment had not passed inspection and now the police were going to dust!

"Sumimasen," she objected. "I'm sorry. Later I will clean."

"Say what?" Officer Nesbitt, forgetting himself, squiggled his nose like a boy lost in math.

"Prease," Motoko begged him. "*Please.* I can do the dusting." And then—oh God, hateful, this—as if the language were now pushing buttons and Motoko could only react—she bowed, first to Nesbitt and then to Davies, a mere maid again in the old Grand Hotel. "*Sumimasen,* because my apartment—"

Ben squeezed her shoulder gently. "Remember what I told you, hon? This is New York City and you're doing fine, just fine. Dusting means for *fingerprints.*"

The dusting took all of five minutes. The woman returned as her partner was attempting to finish his list.

"Take your time," he told Motoko, just barely

stifling a yawn. They had worked their way back to the bedroom and the pattern seemed to be the same from one room to the next.

Motoko pointed to the stand between the two front windows, facing her single futon.

She'd kept the small framed photo there. The pose had been a formal one, in cracked and faded black-and-white. A country girl in her Sunday kimono, wearing the requisite almost-a-smile, but giving nothing to the camera that it could not take.

Through all the years since mother's death, that photo had sustained her: an ordinary snapshot of an ordinary woman who had truly loved her. In no ordinary way. One glance was all it ever took to unlock the floodgates. Now. . .

Special Exercise . . . It's gone . . . All gone . . .

Subvariation . . . Zero . . . Lost . . .

"Dey tayk sumpin' ovah dair, miz?"

Motoko nodded miserably. "He took my mother's picture."

"Awww."

"Photo freak," Nesbitt said. "So far we've got a guy, or guys, who break in here on a Sunday afternoon, to walk off with some photographs . . ." He flipped back to the start of his list. ". . . Books—just the ones in English, nothing Japanese . . . Dishes—all the cheap stuff, but not a good Japanese tea set . . . Not the TV . . . Not the stereo . . . But yes, two dozen rock cassettes . . . One framed poster of the Rocky Mountains . . . Two more of Bruce Springsteen and Elvis . . . What about your dresser, miss?"

Motoko shrugged, still stunned by the missing photograph.

The chest of drawers, a prize junk-store antique, seemed to have been undisturbed. On top, just as she'd left them, were the glitter gifts from Michael: a gold chain and bracelet set, her wedding and engagement rings, gold and diamond earrings, plus seven subway tokens, five or six dollars in change, and three twenty-dollar bills.

"What about inside?" Ben asked.

The question astonished Motoko, who touched her lips and could not speak.

"You should check the whole place while they're here, hon."

"But"—she gestured wildly—"inside is onry crose. *Just clothes!*"

"Remember—"

"Yes, I know. New York."

Noo Yawk . . . Bag ladies pissing in telephone booths . . . Winos stretched in doorway puddles of urine and vomit and feces and teeth . . . And a friendly finger from every passing Michael clawing his way to the top of the heap . . .

This was, she knew, New York, Noo Yawk, and anything might happen here . . . Anytime . . . Anywhere . . .

Slowly, she opened the first drawer.

The second.

And the third.

She murmured first, the language relaxed, her English as good as a schoolgirl's again. "Yes. Yes. It's just fine. Everything is in order here."

Hosiery.

Panties.

Nighties.

Bras.

At the fourth drawer, however, Motoko cried out in confusion, blood flushing from her face like wine from an upended glass. She rocked back toe to heel and reeled, unable to swing back to balance.

Ben caught her in one nimble sweep. Then pulled away with his hand on his back.

"What happened, hon? What was it?"

"I think—" Motoko started. Her attention had fixed on the closets: twin walk-ins with thick sliding doors.

"Miss?"

"Miz?"

"Hon?"

More echoes as she crossed the room.

The first door rattled in its tracks, then smacked into molding.

Motoko stared.

And looked again.

And even her eyelids were trembling as she flipped through the hangers and tried to believe.

"It *was*," she cried out. "It *was* Michael!"

"It *was*."

Ben Shacklette said, "I believe you. Drink this." He'd made himself right at home in the kitchen, finding with minimal clatter everything he needed, his light chatter flowing through the early evening light. ("I do love a logical kitchen. Cups . . . Ah, perfection—exactly where I'd put them . . . Tea . . . No— Here we are . . . Say, that's even better . . .")

Motoko turned the small cup in her palm, savoring the aroma. She took a sip and turned and sighed and murmured, *"Oishii."*

"Means delicious, don't it?" He hastened to add, when she lifted an eyebrow, "Once a week for some ten years I've gone to the same restaurant. Little hole-in-the-wall in the Village. The Yamataka Kiss-a-ten. Sure not much to look at, but, Lord help us all, that soo-shee. And, oh, that tair-ee-yah-kee!"

Motoko half split a gut, laughing. "Takayama" is as common in *Nihongo* as, say, Richards. "Yamataka," on the other hand, falls on the ear like ards-Rich. And "kiss-a-ten" (say kees-sah-ten, with perfect equilibrium) sounded hysterically funny.

"*Sumimasen.* I'm sorry." She lowered her eyes and attempted a tone that grandma might have approved of. "Your Japanese is *jōzu.* Good!" Her voice cracked on the flattery. She'd never been much good at that, though the slightest pretense would drive Michael wild. Motoko felt the fingers on her right hand start to curl, then stop. A shadow movement, really. As if the Special Exercise were waiting on the stoop. She brushed the shadow away with a straightening flick. Then fell under the shadow of Michael again. And felt lost and afraid in the darkness.

"Hon." Ben touched her shoulder lightly and slid a little closer across the nubby foam. Then he did an incredible thing. He reached and in one easy swoop had her circled in his arms. The circle was light and she could have escaped. Instead, Motoko froze in total fascination. No one since mother had ever reached out and simply held her like this. Not even Michael, the night she arrived. She didn't know what to do with her hands. She caught a heady scent of soil, fertilizer, sweat . . . and had a quick impression of rock solidness and strength . . . before he let her go.

"In case you're wondering," the old-timer said, "that is what we call a hug in this here part of the world."

Motoko nodded, misty-eyed.

"Now, hugging"—his voice was low as a horn—"is useful for all kinds of things. We say hi with a hug. We say bye with a hug. We say congratulations or sorry to hear about that with a hug. Oh hell, there's a hug for anything you think of. That's what makes this country great, forget the damned economy. Sometimes, though, the words won't come for what we want to say. That's kind of what the last hug was. Something like—well, like—you know, I believe you about Michael. Even if they don't. Take care."

The police had been gone for an hour. But the walls still seemed to echo with the woman's tortured echoes ("Naooooow, 'member, geddem bahs . . . An' iffyuh ehber seedad Myegle, 'member whaddah toljuh, 'kay?"), with the walrus's grim reassurances (according to statistics, the "perps" would not be back) and his almost abstract pledge to consider the matter of Michael.

Ben tried again to explain why her husband could never be questioned.

—As a senior VP with a top New York firm, Michael was beyond reproach . . .

—With an annual income of nearly a mil . . . a penthouse on the East Side . . . a Mercedes and a brand-new Rolls . . . he seemed to have no motive . . .

On the other hand . . . Ben demonstrated with a palms-up gesture, the left palm rising to his chin, right palm sinking to his waist.

—Michael's weeks-ago threat to deport her meant nothing at all to the cops . . .

—Any prints lifted through "dusting" were useless, for nothing "of value" was taken . . .

"No value," she said gloomily. Then, suddenly grandmother's creature again, Motoko made a demibow.

"*Shikata ga nai.* It can't be helped. Ben-san, thank you for all you have done. And now you rearry must—real-ly must go."

The burble of Shizumi streams had certainly not been as low as Ben's laugh. But if she remembered right, they had been just as soothing. And in the warmth the stream began to rise up into mist.

Lower and lower than low, Ben laughed, all the way down in his *hara,* his soul.

"My sentiments exactly. But hand me that pencil there first, will you, hon, and that rainbow doohickey of paper."

"Doohickey" did not compute. But Scan fixed on "rainbow" and "paper" and followed the old-timer's eyes to the table. Upon which perched resplendently a clear cube filled with paper squares in seven shades of With-it.

The old man settled the cube on his knee. Squared it off fastidiously. Raised the pencil to his lips and gave the point a little lick that made Motoko want to squeal with pleasure and amusement. Ben . . .

Her neighbor started printing in slow, deliberate numbers, each one exquisitely finished before starting on the next. The performance astonished Motoko, as did the incredible contrast between the fastidious script and the old man's gnarled and weathered hands. The hands of a peasant—who wrote like a monk.

Ben handed her the vermilion square. The seven numbers on it had been centered to perfection. With, it seemed, exactly equal spacing in between. The paper was a work of art and Motoko studied it with all due respect.

712-1941

"The magic number," Ben said. "Honey, that's the hot line. Now, you be sure to keep it, 'cause someday it's gonna be worthless."

"Wow." Whoops. *"Dōmo."*

Ben smiled and sat for a moment, still and quiet as a tree. Then he handed the paper cube to Motoko.

"I'll take Michael's number. If you don't object."

"Oh no—"

"Oh yeah. Yeah. You write it down." The old man tapped the cube, a stretch of fuchsia coming up.

"Ben-san, now, you rear—you—"

"Hon, like I keep telling you. This is New York City. Hell on earth for most of us a good seventy percent of the time. Tolerable, maybe twenty. But on rare occasions—ten percent and not one more—the city has its moments. Me, I'm a ten percenter. And if you'll let me make this call, I guarantee it, you'll be too."

"But Ben, you don't know Michael—"

"And hon, I'll tell you somethin': your Michael don't know *me*." Ben shot up now, all the way, and instantly regretted it. He doubled half over, one hand on his back, the other wielding the cane for support. There was nothing old or weak, however, about Ben Shacklette's eyes. They were burning as he spoke.

"I guess I'm a comical poop in some ways." Ben waved Motoko's objection aside—scooting his hand, on the double, to the center of his spine. "My back makes a couple of sounds in the morning that sound just as bad as they feel. My knees pop. My ankles swell. Can't move my goddamn fingers right. And half the time getting out of a chair takes more courage than I've got. But I'll tell you somethin' else." A mighty rap of cane on floor. "In all of New York City, I'm the last man *that* man *ever* wants to mess with! Hell, I've got moves that— Son of a bitch . . ."

Ben's right hand started shaking. He squeezed the cane and steadied it, dolefully shaking his head. "Never learn . . ."

He stood there a moment, looking tired and senile; a geezer dressed, absurdly, in Everlast sweats and Adidas. Then he added softly, "I *will* call your Michael, though. And he will *not* bother you."

"Ben—"

"Uh-uh. You just trust me."

Motoko heard a car pull up. The engine purring quietly outside the front window.

Ben Shacklette pricked his ears. "That'll be your landlord. Mr. Wonderful, Henry Daez. Only son of a bitch in the whole history of creation who can slam a car door smoothly."

Ben had hobbled halfway through the kitchen when the doorbell rang. He raised his finger to his lips. "I'll just slip out this way, honey, if you don't object."

The bell rang two times in succession; then once more as an afterthought.

"You might say there's no love lost between the World's Greatest Lover and me."

Ben paused, just a second, his hand on the knob. Long enough to read the question in Motoko's eyes. "Let's just say it has somethin'—to do with respect for another man's wife . . . Anyway! Don't be a stranger. You need anything at all, just—"

One long steady ring sent him out the door. And Motoko bowed and turned to meet the World's Greatest Lover.

THREE

Henry Alfonse Daez, freshly coiffed and manicured and scented with Obsession, made thoughtful, sympathetic clucks as Motoko related the break-in. Now and then Daez would roll those long-lashed, dark brown eyes of his and make an almost mournful "Tch." Or make a small note in his black leather pad. Or thank God again he was just passing by.

"Your mother's picture. Oh, my my."

At the bedroom door, she paused, suddenly conscious of status.

Motoko said, "Prease," and allowed him to pass her.

"If you don't mind my saying so, you've really made this place your own. Very clean and simple. A nice touch, those plants, Mrs. Leigh."

"Oh. *Sō*. Mr. Dy-ez."

"Day-ez. Call me Henry. Please." The landlord's voice itself was really unremarkable. As hard to get ahold of as was the man by the telephone. But the tone was pure velour and pitched at a seductive purr.

Motoko answered, "Henly-san," squirming just a little.

"Now, doesn't that feel better?" Daez's eyes were warm, concerned, beneath the coal-black arrangement of waves artfully tossed back and blow-dried. His strong nose was straight as an arrow, slightly hooked at the tip over loverboy lips, flanked in turn by two Kirk Douglas dimples and a Cary Grant cleft in the chin.

Motoko answered, "Yes. *Sō.*"

Daez leaned in a little, his face a few inches from hers now. His breath was cool and peppermint sweet.

"I'll bet you can do even better. This time no *san.* Just Henry."

Motoko had turned twenty-six. Lived in two countries. Been single and been married. Learned three hundred Subvariations of the Special Exercise. And yet she blinked and came unglued, so eager to say the right things.

(My door is always open . . . Hi . . .)

"Hen-ry," said Motoko.

"Right! And would you mind—well, I feel a bit shy—but may I call you Motoko?"

"All light," she just managed.

"Motoko," he repeated. "Boy, that sure makes me feel better. You know what I feel like, Motoko?" Daez slipped the long thin pencil slowly into the ring on the side of the pad. "I feel like you're one of the family."

From upstairs, a resounding thump. Followed by a crash. A cry. The sound of someone weeping.

"Whoops. I'll have a talk with Mr. Sloan."

"Prease—no!" The thought was more than she

could bear. Sloan had been here long before her. There would be disharmony.

"Nonsense," Daez told her. "I own seven buildings—that's a total of eighteen apartments—but all of my tenants are family. And, in a family, when there are problems—you talk." Daez was really purring now and Motoko's mind began to drift to thoughts of what he ate. "Well, now that you're part of the family, I think—I *think* I can ask you a question."

"I see," said Motoko. Not really. But still.

"*May* I ask you a question, Motoko?"

"Prease do."

"Now, this question is very important. So, please take your time and consider."

Motoko nodded solemnly.

"All right. If you're ready now. The big question's coming up . . . Come on, Henry, out with it: May I have a glass of water, please?"

Daez set the glass down, cubes tinkling, and half turned, knees facing Motoko's. The black trenchcoat had been folded, far more precisely than she could have done, twice lengthwise—from the outside in—and then again, this time in half, so that the satin lining showed. And the Armani label. He draped his arm over the back of the sofa, intimate vibrations oozing from his every pore.

"Now, I guess you're wondering why I invited you here," Daez said.

Motoko nodded slowly, though in truth her head was spinning. Too much had happened in one afternoon and she'd heard enough English to last her a month. And without the Exercise she couldn't slow the English down. Scan overloaded, in a funk. And the jokes passed by like streetsnots, with their tongues out and thumbs in their ears.

"Relax," he said. "A little joke. You see, when I said— You okay?"

Scan zeroed in. And filled the whole screen with a red letter whirligig.

DIZZY!

"I'm fine," Motoko murmur-croaked. "I think I have been tired now. I mean, I think—"

"Of course you do." Daez tweaked her shoulder, biceps rippling at the bands of his short-sleeved polo. Gold chain softly gleaming on his neck through a thicket of curls.

"Well, shall we get *to* it, then?" Mild fanning of his knees. Double-pleated nubby slacks—baggy *almost* everywhere—with a healthy bulge discreetly semipacked and coiled.

Motoko said nothing for seconds, ignoring the curl of her fingers again. Hoping and hoping that Daez would go, that he hadn't been sent here by brother.

The landlord shifted, five degrees. He crossed his left leg neatly, hitched the fabric at the knee. "Remember what I said before? About how important it is that we talk? I'll bet even in Japan you've heard of New York landlords."

"Welrl . . ."

"Oh, you don't have to say a word. I know our reputation. But I don't let it get me down. I work hard. Six days a week. And I know I'm one of the Good Guys."

Scan singled out "reputation" . . . "get me down" and "good guys" . . .

Daez waited a second. Then coached her, his left knee beginning to swing now. "Suppose we have a little talk—about what you *really need*."

He printed in block letters:

BARS

Daez impressed Motoko with a total transformation to the landlord she'd first met. She wondered where that one had gone to once the deposits were paid. Enter, then, the Invisible Man. Mr. Never Reachable. Except on the first of the month for the rent. Mr. Gosh-I'm-sorry-dear-I-never-got-your-message-and-I-really-like-your-hair-like-that.

Well, Claude Rains was out to lunch. And Henry Daez, Good Guy, was back and on the job.

"Follow me, Motoko. I want to show you something."

The landlord glided catlike from the sofa to the bedroom. His haunches rippled as he moved, tapering to a fine tight ass. At the left window he stopped and gave the shade an easy rise. Then stepped back to admire the view.

"You know what I see when I look through that glass?" The pencil flew in lightning strokes across the clean white page. He turned the sketch to

Motoko: an almost pastoral cartoon that filled her, unaccountably, with a sense of peace.

"That's beautiful," Motoko said.

"That's *freedom,*" Daez answered. "Moonlight in Astoria, a clear view from your lovely apartment. Your window open, just an inch, for a sip of cool night air; no worries, no troubles, just freedom . . . peace . . ."

"Yes," Motoko sighed. "Oh, yes."

"Now, when I mentioned bars before you were thinking Alcatraz. Am I right or am I wrong?"

Motoko figured out the question and said, "Yes, I think you are," her eyes heavy-lidded, desperate for closing time.

A light whiff of Obsession. Daez's warm inviting eyes. A small tattoo she hadn't noticed before, half hidden by his sleeve. Dragon's tail of red-blue blurs on Perma Tan.

The pencil moved light as a shadow.

"Now, there are bars—and there are *bars.* And what I want to show you now is real sophistication. I mean bars that say 'Keep Out,' but say it with an *accent.* Am I right or am I wrong?"

The picture, finished, came at her in waves.

There were bars—and there were *bars.* And there were bars that were not bars, but messages from midnight tides. Powerful and rhythmic. Regular as heartbeats. *(Dōki . . . dōki . . . dōki . . .)*

Daez smiled happily and tucked the pencil over his ear. "Well, don't keep me in suspense! Do you want these or Alcatraz?"

Motoko couldn't stop herself. She touched his arm. And held it. And pleaded, "Henly—*prease.*"

"Don't thank me," he said, minutes later. "In fact, I hate to say this—but I can see how some might say I should've done this sooner. I guess in some respects, though, I'm a little bit like you. Naïve."

Scan raced, as it often did, searching between the words for undetected humor. A sardonic or sarcastic twist.

Daez's eyes, though, matched his words. "Still living in the past. That's me."

(My door is always open . . . Hi . . .)

"Well, times are changing, eh, Motoko? Let's change right on with them. That's two sets for the bedroom . . . one each for the living room, kitchen, and den . . . Oh yeah, and a miniset for the kitchen door."

Motoko said "Thank you" and then added "May I?" glancing at the leather pad.

And Daez—was he blushing now—tore the sketches loose along the perforated edges.

Motoko bowed deeply to catch a short breath. For the day had been a long one, filled with surprises and much too much English, and the corners of her mouth had begun to fail her. Crumbling on the consonants. Bivouacking on the vowels.

Oh welrl . . . Rearly . . . What the helrl . . .

"Thank you," she said slowly. "*Dōmo.* And now, I'm sinking, Henly-san, you weerly have to go."

"You're right. My wife'll kill me. Here."

He scribbled numbers on the pad. Then more just below them.

"If you need to reach me after hours, this is what you do, okay? The top number's my answering service. That's the number you try first. But in a real emergency, use the second number and that'll get you my beeper." Daez snapped his fingers, a castanet click. "Am I one of the Good Guys or what now?"

Motoko, half-dead, bowed and said, "Thank you, Hen-ry. Very much. And now, I sink—I mean—I—oh . . ."

At the door, the World's Greatest Lover returned for one last quick appearance.

"I hope you don't mind if I mention this. But you *do* have an astonishing figure."

"Not at all," Motoko said, meaning every word of it. Her small breasts had never gotten in the way. And though her hips were as slim as *oniisan*'s, her legs were really far too long, her feet were like a child's.

"You serious?" Daez cried. "We're talking *Penthouse* and *Playboy*."

Motoko felt those fingers curl. She straightened them and told him, "Welrl . . . Once I had an Exercise."

"Must have been some exercise."

"It was—Special," she allowed.

"I'd like to see it sometime. —Oops!"

Somehow the notepad had slipped from his hand.

Motoko caught the pad at his right knee. Using her tiny right foot. Instantly regretting it, she raised her foot to ease the pad from two prehensile toes.

Daez said nothing, but stared at her foot.

And she knew that she *shouldn't have done that!*

Oh, *baka, baka*—stupid!

"It's like my mama used to say. A woman needs her exercise. Well, good night, Motoko."

"Good night. Hen-ry. *Dōmo.* Thanks."

Motoko was turning the lock when he knocked, one light-knuckled set of three.

"One last word, Motoko." Daez, almost whispering, pointed to the other door. "Not a word about our little talk to Mister Cotter Sloan."

Motoko nodded heavily, desperate to be alone.

"He gets a little crazy—but he wouldn't hurt a fly."

On cue, all hell broke loose above. A china cabinet maybe, upended and bashed on the floor (pine caving in with a groansplintercrack). Cacophony of glassworks in all phases of disintegration: from crack to shatter and sprinkle to spray. Pictures on the wing and crashing—maddened blinded birds—into walls like windows. Mister Cotter Sloan shrieking, *"Are you fucking satisfied?"*

Silence then. A thump and slide, like a long heavy sack being dragged on the wall. Then a good heavy bump on the floor.

"There he goes," Daez said. "Out like a light for the night. You leave Mr. Sloan to me. Trust me: he's one of the Good Guys."

FOUR

(Good guys . . . Pleased to meechuh . . . Hi . . . My door is always open . . .)

Motoko sat, lotus-style, on the inch-thick crimson rug. The only possession of Michael's that he had allowed her to take. Insisted on it, actually. The color, he'd said jokingly, had changed when she arrived and somehow appeared to be bleeding.

Where mother's picture used to be, two votive candles flickered. Their shadow shows were thrown, now and then, in relief by comet lights of passing cars. Beside the candles Motoko had placed the pictures she'd studied for hours: the wavy and hypnotic bars . . . the moonlit plot across the street . . .

Midnight now. She'd been sitting for hours. Stripped down to bra and panties of matching ultracrimson that seemed, in the dark, to bleed into the rug. The color had started to give her a kick.

Both heady and low-rumbling. Motoko's little secret. Oh, wouldn't it be nice to be . . .

Her thoughts began to stray again, a herd of agitated sheep. Cowgirl Motoko rounded them up till not a curl was uncorralled. Or a ghost of a Subvariation.

No Michael . . . No Daez . . . No burglaries, rapes . . . No threats of deportation . . .

Scan raced through the universe of alien expressions that she had heard today. Motoko's memory had always been—at times to her profound regret—almost photographic. And alone, at ease, like this, she could hear and repeat to perfection *all* the English she had heard. Yesterday . . . The day before . . . Or week . . . Or month . . . Twelve months ago . . . The day that she met Michael . . .

(Christ, Motoko, you're looking *good* . . .)

The problem was not with recovery. But with some central misfire. Some basic failure to relax: a stiffness that obstructed Scan's smooth inner workings and refused to allow her to focus.

The solution: here and now, cross-legged on crimson. She could not allow them to send her back home. Nor could she go forward. Until the "Oh how cute" looks stopped. Until she mastered English.

Motoko felt a red-hot flush that seared her eyes in passing and proceeded to fire her brain. And Scan began to whip right along now through the day's sequence of screens. Ignoring some. Sorting others into little stacks.

FUTURE FILE

Get used to it
Take the couple
What I'm getting at
The world stopped
A woman needs her exercise

LOOK UP

Bro
Foxy
Tossing and turning a storm
Flicked her Bic
Queer suck
Started with a vengeance
Bass drums
Yamataka?

PRACTICE/MEMORIZE

Gonna
Crazy about
You sure?
Nice and easy
I mean, hey
Not exactly
Don't I wish

Scan blipcircled from the blacks to Daez in the hall a few hours ago. When all of the lists were in order, Scan zeroed in on the constants of her nightly Practice list. She set her focus to the max. She'd get these right if it killed her.

"Ree . . ." Motoko tensed her lips, the almonds of her eyes narrowed to mere slits. "Ree . . . Lee . . . Lee . . . Ree . . . Ree . . . Lee . . . Lee . . . Lee . . . Lee . . . Ree . . . Ree . . . Rearry!" That was it! She heard it now. Felt the false configuration of the muscles in her lips. She repeated it over and over. "Ree-ree! Rearry! Ree-ree! Rearry!"—getting this sense of the wrongness into the cells of her tongue.

Motoko then proceeded with a second Waterloo. "Puh . . . Ree . . . Puh . . . Ree . . . Ree . . . Puh . . . Prease!" That was it! She heard it now . . . Wrong, all wrong—com-plete-ly! "Puh . . . Lee . . . Puh . . . Puh . . . Lee . . . Please!

Why, there was nothing to it. When she was alone like this, English was—

"A piece of cake."

Encouraged, she moved on to "Suh . . . Suh . . . Sah . . . See . . . Sah . . . See . . . San . . . San . . . Sanks . . ." That was it! She heard it now. Wrong, wrong, *completely*. "Thuh . . . Thuh . . . Thuh . . . Thuh . . . Thah . . . Thee . . . Thuh . . . Thanks!"

She continued till 12:30 at the radio alarm. The Boss, as luck would have it, was blasting on his *Born* . . . Motoko felt a tingle that began at the roots of her hair. She fired off another round, like a cat burglar grabbing a peach at the door. "Lah . . . Lah . . . Loh . . . Loh . . . Ull . . . Ull . . . Ull . . . Lll . . . Lll . . . Rah . . . Rah . . . Roh . . . Roh . . . Ull . . . Ull . . . Lll . . . Lll . . . Lock and loll . . . Rock and roll!" That was it. She heard it now. She could feel the difference.

"Right on," said Motoko.

She delotused and crossed her legs loosely. Felt little pops and ripples all along the spine. (Twenty-six now . . . Getting old . . . Her "marriage age," twenty-five, had already come and gone . . .) She took one long and slow deep breath. Brought it all the way up to her shoulders. Then on up to the roots of her hair. Held it there, blood tingling, for a good ten seconds. Then exhaled, relaxing completely.

Motoko worked her arches against the crimson rug, tilting her pelvis a little till her forehead cleared her feet. She did not move her arms an inch. She did not lift a finger. She would not have had the strength to. She had focused all the force she had along the twin knife edges of her size-five feet: to hold her position, and now rise above it. When her forehead touched the rug, Motoko really floored it: pressuring her arches through the crimson to the pine.

At the last instant she fudged it with a tiny but powerful spring. The force was more than adequate to carry her onto the crown of her head. Motoko held position, elbows cross-barred at her skull: knees fetal and close to her chest. Her body rocked a little. But Motoko smoothed it with her mind.

No city . . . No subways . . . No Daez . . . No Sloan . . . No Michael . . . No brother . . . No troubles at all . . .

A clear screen . . .

Another chance . . .

Motoko eased her knees up. Halfway up, they rocked some more. But she was almost Home now. And nothing, but nothing, would stop her tonight. She willed her knees up all the way, all the way, her legs too long, but short enough with just a little mind control, her feet too small, but they would do, toes aiming straight for heaven.

Ten . . . Blood flowing down from the soles of your feet . . .

Nine . . . Flowing down, past the ankles . . . the calves . . .

Eight . . . Flowing down past the knees . . . to your thighs . . . strong enough to carry you . . .

Seven . . . Flowing, swift and strong . . . through the thighs to your loins . . . And you *are* going home . . .

Six . . . Charged, from your loins to your hips . . .

Five . . .

Four . . .

Three . . . Yes . . . Blood flowing down through your chest and your throat . . .

Two . . . All the way to your lips . . . She used to call you *aka-chan* . . . She'll always be the only—

One . . . Blood, rich and red and strong, arrives in a rush at the door of your brain . . .

So open the door now.

Just open the door.

Mother's love—the only love that never cheated, never died, was waiting just beyond it.

Motoko took a long deep breath as *aka-chan* opened—

As *aka-chan* opened—

As *aka-chan*—

Iie . . .

No, something was wrong . . .

As *aka-chan* opened—

Come on, won't you, open—

Motoko, meditation shot, began to teeter perilously. Mother was waiting, a spot on her knee, just on the other side. Of the door that wouldn't budge.

Motoko gripped the knob and shook. And suddenly crashed to the floor with a cry.

Helpless on blood crimson.

FIVE

Friday at last. Motoko exited the Double R, discreetly on the watch for hats, as Michael had warned her a good year ago.

"Ninety percent of all subway crime is committed by blacks in their teens," he had said. "Now, you know me—hey, look at us—I'm not a racial kind of guy. But facts are facts, what can I say?" The white horse clopclopped lazily with the velvet-lined buggy in tow. Michael lit a cigarette, snapping the gold Ronson shut with some show. "And fifty percent of that ninety percent—we're talking the serious shit now: murder, rape, armed robbery, mime—is committed by blacks wearing hats."

Scan blipblipped in overdrive, catching the skeletal highlights: ninety percent . . . crime . . . blacks . . . serious shit . . . murder . . . *mime?* . . . When he talked, she *listened*. For Michael—smoothly aggressive and rich—was also a street-smart New Yorker who'd clawed his way out of the Bronx. From the tenement he was born in (first son to a drunken Pole) to the penthouse he now owned. Michael was New York triumphant over the shape in the glass. Hadn't Mikail Lejciechowski become the prince on the white horse . . . the American Dream . . . Michael Leigh? And so she'd squeezed her husband's hand, absorbing Success through the skin.

"So, the first thing you do is look out for the hats. And the next thing you do is remember: the guys who wear the funny hats are not the funny people.

"Take baseball hats, for instance. Now, a baseball hat is serious. Very, very macho, right? Guy puts on a baseball hat and he becomes Clint Eastwood. What he's saying is, Don't mess with me. Muggers just love baseball caps." Michael listed a few other hats to look out for, in a minor sort of way. Toques, porkpies, and berets . . . "Then you have those *funny hats*. You know the ones that have flaps for the ears?" Michael demonstrated, making little Dumbo ears with his flapping fingers. "My father used to wear one and I'd die because he looked so dumb. But you put a nice strapping black boy in one . . . some guy who weighs in at two hundred pounds . . . and somehow it's *different*. You ever see those fellas in the hats with arrows through them? Or the caps with little wings? Do yourself a favor. The next time you see one, if you're not with me, you just cross the street. It's weird, the guys who wear these hats have got that same look in their eyes. Like they're in on some real nifty joke they'd just love to *share* with you."

Michael chuckled darkly then, and Motoko joined him, wondering already if she should have come here. But how could she not have—how,

how—when New York to Tokyo was paved with cherry blossoms?

"Oh, one more thing, my darling."

"Hai?"

Michael had flicked his smoked butt to the street, blowing the smoke through clipped nostrils; diamond-studded cuffs set neatly on his knee.

"Motoko, promise me something, okay? Forget everything else I'm telling you, but remember this one thing. If you ever—I mean ever—see a nigger—I mean black boy—in a Mickey Mouse hat: honey, you open your mouth. And you *scream.*"

Whoooofffff!

Motoko collided with someone, a classic no-see head-on that left them both winded and chalk-faced, Motoko protecting her face with both hands. Her assailant hopscotched back and cowered in front of a turnstile.

Within a couple of seconds they had each other's measure and sailed through the amenities on automatic pilot. The man, well dressed and sixtyish, dusted himself off and grinned. Motoko recaptured his hat off the floor—the Sinatra style ("Come Fly with Me") much affected by Tokyo crooners—and offered it with downcast eyes.

The old man gave her hand a squeeze. "New York," he said and then was gone.

Motoko murmured, "*Hai.* New York."

Someone answered, "Hi, yo'self."

And Motoko did not stop to look. She scurried through the turnstile, past a table of black men in beanies and robes with serious shit-kicking boots underneath, incense burning sweetly in their heavy-knuckled hands and cool eyes saying *You, hey you,* c'mere *now, Allah loves you.*

Past the wino whizzing on the wall, having already filled up the seat of his pants.

Up the last of the filthiest stairs in the world. Concrete covered to the inch with spit and scum and snot and come and piss and gum and blood and wine.

Out of the station and into the light. Where the city came at her in waves once again. Of headlines and towering structures and hats.

BROOKLYN WOMAN SHOT IN FACE
GRANNY SHOTGUNNED OUTSIDE CHURCH
COUPLE TORCHED IN CENTRAL PARK
BABY DROPPED 100 FLOORS LIVES
DRUG WARS BLAZING IN THE BRONX
YUPPIE HANGS UNEMPLOYED LOVER
MAFIA BLOODBATH IN QUEENS BINGO HALL
DEAF NUN BEATEN WITH DEAD CAT
MICHAEL STEALS MOM'S PICTURE

Aa, but *had* he, that was the question! Was it possible for any woman to have been so wrong, even a woman as hungry as she? Could the headlines of last year have all been a joke? Had she missed all the clues, or misread them? Headlines hot and crazy now came spilling all over the page.

"CHERRY BLOSSOMS"* OFFERS HOPE TO SUICIDE'S LOST SISTER
MOTOKO SENDS C.B. A CHECK . . . REFUSES TO SEND PHOTO
MONTHS PASS . . . HOPE FADES . . . LIFE FAILS . . . THEN . . .
LETTER FROM MICHAEL FOUND UNDER DOOR
HANDSOME MICHAEL ASKS FOR PIC
DESPONDENT MOTOKO COMPLIES

---

* An authentic, and reputable, matchmaking club for men in search of Asian brides.

MICHAEL WRITES BACK . . . LIKES HER FACE!
LETTERS NOW COME EVERY DAY
DEEP-VOICED MICHAEL MAKES FIRST CALL
PEN PAL SAYS "YOU'D BETTER KNOW . . . I'M GETTING PRETTY FOND OF YOU . . ."
EMBRAZENED MOTOKO ANSWERS, "AAA . . . I LEARRY, LEARRY RIKE YOU TOO . . ."
MICHAEL STUDIES JAPANESE!
MOTOKO STUDIES ENGLISH II!
FLOWERS ARRIVE EVERY WEEK BY WIRE
MOTOKO RECEIVES DIAMOND RING IN PERSON XMAS DAY!
SURPRISE FIRST VISIT LEADS TO MARRIAGE IN ONE WEEK
HONEYMOON IN TOKYO HILTON BRINGS MOTOKO TO "BIG O"
NEWLYWEDS SEPARATED AFTER WEEKS OF MARRIAGE
ADVERTISING GENIUS VOWS TO HAVE BRIDE IN NEW YORK BY SPRING
MONTHS PASS . . . DAILY CALLS . . . NO WORD FROM IMMIGRATION

and then . . .

MAY BRINGS MARRIAGE VISA TO SISTER OF DEAD KENDO STAR
LOVESTRUCK BRIDE LEAVES ALL BEHIND IN TOKYO APARTMENT
BRIDE FAINTS AT FIRST SIGHT OF RICH HUBBY'S DIGS

and then . . .

MICHAEL PERFECT HUSBAND . . . FOR ONE PERFECT WEEK

Could the Michael of that perfect week—

But . . . If not Michael—who, then?

(Ooooooo—)
No!
(niiiiiii!)
No!

Motoko found herself at Sixth with the sleaze of Times Square well behind her. Dopers, hookers, pimps, and thugs . . . Kung fu and porno palaces: "Drunken Monkey Shaolin Monks Meet Preying Mantis Mothers" and "Debbie Does the Universe" . . . Pinball arcades beside sex shops with come shots and dildo displays . . .

The rush of headlines past her, the other rush began. Bongos in the distance . . . That drive-you-crazy beat . . . The concrete jungle rising through mist from manhole covers . . . Stone and glass . . . Steel and glass . . . The crazed heart of the city rising in sudden and furious bursts of rage to be bigger and better and just more unique . . .

A circle of mid-city landmarks stretched, sacred calves who'd pulled it off, serene in their own gross distinctions.

Ahead, the Chrysler Building, parked for all eternity. An autoerotic traffic jam of fenders, hubcaps, gargoyles, peaking in a prick of blinding stainless steel.

The Pan Am, a behemoth hive, honeycombed with rows on rows of soulless little windows for the worker bees within.

Citicorp. A squared-off clarinet on stilts. Too stuck on the high notes to stoop an inch to harmonize.

Crosstown, circling left, Rockefeller Center's RCA flaunted the chic layered look, the Farrah Fawcett of buildings. A geometric arrangement of varying states of completion, as if the builders had run out of blocks and decided to call it a day.

Crosstown, circling right, older now but still a vamp, grayer now but still a tramp, the Empire State threw back her hair and stretched her long tongue out in search of the sky's.

Within and without the charmed circle on stage proliferated footsteps . . . first tapping, then thundering, as outclassed upstarts, crazed by the competition, made their moves on crazy stilts. No roof too high. No aim too low. No print too blue to be designed. No point too plain to fancy.

The New York Telephone Building. Vertiginous extensions of creamy white and smoky gray, paging heaven, call collect, its own lines just too busy.

The Grace Building. Swaybacked, but positively rigid in its pyramidal posturing. The art of imposition raised to staggering proportions. A poker-faced curve of glass-marbled bluff, raised and raised again. And called before the curve became a homing *kamikaze* dive.

The stage itself was spinning. And the viewers spun around the stage. How lost she felt, and how afraid. How dwarfed beneath the growing weight of alien facades.

Not the least of which were New York City faces. Whites, blacks, Puerto Ricans, Haitians and Dominicans, Hassidic Jews, Nigerians and hordes of chain-smoking Greeks . . .

Maybe one in ten faces that passed her was Asian. Ten percent, at most, of these belonged to *Nihonjins*. In Japan, whatever else, one's status was self-evident: one was either native, on the inside looking out—or one was white and looking in. There were no other options. Money, status, looks aside, one either belonged *somewhere*—or nowhere at all. And this was known at once. On sight.

But in New York City, who belonged? And who could say? The main border seemed to be drawn between those who had just *come* to town and those who had *arrived.* Those who had come might have been there for years—in rags or furs, but *looking.* The *arrivistes* might have stepped off the boat.

Motoko despaired of achieving even this simple distinction. Clearly, she had not arrived. But, more and more, she'd come to feel that she hadn't properly *come* at all. She'd landed in New York. Or happened there. Or been led or drawn there.

But—

For God's sake, you idiot, watch out for the *hats!*

At Fifth she wheeled, sidestepping, to resurvey the rear.

She saw baseball caps, Ivy Leagues, sailor caps and Stetsons, fedoras, beanies, wings and arrows, blue wool toques and brown berets, and Polack Sunday Specials with their long and woolly flaps . . .

But, praise God, no mouse ears.

Safe for now, she rushed to work at New York Nihongo.

"Aaa, Shirata-san, sumimasen!"

Kazumi's voice, as always, was an embryonic bath of soothing, mellifluous vowels. The language washed over Motoko. The sound of it. The sense of it. Kazumi was sorry Motoko was robbed: not sorry just to hear it, but sorry in her very soul. Sorry that the harmony of life had been disrupted. Sorry that her presence might seem to be intrusive, although Motoko had walked in on her. Sorry as if her existence had, in some dreamy unfathomable sense, caused Motoko's misfortune.

Kazumi chanted—bell-like tones such as Motoko still dreamed of—the mist sweeping in and then out like the tides . . . back again just for a moment, to wash over the fear and the filth of the city until the streets were white as sand . . . and she found herself back in Shizumi. Back in the grotto. Back safely before—

Motoko's turn had just come up, Kazumi's amenities past. She felt the old tingle begin in her toes, the language on its way again. Relief coming on, in a well-ordered rush of sound and sense and structure. Everyone and everything in its proper place. And one's response evolving, almost automatically, from each situation. Your turn. My turn. Sorry. Bow.

Motoko heard the difference, and then felt it in her voice. Her blushmaker croak had some range to it now, hardly an octave but still with its notes. The words themselves felt softer, as some inner filter stripped them of the city's hardness, grit.

"Iie, iie, chigaimasu," Motoko half chanted in turn. It was her own fault completely. Her fault and her embarrassment at having brought such bad news to the school. She had disrupted harmony. And Kazumi's unspoken forgiveness—a circle in the circle of that sweet apology—was a debt Motoko must hope to repay.

The language washed over and over Motoko. She surrendered herself to the pull of the tides. She felt contained and confident, in a way she'd feared she might have lost. Along with mother's photograph and the Special Exercise.

"All right now, enough of that." Kazumi gave Motoko the last word in impish grins and placed a tray with a pot and two cups on the lunch room table. The sickly beige almost matched the faded plaster walls. But the green tea worked its magic even as Kazumi poured. Motoko inhaled it like incense and thought: all in all, there were worse fates than teaching Basic Japanese.

Kazumi, a full-timer—though at her most reliable when her "ex-checks" were delayed—would, no doubt, have disagreed. But Kazumi was Kazumi as wind was wind and stars were stars. And even Watanabe Sensei, doddering school president, seemed inclined to put up with her vagaries. Indeed, seemed almost eager to do so.

Certainly, Kazumi was worth every inch of his patience. Five three in her tallest heels, she was every man's dream-Japanese, with hair that half covered a pert little ass that rolled on ball bearings. Kazumi had wonderbig eyes, like a doll's, and the cutest little mouth, rounded almost comically into an undrawn bow. That face alone made hearts skip beats and drove male students half out of their minds. When she spoke, their jaws went slack at finding daddy's girl again, and women's teeth began to grind. And when she walked, Kazumi caused craned necks and major traffic jams. On a taller woman, Kazumi's breasts would have been ample; exceptionally full and firm. On Kazumi, a mere pip, the effect was Partonesque. And those white baggy sweaters drawn in at the waist (no bigger than a D-ring) were models of cunning discretion. They aroused men's curiosity. And their imagination. When Kazumi walked—heels clicking merrily—she was all waves and ripples. One imagined shadows moving on the ocean floor, and felt the sweet steady tug of the tides.

Motoko leaned in close enough to hear the hushed Kazumi, whose breath today seemed exceptionally sweet.

"What is it?" she croakwhispered.

Kazumi's answer was lighter than air. She whispered, "What did they take from your dresser? *Oshiete*—tell me, please!"

Motoko's heart regained its previous lack of composure. It started thumping dully—ga-whump, ga-whump, ga-whump—and then began to pound out loud—puh-Toom, puh-Toom, puh-Toom—as she repeated the terrible loss.

"*Aa, sō desu ka?*" Kazumi squeaked. "If they took mine, I think I'd die!"

Several times that evening Motoko thought she *would* die. Of loneliness. Or horniness. Or selflessness, confusion. A jungle of paranoid thoughts in her head, every branch and shadow filled with threats and accusations.

Motoko, neatly lotused, let it all wash over her, in and out, and in between Scan's efforts to order the day into lists.

The clock radio sounded. Billy Joel was singing "New York State of Mind." Motoko felt that old tingle again, the one that began at the roots of her hair. And she fired off three final rounds, more ripe peaches at the door.

"Leee . . . Reee . . . Reee . . . Leee . . . Leee . . . Reee . . . Really!

"Puh . . . Leee . . . Leee . . . Puh . . . Puh . . . Lee . . . Please!

"Thuh . . . Thuh . . . Thuh . . . Thuh . . . Thee . . . Thhuh . . . Thanks!"

A sudden surge of candle flame. Strong confident sweepings of shadows on walls.

The bars would be up by tomorrow.

Motoko felt a sudden surge of lightness and well-being.

She cleared her mind. She did not think of Michael or mouse ears or muggings or rapes.

She did not hear, not really, the clunking sound below her. Or the slow, sleepy shuffle that followed.

(No way . . .)

She was going to do it, go all the way Home.

She heard the murmur of her heart beneath the blood-red bra.

She took one long and slow deep breath. Brought it all the way up to her shoulders and

(Rrrrrussssstle . . .)

made her way through the paces. Arches working into crimson . . . Pelvis tilted just enough . . . Forehead, easy now, onto the rug . . . Arches through crimson and into the pine . . .

Motoko held position in the semiheadstand, elbows crossbarred and knees at her chest. She did not think of nights alone or Daez or Kazumi.

(Oooo-whuffffff! . . .)

Nor did she wonder—even now—about the sounds in the cellar. If she had chosen to wonder, surely she would have concluded: a mechanical failure . . .

(Rrrrrussssstle . . . Tinnnnnngggggg! . . .)

(Ooooo—)

(No way!)

She hadn't been Home now in nearly a week. And an ache so deep she thought it might divide her up the middle told her tonight was the time. Time to ride back on a wave of

(Plunk . . .)

total concentration.

(Tinnnnngggggg! . . .)

Motoko eased her knees up. Steady, steady, as she goes. Halfway up, they rocked a bit. But she was almost Home now. She'd been doing this for fourteen years. And nothing, but nothing, would stop her tonight.

She'd cleared her mind completely—of even this last thought to clear it. She reached her toes straight for the ceiling. Steady, steady, as she goes.

Tonight would be a perfect

Ten . . . Blood flowing down from the soles of her feet . . . Blood cells tingling with memories of Home . . .

Nine . . .

She made it all the way to Six before she collapsed onto crimson.

She lay there for the longest time, numb with recollections of the last things that Michael had taken.

A moment's silence. And then.

(Ooooo—)

And, though she couldn't be certain—(No way!)—she slipped into her sweatsuit and dialed old Ben.

The phone rang twenty, thirty times. Motoko was relentless, enough of her not caring if Old Ben was sleeping to overrule the part that did.

(My door is always open . . . Hi . . .)

On the forty-second ring, though, she finally surrendered.

The silence now was absolute.

(Maybe . . . Just maybe . . .)

(Impossible!)

(Still . . .)

She wasted no time dialing Daez's emergency number.

Two hours later, still parked by the phone, Motoko fell asleep.

SIX

Saturday. Three P.M. The agitated pacings of Cotter Sloan above her, hard-heeled shoes on knotty pine, revving for a Sunday drunk. Back and forth. Back and forth. Steady and relentless. And nothing at all from the cellar. Oh, shadow shufflings now and then. Those scratching sounds and bumps and klunks. The sound of machinery, on now and working, settling creakily into its ways. Nothing that she couldn't handle.

(**Ooooo . . . Tinklebumpklunk . . . Sighhhhh**)

No reason to sit all day long by the phone.

Daez would call her.

Ben would come home.

She'd have bars on her windows.

And, yes, peace of mind.

Four-thirty. She left a final message with Daez's answering service. The Greek pizza man barely spoke English but managed to convey three things: He did not know where Henry was; he did not care two gyros; if her next phone call wasn't an order, he would bring her a species of sausage that would cause her to slobber for more.

Five-ten. Getting late now, but in New York the world moved at a curious pace: alternating total stalls with fastforward hornhonking blurs of events.

Motoko envisioned the coming together of fragments from two sides of town.

She pictured a storekeeper gathering bars and packing them into red boxes. She saw the driver pulling out, carefully, quite carefully, to keep the bars from jostling.

She saw Daez, in a rich crimson sweater, glance, rebeepered, at his watch. Then race to his blood-red Ferrari, taking off like the devil himself.

Motoko saw wheels spinning, transporting the ingredients of a full and happy life.

Bars, bars, bars for the windows.

While there was still time.

Five-twenty. Motoko had started to doze when bells exploded on the table, inches from her ear.

She answered on the third ring, the first still clanging in her skull.

"*Moshi-moshi!* Henry?"

Kazumi chuckled highly. "*Aa . . . sō . . .* just as I thought! You're being a bad girl on weekends!"

Motoko protested; reverting, in her disappointment, to formal Japanese.

She grew vaguer than Jell-O. And far too polite.

But sly Kazumi understood. She answered with a flight of bells that circled the others in Motoko's ears.

"You can't talk now, am I right? Oh, you are a devil! And who's this Henry, anyway? But listen, the reason I phoned. I know this nice Japanese doctor . . ."

There are sixteen known ways to avoid saying no in the Land of the Rising Sun. A young maid in the Grand Hotel learned the sixteen fast, or else. And grandmother had taught her to parry, evade, and ignore with the best.

Motoko banked her answer off the nearest cushion. "Oh," she cried, "how excellent! I'm so happy for you! But can it be five-thirty now? You really have to go!"

Seven-ten. Much too late. Motoko's solemn vigil ended with the dying light. She stretched in place and rotated her neck, then circled her wrists and her ankles. Arched the toes back on both feet halfway to her shins.

Special Ex—

No-o-o, you don't.

Motoko stood, disgusted by the strength of the delusion. Another New York lunatic who thought her pockets lined with gold when all they were was empty.

She was twenty-six. And Japanese. And lost in New York City.

(**Ooooo . . .**)

And proba—almost certainly—damned to hell besides.

(**Ooooo-whuffff!**)

For a minute she just stood there staring at the cellar door. Then at the yellow Princess phone that seemed to be there just for show. Finally, she cried out in loneliness and anger.

"Why won't you answer me? Call me!"

Eight sharp. Much darker now. Motoko set the number down, willing herself not to dial. *Shikata ga nai:* not a thing to be done. The whole of Japanese history, captured in three tiny words. If she was safe, so it went, she was safe. If she was not, then she wasn't.

Either way, one did one's best and all the rest was

Karma . . .

For the moment, this one moment, she felt somehow complete in her serene conviction that really and truly

Shikata ga nai . . .

For the moment, tonight, she was safe.

Not a sound in the basement for nearly an hour. Even the footsteps above her had hushed.

Motoko considered her options. One of which made her mouth water. She smiled for the first time this longest of days and, feeling almost funky, dialed.

"Yo! Stan's Pizzeria."

"Hi—*Yo!*—it's me again."

The Greek exploded, a four-star eruption that put Mount Fuji's last to shame.

Motoko kept her left hand on her belly, a quick quality check on her breathing. Steady now. Nice and deep. In and out, no flutters. As smooth and long and rhythmic as the Greek's was coarse and choppy.

"Are you finished?" she asked him politely.

"Zxymgphh?"

"I would like to order, please."

"Xymgzpgchclbgklmp?"

"I believe so."

"Xymgzpgchclbgklmp?"

"Yes. *Yes*—exact-ly."

His guard lowered, the Greek laughed. He made a joke she did not catch and then said, "Ha! It's groovy."

Motoko concurred. *"Hai."*

"Hi!"

"*Yes*, I mean. It is. *Far out*."

"Okay, darling, now what can I do you?"

"Please send me small pizza with everything in it. And lots of little fishies."

The Greek thanked her and told her that Daez had phoned in. Oh, about an hour ago. But just between the two of them—the Greek was almost whispering—Henry Daez was a bit of a shit when it came to returning his calls.

Nine-fifteen. Motoko's stomach rumbled and made plaintive sounds, unfed since noon and frankly thrilled at the prospect of hot cheesy junk food.

She heard a car door shut in front. Then footsteps on the walk.

Clopclop, clopclop, clopclop.

Strange how footsteps all sounded the same after dark.

All of them vaguely familiar . . .

Motoko felt her system shift into basic overdrive, the roots of her hair atingle. Blood cells rushing to the bank; returning, pockets loaded with adrenaline alerts.

Footsteps getting closer now.

Closer.

Clopclop. Clopclop.

Odd. Footsteps swinging to the left. And passing through the alleyway. Pizzaman making good time in those cloppers. A ripple of ghost clops still climbing the walls as he rounded the back of the house. Clopclops nice and cool and crisp on the concrete patio. Pizzaman making a back door delivery, the lights in the front of the house being off. A kid, no doubt—just starting out—and saving his pennies for college. Grateful for a dollar tip.

Two brisk klumps of heels on steps.

Motoko raised the tip to two.

Knuckles rapping, light but sharp, in twin sets of three.

Motoko reconsidered. The night was cool. The drive was long.

A dry cough. "Duh-*lih*-bree."

Well, tonight, just tonight, for all the trouble she had been . . .

Knocks on wood.

All right, three bucks.

She called out, "Just a minute!" padding on into the kitchen. Where Michael's instructions for opening doors came at her through a megaphone installed, dead center, in her brain.

WHEN YOU'RE ALONE DO NOT OPEN THE DOOR UNLESS YOU REALLY HAVE TO. FOR DELIVERIES HAVE THE EXACT CHANGE IN HAND. BE MODESTLY—AND PLAINLY—DRESSED, WITH NO ASSETS SHOWING AND YOUR FACE AS MUCH A LIABILITY AS YOU CAN POSSIBLY MAKE IT. GIVE THE IMPRESSION THAT SOMEONE IS WITH YOU—BECAUSE SOME PERVERTS PREFER WOMEN PLAIN.

It was the duh-*lih*-bree boy.

She had twelve dollars right there in her hand.

She wore no makeup and had changed to the no-nonsense sweatsuit she'd bought in Japan. A pale gray richly suited to the life she intended to lead behind bars, if Henry ever installed them.

Three out of four down and still going strong. Motoko went the distance, calling out distinctly, "The pizza's here—I'll buy it!"

Motoko was still wondering how she might check without giving offense—when the small voice shivered.

"Pleazzze, mizzz, idz geddin' collld!"

And, well, she *had* to smile. Because the voice sounded so young and so small. A stranger, like she was, and out of it, lost. A boy who had no business being kept in the dark on a cool night like this. With the weeds in her yard halfway to her chin. The rich perfume of roses—all of them vaguely familiar—next door. Like the footsteps that all sounded so much the same. And even the voice of this boy in the dark . . . coming in as it did from the cold . . . an old friend . . .

"Awww, mizzz, yuh godda, heyyy . . ."

Motoko turned the knob an inch, pausing a second to wonder again. Perhaps just a peek through the curtain before—

The knob twisted, a swift vicious circle that brutalized her wrist. Motoko cried out from the pain and surprise. Then suddenly some lost part of Matsuo reclaimed her. She threw herself straight through the pain at the door.

The move was almost fast enough.

But this was New York City. The counterslam sent her flying in a shower of shattering glass.

Motoko landed painfully, reverse-rolling onto the balls of her feet with a muscular flip of her shoulders.

For a moment she thought she might handle herself. Scan worked from the bottom up, strobe-flashing on the details: expensive wingtips . . . aggressively vulnerable front stance, crotch a tailored "Kick Me" sign under charcoal chinos . . . broad chest heaving underneath a tweedy black wool turtleneck . . . brown bull-neck supporting a walnut-colored mask of rage: a teeth-bared, nose-flared, drumskin-tight-skin kind of fit . . .

Underneath two mouse ears . . .

Motoko gasped and raised her hands, certain *onii-san* had found her at last.

(Ooooo—)

No!
(niiiii!)
No!
Her heart stopped.
Her bladder gave.
She wept and croaked, "Oh, Michael!"

SEVEN

Michael stood there a couple of seconds, daring her to make a sound.

Then he kicked the door shut behind him, another pane imploding, and threw the mouse hat to the floor.

Streaked three fingers through the shoewax covering his face, leaving tracks of creamy skin flushed hot with anger.

Crunchstepped through the just-iced glass.

"Well, hell, what are you looking so shittyassed *frightened* about? I used the window last time, right? So this time I figured, hey, why not go the distance, eh, and come calling properly. Presto. Bingo. Here I am, one of your niggers in mouse ears. No flies on you, my darling. No-o-o. You've got the whole thing figured out: You're married to a psycho!"

Scan blipraced and shut down, shorted by the sudden force of alternating currents: his actual physical presence . . . the righteously sarcastic tone . . . the accusation blazing in his crystalline blue eyes . . .

Images came of his study, lined with books like guns and knives, all of them internalized. *Power . . . Success . . . Looking Out for Number One . . . The Art of Imposition . . . How to Buy the Perfect Suit . . .*

And all of her memories faded away: the thousand and one little put-downs and hurts that had driven her away from him, reduced to one impression. Herself as the betrayer of her own answered prayers.

Michael's eyes, projectors, unreeled a steady stream of cherry-blossom heartaches.

And his voice was the only voice that Motoko could hear in her mind. An instrument as finely honed as the razor that layered his sandy gray hair.

The Inquisition had arrived. And she wasn't asking the questions.

Michael crunchstepped to the left to swipe a vase off the table. It shattered in a spray of blue porcelain and blood.

"Stay there," he commanded.

"Mi—"

"Hey, I've been bleeding for weeks, since you left. What's a little more blood between friends?"

"Michael, please—"

"Shut up!"

Two stomps above from Cotter Sloan, who needed rest this evening for his Sunday matinee.

Michael grabbed the nearest chair, raised it back over his head like a ball, and pitched it at the ceiling. The chair fell between them in a rain of white. Encore stomps from Cotter Sloan sent more plaster flying.

"You want to play games? Fine, I know a good

one. Let's play Twenty Questions, eh? Who brought you into this country?"

"You . . ."

"Who got you your green card? Who paid for the lawyer?"

"You did, Michael. You did."

She could barely hold the tears back, the headlines coming at her now in a furious, heartbreaking rush.

"Who paid for your plane fare? Who paid for the penthouse? Who paid for the taxis, the limos, the trips? Who filled two closets with clothes out of *Vogue*?"

From her own eyes—nothing now.

From *his* eyes—everything.

Motoko felt dwarfed by her failure to be an acceptable wife. And so she answered, "You."

"You're goddamn right it was me. I was *there.* I even helped you move into this dreamy little cottage."

"Yes."

"And that, of course, explains why I hustled my lazy ass down here to Queens . . . one of those typical Sundays, you know, when I don't have a *damn thing* to do . . . and I slipped in through the window—or, wait, did I jimmy open the door—to steal your mother's picture . . . your Bruce Springsteen poster . . . and your *fucking blue jeans!!!*"

His voice now at a fever pitch, he crunchstepped in, a few furious steps, blue eyes blazing and teeth bared. Suddenly he stopped, mid-step, and glared at Motoko in stunned disbelief.

"Don't you raise your foot to me!"

"Don't come any closer!"

"You put that down this minute!"

She followed his eyes, as astonished as he was. Her right foot hung suspended, toes right-angled to the floor, heel level with her knee. The foot felt loose and flexible, almost detached from her body; her leg, like one of those long rubber strings attached to a paddywhack paddle. It had been a good long time since she had attempted this Subvariation. Not since the day she left Japan. But it occurred to Motoko—though her legs were in sore need of stretching—that she could do it, just like that. Throw her foot out like a steel paddleball and snap it against Michael's ear.

She said, "Go."

Michael eyed the floating foot. "What, have you been watching 'Kung Fu' on TV?"

He advanced another step.

Motoko did not move.

"That's good. You just fucking *stand* there." Michael threw his shoulders back. A tiny little iron man with a king-sized attitude growing by the second. If he couldn't buy it, he'd beat it; if he couldn't beat it, he'd take it to court.

"You know, I've never pushed the point, but maybe now's the time to start. *You're* the woman, *I'm* the man, and if you *ever* move on me, I swear to Christ I'll drop you. I was born in the worst part of town. —Oh, my God!"

Her husband froze, eyes wide with shock. "Mo, what happened to your hand?"

She followed his eyes to her wrist, a deep purple swollen half double. And the sight released red waves of pain that set her temples throbbing.

Michael radiated affection and concern. He seemed almost too open and lonely to see. "Hon'," he begged her, "come home now."

(Do come home to the white silk kimono . . . Do come home to the dream-designed penthouse . . . Do honor me and do serve tea to guests who grow faint from your *dōmo*'s . . .)

Motoko's foot was quivering. From the tension of keeping away from that tag.

The bloodred tag on Michael's ear.

"Don't come closer—I can't stop!"

(A woman needs . . .

a woman needs . . . !)

Michael crunchstepped, left-right-left, like a bull snorting up for the charge.

"You're my *wife,*" he told her.

"Go."

"You're my goddamn wife!" he screamed.

Motoko shook with anger. "No!"

She saw the first slap coming long before he raised his hand. But he'd hit on the magic word. And wife . . . *wife* . . . wife . . . *wife* . . . splashed in red waves on the wall as Michael started in on her.

Fronthand slaps to start with, firing his fingerprints into her skin. Then, for good measure, a backhand that loosened a fine mist of blood from her mouth.

Motoko fell, surrendering to the knowledge that it ended here, with Michael on top, screaming, *"You fucking cunt!"*

Red waves splashing on the walls.

Angry stomps came from the sky. Then a quick charge of low rumbling thunder that stopped with a series of *booms* on her door.

Motoko fixed on Michael's face, seeing worlds of angry ghosts in his screaming eyes. Her ears, ringing with his screams, heard frenzied scratchings at the lock.

"You're coming home! *You're coming home!*"

(Hi there . . .

Nice to—)

WHAM!!!

A sudden explosion of wood into wall. Footsteps

crashing down the hall with a roar for the end of the world. Michael, in a state of shock that certainly rivaled Motoko's, turning head and shoulders.

To meet the vast unsmiling fist of Mr. Cotter Sloan.

EIGHT

Blood and shoewax on the walls. Chips of pearly teeth on pine. And through the front door, slamming shut, raging cries from Michael, who'd been beaten clear back to the Bronx.

"I been in Adweek *five yeahs innarow! I god five hunnerd towsan' bugs in stogs 'n' fuggin' eye-are-ays! I wantcha mommy's pigchuh, I'll fuggin' buy it from yuh!"*

Cotter Sloan, who'd said nothing throughout the eviction, stood at the apartment door. Said "Should I?" Shrugged. Then reconsidered. And John Wayned his way out the door to the street.

Motoko flinched, unable to stop Sloan or even watch through the window.

The slides kept flashing in her brain. Sloan pinning Michael to the floor for a rampage of triphammer shots to the mouth . . . smashing his face, contentedly, against a succession of reddening walls . . . then strapping on the mouse ears over Michael's blackened eyes . . .

The show continued outside with Michael screaming, *"Bumboy!"*

Motoko could not see the slap. But even from this distance the report was awesome. The slap was followed by a squeak.

Cotter Sloan said, "You like this?"

The squeak crescendoed to a squeal.

"How 'bout *this?* This better?"

"Eeeeeee!"

"You wanna keep 'em? Don't come back!"

"Mo—I'll fuggin' geddddd jewwwww!"

Sloan closed the oak door behind him and, with a small wave and a yawn at Motoko, started up the stairs.

Galvanized, she cried out "Wait!" and scurried after her vanishing knight. That Sunday drunk. And Good Guy. Who checked his ascension midflight to turn and smile serenely.

"Let me guess. You're wondering. Where on earth I got the key!" Sloan produced a key ring from his right front pocket and made it dance and jingle. He considered the sight for a moment, nursing the full scruff of beard on his chin while he rumbled sweetly on.

"I admit it *is* a mystery. It *really* has me baffled." He studied Motoko a moment, something different in his eyes, but nothing in his tone to tell exactly what his drift was. Or what her reaction should be. "Of course—now wait a minute—yes! Wait, I think I've got it now. Could it be . . . Do you possibly think . . ." Cotter Sloan's eyes widened with wonder and excitement. "Could there be a teensy chance that maybe—that's all, maybe—these are in my pocket . . . 'cause I've just been made the *handyman?*"

The last word was snarled with such venom that

Motoko jumped in sections, beginning with her feet. For a moment Cotter Sloan loomed, six good steps above her: rapacious-looking, hooded-eyed, and eager to be on the wing. The bird of prey transformed then before Motoko's startled eyes into a musical purrbox. The very heart and soul of furry catagreeability. "Well, Lord, look at me, turning on a friend like that. Not just a friend, a *neighbor*. Hi. Guess I've had a long tough day. Guess life's just not turning out to be what I expected. Should've known—my God, I'm daft—you weren't here about the keys. You never thought for a sec it was *me*. You wanted to say—thank you!"

Cotter Sloan performing now a gross exaggeration of a Little Nipper smile. Scan, greased and out of it, was slippin' and slidin' through the maze of shifting tones. She turned to his eyes for a sign, any sign. And instantly wished that she hadn't. More comfort in a cobra's eyes.

"You scumbunny bitch of a fishlicking whore." Sloan stretched closer to the roof, sloughing off disagreeable humor and warmth. His low voice slinking through a rising bath of acid. "You Jap cunt. You slanty-eyed slut. You Yokohama yo-yo. How'd you like the little show with Iddy Mikey Mouse Ears? Not really much of a workout, of course. You already had his balls. I said to myself the first time I met him: Whoops, there goes another one! Another outstanding American man pussywhipped to an inch of his life by some bowing little geisha with ice in her heart and cash-register eyes. And a silk cunt lined with shark teeth."

Cotter Sloan stomped down a step.

Motoko cried, "Pl—"

"Shut your hole. I cleaned your house, I'll talk a spell." Sloan's cobra gaze was rimmed with fire, but the low voice snaked just as smooth as could be. "I love the way you *ladies* work, none of this women's lib shit in Japan. Fetch my slippers. Cook my rice. Clean my chopsticks. Bring my beer. Have my baby. Kiss my ass. And keep your fucking mouth shut unless you want to suck some more."

Cotter Sloan took one more step, an evil grin across his face.

"But here you are—America! All you've got to do is bow. Smile that famous inscrutable smile. And soon enough your prince will come: some rich clown who hasn't had a blowjob in a year."

Cotter Sloan took one more step, three above Motoko now.

"Some poor schmuck who just can't cope, not one second longer, with the new, aggressive, hard, ballsy Liberated Woman. You know, the one who Wants It All—and still likes her doors opened. She beats him in the boardroom. She creams him in the sack. He's distraught. He's dizzy. Is he coming, is he going, will he ever really come again?"

Sloan two steps above her now and looking as if he might mow her right down.

"You make him feel like something he hasn't felt close to in years—I mean *years:* you make him feel like a Man. You clean his pipes. You clean his house. You smile and smile and smile and bow. And then one day, no special day, he's looking in the mirror, thinking how lucky he is. And he notices something peculiar. A queer shape around his neck. Something like a collar but—how could it be, it feels so *nice*—and what's that thing—is that a chain? Why, hot damn, hear it jingle!"

Scan screaming for attention now, for a glimpse of the first provocation. What she had done. What he'd seen in her eyes that had opened the floodgates upon her like this.

Red waves roaring, high as houses, crashing on and through the walls.

(Have my baby . . . Cook my rice . . . You're the woman, I'm the man . . . Suck some more . . . Kiss my ass . . . You bitch . . . *I'll fuggin' geddddd jewwwww* . . .)

Motoko dying truly with the burning need to know)

(Ooooo—)

No!

(niiiii!)

No!

—how brother could travel so far and so sure and strike with such cruel precision . . . over and over again . . .

Sloan waved his palms before her face. Whistled. "Anybody home?" Shook his head and rolled his eyes. And said, "No-o-ope, I guess not. Oh well. I guess you got the message, eh? I *piss* on the ground you walk on. So, save the silk and sushi bull for some other sucker. Some clown who ends up with his head up your ass thinking your shit smells like roses. I helped you 'cause—Oh, Christ! I *know* you douche with Raid.

"Good night."

NINE

Twenty minutes later. Motoko sitting, lotus-style, on the inch-thick crimson rug. Beside the candles she still keeps the pictures of wavy and hypnotic bars and tombstones lit by moonlight . . . On the floor, beside her foot, Daez's magic number . . . and the long-awaited pizza—cold . . .

"Call," Motoko whispers. "Prease."

Call me . . . I'm a person . . .

She shifts her mind. She seals her mind. Stripped down to bra and panties that match the ultracrimson wave that bleeds drop by drop into her tampon.

No Sloan . . . No Michael . . . No Daez . . . No mouse ears or green cards or bigboobed Kazumis . . .

The entire ritual flashes through her mind. And this time she can see herself floating clean through to the end, through the sharp and terrible pain of her wrist.

She imagines her arches clear through to the pine . . . sees the powerful spring to the crown of her head . . . the blood flowing homeward to mother at last . . .

She's ready, truly ready, when the pounding begins on her door.

Motoko springs to the balls of her feet. She has barely recovered her balance when the pounding starts again. Louder by ten decibels.

She slips into her sweatpants, heart trapped and pounding in her throat. She tightens the Ace—

Boom! Boom!

She scrambles into the matching gray top, panicking (too much, too fast!), not so much from fear itself—*shikata ga nai, hai,* it just can't be helped—as from the lack of ritual . . . rules clearly stated and precisely understood . . . acceptable guidelines that—

Boom! Boom! The sledgehammer blows rattle the door on its hinges.

"Open up! Police!"

The voice of doom. The voice of God. The voice of Law itself.

Boomboomboomboomboomboomboom!!!

"Open, you! We're coming in!"

She turns to the window. She wheels to the door. There is no time to think or plan. The voice cannot be reasoned with. The voice cannot be stalled. Michael's Rules do not apply. She has done something terribly Wrong and *They've* come.

Boomboomboom!

Boom!

Boomboom! Boomboom! Boomboomboom!

"We'll count to three! Surrender! One!"

A last desperate glance at the window. Michael's Rules . . .

"TWO! WE'LL SHOOT!"

Boomboomboomboomboomboomboom!

There is no time . . . The time is now . . . Motoko scurries through the hall, on the wings of destiny . . .

Ready to die, yes, and willing to pay . . . But eager for some ritual, just the barest guidelines, and just one glimpse of home before—

BOOMBOOMBOOMBOOMBOOMBOOMBOOM-BOOMBOOMBOOMBOOMBOOMBOOM!!!

"THREEEEEEEEEEEE!"

Motoko whips open the door with a scream that dies, stillborn, in her throat.

The longest barrel of the world's largest gun is stuck between her eyes.

And Cotter Sloan, standing behind it, is wearing the craziest grin.

"Well, well, well," he drawls. "This was just too much to hope for. Shame. Falling for the same trick twice."

Shikata ga nai . . . Shikata ga nai . . .

Some wicked, unrelinquished part cries out in the heart of her. She feels her fingers start to curl, foolishly hopeful right up to the end.

Shikata gai nai, though . . . *Shikata ga nai . . .*

Brother is faster than she is.

Sloan cocks the hammer with a click that thunders in her ears. His nutty grin gets crazier.

"Girl, you'd better get smart, fast. Or you won't last the summer."

His gun hand begins to tremble, his eyes certifiably whacko.

And yet Motoko cannot move or think to close her own eyes.

There is no time . . . The time is now . . .

Oh, mother . . . *Oka-san* . . . I'm coming . . .

"Then again," cries Cotter Sloan, "maybe I won't last *the night*!"

And Motoko *knows* he's crazy when he jams the barrel in his mouth.

And pulls the trigger.

Twice.

TEN

"Oh Motoko, Motoko, I'm sorry!"

Henry Daez, in funereal black, gave his head two mournful shakes, pinching the bridge of his nose. He was seated, discreetly today, at the opposite end of the sofa, and had heard the impassioned recital without interrupting her once or moving more than his eyelids, to blink in sadness, disbelief.

It was Sunday and things were in order again. Robins chirping on the wire.

And through the screen behind her, the metronomic rise and fall of Ben Shacklette's scythe.

That heady, tantalizing rush, exotic yet vaguely familiar. As far as the moon yet as close as his card: the exquisitely hand-lettered note inviting her this Saturday. A special advance screening of Ben Shacklette's garden of delights.

And P.S.: Don't tell Henry.

Why?

Ben and Henry . . . Ben and Henry . . .

(Something to do with another man's . . .)

How, though?

Why, Henry was thirty years younger than Ben. And the old man had told her that he lived alone. And if Ben had ever been married . . . Motoko tried but could not Scan the obvious scenarios. The World's Greatest Lover with Ben's old wife . . . or Ben with The World's wife . . .

No rituals. No guidelines. No clues that she could fathom.

While Henry Daez murmured his stream of vague apologies, Motoko watched his eyes, his mouth, his neatly folded hands; wondered if The World's Greatest Lover had ever been there. For, Henry, though American, was positively *yasashii.* Gentle, thoughtful, kind. "I really can't tell you how sorry I am. This is just—why, it's disgraceful."

Daez waved a manicured hand at the battered ceiling, then at the ring of purple-black surrounding the Ace bandage. Then he fixed her with a look that melted her completely.

"May I be honest with you?"

"Sure."

"I have a small confession."

"Oh."

"When I got back this morning—I heard how many times you called. I felt so bad I didn't think that I could even come."

"I see."

"I thought, why not just phone and say that mother died and drop it."

Motoko gasped. "Your mother died!"

He raised a hand to stop her. The palm was surprisingly callused. "She was sick a long, long while. It only seemed sudden, you know, at the time."

"Oh, Henry."

"*Bars.* No excuses. I should've called you Friday night. I was just too busy feeling sorry for myself."

"No."

"Oh yes. It's true. I was. But—we buried mother this morning. And if you'll be kind enough to accept my apology . . ."

Motoko said *"Dōmo"* and "Thank you" and "Yes," knowing that she had been wrong. That this man was no more, no less, than what he had proclaimed to be.

Landlord.

Good Guy.

Family.

Friend.

A sudden, glass-shattering scream from above. The reupended cabinet making great headway through pine.

Motoko shot back an inch on the sofa, sealing her lips with one hand.

Henry Daez clucked his tongue and raised his eyebrows slowly, as if they weighed a ton.

"Oh my," he said. "Oh my, my, my. Will you excuse me for a minute, please?"

It lasted barely three. Motoko heard Daez's key in the lock . . . the catlike pad of his steps up the stairs . . . and the quiet "Hello? Mr. Sloan?" Silence, then a cry that sounded half surprise, half pain. Then quiet, urgent questions put to Mr. Cotter Sloan, who cried out in misery, "Yes! Yes!"

And then Daez was back, holding the gun by the barrel as if he were Sloan with the rat by the tail. He set it on the table with evident distaste and sat back, sighing and crossing his legs.

Weeping up above them now. Quiet and despondent, from the bottom of the soul.

"I think you know how important it is . . . that we keep this in our family." She followed his eyes to the oversized gun. "You and I know the thing wasn't loaded. But the cops? They might not understand. And we don't want big trouble, right?"

Motoko shook her head, emphatically agreeing, "Yes"—then correcting herself, with a furious blush.

"No," she blurted. "No we don't."

Daez shifted position, as if shifting gears. A silent humming in the air, reflected in his slow, sloe eyes. His voice, like music to Motoko. Manners straight from heaven.

(Hi . . .)

"I probably shouldn't be telling you this. I mean, in every family there've got to be some secrets. You see, about two months ago Mr. Sloan came home to learn his wife had upped and gone."

"His wife?"

"They'd been married just under a year. A really remarkable woman. Beautiful. Just beautiful. It hit him like a ton of bricks. I'd like to give him one more chance . . . if that's all right with you."

Motoko, who knew about loss, said of course, the tide pulling her gently again out to sea.

I'm twenty-six years old, she thought. I came from a good family. I lost my mother and I lived. I lost my brother and still lived, though there is no escaping. I lost myself in Tokyo and somehow I survived. Michael found me; I survived. I know four thousand *kanji*. This is my second language. But I am having *trouble* here.

(Something to do with another man's . . .)

(Hi . . .)

"You look tired," he told her. "I guess I'd better be getting along. Before I go, though, listen. I want you to go to bed early tonight. Get a good long restful sleep. Forget about last night, last week. 'Cause tomorrow night, when you get home, this place'll be a *fortress*. Come on, let me show you."

Daez led Motoko through a paint-by-number picture of the scheduled refortifications.

Bars . . . Impregnable cast-iron bars covering all of the windows, even the panes on the rear kitchen door . . . Wavy and hypnotic bars weaving a spell to protect her from

(Ooooo—)

anyone and anything that she might need protection from . . . and nobody and nothing

(niiii!)

coming in, not on her life, without a fucking blowtorch, if she'd excuse his language . . . And on top of the bars he was throwing in

Locks . . . Not just locks, but deadbolts—two premium, eight-lever Medeco deadbolts . . .

A peephole for the door . . .

New lighting for the hall . . .

"And, of course, lest we forget . . ." He crossed, in a few catlike strides, to the special security door. He slid the bolts back and forth in their housings . . . back and forth . . . and back . . .

"Remember what I told you. One person—me—has a key to this door. I can get to the basement from this side. But no one—I mean no one—can come in here from *that* side. What we're talking about"—Daez leveled his gaze—"is the closest thing you'll ever see to absolute security."

Motoko said *Dōmo* and held herself back, the temptation to run to Daez was so strong.

Oh Henry . . .

(Bars . . .)

Security . . .

A small touch of home in one spot of New York . . .

Absolute . . .

(My door . . . You cunt . . .)

"That is . . ." A small but pregnant pause. A twinkle born, a set of twins, in those sloe-ly smiling eyes. "Unless you think it was me."

ELEVEN

Inconceivable!

Outrageous!

Flashes from the Grand Hotel were still beaming at her long after he'd gone.

Not even the World's Greatest Lover could—

No . . .

True, this was New York City . . .

Still, one situation brought all men together, regardless of custom or personal creed. Daez was a Property Holder. And built into the core of *that* was a certain inviolate sense—

By the gods! If you couldn't trust your landlord, then who in the world could you trust?

Fifteen minutes later. The thought had settled in her mind with a mellow aura. She had good feelings about this last thought and was pleased that it had come to her. If you couldn't trust your landlord . . . Yes . . . This was New York City, but here and there and everywhere there still existed inviolate Rules . . .

Motoko was pouring her tea when she heard the first sound in the basement. A clicking sound, like a door being shut.

"Henry?"

Shuffle . . . Shuffle . . .

Pause . . .

Then . . .

Hell let loose in pointillist sounds like buckshot through the basement. Over here! Over there!

Rrrrrrrrusssssssstle!

CRASH!

Shuffle . . .

Shuffle . . .

MumblesomethingmaybeShit . . .

Clopclopclopclop!

Rrrrrrrrusssssssstle!

WHAP!

A shrill, almost birdy,

BLEEEEAUGGGGGHHHHHKKKKKK!

And

WHAPPPPPPPPPPPPP!

And

B l e e e e a a a a u g g g g h h h h h k k k k . . .

STOMP!

Oh my God . . .

Oh, "Henry?"

(*Bars!*)

"Henry?"

Silence.

Nothing.

Then.

Shuffle . . . Shuffle . . .

"Henry?"

Creeeeeaaaaakkkkk . . . Something coming up the stairs . . .

Motoko, frozen where she stood with the steaming kettle. Absolute paralysis; the moment, long awaited, here faster than she could have hoped for. Not absolution, but something as good. The final squaring of accounts.

The debt collected.

Darkness.

Sleep.

(**Ooooo—**)

Yes . . .

(**niiiii!**)

Yes . . .

No excuses, no regrets. Brother coming up the stairs, with grandma and grandpa behind him, to crush her completely now, once and for all.

Heart pounding, not so much with fear—

(Shikata ga nai . . . Shikata ga nai . . .)

as with the certain knowledge that brother was writing his finest *kaidan.* And it would end any second with her.

Crrrreeeeeaaaaakkkkk . . . Crrrreeeeeaaaaakkkkk

Stttttepppppp by stttttepppppp . . .

A low moan escaping from the depths of brother's soul:

"Ohhhhh—"

God!

"Grrrrroooooosssss!"

What?

The doorknob turning slowly . . .

The door opening now with a long lazy creak . . .

The head of Henry Daez materializing inch by inch, with an almost boyish smile.

"Hello there! I hope I didn't alarm you. I was driving home and I started to wonder if I shut the bolts right. Chee! Do yourself a favor, eh, and double-check them every night. You just can't be too careful."

Again, that odd smile—embarrassed, it seemed—Daez's head alone extending around the security door. "Uh, you're probably wondering . . . I don't usually hide like this . . . Actually, I need a small favor."

Motoko, still frozen, just managed to nod.

What *was* brother up to?

"As long as I was here, I thought, why not check out the basement? Uhhh . . . How's your stomach? Is it strong? I've had a little—accident."

Motoko dropped the kettle and scurried to the door, transmissions from the Grand Hotel roaring in her ears. Henry was family—*uchi*—and hurt. She had clear obligations.

"Gomen!" she cried; and pulled open the door; and stepped back with a croaktinny sound in her throat.

In his left glove Daez held the crushed, bloody corpse of an albino pigeon, one red eye fixed on Motoko. His right glove was half covered with pigeon blood and feathers. The trail continued on one shoe, with a liberal splatter of shit on the toe.

"I hate these birds. I swear to God. They gross me out completely. Have you got a bag or box or something I can put this in?"

Motoko returned with a green plastic bag and handed it to him at arm's length. Daez closed his eyes as he dropped the bird in.

"Cheez. Must've been from Brooklyn."

"What?" Motoko was still thinking of the redness of that eye.

Daez dusted his gloves free of feathers. He held up his right for Motoko to see. The leather, expensive and suitably thin, was shredded through the knuckles.

"What happened?"

Daez looked at her, that certain something in his eyes, that secret you-and-me look. He lowered his eyes from her face to her foot, then looked up without missing a beat. "Hey . . . what are Good Guys for?" he asked.

A SUMMER'S END FORETOLD: II

JULY 1985

The footsteps sounded strange today, almost inhumanly heavy and slow.

(**Shuffle . . . Shuffle . . .**)

(**Ooooo . . . Ooooo . . .**)

She heard his breathing—his, *not* his—and shuddered, naked, in the heat, straining at the shackles.

Footsteps creaking down the hall, like two trunks of oak on feet.

Footsteps stopping halfway there.

Concentrated breathing.

(**Ooooo . . .**)

She took, and held, a sip of air, afraid that if she let it go she might miss some vital clue. Some sound or signal in the air, some secret electrical impulse. For, more than the fear, and more than the pain, the sense of having missed the signs ate away deep in her soul.

She was going to die. She had known from the

start. If only she could go believing that the gods were satisfied.

(Crimes against family . . .

Husband . . .

Japan . . .)

She heard the other door creak open slowly down the hall. It swung on haunted hinges and the sound did nothing for her faith. She heard his breathing quicken. She heard him shuffle, foot to foot, like a rogue bull getting ready to charge. Then the door slammed shut again. She heard a torn but mighty howl, half anguish and half war cry.

The silence that followed unhinged her completely.

And she went half mad from grief, knowing it was, in the end, nothing more than a foolish and tragic mistake.

Just then the silence ended in a furious rushing of footsteps and screams.

His, as he opened the door to her room.

Hers, as she looked at the change in his face.

PART TWO

ACTIVIST

TWELVE

i. MONDAY: 8:00 A.M.

In the distance the sound of a crow.

That was queer, for the dream was of roses and robins and wine.

Cotter Sloan knew he was dreaming, never having been that keen on any of the three. But what the hell, the dream was his, and no fool crow was buzzing it.

He tossed and bumped on the bed of pine feathers, settling finally on his right side.

Sweet vision of roses and robins and wine. Sloan and Maureen on a small shady knoll in 1967. In tie-dyed tees and faded blue jeans patched with PEACE and LOVE and STONED. Sloan's hair a lustrous shade of long he'd never live to see again. Hers, blond and like the sun and blazing a trail to her ass through the lawn.

Sloan leaned over her, sipping his wine. "Love,"

he said. "Peace," she said. And in the background—Christ, some dream—six medieval troubadors started luting "All You Need . . ." in sync with a chorus of robins.

Sloan inhaled the heady perfume of all the invisible roses.

Young again . . .

Alive again . . .

In love again . . .

Complete again . . .

Sloan and his woman looked over the hill at the next horizons. Each one bluer than the last.

"I love this dream," he said to her.

"I rove it too," he heard her say.

But when he turned, Maureen was gone. He was there with Charlie's wife, a mad-eyed gook with Charlie's brains splattered all over her face like a mask. She was screaming and swinging her cleaver. And he didn't speak the language but he knew it wasn't Peace or Love. And in another time or place he might have taken the time to explain. But bombs and screams were everywhere and now was all the time he had. And before he could stop it, his hand with the knife—

The buzz of the crow like a chainsaw.

Cawwwwwwwwww!

The red-eye express coming at him. Rabid flight of coal-black wings. Beak, a flaming arrowhead destined for his heart.

Cawwwwwwwwww!

Sloan bolted upright, naked on the pinewood floor, splinters sticking in his ass, the buzzer roaring in his ears.

Someone pounding at the door.

"Mr. Sloan? Hey, Cotter?"

Cawwwwwwwwww!

"Cotter? Coming up now!"

A jingling of keys and then one in the lock.

"Cotter? Yo! You dead or what?"

Footsteps creaking on two steps. Then, slowly, up another.

Sloan upchucked in his hand and swallowed it whole in disgust and despair. He held it down . . . he held it down . . .

Daez taking two more steps, as if he owned them, which he did.

"Cotter? Hey, come on now. I thought we made a deal last night."

A throbbing at his elbow. A half-remembered purple bruise. (Henry digging in one thumb halfway to the bone.)

"Do the work or pay the rent."

Footsteps heading down the stairs. And with them his salvation.

Sloan screamed "I'm up! I'm up!" and scrambled to his feet.

God only knew, there was work to be done.

Oh yes, a man's work to be done.

He stumbled seven steps and crashed against the bathroom door.

A Sunday drunk . . . A *Sunday drunk* . . .

Oh God, his head was splitting! But— Come on, that's it, use it, think: He'd been drunk . . . a Sunday drunk . . . Therefore, it was Monday . . . Good! . . . The sun coming in from the kitchen . . . All right . . . Make that Monday morning . . . Queens . . . Sounds of hammers from below . . . Hey guys, wait up, I'm almost there . . . Queens— no, wait, Astoria . . . Okay, I'm in Astoria . . . I can think of worse places to be, give me time . . . Hammers, Henry, Christ my elbow, how'd a little prick like that . . .

Hammers pounding in his skull. Heavy-metal do or die. A red-hot transmission from the landlord to the troops: The rent is due, pay up or else . . .

Hammers pounding . . .

Red waves splashing . . .

Fear coming at him in waves from his arm . . .

How *did* a little prick like that . . .

He riveted his haunted eyes to the mirror that hadn't been cleaned since she'd gone.

I'm not a drunk . . . I'm *not* a drunk . . .

Sloan promised himself, there were tears in his eyes.

I *will not be* some zonked-out vet . . .

He slipped into the same shorts he'd worn for two days and the jeans that he'd worn for a week now. Higher than a kite again on the old sense of mission.

To get his act together.

To keep his act together.

Until he could find his wife.

His darling, adorable, beautiful wife.

And proceed to break her neck.

ii. MONDAY: 9:30 A.M.

Michael was taking his first day off sick in almost seven years. And spending every second of it regretting the day he was born.

With nine stitches in it, his upper lip resembled a badly stuffed tomato. One of his front upper teeth, though intact, had been jammed back some forty degrees. Two more uppers had been halved and the lowers smashed into ragged pickets.

The oral surgeon who lived down the hall had yanked the upper back to flush. Only an hour had passed, but already Michael wished Dr. Reuth had pulled every tooth in his head. Root canals, from two to four, were scheduled starting Friday. And then some extensive recapping.

In the meantime, Gerber's.

The finest painkillers money could buy.
Visions of Motoko.
And a little late May snow.
Michael razor-edged the candy in a tidy little row. Stopped one nostril. Snorted up. Just like they did in the movies.
Oooooo . . .
The snow had started falling when the cherry blossoms stopped. Michael had had his first hit at a party the week Motoko walked.
Ohhhhh boyyyyy . . .
One of the nerves in his mouth screamed a little but Michael was already sailing along. That was the thing about candy, yeah, the beautiful thing about snow.
Sooooo fiiiiinnnnne . . .
Michael, in a party mood, hit the other nostril.
Oooooooooooooooo . . .
There you are on a luxury liner and you're making the smoothest incredible waves. You've done it. Oh rogue sailor. Wave goodbye to the pain of your life on the shore.
Michael did.
And did again.
He'd never come so far before. He'd left it all behind him now: six-day, eighty-hour weeks . . . jingles . . . games and politics . . . bullshit, Mad Ave greed, deceit . . . miles and miles behind him, with Ivory Snow and Camels and Milk Week . . . Johnny Walker and Spam and Isuzus . . .
He'd come so far, from there to here: the vision of Motoko in the silk kimono he'd bought her for ten thousand dollars: virgin white with cherry blossoms fallen straight from heaven.
Ahhhhh . . .
Michael sailed across the room on waves and waves of visions.
Oooooooooo . . .

Motoko brushing her hair that first night . . . fifty strokes, a hundred, two . . . applying cold cream to her skin in concentrated circles, as if he weren't even there in the room . . . Motoko crossing the room in her robe—truly surprisingly crimson—and folding neatly in his arms without a trace of shyness . . . No, not shyness, something else: a sort of sad sensuality, a not-quite-letting-go-but-then . . .

(I never really knew you . . . I should've fucked you harder, longer . . . Should've tried it up the ass . . . Books say you girls are kinky . . . Mo? . . .)

Michael sailed into the kitchen, chic waves of snowy white and chrome, and opened the second left drawer. A ricocheting flash of steel. And he was really sailing.

Oooooooooo . . .

Motoko waiting at the door . . . Reliable . . . Conventional . . . Happy to see him and glad to be there . . .

(I should've been home earlier . . . I should've left my work behind . . . along with my agency bullshit . . .)

Michael dropped anchor right there where he stood, and sailed his right hand like a skiff to the knife. The pleasure came at him in waves from the blade, so long and so wicked and gleaming and sharp.

Motoko bowing . . . serving drinks . . . smiling at each honored guest as if the world hung in the balance . . .

(What was the problem? . . . I really don't see it . . . You should've told me it bothered you so . . .)

The knife kept floating back and forth. Michael watched it, mesmerized. Mo had always liked this knife . . . for slicing and

dicing and

lopping and
chopping and . . .

Motoko pulling back from him . . . to some secret inner place where he could never reach her . . . not even when he touched her . . . especially when he touched her . . . The black art of being there when you are gone . . . And then one day she was gone . . .

Oooooooooo . . .

Michael flicked the little switch. The humming noise came at him from a distance in the warmest waves. And he rode them until he was sailing again. With the blade on the sharpener sending off sparks.

(You felt nervous around me . . . I know that . . . I'm difficult and moody . . .)

The sparks were really flying now and Michael sailed beyond them on a blissful wave of love.

(I guess I wasn't strong enough to tell you this before: but I found it hard to relax around you . . . I wanted to impress you . . . I wanted you to think Oh Wow . . . I should've been more mellow . . . I mean like I'm feeling now . . .)

Michael drew the sharpened blade in a feathery arc on his thumb.

Red waves . . .

He could let her go, of course.

But, then again, he had the knife.

He couldn't.

He might, though.

He *couldn't.*

Why *not,* though?

Why *not* put it all on the line?

iii. TUESDAY: 1:00 A.M.

"And now, *ret's* have a nice big hand for a *rearry speshuh rady* . . ."

Ed, of course, begins to laugh, as only Ed McMahon can do. And the audience, pre-Carsonized, finds the sound infectious.

Johnny holds their rapt attention with an upraised finger. Though wearing a suit—and by no means a cheap one—he resembles, somehow, an Upper East Side sushi chef. Some subtle triumph of makeup, perhaps, or a sly way of using his eyes.

Motoko cools it in the wings, stilling the thumpity-thump of her heart.

Finally, when they can stand it no more, the drum roll begins. Like the purr of a cat.

"*A* rearry speshuh *rady* . . .

"Motoko . . . Shirata . . . Leigh!"

The roar of the crowd. Wave on wave of applause. Motoko, oddly confident in Michael's white kimono, with hair long like Kazumi's, crosses the stage in smooth elegant strides.

Motoko sighed, turning over on the crimson sheets. It was sometime after midnight and she guessed that she was dreaming. But she'd never been a guest on the Johnny Carson show and did not choose to argue. Despite the difference in her hair. And the whistles that followed the sway in her walk.

Motoko throws the crowd a kiss and takes a seat beside Johnny, demurely crossing her legs. Doc brings the junket music to a screechy funky close. And Johnny Carson raises his hand to bring the crowd under control.

J.C.: (*Peeling layers of rubber off his eyes and upper lip.*) I'd better tell you something. I'm not *rearry* Japanese.

M.L.: (*Smiling, does the same. Then does something to her hair that turns it a bright golden Marilyn blond. She still looks vaguely Asian but . . .*) Well, Johnny, I have a small confession too. I'm not *completely* either. In fact . . .

Motoko stands and raises one finger and holds

the crowd just as he did before. The drummer, getting into it, initiates a purring roll. And Motoko starts peeling down a zipper that hadn't been there before. The drum purr grows, the zipper falls. The drum roars, a mighty clash, and then a gasp throughout the crowd. To see Motoko standing there, the silk kimono in one hand—pure Kazumi underneath.

Motoko gives her hips a wiggle under the red leather mini. And the movement starts those shadows rippling under the black cotton turtle. Her breasts are truly Partonesque. Her slip of a waist, like a D-ring. And throughout the audience grown men are heard to weep. Motoko, smiling, takes her seat. And Johnny, though still Johnny—look, this *is* Johnny Carson—is nowhere near so arch.

J.C.: That's quite a trick. *Mo Leigh!*

M.L.: (*Waits for the whistles to end.*) Thank you. It was nothing. I do it all the time.

J.C.: You know, Mo, I've heard so much about how—*deep* your voice is. I was expecting Sylvester Stallone. (*Mugs it with a Rocky face. Waits for the laughter to end.*) Your voice is really something, though. At the risk of sounding a little chauvinistic, I think it's really *feminine.*

M.L.: (*Waits for applause and more whistles to end.*) Thank you, Johnny. So is—

No, Johnny is too fast for her. The band starts up. And old Ed chuckles ripely as Johnny reaches to the side and comes up with a set of bars. He holds them up before his face.

J.C.: And this is where *I'm* gonna be if we don't stop this instant for a short commercial!

Motoko tossed and turned some more, vaguely agitated. The screen seemed to have drawn a blank, although she did hear music, a low cello in the background. She tossed again. Turned again. Something not quite right here. Then Michael's voice came on over the cello. "Lights out . . . Sweet dreams . . . Day is done . . ." Another cello joined the first. The mood was growing ominous. And Michael's new Price-Karloff voice wasn't really helping. "You're home . . . Alone . . . You're all alone . . . Here in New York City!" Sounds of pounding at the door. Scratchings at the windows. Screech-screech-eek-eeks crawling all over the cellos. A heart-stopping collective "Ooooooo" from the graves across the street. And before she could think to react . . . or to check somehow if she was dreaming . . . the right window imploded in a million waves of bloodred glass . . . and

(Ooooo—)

No!

(niiii!)

No!

brother—no, something like brother—was on her. And nothing could stop him

from cutting her off . . . with a blow that began at the ceiling . . . and then circled on through, like the breeze, through her neck . . . "Don't lose your head over safety," Price-Karloff continued. "When for just a little more you can have new Sexy Bars."

Cut now to Johnny and Stage Mo. A thundering ovation. Johnny just chuckles and tickles his nose until the crowd falls silent.

J.C.: Was that your first commercial?

M.L.: (*Blushing prettily.*) Why yes, it was, as a matter of fact.

J.C.: So how does it feel to be safe behind bars?

M.L.: (*Fine now. Back on breezy turf.*) Johnny, I can't tell you—

Man #1: Funky!

Man #2: Come on, girl, get down!

J.C.: Mo?

M.L.: (*With a seated wiggle that sets those shad-*

ows quivering.) It's out of sight. It's just so-o-o cool. It really blows my mind.

J.C.: (*Chuckles and tickles his nose.*) It *rearry brows—*

M.L.: (*Smiling sweetly. In a high Kazumi voice.*) If you say that one more time, I'm gonna cut—

Commercial! Motoko turned right into it, helpless again on blood crimson as the small screen divided in two. Henry on the one side, old Ben on the other. Ed McMahon, grown serious, announced "About other men's wives . . ." And Motoko turned again, straining to hear as the screen washed away.

J.C.: So the bars are up. You have new locks.

M.L.: No, Johnny, actually the locks didn't come yet.

J.C.: You're kidding.

M.L.: No, he left a note. (*Withdraws a slip of paper from her disco glitter handbag.*) "Dear Motoko, enjoy your new life behind bars. The deadbolts are on order."

Man #1: Uh-huh.

Man #2: Yeah, right.

M.L.: No, *really*. Listen! Like, Henry is one of the Good Guys.

Man #3: Aughhhhhhh.

M.L.: I mean, like wow, the bars are up. He fixed the ceiling. He painted the walls.

J.C.: (*Fixes Mo with an amused, ironic look. Then turns to the audience.*) But will the man answer his beeper?

Motoko folded into a center of absolute silence and peace. Ready for whatever came. Even "The Tonight Show." Because Henry was with her. Henry and Ben. And the bars were up. And the deadbolts were coming. And tonight before bed

(*Make no mistake!*)

Mo Leigh had taken—a Vow.

iv. TUESDAY: 1:00 A.M.

Ben slept as always, upon his right side, having learned long ago what turning front or back could do . . .

(*Tell me, tell me, darling boy* . . .)

He could sleep through trucks and planes, through screaming babies, barking dogs. The alarm clock had not been invented that could raise Ben Shacklette from his sleep. But Ben knew this dream like the back of his hand and could spot it a mile away—in his sleep. In the distance, the sound of an engine. A far-off, sweet, contented purr that raised the hackles on his neck along with a thin sheen of sweat on his brow. Easy, Ben, you've had this dream sixteen thousand times before . . . Steady, steady, as she goes . . .

The singular purr kept on coming, no hurry, by inches at first . . . and then feet . . . and then yards . . . It was ever so sweet. And it did take its time so, you'd think it had all the time in the world, cruising this fine warm June day the first week in December.

(*Oh, my darling, little boy* . . .)

And, though he knew every inch of this dream, he listened with genuine wonder and awe as the purr closed the gap now by miles not yards . . . the sound now a low and malevolent growl . . .

(*How does this feel, darling boy* . . .)

The sweat now bubbling, hot and screamy, in the tracks of jagged scars. A furious chorus of candles roaring into view on engines of destruction.

Steady, steady, as she goes . . .

The sky was filled with candles and a row of flaming pearls . . .

Ben Shacklette opened his eyes.

Just in time.

He listened and heard not a peep in the house.
He checked the sheets, found them runny with sweat.
Checked his pulse, found it racy but strong.
Considered long and thoroughly precisely what had to be done.

v. TUESDAY: 1:30 A.M.

M.L.: (*Shocked*) Are we still on?
J.C.: (*Chuckles and tickles his nose.*) Well, I guess if you don't want your cake . . .
Out of nowhere Ed McMahon appears with a three-layer chocolate cake and sets it down before her. Mo blows the dozen candles out and reads the pink script on the icing: "Congratulations on surviving your first year in Manhattan!"
M.L.: Thank you, eblybody— Oh!
J.C.: (*Smiling wickedly.*) We've been waiting for that.
E.M.: Oh-ho-hooooo!
Man #1: Chop chop!
Man #2: Cut it off!
Mo sits there for a moment, grinning rather sheepishly. How had he learned of the Vow? (*No mistakes!*) She wiggles and giggles and tries to Kazumi her way out of this terrible jam. But this is "The Tonight Show" and there can be no sly escape.
J.C.: Don't fuck with *us*, young lady.
E.M.: Oh-ho-hooooo!
Man #1: Chop chop!
Man #2: Cut it off!
Man #3: Get down, sugar, *do* it!
Mo Leigh watches, in a funk, as Johnny plops a butcher block on top of her chocolate cake, then

whacks down a great machete in the center. Cake and frosting everywhere.

M.L.: Well, I guess if you insist.

All: *Cut it! Cut it! Cut it* off!

J.C.: Come on—a deal's a *dearl*, my dear.

Mo raises the machete above her outstretched pinkie with almost maniacal glee. Her finger twitches. This could be fun. A *deal's* a *dearl:* one finger lopped for every time she *brows* it. Unless . . . Unless . . .

J.C.: Goddamn! She's gonna go for it! It's double or nothing, folks, and here we go! Sixty seconds, double time, of nonstop, total Funky. Or she'll chop *two fingers off!*

A classic "Tonight" drum roll. Charo or Kreskin could not ask for more. Ed cocks his head for a sign from Mo Leigh, who nods and takes a sip of air and begins to Funky as Ed hits the stopwatch.

M.L.: YakatamaFugyoucuntGetdownnnnnYuh wannagedzumbahhhhhsIgodfivehunnerdtowsan bugsinstogs'n'fuggineye-are-aysIwanyourmommy's pigchuhHiMydoorisalwaysopenWaitnowcouldthere beateenychance ....

....

....

Fifty seconds . . . Forty-five . . . Mo Leigh's voice was spinning down a long wide-open freeway. The night was dark. She could not see beyond her speeding headlights. But there was a chance she might make it.

M.L.: PenthousematerialAmIrightoramIwrong GetrightintothepicturePeaceThat'sagoodgirlIwon't biteNowtherearebarsandtherearebarsTrustmeHe's oneoftheGoodGuys ....

....

....

Thirty seconds . . . Twenty-five . . .

vi. TUESDAY: 1:30 A.M.

Daez slipped in on Cloud Six-and-a-half with lipstick rings around his dick and a terrible ache in his heart for Cloud Nine. He took his pleasure where he found it, but found himself thinking these days more and more of Motoko . . . Motoko . . . Motoko . . .

He padded to the living room, to find Cloud Zero waiting up with rose curlers in her hair and murder in her eyes.

"Hen-reee, where the hell you been?"

Daez answered, "You know . . . I, uh—"

"Don't sweet-talk me, you slick son-of-a-bitch. I own half your mortgages. You call me, you're out late like this."

"Sorry. Get you something?"

"Bring your old mother a bottle of beer and start earning your keep around here."

"Sure, ma."

"And send that bitch wife of yours her goddamn check before she drives me clear out of my mind."

"Yes, ma." Daez shuffled off and thanked the Lord he had Cloud Nine.

Thank God for Motoko.

From the kitchen he heard mother chuckle. "Someday that damn-fool pecker is gonna be the death of you."

vii. TUESDAY: 1:35 A.M.

Eight . . . Seven . . . Six . . . Five . . .

Mo Leigh, turning blue, catches a glimpse of checkered flag and barrels down the runway on the heels of her salvation.

"Yourockin'likearockin'chairYoEverything'sin orderHuhhhhhTooweirdforwordsWhoopsBlessmy starsJuhwannataykustroopleasemizDaydidden tayknofoinuhjuhIswearI'llfuggingeddddjewww ww!"

The buzzer sounds.

The crowd roars.

Balloons and streamers filled the air, with sounds of New Year's Eve kazoos.

J.C.: Mo, that was phenomenal.

M.L.: (*Winded, but flushing with pride.*) Thank you, *ev-ery-bod-y*!

J.C.: And nowwwww . . . (*A little fanfare from the band, climaxing with a cymbal clash.*) Mo, we want you to know how we feel. I mean, really deep inside.

Johnny reaches in his jacket . . . holds the pose dramatically . . . and produces, with a flourish, an envelope.

J.C.: (*Offering the envelope to Mo.*) Go on, take it. I insist.

Giggles, chuckles from the crowd as Mo Leigh opens the envelope. And then roars of laughter as she slips the ticket from its sheath.

A one-way ticket from New York.

Back to the Grand Hotel.

Motoko awakened at dawn. Just a dream. But the butcher knife was where she'd put it, half hidden in the shadows of the guttered candles' light.

viii. TUESDAY: 6:15 A.M.

Daez hooked his right heel in the strap and then hoisted. Held it for a count of ten. Did two sets of twenty. Then switched to the left. Thinking of

Motoko. Half out of his mind from the heat in his heart.

In the end, it had all come down so clearly to *her*.

After the war he'd gone East to study. Had been praised, in fact, for speed, dexterity, and power. He broke boards with the best of them, using feet and hands and head. Meditated by the hour. Shattered toes and fingers sparring on wood floors in dojos where his life was on the line. In time, he racked up a small rainbow of belts. But always black eluded him as he grew restless and moved on. Korea. China. Thailand. To master the basics again and again while he himself was mastered by the legions of ripe Asian pussy. So exotic and willing and—*easy*.

(Hey, Joe!)

But now he knew the easy life had proven the hardest of all. Thirty-nine years old, without a goddamn pot to piss in! And he'd grown soft on top of it.

She'd shown him, in that single flash—must've been some exercise—what a Master was capable of.

He switched and started hoisting his right leg from the side. Chest high . . . Chin high . . . Easy . . . Up! . . . With his arch almost touching the ceiling, he counted. This time up to thirty. Sets of five. Then right to left.

The pain was unendurable. He welcomed it and wanted more.

Motoko, Motoko, Motoko!

That funny voice . . . that broken nose . . . that almost boyish body . . . You looked at her once and thought, What a dog . . . You listened, but she didn't bark . . . You looked again . . . you passed again . . . you couldn't take your eyes off, though—there was something, just something about her . . . By degrees that voice of hers didn't seem so funny . . . that nose began, it seemed, to curve . . . You looked again . . . she made you see the way she moved her body . . . the subtle ways she moved her mind . . . with purity and inner strength and total concentration . . . and then one day, that fateful day, she surrendered and gave you the slightest of peeks . . . she reached up with her *foot,* just as cool as you please, and caught the notepad—with her *toes* . . . The most natural thing in the world . . . The hard life, the good life, made easy . . .

That instant she became Cloud Nine. And he knew he must have her, whatever the cost. Or die without ever tapping, as she had, the Source.

Stretched out now and limber, he ambled to the workout bag. He stood before it, loose and hungry in a way he'd never known. He took a sip of air and exhaled it deliberately, working his diaphragm down to his gut.

He imagined a face on the bag, one of many faces he'd use throughout the workout: this first one of Rambo the Pigeon.

He saw the red eyes coming at him from across the room again. Mad red eyes, like no others he'd seen. And though the light in the cellar had been very dim, he'd had the impression of needlepoint teeth. The bird coming quick as a shot for his throat.

He threw a left hook, then his foot in a roundhouse that rattled the bag on its chain. A bloody blur of feathers exploded in his mind.

Hot stuff, he had thought. Rough and tough, dramatic.

She'd catch it with her toes, though, or some sly and subtle move that looked like a ballet.

Must've been *some* exercise!

The Masters never strut their stuff. The Masters

never sweat. The Masters never even move, the movements just flow through them.

Daez settled into the bag, fast and mean, with a flurry of high-powered blows. The Power rippled through him, exploding in shock combinations of lightning feet and hammer fists. The tattoos glowed beneath the sweat that rushed from him in waves.

Flashes . . . He knew flashes now . . . Motoko, however, tapped into the Source . . .

One night, just one night, with her!

He placed her image on the bag and focused on it wordlessly. Thoughtlessly. Completely.

Suddenly, he whirled: as if a tight-packed coil of steel had suddenly snapped from the tension. His right leg, outstretched like a hammer, connected at the heel—in a kick so exquisitely angled and timed it launched the bag clear off the hook to the wall.

"Oh, baby, you'll be good for me!"

ix. TUESDAY: 6:10 P.M.

When the new student entered the classroom, Motoko's heart skipped a couple of beats.

He bowed, then looked around the room. *"Boku wa osoi kara taihen sumanai."* Sorry that I'm late, he said, affecting the informal level of speech.

She figured his age at about twenty-two. And the way he flaunted his hairdo—a sort of reversed Mohawk, with long hair brushed back on the sides and the center mowed half to the skull—said he might spell trouble.

"Bryant-san, welcome. *Irrasshaimase.*" She proceeded slowly through the introductions: status being of all things the slipperiest to express.

Mr. Walker, president of Walker International . . . Miss Beirut, traffic manager of Times

Square Distributors . . . Mr. Kasimir Wojciechowski, senior clerk at Blue Collar Temps . . . Miss Casey . . .

Bryant-san stifled a yawn and seated himself at the end, propping a long canvas case at his side. He leaned back and stretched his legs, silver studs on cycle boots gleaming in fluorescent lights. *"Sumimasen? Anata ga osku hanashite iru kara boku wa wakaranakatta."*

The eyes around the table glazed. The class nightmare had arrived, wearing a Nuke 'Em High T-shirt and sporting an attitude problem that steepled the Empire State. The creature's thick lips rat-a-tatted street-level declensions of verbs they scarcely knew.

Motoko repeated the charges, translating the verbs to the more formal levels of textbook Nihongo. She spoke slowly and precisely, noting the look of relief that spread from manager to president.

"Watashi ga osoku hanashite imasu *kara . . . anata wa . . . watashi ga* wakarimasen deshita." Because I am speaking too slowly . . . you cannot understand me . . . Why don't we speak it like real Japanese?

Watanabe Sensei stood in the doorway observing and frowning at her bandaged wrist.

Motoko cleared her throat. The Party Line, well known to all, was crystallizing in her mind.

Ah so, Bryant-san. How well we all share your frustration. Even native *Nihonjins* find it incredibly hard sometimes to speak like Japanese. There are too many endings for verbs: indicative, imperative, presumptive and provisional, conditional, alternative, passive and potential, causative, causative passive. Too many intricate levels of speech: slang, plain, humble, honorific. And the rules to tell which level is correct for which situation are not at all well defined. A native *Nihonjin* makes countless day-to-day decisions, shifting gears over and over, from one level to the next. Depending on the place and time, the person he is with. Our job is to get you there. To provide a sound footing on a level of speech that is in itself rather slippery: the always appropriate humble.

Motoko knew the Party Line and was about to give it—when something caught between their eyes. She saw the boy in Tokyo. Giggles as he made his way, with that Day-Glo hairdo and his idiot *Nihongo*. *Konnichi wa! Genki desu ka? Yoi tenki desu ne? Good day, sir, nice to meet you! My, it sure is lovely weather, eh?* She could see him tuning in, almost, not quite, getting the harder, cooler inflections of verbs; breezy, slangy turns of phrase; words that had that live-wire, funky sound about them. Close, close, but no cigar because he was a *gaijin* . . .

And somehow, though the Party Line was there and necessary, the words just got lost on the way.

Hands on hips, Motoko did a passable impression of teenybop *Nihongo* that lowered the president's jaw. She asked where big boy made his bucks. And what was in his groovy case.

Watanabe Sensei stormed off in a thunderous series of clicks.

Motoko gathered that she was in serious shit. But when the boy answered the first of her questions, her eyes lit up like Christmas trees.

He never answered the second.

X. WEDNESDAY: 10:00 P.M.

Motoko padded through the apartment, squeezing the tennis ball in her right hand. The wrist still throbbed relentlessly and her grip was tenuous. Still . . . The doors were locked, front and back—

and Henry had *answered his beeper* to tell her the deadbolts were due any day! Motoko checked the security door; rattled the knob; slid the bolts back and forth. She returned to the bedroom, where the candles still flickered, and knelt before the block that sat awaiting one cutting remark.

Makoto? she thought. Fine, I'll give you *makoto.*

She slid the left palm to the edge of the block till only the pinkie remained. She stared at it for a good time, the cleaver shaking in her hand.

"No more mistakes," she murmured.

"*Absolutely* no mistakes."

Motoko smoothed the MTA subway map before her. Graduation day had arrived. Green, blue, and orange lines; fuchsia and bold crimson, crossed the map like arteries. And the craving came on her to go with the flow and find her new life in the city.

Why, she could switch at Queensboro to the 7 from the Double R, change again at Forty-second to the 1 train for the West Side, or she might change at Thirty-fourth to the F train for the Village . . .

Soho . . . Little Italy . . . Chinatown . . . Tribeca . . .

The map seemed to glow in the candle- and moonlight; the spell it cast, enhanced by the shadow bars across the page.

Manhattan gridlock, compounded. No prison now, the checkerboard on which New Yorkers made their moves. Her turn now.

Where was it?

Where *was* the real, the *Mo,* New York?

Motoko's eyes began to roam.

She let them wander where they would and pictured herself where they took her. She had no special preference. But nonetheless was not surprised to see where they finally settled.

xi. WEDNESDAY: 11:30 P.M.

"I asked you nicely," Sloan said.

"Wise." The fat man outweighed Sloan by, say, half a ton. "Now suppose you ask again, real nice—oh, about a week from now when I'm in Miami. Blow."

He sounded like Joe Cocker hoarse. His features were coarse and queerly arranged: a pig's face on a party cake stepped on in the rain. But then, the whole bar was peculiar . . .

"You're sweating, babe," the fat man said.

Sloan wiped down his brow with a napkin. He set *her* photo on the bar. He grabbed his glass, allowed himself a sip. Just one more to stop the shakes.

Finally, he managed, "Look."

The fat man leaned over, both hands on the bar. "Do yourself a favor, sport. You take a look around instead. See those two girls dancing? Those two boys at the end of the bar?"

Sloan followed the bouncing ball of the fat man's shining dome. Mr. Clean with a pair of gold earrings. And a red bandana tied around his oceanic neck. He nodded sagely. He'd gathered as much from the pink-lettered sign, The White Swallow.

"Your cunt a pussy licker?"

Sloan choked back the crazies and let the sadness hang its load. He smiled for the fat man. "I honestly don't know," he said. "It's so hard to tell these days. She said she'd be in here to see *you* tonight."

"I really want you out of here." The fat man laid

a billy club the size of a junior league bat on the bar. He knocked wood a couple of times and growled, "Go."

Sloan wiped his face with his sleeve. And he begged, "All I'm asking is, just look."

One pink sausage finger flicked the photo from the bar.

Sloan squatted to salvage his wife, who had fallen facedown in the filth.

"This was my favorite photo." He slipped it in his pocket and felt his shoulders go to hell.

The fat man laid a heavy rap of nightstick on the bar.

Whapbap . . . Whapbap . . . Whapbappabipbap-bipbapbap . . .

The girls and boys were watching them. Show time was about to start.

"I even wore a sport coat."

Whapbap . . . Whapbap . . . Whapbappabipbap-bipbapbap—*Crash!*

Sloan's glass went to pieces in a thousand different ways. He surely could have used a sip, and wondered how much sweat was in him.

"I think, sir," he said to the fat man, "that you are a very bad dude."

Whapbappabipbappa . . . *Whapbappabipbappa* . . .

The fat voice, almost playful, snarled, "That's what I keep *trying* to tell you."

Sloan trembled and sweated and took it all in: the distance between the two dykes and himself . . . the position of the fat man's glass . . . the angle of the billy club . . . the stance of the behemoth . . . height . . .

"Let me just leave you my address, okay?"

Sloan fluttered his eyelids and reached for his pen, a modified Bic he had brought just in case. He slipped the blue cap off, licked his lips, and printed on a napkin.

"Hhhhhh . . . Eeeee . . . Nnnnn . . . Rrrrr . . ."

White letters, huge and childlike, each gone over several times in madcap concentration. The napkin drenched with beer and sweat. The pen point he had filed for hours tearing the paper to pieces.

Sloan looked at the pen with alarm and dismay. Shook it. Tried it on his palm. Shook it. Turned it upside down.

"I really, *really* want you to go!" *Whapbipbipbip-pabipbapwhap!* Fatso stroking the head of the club in lewd anticipation.

Sloan held the fat man's piggy eyes while his fingers curled around the pen. The fist they made was lethal and could break with ease through boards and bricks. "Thanks," he said, "I needed this."

The fat man was fast. But his stance was all wrong. And he lacked both time and distance to maneuver the club into place.

Sloan rammed the Bic in a murderous arc through the hollow under the runaway chins. The honed tip surfaced with a splash through the dorsum of the tongue.

"Don't you fucking move!" Sloan tugged the Bic toward him; the tongue screamed some more. And bucked and spat more gouts of blood. Sloan purred, "This may hurt a little, but you'll get the hang of it. Now . . . I believe you and I were discussing my *wife.*"

xii. THURSDAY: 11:00 A.M.

Daez slipped the door shut behind him. He felt vaguely foolish, but moved on ahead. One foot leading gingerly. Coiled and ready for action. Professional Good Guy, and dressed all in black. Because he still had *feelings*—

(Ooooo—)

about those crazy flaming eyes, coming at him, going for his throat . . . Rows of needle-pointed teeth . . . Who'd ever seen a damned pigeon like that . . . The more he thought about it, the more alarmed he felt—but a Master, a real one, would just have to *know* . . .

He flicked the switch. Light crackled and popped as the newest bulb died.

Shifting clouds allowed scant light through the broken window from which the bird had come. He catwalked to room center, stopped. Another cloud eclipsed the sun. And he could not be certain, but in a single strobelike flash he thought he saw something peculiar.

Or rather, more queer, he did not see something.

Not one feather.

Not one red drop.

Wait now . . . That *was* curious.

Daez wheeled slowly to the left, leading with his nose.

Good God.

He sniffed and grimaced in disgust. From the boiler area. Mild wafting of decay. Almost undetectable, yet totally offensive in a way he'd never known. Something rotting slowly and reveling in the prolongment. A woodchuck or rat in the piping. More pigeons dressing their festering wounds with beakfuls of white oozy shit.

Why not just let Cotter Sloan . . .

No. A Master went the distance.

Daez felt sleek and lithe and quick, muscles rippling underneath his black Armani T-shirt. Another step . . . Another . . .

The smell grew progressively worse—though,

somehow, as faint as before. A six-day down-home chili fart was roses in comparison.

In all truth, who could blame him if he chucked this and phoned Cotter Sloan?

All the way in, pal . . . Come on, all the way . . .

Motoko's silken pussy waiting for him at the Source . . .

He made it to the boiler when an icy rush assailed him and he started to shiver like crazy.

(Ooooo—)

xiii. THURSDAY: 11:02 A.M.

It studied him and swelled with rage.

In its spare moments, of which there were many, it built its strength with exercise. Amused itself with little games. It dragged boxes on the floor, unable yet to lift them. It made smaller bottles *ping.* Levitated tools and nails. Erased the blood and feathers of its first attempt to Be.

And if it had a mind to, it might just be able to finish him now. Freeze him for starters, then when he was down, it would take him and break him and take its sweet time, the screams white music to its soul.

For it had slept so very long. Waited with infinite patience and craft for just the right time, the right chain of events.

Here it was now, here at last. So close that it could taste her blood and hear bones crushed to powder.

(Ooooo—)

First the gods had sent the rat: a small step in its quest for form, seized almost on sight.

Next had come the bearded one: a painful lesson

from the gods. For, it—in all its innocence and eager longing—had joyously leapt with a scream for his throat. And suddenly found itself formless again.

But the gods in all their mercy then had sent the flying rat-thing. And, trembling with joy, it had taken the bird. Waited this time patiently. Till the right time arrived and the slick one walked in.

It remembered the savage red rush in its heart . . . the furious heat in its eyes as it flew . . . already eating his soul . . . through the mouth.

Form!

Life!

Speed!

Force!

When suddenly, then—out of nowhere—that *kick* . . .

The shock of recognition: that the time was too soon and mere men had more force and its precious form was lost again, spent chances bleeding through its eyes, wrecked neck spasming on cement. Painfully conscious of failure as the heel fell again and again. Until it was formless as air.

Saa, nani o shimashō ka ne? What else was there to do, but wait?

Form . . .

Life . . .

Speed . . .

Force . . .

All these it would have again, when the time was right.

Its lineage was ancient.

It had not been created to fail, and would not.

It studied the man and shrank further and further within its burgeoning sense of itself.

It looked into his mind and it played little games, concentrating fiercely with all its youthful power.

It made him feel tingly all over and warm, confident and in control . . . mindless of his former fears . . . forgetful of why he was here . . .

It assured him that Sloan had . . . who else . . . cleaned the floor . . .

It made him smell Ben's roses, then filled his heart with white lust for Motoko, made his one-eyed snake stretch tall with visions of those gorgeous lips.

It watched him walk away and thought: You belong to me.

Next time.

xiv. THURSDAY: 11:15 A.M.

Ben lifted the edge of one curtain an inch, enough to see the World's Greatest Lover circle back to the newly barred door.

Daez shot furtive glances from one side to the other, key ring jangling in one hand. Then he directed his gaze, unexpectedly, to the window where Ben had been standing.

With a speed that nearly rivaled the pounding of his heart, the old man two-stepped to the side, gone before his fingers had released the slip of lace.

Daez in Motoko's apartment!

Daez!

Ben choked back a surge of bile.

He was fifty-nine years old and scarred in places he still couldn't look. Daez was young and quick and lithe. The old man sensed danger and madness and death. But the thought of the World's Greatest Lover—in *there!*

Under the window, attached to the wall, was a small bar that Ben used for sit-ups. He laid into the day's set of twenty and felt, instead of the usual stiffness, a charge. Almost like a youth again.

Fifty-seven . . .

Fifty-six . . .

XV. THURSDAY: 11:16 A.M.

Daez slipped the door shut behind him and padded to the living room, away from the windows and strong morning light.

She *practiced* in here, he could feel it.

Right here.

He flicked on the light switch, surveying with a reverent eye.

The alley curtain, neatly drawn.

A sofa, table, TV, chair: laid down like *sumie* brush strokes—boldly, with force and precision.

No frills. Get in there and get to it.

A blue ceramic cup beside a gold-covered text and a soft yellow pad.

The knotty pine buffed to perfection. No mats. He guessed that she could fall on it from ceiling height without a sound. And a rush of images flooded through his mind.

Motoko doing sweet samurai shit every morning, noon, and night, the real stuff, man, the right stuff, yeah: catching paper with her toes, cartwheels, backflips, leaping side kicks, blowjobs fit for *shōguns* . . .

Daez crossed, in an agony of guilt and heat and self-disgust, and opened the door to the bedroom.

This was where she slept.

Right here.

At the sight of the rich crimson sheets—a ribbon of satin tucked over discreetly like a subtle glimpse of thigh—the blood roared in Daez's ears. He rubbed his swollen cock and came, with a cry of despair, in his shorts.

xvi. THURSDAY: 6:20 P.M.

Watanabe Sensei presided from his doorway like a chain-smoking, horny, old hoot owl. Motoko had heard the first resonant *whoooooffffff* of his coughing down the hall, his eyes copping feels with a rustle of feathers before he landed on his perch. What a sly old bird he was. But eminently pleased right now with the class in progress. And possibly disposed to forget the unfortunate outburst of Funky and her blunt refusal to explain the Ace. Motoko needed the hours, or she'd have to start using her savings for rent. And $1500 wouldn't last the summer.

She adjusted her bangs, feeling quaint and uneasy under the intense blue stare of the outrageous Bryant. Still with his strange canvas case.

"Walker-san," Motoko croaked. *"Tokyo to Kyoto to* dochira ga okii *desu ka?"* Tokyo and Kyoto . . . Which is the bigger of the two?

The strapping president of Walker International showed his executive mettle. "Tokyo no hō ga *okii desu!"* Tokyo is bigger.

Motoko smiled. Bryant stretched. Watanabe nodded, pleased.

"Beirut-san," Motoko said. *"Shinkansen to hikōki to* dochira ha hayai *desu ka?"* The bullet train or airplane . . . Which is faster of the two?

The traffic manager of Times Square Distributors lost no time in shipping the right answer to the class. "Shinkansen no hō ga *hayai desu."*

Motoko smiled. Bryant yawned. Watanabe Sensei beamed.

"Wojciechowski-san. *Sake to biru to* dochira no hō ga *oishii desu ka?*" Which tastes better, sake or beer?

The senior clerk at Blue Collar Temps stammered and blurted and mopped his bald pate.

Bryant-san raised his hand with a yawn, sporting a blue FUNK ME T-shirt tonight, a bold stripe of orange on top of his skull.

Motoko saw her chances fading right before her eyes.

But he gave her the answer, lickety-split, in perfectly formal *Nihongo.*

Motoko smiled gratefully, a little moist between the thighs. Watanabe Sensei sighed. And the look never left the boy's eyes for a second: You're ready . . . I can tell . . . Come on . . . You really want to, *don't* you?

xvii. THURSDAY: 11:20 P.M.

Somehow the knife seemed lovelier every time he sharpened it.

And increasingly more—to the point.

The *point.*

Back and forth . . . Back and forth . . . The power of suggestion . . . Hi . . . You are feeling very . . . Ooooo . . . The point of it shifting, again and again, before his snowbound eyes . . .

The *point.*

The point was, he'd been beaten to a goddamn bloody pulp and was scheduled in the morning for a dreaded root canal.

The *point.*

Get a grip on yourself . . .

Michael did a grip. He raised the knife over his head *Psycho*-style, baring his stubs in a mock silent scream.

Hard to admit, though: his heart wasn't in it.

Mouse ears . . . Shoeblack . . . Fun and games . . .

The point was, a man mustn't lose it!

Control.

Michael, in a responsible mood, razor-edged more candy in a thin efficient line. Stopped one nostril. Snorted up. Hit the other. Highdeehoooooo! Hostility sailing the blue tranquil waters on board the luxury liner. Making the smoothest incredible waves. Michael on shore, a *responsible* man, coming to grips at long last with the point, which flew back and forth like a snowball between two extremes. Michael sailing after it on waves and waves of visions.

The point was: Cut your losses . . . Motoko in the silk kimono he'd bought her for ten thousand dollars was gone . . . Lost virgin-white with cherry blossoms fallen straight from heaven . . . Cut your losses . . . Cut them . . . Cut . . .

The point, sweet snowball, floated back with Michael, sky-high, in pursuit. Another way of seeing it: The point was . . . Ah, yes, *here* . . . The *point* . . . She shouldn't have left him . . . that cold winter night . . . dressed in those blue jeans, American bitch . . .

(Oh, cut your losses . . . Cut them . . . Cut . . .)

The point, so wicked and gleaming and sharp, stood—now fixed—before his eyes: There were moments when love was a man with a knife . . .

The point was . . .

If you loved someone . . .

Sometimes you had to—

(Cut them . . . Cut . . .)

Sometimes you had to let them go . . .

From the kitchen he studied the foyer, another forty feet away, over a carpet as white as the Arctic and a ring of Chippendales around a great table of oak of the gods. The front door had been hammered from premium Portuguese steel; sand-blasted down to a foggy-day gray. The matching panels on the sides were spring-latched walk-in closets, each able to handle some two dozen coats. On the left, a cut-off stretch of softly mottled plaster, the fog disappearing at midpoint to show a wide beam of beautiful ash. Michael could see two inches of a masterwork by Dalí, with a frame that had cost a half grand in itself. Melting clocks and melting checks.

And melting snowballs on the door . . .

A lifetime on the line . . .

Control . . .

The point was, that door was the door to his world. A world that revered the grand entrance. And dreaded the ultimate shutout. Where the locks were changed by the hour. New memberships granted. Cards taken away. And once you lost yours, that was it.

Michael flashed, reseated at his mahogany throne on Mad Ave. His various futures before him like so many cartoon storyboards. All of them possible. One of them right. The difference between him and those outside the door, the power to make, over and over, decisions that cost one an arm and a leg.

(Cut your losses . . . Cut them . . . off . . .)

He sent the knife clattering into the sink. And, with no waste of sentiment, sent the other string of candy flying in a puff of smoke.

He loaded a Glad bag halfway to the top with Motoko's last remains. And when he was done, he thought, Well, there you have it.

Sayonara, baby.

xviii. FRIDAY: 11:45 A.M.

The problem of doors still remained; and still would.

(Form . . .

Life . . .

Speed . . .

Force . . .)

But it practiced constantly; and its powers, though limited, grew more refined.

No longer contented with hammers and nails, it sent whole gangs of boxes flying, with posses of bottles in tow. And, playtime done, it landed all, most times without a sound. An occasional shuffle (*shikata ga nai*) or crash (well, it *was* very young).

It could change humidity—now within a ten-foot range of its baleful soulspace. It showed a special talent for the sickeningly clammy. And had recently started on changes in mood to accompany its atmospheres. (The Kung Fu Kid, whom it *would* eat, had responded nicely.)

It heard the open and close of a door, the jingle of keys in the lock.

She was going out again. It wished that it could follow her.

It willed the most minuscule part of itself under the special security door that it would soon smash to pieces. And, waiting, it encouraged her.

xix. FRIDAY: 1:00 P.M.

Encouragement seemed to fill the air; a gentle northeaster teased her hair and tugged at the hem of her skirt. Motoko looking Funky—well, working on it anyway—in white Reeboks and red cotton sweater with doves. A touch of frosted lipstick.

(Ooooo—)

And five hours to kill before class time.

And here, on her own, in the Village at last.

The F train ridden—a lump in her throat—like a verb in an alien language. Each stop a heart-stopping declension.

Here though, somehow, with Famous Ray's Pizza behind her. Blacks in toques and baseball caps, on the court across the street, shooting basketballs like bullets. Funky people everywhere, in jeans and tees and ratty sweats, with cigarettes between their lips and freedom in their eyes. The real, the true, the Mo New York falling upon her in wave upon wave.

Bleecker just up thataway. Solid blocks of hot boutiques for leather and denim and posters and things. Hip cafes and jazz and folk and funky, funky theater. Each small step another step of freedom from the Grand Hotel. The old ghosts dying peacefully this summer afternoon.

New York . . .

The thought, like the sunlight, was gentle and easy. And the voice in her ear was surprisingly kind.

Come on, girl . . . you can do it . . . The city's waiting for you . . . come . . . open up your heart to us . . . do take down the rigid wall . . . What's past is gone, what's done is done, you're here, won't you be one of us . . . do let us reach you where you live . . . do kick back and grow Funky . . . Girl . . .

And yet she feared her heart would fall before she went the distance.

To the outrageous Bryant-san.

Tomorrow, though . . .

What of tomorrow?

xx. FRIDAY: 5:55 P.M.

"Hello?" Motoko held the phone close to her ear, Watanabe Sensei straining not to listen.

"Shirata Sensei desu ka?"

Motoko knew the soft drawl well. She turned a little and said, *"Hai."*

"This is Bill Bryant here. Sorry to bug you. But I was having trouble with the lesson for this week."

"*Aa. Aa.* I see," she said. Her heart sank just a little. Yet what had she expected, a broken-nosed, small-breasted wreck from Japan with a voice like a frog and a sad trail of ghosts? And—

"I mean, I got a little stuck on the *'to omoimasu.'* Think you might give me a hand?"

The boy had shown no signs of trouble with the "I think" construction. Motoko turned a little more from Watanabe's prying eyes.

"Mochiron," she said. "Of course."

"All right, here's where I got stuck." Bryant-san translated then, in flawless Japanese, "'I was waiting all day for my new friend to come. But I think she lost her nerve.'"

"Collect," she said. "Exactry."

xxi. FRIDAY: 11:30 P.M.

Makoto . . . All right then, *makoto* it is . . . You've come back for your pound of *makoto* . . .

Motoko, in gray sweats and red underneath, padded through the apartment, squeezing and squeezing and squeezing the ball. The doors were locked, front and back, and Henry had answered his beeper right off to tell her the deadbolts were—*due any day.*

She cocked her ear, half thinking she'd heard a low sound in the cellar. She slid the two bolts back and forth. And returned to the bedroom, where two candles flickered, the bars coming at her, and at her, in waves.

Motoko knelt before the block.

"Collect?" she cried. "*Exactry?* I told you, fingers, no mistakes!"

She worked the left palm to the edge of the block, two fingers in position. She stared at them a good long time, making stronger chopping movements with the eager cleaver.

"You thought I was kidding, *ne?*"

Motoko set the cleaver down and picked up the stopwatch. She bounced it lightly off her palm.

"You owe me sixty seconds!"

Motoko set the Timex down and hit the timer button, breaking into a frenzy of Funky as she raised the cleaver high over her head.

(*Ooooo—*)

(Hoooo!)

(Cut 'em off!)

"YakatamaFugyoucuntYuhwannageddemdead boldsdeahTheendisalwaysbetterwhen.......... ...."

xxii. SATURDAY: 8:00 A.M.

Swoosh, swish! Swoosh, swish!

The metronomic rise and fall of *onii-san*'s mighty scythe through fields of cherry blossoms. Green stands filled with spectators watching her deliverance: Mother . . . grandpa . . . grandma . . . Michael . . . Cotter Sloan . . . and Ben . . . Henry running through the field with two new sets of deadbolts . . .

Swoosh, swish! Swoosh, swish!

Chotto . . . Just a minute . . . *Aa* . . .

She slipped out of her life's strangest dream with an ease that half astonished her. And the sense that this awakening was a general coming to life. Nothing had changed overnight, that she knew. Yet an intricate crossing that had lasted years had finally brought her to shore.

Mo Leigh, in love with the sound of her name, slid out from under the rich satin sheets and bounded to the closet, small breasts bobbing happily.

The acid-washed black denims were hanging in a tidy row, with white and pink and jet-black tees, and spanking new black Reeboks.

She *hadn't* been dreaming. She'd *taken* the F. She'd *gone* to the Village, though not where she'd planned. But tomorrow was here if her heart didn't fail her and—

Swoosh, swish! Swoosh, swish!

Ben, in his garden, was at it again.

Old Ben . . . Gentle Ben . . .

Mo chose one of the three jeans she'd bought, a snug fit that had taken some tugging at first. But, on, they'd felt *so*—well, so *Mo.* A second skin that dipped low at the waist and so realigned her proportions—her torso, more *fluid,* was up to those legs; her fine ass, dramatically centered.

Okay, she thought . . . I am okay . . . I wish my breasts were bigger . . . But . . .

Swoosh, swish! Swoosh, swish!

(That was odd . . .

Well, maybe not . . .)

Mo slipped the pink tee on over her head and tucked the end in nice and snug. No high rise of excitement there, but firm and pertly rounded slopes. Tips responding nicely to the soft touch of fresh cotton.

Fine . . .

Swoosh, swish! Swoosh, swish!

(The sound *was* coming from the back . . .)

Mo padded through the living room, stopping at the security door, from which—an illusion, she guessed . . . she was *sure*—an eerie chill air trickled. Faded. And was gone.

Swoosh!

(Make a note . . . Phone Henry . . .)

Swiiiiissssshhhhh!

Mo turned her head back and marched, head high, in purposeful strides through the kitchen.

She parted the white flowered curtains an inch. To see the happy smiling face of the arch-fiend Cotter Sloan: his biceps rippling, slick with sweat, as he leveled the yard with long strokes of the scythe.

And at that moment Mo Leigh knew that everything would be just fine.

xxiii. SATURDAY: 8:00 A.M.

"Hey," he whispered. "Wait. Don't go."

She turned before he pitched that "Hey." But Saturdays were all the same: the *unbeerable* lightness of being that tormented him Monday through Friday gave good weight on Saturday, its gravity mercifully freighted with hope, before the weekly crack-up on Sunday's drunken edge . . . His world into atoms and eves spent alone . . .

But today was Saturday. Impossible to think of that. Impossible not to believe that she'd call, as she'd called every Sunday these long months she'd been gone. Impossible not to imagine himself hearing her voice again, bells in the wind again, sending old-time sexy shivers up and down his spine again. This week's fix delivered in a chime that thrilled him to the quick. This week's clue. The real one.

Sloan was still eyeing the window when he heard the front door close. The smile did not leave his face.

She was cute as a button.

A really nice girl.

And Sloan had no trouble imagining how, in another time or place, a man might overcome the weight of—potent *similarities*.

He thought about her sometimes, just as he was thinking now. The way she smiled and cocked her head. The way she'd stood up to him once in the hall. An inner surge of confidence flowing somewhere underneath. Courage there. And dignity. What was she wearing underneath . . .

(Ohhhhh,

noooooo,

cut it off!

Don't even think about it . . .)

Well . . .

The air was fresh, the sun was light, and Sloan started swinging the scythe as he wished that he could simply tell her.

Just tell her, plain and simple.

That it was nothing personal.

He ached with sorrow in his bones.

To think of things he'd said and done.

Would say.

And do.

For love.

Sweet love.

xxiv. SATURDAY: 10:15 A.M.

"Now, this won't hurt a bit," he said. "Come on, relax, don't be so stiff." In the madness that surrounded them, the outrageous Bryant-san seemed right in his element.

Orange hair, shocking-pink, lime-green, grape and fuchsia . . .

Spiked hair, funky crews and shags, Mohawks, rattails, combos . . .

On the left, an androgynous dome had been shaved into neat rows of sixes and nines. On the right, a cherry braid snaked out of a gold Lurexed skull.

The Astor Place was jumping. And tomorrow was here, if her hair didn't fail.

"Shirata Sensei."

"Mo. And—"

"Bill."

He stood behind the swivel chair. And ran his fingers through her hair, almost like a lover. He extended two strands of her country-girl cut and held the sections out like wings.

"Anything you want," he said. "As far out as you want to go. I mean, I can take your hair right out to *The Twilight Zone*."

Mo bit her lip. "Welrl, not that far."

He started cutting. "Mo, believe me. The time has arrived to get *funky*."

THIRTEEN

"Why, I thought you'd forgotten about it!"

Mo heard Ben's voice through the door to the garden before she had a chance to knock.

The cedar bridged the house's bricking and the garden wall—thatched cedar topping more glorious brick. An orgy of scimmia climbers curled their vines in lush designs around the crowning panels. And over the climbers, just through the door, the source of the peculiar scents that had teased and perplexed Mo Leigh's senses for months. Vaguely familiar, impossibly strange. An old question trying to surface at times, the tip of it rising, then lost under waves of the glorious sense of the scents in themselves. Now lost again in a wave like no other as Ben Shacklette opened the great cedar door.

His surprise, apparently, more or less equaled her own.

He pulled his jaw up by invisible wires; muttered something to himself, and continued to stare at her hair: a spiked shag with a long string tail and fiery streakings of crimson.

Ben chuckled softly and tugged at his beard. "Blow me down," he muttered. "I reckon it's been about forty years since I've felt *this* surprised."

Mo Leigh smiled impishly, materializing her hidden left hand, with the minicake flush in the palm.

(Hi there . . . Nice to meechuh . . . Whoa . . .)

Mo thought old Ben might be having a stroke. He took a step back, then another one, reeling. He looked ashen and bug-eyed and slack in the mouth. He sputtered. And stammered. And finally managed, "For God's sake—put that candle out!"

"I can't believe I said that."

They were seated on the patio, a happy combination of pale rust-colored pavier bricks (fired, he told her, for hardness and strength) and tawny-colored furniture, hand-carved from the ripest oak. Above them, the cedar pergola supported climbing honeysuckles of almost blinding whiteness, the shadows of its crossbeams like long bars to the ground.

The sense of enclosure was neat and dramatic. Mo felt as if they were on stage, watched in eerie silence by the wonders of Ben's garden. All were rearranged beyond recognition into a whole of such power and beauty it took her breath away. And left something lighter, and darker, than air: a curious sense of *knowing* this place. In all of its particulars. And in their odd combinations.

"It's a terrible thing, getting old, dear. You start losing it from the top down, I'm afraid."

Ben stretched and didn't look so old, his eyes a splashing shade of blue. His dress navy sweatshirt rose up a couple of inches. Mo was treated to a flash of surprisingly taut, hairy belly. She had not caught a glimpse so far of his habitual stoop. He looked ten years younger.

"You're not so old," she scolded. "I think you look—fit as the fiddle today."

"You think so? I'm sure *feeling* good. I'd guess a bit fitter than you feel with that wrist of yours. Say, what—"

Mo said firmly, "I like spring."

Something in her voice caused Ben to drop the question. "Yeah," he said. "Me too. What's been planted, coming up. What's gone around, coming around once again."

He directed her attention with a flourish of his hand. And the garden came at her in waves once again, the tide washing over all tension and doubt, along with the questions she'd wanted to ask.

(Say, Ben, about that candle, please . . . And what did you mean about What's gone around . . . And—)

"Come on, I'll show you what I mean."

The long, narrow yard had been sculpted, from stone and grass and tended seed, into a magnificent triptych. Each panel set between a wall of mellow brick and cedar and a footpath of gray flagstone paving, randomly set in a careful design. The footpath, in turn, framed a perfectly trimmed square of pure emerald-green.

Mo trailed Ben's sprightly figure along the flagstones in front of the left wall. Most of the shrub names were alien to her: Latin-sounding and hard to pronounce. But the flowers, pale to the point of translucence, harmonized rhapsodically. And teased her in some unfathomable way.

Ben stopped and turned, lightly scratching his head. "Now, what did I just call that thing, the second one we looked at? Drat!"

Scan followed Mo's eyes from the daylilies, with their straplike, brilliant emerald leaves and creamy yellow flowers, to the filigree silvery evergreen leaves with blossoms as white as the kisses of gods . . .

"San-ta-lee-na," Mo recalled.

"*Santolina*—excellent! My word, you go to the head of the class."

Mo beamed and said happily, "*Dōmo*. I have, how do you say it, a pornographic memory. For words and names and certain things. But, as for the flowers themselves, *saa*, I can never tell one from another."

"That's very interesting," Ben told her. "I really *must* remember that. My memory's like a bloody sieve. Sometimes I'm hard-pressed to remember my name. But, I guess you might say with a couple of things my memory's pornographic too. With one or two faces or places or dates."

"I see," Mo said. "This one, what's this?"

"Ah yes, the *Azalea pontica*. It's a type of rhododendron."

"Roh-doh-den-drun," Mo repeated. "Ah-zay-lee-ah pon-tee-kah."

"Mo, I swear, you amaze me. I never, never would have guessed."

"You're an artist," she said.

"An old geezer. Come on."

Ben had built a small five-sided shed in the corner. The cedar matched the fencing and propped up one end of the viny pergola along the north wall.

"You like roses?" he asked her.

"Oh yes, Ben. They're—lovely!"

Ben took her arm. "Stand over here. This baby is one of my favorites. It's called *mutabilis*."

"Myew-tah-bee-lees," Mo repeated.

"Yes, that's it, exactly!" The flowers grew singly

and were, at the moment, a yellow as pale as young butterfly wings. But the color, Ben told her, changed daily. "That's the ticket, eh, Mo? *Change.* Tomorrow the flower we're looking at now . . ." Floating palms. A wistful shrug. ". . . might just be sporting a Mohawk or a purple or pink streak."

Mo Leigh giggled, solitaire, and changed the subject smoothly.

"What color," she asked, "does it change to?"

Ben gave her elbow another light tweak. "Come back in a month and see!"

He directed her gaze to the creamy white flowers in umbrella clusters. "Mrs. Wilson's Rose," he said.

"Mrs. Will's Son's Rose."

"That's it. And here, Frau Dagmar Hartopp."

"Frow Dagg-marr Hard-top."

"You *are* good. You're very good. Don't be shy, look closely now."

The last had single flowers of the clearest shell-pink imaginable, with 14-karat stamens gleaming in the sun.

"I see," she said vaguely.

"Oh, I'm sure you do. You just don't know you know it yet. Follow the line of the garden again, from the daylilies there to Frau Dagmar."

Mo did, with rueful frustration. She had never been skillful at puzzles. But from the instant she'd walked through the garden she'd known that—there was *something* about it.

From the softest of yellows . . . to the purest of pinks . . .

"Don't let the names mislead you, dear. Just follow the *line* of the garden. The natural progression. From the daylilies there, to Frau Dagmar, to here . . ."

Ben led Mo to the final panel, the center of which was the heart of the place.

And the only name she knew.

"Osakazuki," she murmured.

"Uh-huh."

The Japanese maple, as high as the wall, was sturdy, straight, and impeccably trimmed, a mushroom of foliage traced with a slide rule. The greenglorious leaves were exquisitely shaped, as deeply cut as fingers.

(Green . . .)

(Don't let the names mislead you . . .)

(Green . . .)

"The redvein enkianthus, Mo."

"Sorry, I was—thinking."

"Good."

Mo had long since despaired of the cryptic remarks and focused instead on the curious names. She'd been warned they would only mislead her. But Scan was still crazy to plenish her pornographic memory.

"Red-vain en-kee-yahn-thoos."

"Yes!"

Pendulous, bell-shaped flowers hung in inverted clusters, creamed-gold blossoms tipped with bold splashes of bloodred.

"The Adolphe Audusson," Ben said.

"Aid-awlf oh-doos-sohn?"

"Oh, yes!"

A rare and exquisite camellia, its bloodred petals redoubled around a tuft of incomparable gold.

(Red . . .)

"So, what do you think?" old Ben asked Mo. His eyes were so hopeful and intense that she had to think twice of her answer.

"Wakaranai," she murmured, Scan idling nowhere in sight.

"Wah-kar-ah-nye," Ben said. "Hot damn. That means you don't get it, right?"

"Yes," Mo said. "You—lost me. You took me out to lunch."

"Well, I just know you'll get it, Mo. To me, it's as plain as the nose on your face. What got planted . . . Hey, come on. Why don't we go have that cake?"

Ben shoveled in a mighty load and chewed with maniacal gusto. Halfway through, he asked her in a spray of chocolate, "You got any oh-knees?"

And that was when Mo dropped her fork and—

(Ooooo—)

(No!)

(niiiii!)

(No!)

opened her mouth in a wide silent scream.

FOURTEEN

Ben towered over Mo, tall as an oak, with straight, sturdy branches: soothing words, low murmurings, assurances that she was fine.

Branches to shade and protect her, and perch her hopes of safety on.

Ben rubbed her shoulders, massaging her neck. And the branches continued to throw down their shade.

"It's okay. Hey, hon, you're fine. You're fine, you hear? You're fine, just fine. You know, I *like* your hair like that. And I promise never to ask you again about your brothers and sisters, or—"

"*Nani?*"

"Cross my heart, hope to die. No more oh-knee, ah-knee talk. Sure wish to God they'd told me at the Yamataka Kiss-a—"

"Ben." Mo started to chuckle, softly at first . . . then a real croak-giggle, outrageous and low, from the belly and down.

"*Sumimasen,* please, for laughing," she said. "But you make a mix-up, *ne?* My brother is my *onii,* if he is older than I am. My older sister is *anē.*"

Ben scratched his head and took his seat. "I thought—"

"You said, do I have any *onis*. *Oni* and *onii,* Ben-san, are different like the day and night."

"Say it again, eh? They sure *sound* alike."

"*Hai. Sō desu.* I know they do. Listen, please, and repeat after me. *Onii,*" she said slowly. She exaggerated slightly so that it sounded like "Oh-kneeeee" and Ben could hear the hold note.

"Oh-kneee," Ben repeated.

"Good. My *onii-san* is my brother. Now, please listen carefully. *O-ni,*" she said slowly, each syllable the same length.

"Oh-knee!" he repeated.

"Good. If I have *onii-san,* Ben, sometimes it is good, sometimes it is not so good. But if I have an *oni*—then my life can only be bad."

Mo Leigh set her fork down, thinking she had said enough.

But the World's Greatest Neighbor pressed on. "What exactly *is* an oh-knee, hon, if you don't mind my asking?"

There were sixteen known ways to avoid saying no. But not one of the ways she had mastered came to her service now. For the mist had been thickening all afternoon, since her eyes had first set on the garden . . . And so, she bowed and said, "Oh . . . Welrl . . ."

In Japan, people say, there are eight million gods in the heavens and on earth. There are gods in mountains; in oceans, lakes, and pools of rain; in trees and plants; in homes and barns; in stoves and clocks and toilets. The gods themselves, it is believed, are usually benign. But they do sometimes react to agitated states of mind.

The Japanese are trained from birth in the absolute imperative of inner equilibrium.

For there are also demons, too numerous to mention, who play an active part in causing loss of balance. Demons of sickness and hunger and hate; of greed and desire and war.

"Gets a little crowded over there," Ben said.

Mo Leigh smiled grimly. "It is sometimes known as 'the rush hour of the gods,'" she said.

"How 'bout that. And these oh-knees—"

"*Iie.* An *oni* is, how do you say, *something else.*"

There were levels, and levels, of demons. With gradients of power ranging from playful to eerie to awesome. Demons from the bush leagues might transform themselves into foxes or snakes, and wreak all manner of mischief. No special reason. No serious harm. Tricks. Pranks. Banana peels left for the spirit to slip on. A pratfall was good for a laugh in itself.

On the middle levels, tricks and jokes were child's play. Demons had more muscle to flex: were able to transform themselves into lightning and thunder and fire and more. And cause actual physical mayhem. They took malevolent pleasure in causing loss of balance—and setting the gods, who outnumbered them so, at the throats of humans. They specialized in confusion and sweat, but were not too proud to stoop to jealousy, pettiness, envy, or spite.

On the upper levels, the worst of the lot went about their business with unrivaled dedication. And the worst of the worst were the *onis*. Of all the demons known to man, none craved destruction and death more than these.

"The Wild Bunch," Ben murmured.

"*Hai.*"

The *onis* themselves could be located on a sliding scale of danger. The smallest might drive a man mad in a week. The greatest could rip one's arms out of the sockets.

"Good Lord," Ben said. "They're demons, though!"

Mo nodded, realizing where his tack was headed.

The *onis* were spirits indeed—to begin with. But their particular genius lay in finding and taking on physical form.

Ben slid to the edge of his chair, propping his chin on a tight-knuckled fist. "And just how does it do that?" he said.

Mo shivered and said, "*Saa* . . . Welrl . . . This is how I learned the tale in Shizumi, the town I was born in . . ."

An *oni*'s potential was fearsome, for certain, but before it could move it must pass through two doors. The first was the doorway to physical form, a passage that might take it many long years.

"Oh yes," Ben said, "I can see that. I can. Why, an oh-knee does have all the time in the world."

Exactly. But one day, when the moment had come, when an intricate chain of events had conspired to produce an atmosphere so *right*, so ripe for evil and pain . . .

"Bad vibes," Ben said softly.

"Ee?"

"Bad vibrations. In the air."

Then, and only then, could an *oni* make its first tentative move.

"Tentative, you say. You mean . . ."

Mo nodded solemnly. At this particular stage, the *oni*'s powers were still limited. In its quest for form, small creatures made for easy prey. And an *oni* might work up the ladder from worm . . . to snake . . . to bird . . . to dog . . . until it had found the right form for its work.

"But how, Mo—how exactly . . . ?"

The old man seemed beside himself. And Mo lost herself in the narration, as if she were simply returning his tale of that long-ago Sunday in May.

"The *oni,*" she told him, "comes in through the mouth."

"Lord God Almighty! I'll bet it hurts like *hell,* eh, Mo?"

Her stomach growled. She flushed and said, "Welrl . . . So people say."

"And bloody? I'll bet it's bloody as—"

"Hai . . ."

Ben grinned and nodded happily. "Jesus Christ, the two of us and our damned ghost stories, eh?"

Mo nodded, half anesthetized by the putting of fear into fable.

"But the one thing I don't get is *this.*" Ben screwed his eyes into a curious squint. "I mean now, when push comes to shove, what gets an oh-knee going? I mean, what sticks in their craws? What pisses 'em off? What sets 'em loose? What—"

"Hai," Mo said. "I understand. What starts their *rains of terror?"*

"Yes, you've got my meaning now. What really, truly turns their cranks?"

"Ben," she said softly, "do you understand *rōnin?"*

Ben stroked his beard with an uncertain thumb. "Seems to me I do," he said. "Weren't them roh-neens renegades—you know, outlaw sam-ur-eyes?"

"Exact-ly," Mo said. "Out-laws. Like *onis,* all for hire."

The old man's eyes strained against the confines

of their sockets. "Wait now, just a minute there. You don't mean that—you or me . . ."

"Oh, no, *no*," Mo answered. "Has to start the other side. *Onis* hate all humans."

"But *who* does the hiring, then? *Who* gets 'em going?"

Mo looked at her watch. There were sixteen known ways—

But the old man, grown relentless, reached across and seized her hand. "Lord have mercy on my soul, you can't leave me hanging now!"

"*Saa* . . . *So* . . . You see, it's like this . . ."

Human spirits also traffic in the "rush hour of the gods"—the ultimate goal of life being *sorei:* the long line of ancestral spirits protecting the family's welfare. After death, however, the soul is ragged and impure. And these soiled, unready spirits, called *aramitama,* rely on human rituals of appeasement and purification. There are, from time to time, however, certain—complications, and the spirit, trapped, continues to float between death and afterlife.

"I see. Now ain't that somethin'. What *kind* of complications, though? You lost me a turn or two back there on the long pike to *so-ray.*"

If the rituals were not performed consistently for seven years, by all of the family members . . .

If the rituals were not performed with absolute love and devotion . . .

Or, if at the very verge of death . . . at the *precise instant* of dying . . . the soul was not released from an extreme state of emotion . . .

If the person died quite painfully, or died burning for revenge . . .

"You mean, this a-rah-mee-tah-mah spook is stuck out there in limbo?"

"*Hai.* Until it can have its revenge. But, you see, the real complication—"

"Uh-huh. There just ain't that much a mere spirit can *do,* short of stopping your ticker or driving you nuts. And from what you're telling me, that just might not be enough. I mean, for a screaming, red-hot a-rah-mee-tah-mah."

"So . . ."

The spirit's bid for services would pass along thc sliding scale until an available *oni* of the right size and awesomeness agreed to take the case.

"So the a-rah-mee-tah-mah has everything at stake: so-ray if the oh-nee wins, lights out if it loses, eh?"

"All or nothing," Mo agreed.

"But—wait, let me think how to put this now—what's in it for the oh-knee, eh? They got some special currency over on the other side?"

"Wakaranai," Mo answered. "What does special—"

"Money, honey. Payoff time. What exactly is an oh-knee's reward?"

"Ah," Mo said. "That's easy, Ben. Every day is Christmas when an *oni* has a kill."

Ben sat in stunned amazement as she slid her chair back to go. "You can't go yet."

"It's getting late."

"Just tell me what they look like, eh?"

Mo straightened and chewed on the question a moment.

There were pictures of *onis,* she told him, from knee-high to seven feet. The smallest had pig snouts and long-pointed ears, while the lords of the *onis* were hulking creations with murder and hate in their fiery eyes.

"My *word,*" Ben said. "That's as scary as sin. It sure don't sound as if a human has a chance in Hades."

"Maybe one," she answered. "The *oni*'s second door."

"What's that?"

"An *oni,* you see, cannot enter your home, unless it is invited."

"Well-l-l." Ben slipped to his feet, smooth as Henry Daez, and showed her the way to the gate. "I feel a whole lot better knowing no oh-knee broke into your place."

Mo thought about that and agreed it made sense.

"'Course the trick now's not to ask any in."

"Exact-ly," she said. "Ben?"

"Uh-huh?"

"May I ask you something?"

"Shoot."

"Do you remember you said—about somebody's wife?"

"I remember. Very well."

"Ben, I know Henry is—*s'teki*—a wolf? But I think in his heart . . . Was she—yours?"

"Oh, Lord in heaven, no, child. You think that young peacock would strut his stuff for an old bag of bones about *my* age?"

Scan screeched and skidded, and Mo caught the drift, but could not, for the life of her—

"Cotter's."

"Ee?"

"He was putting the blocks, that landlord of yours, to *Mrs.* Cotter Sloan."

Mo stepped out the door to the alley and turned, free of the mist and the garden.

Ben's eyes told her nothing she wanted to hear.

It was true, it was true.

The World's Greatest Lover . . .

"Oh, by the way . . . I plumb forgot. That damned husband of yours was around Friday morning. Think he took something out of your mailbox."

Mo was halfway to her door when the old man called to her. "Not a word to Henry, eh?"

FIFTEEN

"Ben?"

"Henry? Is that you?"

"Yeah, pops, how you doin'?"

"Fine."

"You sound a little out of breath." Daez cradled the phone with his chin on his shoulder, and hooked his right leg in the sling. He hoisted smoothly, held the stretch.

"Ah, you know, at my age. Wait—" Ben whipped off the last seven sit-ups, completing his third set of thirty since Mo Leigh had gone. He panted a bit, just for effect, into the pearly receiver. "Just cleaning up around the house. Now then, Mr. Daez, what can I do you for?"

"Ben, about those deadbolts. The ones for Mrs. Leigh."

The old man chuckled ruefully. "They're still waiting at the shop."

"Say, Ben. Look, on second thought . . ."

Ben cupped the receiver intensely, as if reeling in the line.

"Ma—I mean, *my*, uh, thinking is, it's just not cost-effective. I put the locks in, she moves out, I've gotta change the locks and—"

"Yeah, I'll tell you, Henry, your mother makes Jack Benny look like Jesus handing out the fish."

"*Tell* me," Daez said. He slipped his right foot from the sling and through a slow high kick in place at an image of his mother. With a pigeon for a face.

Ben lowered his pitch a half octave to its deepest, richest Sunday best.

"Let's say I *give* them to you."

"*What?*" Daez dropped his foot and came to, unaware of the footsteps behind him.

"No charge," Ben said. "A freebie. Only met her once, in passing, but she seems like a nice enough girl. Supposin' we just give her a little peace of mind?"

"Oh, I couldn't," Daez said. "I couldn't—for free?" He thought he heard somcthing; half turned; changed his mind.

"You've *got* to," Ben urged him. "I mean—Henry, please. I thought you were one of the Good Guys." Ben squeezed the pearl so tightly he heard it make a little crack.

"Well, if you put it that way."

"Yep-p-p."

"I'll drop by Monday morning."

"Good."

Daez clicked the receiver and turned with a smile—that disappeared on contact with mother's granite palm.

"You slick prick little weasel, you, did I just hear you almost pass up a *freebie* from Ben Shacklette?"

SIXTEEN

Well, it's Saturday midnight, you're out on the town . . . You're getting much better, *much better,* at this. You're a veteran now of the R train . . . the F . . . and other trains await to speed you down new lengths of rail . . . Keep on stretching . . . Ride 'em, girl . . . the 2 . . . the 3 . . . the A . . . the E . . . Are you worried? . . . A little? . . . Well, don't be . . . Your body language is superb . . . Your pink T-shirt's out of sight . . . Safe again, you're you again . . . Do let us into your garden . . . Unfold . . . You amazing and shy and mysterious flower . . .

On stage an unspeakable voice met its match in a snatch of unsingable Dylan. The sixties re-emerging. And duly bound for Tokyo, where the fifties were still in a big kind of way, around the year 2000.

Profs in cord jackets with suede elbow patches . . . Beats with moustaches and days' growths of beards, berets cocked at radical angles . . . Day clerks, out of uniform, were now hungry actors in blue jeans . . . Women in T-shirts and old rumpled sweaters, with minds of their own and ideas in their eyes . . .

Mo's cappuccino had grown cold, the foam fizzled down to a pale slick of cream. She forced another sipful. Over the rim of her white and black mug, a distant mirror image.

(Hi!)

Funky . . . Truly . . . Out of sight . . . Foxy as all get-out . . .

(*Hai!*)

One of *them* . . . Belonging here . . . With a mind of her own and ideas in her eyes . . .

Calling . . . Calling . . . Loud and clear . . .

(Help me . . .)

(Won't you help me . . .)

(I'd rather be dead than outside you like this . . .)

(I'd rather be gone than go back to the past . . .)

(I'd rather be finished than not start again . . .)

(I want a chance . . .)

(I want someone . . .)

(I'm lonely . . .)

(I'm so horny . . .)

(Please, won't somebody fuck me . . .)

(*Please* . . .)

SEVENTEEN

Young again!

Alive again!

Complete again!

In love again!

Sloan knew he was dreaming, had to be dreaming, never having been that young, or that alive, or that complete. But a part of him seemed to recall that he had, in fact, been so in love. So, he followed the dream where it led him, through the visions of roses and robins and wine.

Sloan was back with his old flame, Maureen, on the knoll. Time out for T-shirts and denims and patches. Time out for long hair and sky-high ideals.

PEACE . . . LOVE . . . HARMONY . . .

Hippies everywhere in tunics and togas and LSD gowns. And, in the background, six troubadors luting the rich mines of Aquarian Gold: "Lucy in the Sky" . . . "Strawberry Fields" . . .

Sloan's hair a lustrous black he'd never, never dream like this again.

Reflections in her emerald eyes of a self he'd lost forever.

(But if he could dream it, could it be lost?)

Sloan looked up and over the hills at the next horizons, each one truer than the last.

"I love this dream," he told her.

"I rove it too."

And there she was, screaming and swinging her cleaver again as he rolled away, frantic, and jumped to his feet. And he didn't speak the language but he knew it wasn't Peace or Love. And he knew if the phone didn't ring pretty soon he'd have to do it all over again. But the clock in the dream said a minute to twelve, so he scrambled, barely, out of reach, for a minute, one minute, of dream time. The White Album, a shield on his left arm. In his right hand, the great Rambo knife. Bombs and screaming everywhere, with just thirty seconds to ring time. A parry, a block with the album. And just twenty seconds to ring time. Charlie's mad-eyed, pint-sized wife circling and screaming and crazy to kill. And just fifteen seconds to ring time.

Another charge . . . A parry . . . Good! . . . Come on, ten more seconds to ring time . . . You can do it . . . Sure you can . . . *All you need . . . All you need . . . Lucy in the Sky-y-y-y . . .*

"EEEEEEE!!!" . . .

In a wild spray of foam and blood, she swung the cleaver at his heart. And before he could stop it, his hand with the knife—twelve inches long and snaggle-toothed—slit her, womb to sternum, and came out again near her throat: with a small head—too cruelly aborted—impaled through the ear on the tip. The fetal body, torn off at the neck, slipped through her red fingers as the dying woman fell. All the while screaming.

"EEEEEEE!!!"

Screaming . . .

He was . . .

Scringing . . .

Ringing . . .

Sloan reached for the phone like a lifeline and cried out as it slipped through sweaty fingers to the floor. He thought it might break and so shatter her voice. And then she would be gone for good. But he heard her small voice, made a million times smaller, just there inside the receiver.

She said, "Cotter . . ."

"Come home."

She said, "I—"

And said, "I—"

And said, "Ohh . . ."

He said, "No questions asked. Just come."

She'd been phoning two months, every Sunday at twelve, to let him know where he might find her. This week.

For a second he thought she was crying. But then it started up again, the tired droning repetition of the weekly mantra. "I'm nothing. I'm not worth the pain I've caused you. I'm not worth a single candle burning in your heart."

"Fuck this horseshit. Just tell me where you'll be."

"Tuesday. Ten o'clock at 'Pete's.'" Her voice was slurred. She sounded stoned.

"I wait for fifteen minutes."

"Darling." Whiny. Not like her.

Sloan was grooving on the change. "I wait and then I cut you off."

"Cotter!"

"I will cut. You. Off!"

EIGHTEEN

Mo Leigh had also selected a set of black and crimson cotton sweats, her gray days gone forevermore.

She was breaking them in on the thick crimson rug when the telephone began to ring. Her mind was calm; her focus, sharp; the general prognosis, good—progress slow, but *what the hey.*

"'CoursethetricknowsBlowmedownIreckonit's beenaboutfortyyearsForGod'ssakeblowthatcandle out ...."

Twin candles burning in the hollow where mom's picture used to be. The aching left in Mo Leigh's heart already healing with her wrist. Her heartbeat as smooth as a marshmallow bounding on a thick layer of foam.

Scan purring and spinning and stopping on dimes, first in succession and then quite at random, thoughtless of all but the words in themselves and the high road to Funky.

"You'rereadyIcantellComeonIhatethesebirdsI sweartoGodTheygrossmeoutcompletelyCheez Must'vebeenfromBrooklyn ...."

Scan humming and purring and Mo right at ease. Filled with the sense of herself on the edge of the start of the rest of her life. Things falling somehow into place, in their own unfathomable, puzzling way.

So, the World's Greatest Lover had turned out a hybrid of World's Greatest Landlord and Shit. His phone call last midnight was fresh in her ears. ("Did I wake you up, Motoko? . . . Mo . . . I just phoned to tell you—Mo—that your new locks are in . . . That's right . . . Mr. Sloan will install them on Monday, how's that? . . .")

Cotter Sloan had smiled again and hadn't made a peep all day.

Ben was a loyal, if puzzling friend.

And Michael, whacko in the end, was no longer the threat she'd perceived him to be.

She had bars on her windows.

Soon, locks on her door.

And if only the phone would stop ringing . . .

Mo Leigh sighed, thought *Fuck a duck,* and bounded smoothly to her feet. She reached the phone in six slow strides, thinking—hoping—that it might be Bill.

"Mo!" The voice was frantic.

She stared at the bars and said, "Michael."

"Don't hang up the telephone."

She picked up the rubber ball and started squeezing away.

(*I'm your goddamn husband!!!*)

The words burned in her throat. "You were here the other day."

"I—took something."

Squeeze.

"I heard."

"Mo, what I took was a letter. From my lawyer, about deportation."

"I don't understand."

"I mean—there's no way I can do it."

"Oh, Michael," she murmured.

"Yeah," he said. "And listen, about that other night . . ."

"Forget, please," she said. "Thank you."

"Yeah . . . Mo— Aw, this is tough . . . I just got a wire. Your moth—your *second* mother doesn't have your address. Your father's really sick this time."

Mo stared at the receiver, stunned, wondering how to react. Except to keep squeezing away.

"I see," she managed finally.

"Look, I know you— Call her."

Squeeze.

"We don't speak for many years."

"You've got to go."

"I think so. Yes."

"Have you got the money, Mo?"

". . ."

"Stupid question. You and your goddamn Japanese pride. Well, here's what you do when you hang up the phone. You start packing your bags—"

"Michael, please."

"Just do it. Because you're on the first plane out."

"Dekinai." She dropped the ball.

"You *can*. And I won't take no for an answer. So,

get a good night's sleep, okay? I'll send the limo over at noon with your ticket and a couple grand."

"But Michael—"

"Bye, Mo."

"I'll pay—"

Click.

NINETEEN

From Tokyo, by Shinkansen, Shizumi was only a two-hour ride. But the flight had been some fourteen more, with two hours' detention at Customs (her hair the source of a number of jokes and a panty-by-panty search of her bags). At six, when she debarked the train, her bearings were already spinning. She felt hungry and tired and vaguely depressed and semidiarrheic.

Swarms of hotel agents clamored for attention, leading the trickle of tourists to cabs. In the corner, a wino—good help, hard to find—smoked disconsolately. Between his feet, a tattered sign:

"GRAND HOTEL . . . SURPASSINGLY ELEGANT . . . SURPRISINGLY CHEAP . . ."

She ignored the agents. As they did their best to ignore her in turn, with their cool, perfunctory bows. Shizumi had come a long way since the war . . . but not so far it could afford the changes that *her* kind might bring. Here she was, a young Tokyo chick, with crimson streak and crazy shag . . . in her black tee with pink "Groovy" *kana* . . .

Motoko gave back just as good as she got. She started sending signals, unmistakable transmissions, with her hurt and angry eyes.

I. Do. Not. Be. Long. Here.

I. Don't. Want. To. Be. Here.

Nobody asked to help carry her bags.

Nobody stood in her way.

Shizumi, like Motoko, was small but on the make; with a past and a yen for the big town. It was perhaps inevitable that their destinies should clash.

Well situated in the southeast corner of the Hyogo Prefecture, between Osaka and Kobe, Shizumi was 49.21 square kilometers, with a population of 70,000. Running through it, east to west, were the Hanshin Railroad, the National Tokaido, and the smaller lines. From north to south, four rivers crossed the aggressive expansion of rails: the Kanzaki, Shoge, Yomo, and Muko.

Shizumi fancied itself the industrial center of the Hanshin Zone, with a proliferation of iron, chemical, and metalworking plants in the far northern parts of the city. By 1980, the value of exported goods amounted to two million yen.

The Good Life had come late to Shizumi, but the trappings of Civilization were embraced with trembling arms. The lowliest serfs in their ramshackle huts now listened to Mozart on compact discs, while eating rice with chopsticks.

The North and Northwest sections sported vast apartment towers . . . shopping malls with Calvin Kleins . . . Western-style restaurants . . . office buildings . . . cinemas . . . three nude-dancer nightclubs . . .

Motoko turned south from the station, directing her steps to the old Quiet Sea. The road tapered a half-mile out to two lanes and she walked at a brisk New York clip on one side, ignoring the gawks from odd drivers. A mile from the station she came to a fork in the road and turned left, the sign all the sign that she needed of the section's disrepair.

No high-rises here. No offices or *nūdo* bars. The road to the old Shizumi, of white beaches and the Grand Hotel, was lined with shacks of fishermen, dumps of once-prosperous tour guides and cocky, strutting *shizoku,* sons of sons of samurais.

Her thoughts were never darker than when she returned to the source of it all.

Through these long and narrow streets with their half-naked children and gold-toothed, old crones.

Through the maze of her first memories: the calm smell of rice steaming, the sounds of small women, with faces like geishas, noisily slurping their noodles and soup.

And onward, just a few blocks down, to the corner where mother had borne her—and given, for a few short years, the greatest of all gifts: *amae**.

Father had sold the house when he remarried, of course. And the place was sold again, twice after that. As if mother had not quite resigned herself yet to her tragic dispossession and kept spooking the new owners out. But Motoko knew better than that, then and now. No soul had been gentler than mother's, or more eager for life to go on.

In any case, mother's poor wandering spirit had long since attained *sorei.* And the old house had prospered, for almost a decade, as a tiny coffee shop. Motoko admired, begrudgingly, the pastries

---

*In Japan, a parent's total surrender to the child's self-indulgence and displays of dependent behavior.

in the window and passed on through the dwindling maze of hovels to the shore.

For years after the *accident* the grotto had been unattended. Three years before Motoko left Shizumi, grandpa funded an earnest attempt to undo the years of neglect. The effort never took, though, and by summer the orchard was starting to look haunted all over again.

Motoko blinked and turned away, starkly aware of the pull of the tides.

(What's been planted, coming up . . .)

(Three feet of freshly razored steel . . .)

She started walking, quickly now, putting good distance between herself and the abandoned grotto.

(*Makoto! I tell you, you take up the sword* . . .)

The shoreline still afforded a majestic view and Motoko narrowed her focus, squeezing the scene from her mind.

(*Will you ruin my story then?* . . .)

The Quiet Sea was still, in places, the most remarkable blue. And stretches of the beach remained the old Shizumi white. A sightseeing boat—the lone survivor—gave a single doleful toot as it made a slow round of the bay. There were, of course, no fishing boats; the factories had poisoned the fish long ago.

(*Did you really think I'd kill myself?* . . .)

Still, if she narrowed her focus—to a tiny stretch of the old blue, a single length of virgin sand—Motoko could remember what Shizumi had been like.

The boom resort with the world-famous spa . . . Mother pointing one fine evening to the distant Grand Hotel, a dream straight out of Disneyland . . . As if to say, One day, my dear, you will stay there overnight . . .

(*Well, what's a good story without one? . . . Surprise! . . .*)

Motoko turned abruptly, the grotto just perceptible. She did not weep. She could not burn. She muttered, and meant it, "You bastard."

(A raw smell filled the air—pungent, overpowering—followed by another smell as brother, all crazy-eyed, cried to the gods:

Ooooo—)

No!

(**—niiii!**)

No!

(**Oni!** Demon **oni!**)

No! Goddamn you to hell!

TWENTY

Monday. 2:06 P.M.

According to the note, she'd left for JFK at noon and would be gone all week.

Six days!

The World's Greatest promptly dispatched Cotter Sloan on a round of red-herring repairs. Mrs. Murphy's month-plugged drain . . . Mr. Meecker's roaches . . .

Daez moved at his leisure now, on this, his second visit, playing with her panties without undue concern.

The locks could wait a day or two. Someone else had been in here a few weeks before; and, just in case she'd rigged the place in some improbable fashion (a snippet of hair that he'd missed on a drawer, a preordered stacking of sweet things), this way he covered his bases.

What a mystery her mind was!

What secret strengths were locked in there?

He raised the panties to his nose, inhaling in a swoon. His cock snorted and buckled. And whinnied. And reared. And tried to take off at the gate through his slacks.

He would have her, by Jesus, the night she returned!

The thought was too much for him. He buried his face in the crimson and lace as if somehow he might reach her. A direct connection through the scented soap and softener. And in the rustle of a zipper . . . the quick flip of a flap . . . the pride of Astoria, joy of his life, was out and in the running . . . nine inches ahead of the great dangling balls . . . the head a shade of purple so rich it cried out for a crown of its own. Shove it down her throat so far he'd cream royal shooting stars out that silky cunt of hers, a fine spray that fell like white rain on her toes.

The image amazed him. He cried out for more, tumbling on the black and blood of her sweet futon. He'd never fallen quite so low. The appalling sensation reclaimed him.

"This is bad," he murmured. "Oh man, oh man, oh shit, oh boy." He inhaled deeply, through both nose and mouth, the cloth attempting passage through any port of call. "I'm crazy about you, come on, suck it up! Oh, I can't believe it, I'm getting so bad! I've never been this bad before!"

Daez folded the panties, then folded them again: a thick-wadded square he fit into his palm, then cupped over the glistening eye of his cock.

"Fucking unbelievable."

She'd miss the panties, sure as hell.

Should he wash them? Replace them?

"Oh Jesus, I don't give a shit. I'm gonna fuck her brains out. Mo-o-o."

Daez surrendered, mad and bad and dangerous to know. Visions flashing in his eyes: bouncing her head like a speedball, pattapattapattapat, from lips to gullet, on his lap . . . the red-eye express coming at him again . . . a snapkick . . . a backfist . . . and Mo, by his side . . . tamed and wholly his at last . . .

He shouted, stunned by the love pumping through him.

He cut the cry, then, suddenly—squiggling, absurdly, in heat.

Something in the cellar.

(Bump!)

And then, nothing. Or something like nothing. But—

(Ooooo . . .)

Shooting stars through crimson, melting on his flaming palm.

And then, slow and stealthy, a key fitting in the back door.

TWENTY-ONE

"Dōzo," her stepmother said. Please come in.

They waited for the maid to go.

The old woman, the last *gejo,* scurried backward to the door, where she bowed still more deeply, then wheeled and rushed off. Perhaps, Motoko thought sadly, to a better year.

Motoko would not soon forget her first return impressions: rank weeds drilling through the cracks of the front stone walkway . . . the banister, once polished to a mighty luster, now worn and splintered and crying for paint . . . the rug in the lobby worn through in two places . . . spots on the mirrors . . . dust on the phone . . .

Stepmother's voice had been beautiful once: high as a wind chime, clear as a stream, tinkling with cool confidence as it flowed through the halls with grandfather's commands. It slipped between the cracks now, the quivers reflecting the gold of her teeth. But her voice had not lost all, and when she repeated, "Please, child, come in," Motoko stepped into the parlor.

Room center, a low table was set for tea. Stepmother sat, legs crossed, beneath the old family portrait: grandpa, as stiff as the back of his sword, the very soul of Old Japan; grandma, wearing her slyest of smiles . . . with her porcelain-perfect expression of peace, her iron fist, her heart of ice; and, in the center, fading in, stepmother at thirty: a schemer who would steal a family's lost knight.

(Father started disappearing months after mother passed on, his footsteps always leading him in the same direction. But who could have guessed where those trips would all lead?)

Motoko sat and crossed her legs, and kept her eyes from stepmother's.

("This will be your mother, and that is where we will live in one month." Father, not yet broken, had brought the rather plain invader to their house at last. He pointed to the Grand Hotel; awaited their reaction. Motoko, four, and Matsuo, ten, stared at the horsey-faced thief in the night. Then they looked at each other and started to cry.)

"How is he?" Motoko said quickly.

"*Saa* . . . He will live till after tea."

Motoko sat, chastened as always when here, by her failure to grasp the essentials.

Stepmother added the tea leaves to the priceless, hand-painted, porcelain pot.

"Remember this, Motoko-san?"

(Oh yes, I remember . . . I remember the day we arrived here. Father had scrubbed us until we both squeaked. We appeared in the lobby at ten o'clock sharp, the day before the wedding. The three of us, lined in a neat little row. Father's hands trembled like leaves at his sides. Grandpa gave him just one glance that told us in an instant what a *mukuyoshi** marriage meant. And though we were just children we understood completely that from that moment on: it was us against you. Grandfather settled his gaze on Matsuo. Grandmother leveled her own sights on me. Our hearts sank. They had plans for us.)

Stepmother began to stir, a ballet of intricate moves with her hands. As she worked, she chatted in the faded remains of her voice. ". . . and I guess you still remember the old village broadcasting system. They discontinued it—*saa,* let me see—about five years ago. Too quaint for the tourists, some people said. *What* tourists, I answered. Well, *shikata ga nai,* of course, and all that. But I always did consider it—well, so Japanese. All those little announcements on all the overhead speakers outside. '*Ohayō gozaimasu, Shizumi no minna-sama* . . . Good morning, everybody in our village of Shizumi . . . The weather is lovely today. A bit cool at this time in the morning. But don't forget your parasols for the hotter noontime sun. And, might I remind you, the unexpected showers for which our dear town is so famous.'"

(Grandfather clapped, like thunder, and boomed from the depths of his soul: "You will have your first lesson in kendo. *Kite!*" At the door, he turned and bowed, allowing Matsuo to pass him. There was a swirl of movement as the wood *shinai* cracked brother's skull. I heard grandfather roar, *"You will be a samurai—or, by the gods, I'll bury you!"* The great door closed. I saw no more.)

Stepmother began to pour, making circles with the cups that held Motoko's eyes.

"The seventies, of course, were hard. Not just for us, but all the hotels. At least along the shore-

---

* A marriage where the male marries into the wife's family. Children often see the father as emasculated.

line. When my father died we were, just barely, able to manage a profit. Now we are able, just barely, to continue the family name."

("You are a Shirata now." Grandmother sighed. "I don't see how, but I will try to turn you into a lady, my dunce." I followed her here to the parlor. She closed the door. And we began.)

Stepmother handed a cup to Motoko, turning it first in her palms.

"*Dōzo.* Let us drink our tea. Then we will visit your father. After you put on a kimono, of course, and do something with your hair."

Motoko had been waiting for this since she came. She matched stepmother's smooth turns of the cup and raised hers to her lips, inhaled. *"Iie,"* she said simply. *"Dekinai."* I can't.

Her stepmother blinked once, then lowered her gaze. "I see."

Father had been dying, in his own mind, since they came here. Indigestion . . . Headaches . . . Insomnia . . . Runs . . .

Grandfather's death, of a stroke on the steps, had only unsettled him more. The symptoms became more exotic. Catarrh . . . Vague congestion . . . A murmur in his prostate . . .

Sō . . . Father's body had caught up, at last, with his mind. At his peak, he'd weighed no more than one-ten, at five five. By check-out time, he'd halved his weight and thrown in an inch for good measure. He'd primed himself so long for death that life could not defeat him now. Swaddled in blankets to combat the chill, he scarcely appeared to be breathing.

Motoko whispered with her eyes.

"He comes and goes," stepmother said.

"How long before—"

"Dr. Nagura says Friday. And he's not often

wrong, you know. He predicted your grandmother's death to the hour. And he warned your grandfather two days before."

Just then father had a moment. He glanced around the room with a glazed expression, then closed his eyes. And sighed. And slept.

The maid gave them a withering look. (Leave it to father, Motoko thought sadly: a master at last—on his deathbed!) Motoko knelt across from her, stepmother by her husband's feet. The maid tucked the blankets in snugly. She felt father's hands, made a grunt of approval; and approved of his pulse with a sigh. She lit another candle, the second in the second row of the ten-by-ten rack by his bed.

Motoko murmured, *"Ee? Hyaku monogatari!"*

One hundred candles . . .

Stepmother made no attempt to conceal the teardrops falling from her eyes.

Motoko fought her own tears back. In this single, last heroic act father slipped forever from her superior sense of the man. *Hyaku monogatari* . . . One candle lit for each demon quelled . . . Eighty-eight candles to go in the night . . .

"He can't complete," Motoko said.

Stepmother whispered, *"Shikata ga nai."*

The maid's eyes flared angrily. She raised a crooked finger to her crooked lips. And Motoko and her stepmother settled back on their heels for a very long wait.

At midnight, exactly, father sat up. The blanket fell away from him. Motoko gasped at the bones underneath. But father's eyes were cognizant. The look of a man at eight in the morning, on the verge of a long-earned vacation. He grinned eerily at the old *gejo*. *"Konnichi wa,"* he said. Good day. The maid's voice quivered, answering. *"Otenki ga ii?"* father asked her. *"Hai, subarashii desu,"* she replied. The weather's really splendid. "Good." Father turned to the foot of the bed, with the same eerie grin for his wife. *"Okā-san,"* he said to her. Mother . . . *"Domo arigato gozaimashita."* Stepmother gave him a slight formal bow. *"Otō-san,"* she said. Father . . . "See who has come to be with us tonight."

The bag of bones turned, somehow without clicking, till father was facing Motoko. The eerie grin diminished slowly into a questioning purse of his lips. He cocked his head. Considered. And just when Motoko was starting to think she should have put on the kimono, father's eyes moved from her face to her hair. He bolted upright, saucer-eyed, and cried out in a strangled voice, "*Matsuo! Onii-san!* Still bleeding after all these years!"

He clutched at his heart then; and fell back; and died.

TWENTY-TWO

The World's Greatest Lover had had his close calls. He'd taken his share of rear windows; had hit the steps two, even three, at a time. But till now he had been spared having to hide in a closet like this.

The footsteps moved, surefooted, from the kitchen to the living room. Daez slid his pants from his knees to his hips over the dribble of semen that ran down his thigh. He raised the zipper—not a sound—and fastened the clasp, a respectable man. The World's Greatest Landlord in action again.

Here in Mo Leigh's closet . . .

Why?

Uh— Well, for one thing— Er . . .

Daez cocked an ear to the closed cedar panel. Footsteps in the living room, lightly moving here and there, as if they belonged here. This was no intruder. Whoever it was had been inside before and knew what he was here for now.

A light taptapping on one of the walls. A nail going in for a picture, perhaps.

More footsteps, calm and confident. To the kitchen and back.

Taptap. Taptap.

Footsteps here. Footsteps there.

Whistling softly to himself.

Taking care of business.

Now . . .

Daez could almost hear the man quietly study his work.

Just so . . .

Footsteps to the kitchen.

Footsteps to the bedroom.

A rustling, smooth as silk, on the bed.

Footsteps to the dresser.

A muted sound, like beads clicking through cloth.

Whistling softly as he took one step, two steps, three steps back.

Stopping to consider.

So . . .

Footsteps to—

A sudden stop.

An unsettling pause.

And then two sniffs, one short, one long.

Footsteps starting up again.

And heading for the closet.

Daez cocked one foot halfway to his shin.

All right, kiddies, here we go.

TWENTY-THREE

"*Gomen nasai,*" stepmother said.

So sorry that you will, please, go.

Motoko bowed. "*Iie.* I will catch the first train in the morning."

The women stood at the foot of the hall. The old maid had more or less dusted. But the west wing, from the look of things, had been shut down for years. The doors had been shut all the way to the end, except for the last on the right.

"The *gejo* has made up your room. It has been changed a little, but I think you will be comfortable. A cab will arrive here at eight-thirty sharp to take you to the station."

"That will be fine," Motoko said.

"You will understand, I hope, if I don't see you off."

"Of course."

Mochiron . . . *Mochiron* . . . It is all understood . . .

But then, with all the nerve in her, she said, "I regret I must ask you a favor. May I please—forgive me—see *onii-san*'s room?"

She had not entered since that day.

Oya-san took a few seconds, then shrugged. "What does it matter now? Take what you like. Why not take *it?* Take the family honor, the shame of us all."

What remained of her past up to '76, the year she left for Tokyo, was packed in thirteen boxes, with a chart in father's meticulous *kanji* hanging by the closet door.

Aside from his genius for following orders, he'd been enamored of lists and had loved to make longhand copies of important documents. (A good-for-nothing, grandpa said, who turned out to be good for one thing after all. A sort of human Xerox. *Saa* . . .) At the top of the list, he had printed her name, so neatly it might have been done by machine. Beneath her name the boxes, numbered, had their contents itemized. Knowing father, Motoko suspected he'd prefigured the postage as well.

A life reduced to thirteen lines on a five-by-six card on the wall.

Box One: schoolbooks, diaries, papers.

Box Two: photo albums.

Box Three: old favorite dolls.

Box Four . . .

Motoko turned and faced herself in every square inch of this cool empty room, stripped down to four naked walls, tatami mats, her old futon.

She would spend the night here, yes.

Then say goodbye forever.

But first there was one more small stop to be made.

Motoko took a sip of air and crossed the hall to brother's room.

TWENTY-FOUR

The footsteps stopped a few feet from the closet.

His balls went as hard as two nuts in a shell. He was sweating, certainly—close quarters gave him the willies—but still . . .

Come on, think now, work it out!

Whoever it was had a key . . . Well, all right . . .

Whoever it was seemed to be right at home . . .

Come on, Henry, use your bean!

(Taptap, taptap, rustle, whistle.)

(Really, what the fucking *hell?*)

The Alvarezes, maybe. But he'd been called two months ago from Pittsburgh to give them a reference.

That crazy husband, Michael. But Sloan had given him reason enough to steer clear of the place for a life and a half.

Sloan, yes, had a key. But was earning his keep at the Murphys'.

The footsteps came within reach of the door. He

heard a graze of fingertips brush lightly over the surface, as if taking a reading through cedar.

Come on, Henry, think it out!

You can only hear heartbeats in the movies . . . Relax . . .

She'd given her keys to someone—yes!—who'd come by to do a few small odds and ends.

(With a taptap, taptap, rustle, whistle.)

(And—what's that—a *crash in the basement?*)

Come on!

Footsteps slowly backing off. The other man turning now, curious too.

Daez listened intently, not fearful, but *thinking* how grateful he'd be if the man would just leave.

Footsteps then to the futon.

A flurry of rustles. Ah, there, that was right.

Footsteps to the dresser.

That same soft click of beads through cloth.

Footsteps to the living room. The lazy, ambling shuffle of a man going over his work step by step.

To the kitchen then.

Then back again. Unbelievably back through the bedroom—oh Jesus!—to stand there for seconds—and *sniff.*

Daez screamed inside from the anger and shame, swearing on all that was holy, if the footsteps did not leave right *now* . . .

Footsteps to the living room. A knock-knock on the security door, with a low here-doggy whistle. *Whuhhh-Wheeeee-Whooooo!* Silence. That low chuckle. Then—

Footsteps, brisk ones, through the kitchen.

Out the door.

Down the steps.

Coming down the alley.

Move!

The World's Greatest slipped from the closet and scurried—

stopped, by a side flash of color.

Daez turned to the rainbow upon the futon.

His heart leapt.

He murmured, "Wow!"

TWENTY-FIVE

"Saa!"

Motoko guessed *onii-san* would never really leave this room. Grandfather had insisted, until his dying day, that nothing here must be disturbed, right down to the unmade futon. As if Matsuo might somehow return and feel lost. Motoko had taken for granted that at some point through the years, the others had managed to—give up the ghost. To file *onii-san*'s possessions, black pages of a red *kaidan*, into a series of boxes, like hers. She saw now the futility. The more you might try to deny it, the more *brother's* the damned room would be. Close your eyes, the vision cleared, as if freed of a mist, in your mind. Turn away and there he was: *onii-san* . . . brother . . . lover . . .

(!!!!!)

Motoko felt her heart grow cold, iced fury bubbling in her eyes.

(*Jū-ni-nen dake desu!* I was only twelve years old!)

Motoko heard her knuckles crack—

(Mo, believe me, the time has arrived . . .)
and surrendered, just this once—

(A woman *needs* her Exercise . . .)
stepping onto the tatami mats with a wary half bow.

Fists clenched, she moved on the balls of her feet, ready for a chance attack by any half-sprung part of him: a piece of cloth, a photograph, an echo of some lost brotherly word.

Nothing had been touched here, except by the curator-*gejo,* who kept the clock set at that last day in May.

Brother, brother everywhere . . .

And not a—

Stop

to think . . .

I can't!

Everywhere I look, I see—

*Shibumi** . . .

Makoto . . .

Onii-san . . .

The gods had you in mind when they thought of these words. These visions were etched in their hearts and their minds countless eons before you were born:

the rakish tilt of your *shinai,* propped in passing against the west wall . . .

your slippers, casually kicked, left then right, into artless symmetry . . .

---

*A sort of spartan elegance; quiet, effortless grace.

your desktop a singular clutter of books: novels by Mishima . . . kendo and Bushido texts . . .

a fifty-pound weight on each side of your chair . . .

a single sheet of rice paper . . . with a perfectly calligraphed *kanji: Go* . . . The Japanese letter for "five" . . .

You arrived after midnight, while all of us slept. You pumped your muscles while you read, arranging your mind and your body. You left us a calligraphed puzzle. You rehearsed your last *kaidan* on earth with your very first *shinai,* now a mere mass of splinters. And then, a proper lunatic, you lay down for a little nap before getting on with the end of your life.

What were you thinking of?

What went so wrong?

What in God's name was your *Five?*

Motoko circled, still light on her feet, though her hands, long unclenched, had grown moist in the palms. And her fingers were trembling a little.

It was no use fighting brother.

No one could win against brother.

The insane courage of his death defeated her unendingly. And crushed her now, as always, with its utter contempt for the hopes of her life.

Motoko shuffled, heavier, to the photo montage on the wall near the door: a young man's ten-year odyssey from the first crashes of a *shinai* on his skull to the twelve trophies queued by the window . . . Brother with grandpa . . . Brother with grandpa . . . Brother pumping iron here . . . Brother starting judo when he turned fourteen . . . Brother with grandpa, their samurai poses, a slice of my kimono showing in between their egos . . . Brother first meeting Mishima in the summer of

'66 . . . Grandmother, always offstage, as she wished, but working her will in the wings—as brother here enters Azalu, the junior high "staircase" to Tokyo U . . . strings pulled by his steely "Education Mama" . . .

Motoko shuffled back to Matsuo's desk.

The pressure . . . The terrible pressure . . . The six-day, hundred-hour weeks . . . with the four-hour round-trip each Sunday for more tutoring in Tokyo . . .

When they slept, I would sneak to your room, sit quietly there in the corner and watch you light into some *kata,* smooth as a shadow and quick as a bolt. And when you were finished, the hour grown late, you'd light a candle and turn off the light and then tell me a horrible story.

Oh, *you* . . .

By the closet, solo, was the picture Motoko remembered the best. Summer, 1968. The year before Tokyo U.

Onii-san stood immortalized on the beach outside the grotto, bathing in the eerie glow of one hundred candles. He'd just set a record for all of Japan in Shizumi's *hyaku monogatari*—one hundred *improvised* tales in a row. One candle relighted for each one he'd told. Baby sister worshipping at big brother's feet.

"No more," Motoko said.

"Goodbye. I leave this room. I leave you here. I love you, but I leave you here. You made your choices. I make mine!"

Motoko turned, the heaviness gone, lightness flowing on up through her feet, vigor instilled in her hairline again.

No, brother couldn't be beaten, she knew.

His lone puzzle might never be entered.

(That Five . . .)

But brother could be *left.*

Like this.

The first step was easy; the second, a breeze; and they kept getting lighter each step of the way. At the door Motoko paused to study two gleaming additions.

The family honor, retrieved from the grotto, had been polished and put back in place on the wall: grandfather's grandfather's grandfather's sword—an authentic, it was rumored, Muramasa* blade; above it, the foot-long *yoroidoshi.* One used, the other un-; one at rest, the other not.

(Balance, the spirit needs balance, Ben, or—)

Motoko pressed three fingers lightly to her lips, then transferred the kiss to the dagger. She did not disturb its peace, but relieved the brackets below it of their far heavier burden.

She eased the great blade halfway out of its sheath. The light reflected from it might well have illuminated the entire west wing. She had listened that night at the door when grandfather presented it.

The peerless Muramasa blades were forged, he said, with hammer blows from the heart of madness . . . tempered at a maximum of 1350 degrees. The steel was the finest in all of Japan—*hontō no kotetsu*—with a carbon content of .9 percent and a phosphorus of only .003. The Muramasa blades could readily cut through sheet metal, nails, steel hawsers, and men's helmets . . . And the brilliant steel reflected the shining of the true samurai soul. I present you with the honor of our family's history, today on your birthday, my son . . .

---

*Muramasa Senzo (b. circa 1341), a brilliant but demented swordsmith.

Motoko smiled grimly, rehousing the blade to the hilt in its sheath, game wrist throbbing from the weight.

(Take the family honor, the shame of us all . . .)

She turned back to the room and she bowed and she said, "You won't be needing this. Goodbye."

Then, to the sword, "You come with me."

TWENTY-SIX

Still panting from the two-flight run, but in a heady mood today, he studied the World's Greatest Lover through a sliver of space in the pearly white drapes. Slick was getting cagey there, parking that little toy sports car of his down the road before having his fun at Mo Leigh's.

It had been close today, yes, much too close. He'd been whistling and tapping and doing his thing, getting closer by the day now to the good old Pearly Gates, when suddenly he'd *known* for a fact that he was not alone.

The sense and the scent came in tandem. The bristling, the corneal zing, and the whiff of that godawful horny cologne.

Daez in the room with him . . . in the closet . . . trapped like the insect he was . . .

And, though the risk was very great—he'd waited now so *many* years—how could he help himself, how could he stop, he just followed his feet to the closet—and *sniffed.*

The World's Greatest Lover . . .

The World's Greatest *Prick* . . .

Ben flinched at the phrasing and shuddered as the World's Greatest rounded the block to his car.

He stroked his candle—call it that—wistfully, remembering the first hot pearly drops she'd licked like drops of melting wax.

(*Tell me, tell me, darling boy . . . Oshiete kudasai . . .*)

Tortuous grazings of teeth on the shaft . . . What did it matter? . . . Oh, who could object? She wanted numbers, that was all . . . And hadn't she told him how *hard* life would be for a woman like her in a place such as this . . . at a time—of all times—like the present. To have fallen in love with a boy, when the price of her failure was her life itself . . . Numbers, useless numbers . . . That was all she needed . . . to milk his candle dry . . . like this . . .

The memory was too much for him. He sat and swiveled back and forth in the Admiral's black leather chair, the stark room's only furnishing. The tears were streaming from his eyes. His hands had not stopped shaking since he walked into the room.

It cost him two matches to light the left wick; he managed the right in a match and a half. The twin candles lit up the arm rests like endpanel lights in a cockpit.

The sky was filled with candles and Ben again was one of them, roaring into view on engines of destruction.

The sky was filled with shooting stars and rows on rows of falling Pearls.

Ben felt himself shrinking again down to size. The floppy-eared flight cap again back in place.

Little Nipper megaspecs. The old pencil moustache. A fine buck to his choppers.

He worked the joystick wildly, cockpit swinging in the sky like a game in a penny arcade.

The candle burned home and he screamed, "*Tennō heika banzai!*"

(For the emperor! The emperor!)

His fine scores recorded forever in three dozen photos on the wall.

(*Tell me, oh, my darling boy!*)

Burning ships . . .

Exploding planes . . .

Under the cool watchful eye of the moon . . . Pearl of the Pacific sky . . .

He flew for hours looking for the body of his father.

Found it nowhere.

And despaired.

Landed at length on a photo that grounded him completely.

Boy Wonder at the radio—fifteen and a regular sailor for sure . . . Look at him there in his crewcut and whites, "hamming" it up while the Admiral watched . . .

(Numbers . . . Only numbers . . .)

(Dad . . .)

(Oh, who will know, my lovely boy . . .)

Ben rose, his body slick with sweat, bleeding Pearls from every pore.

He took the steps two at a time, scarcely stopping to grab Mo Leigh's keys on the way.

Young again . . .

Alive again . . .

Complete again . . .

In love again . . .

with the magical scents of the garden . . .

Oh, yes . . .
What's been planted, coming up.
What's gone around, coming around once again.
"Here it comes," he told himself.
Do it.
Go on—all the way!

TWENTY-SEVEN

Yamada Sensei delivered the goods. From Times Square to Tokyo, chopsock aficionados recognized his cool arrogant eyes, his short angry slash of a mouth.

No one knew exactly how many films he'd made. Two walls in the dojo lounge were covered with his Greatest Scenes. Seven shots had jeweled frames: a step-by-step unreeling of his death at the hands of . . . Toshiro Mifune!

The flow of choicer parts these days was thinning to a trickle. But Sensei, at sixty, still staged his own fights and would die before using a stuntman.

On the third wall, hung over the desk, were three other prized possessions: calligraphs exquisitely done, it was said, by Musashi himself—*Itto-sai . . . Itto-ryu . . . Kiriotoshi . . .*

One sword . . .

One school . . .

One technique . . .

Sensei clapped his hands to start at twelve o'clock precisely. Nine students circled around him: two with staves; three with spears; four with real swords from the film.

Sensei alone used a *bokken** in his life's supreme reversal. Today, as every day at noon, it was he, not Mifune, starring in those jeweled frames. Sensei racing with the clock to meet the actor's record time of five seconds flat.

He warmed his hands, Mifune-style, inside his *hakama*. And paused, to admire a snowflake perhaps, or improvise a haiku.

Motoko hit the stopwatch as he sprang into motion.

He unsheathed the sword with his left hand and thrust it in a blinding flash into the assailant behind him. As the first man fell . . .

Sensei switched hands on the *bokken*, eliminating with one sweep the two men charging on the right. Even as their bodies fell . . .

The fourth assailant, sword undrawn, was cut down on the back swing, which also beheaded the first. And as the fourth fell screaming . . .

The master felled the fifth and sixth with the *kegasake*, a whiplike slashing of the blade. Before the two men reached their knees . . .

Sensei pivoted sharply, dropping the seventh assailant with the flash of a flip of his blade. The man fell like a stone as . . .

The eighth and ninth were halved at the waist with the master's forte: a single slash of lightning, the fabled stroke—*do-giri*.

He resheathed the *bokken*, the guard making the

---

*Extremely hard wooden practice sword: the same size and weight as a real one.

faintest of clicks as it homed. And the "dead" bodies rose to their feet.

He caught Motoko's eyes and smiled. She smiled back and bowed, discreetly eyeing the stopwatch.

"So, you have returned to your Sensei."

"*Sō desu ne.* Today you were faster than ever, I think."

"*Sore hodo demo nai,*" he said. Nothing of the sort.

But Motoko insisted and thanked him and bowed.

"A four-point-nine, I'm sure, today. If you forgive my saying so."

"*Hontō?*" Sensei asked her.

"*Hai.*"

From the dojo a series of bloodcurdling screams, synchronized with mighty stomps, brought a smile to Sensei's face. He clasped his hands behind his head.

"Four-point-nine. That would be nice. But you don't think, perhaps—"

(Yes, I don't, sir . . . No, I do . . .)

"—just perhaps a six?" Sensei held one palm outstretched. "*Misete,*" he said. Show me.

Motoko reached in her handbag, not knowing how he'd seen the watch.

"*Shimatte!*" Sensei muttered, with one of his world-famous scowls.

Five-point-eight seconds exactly.

"*Saa,* even my timing has left me."

"*Gomen nasai,*" Motoko said. I'm sorry. Please forgive me. For coming here. For seeing this. For causing your embarrassment. For being much younger than you are. For thinking that it mattered, to see your Special—

"Motoko-san."

She looked up. She met his eyes. She could not hold that infinitely shrewd and tender gaze.

Motoko cried, "Oh, Sensei!"

"You will look at your Sensei, please, when you break down."

Motoko did, the waterworks trying to start up in earnest.

He said, "I hope your trouble—is not connected with your hair."

Motoko sniffled, better now for a little touch of wry.

"I leave at three," she told him.

"*Sō* . . . Excuse me for a moment."

Sensei rearranged his face—very much the grand master again—before gliding into the dojo.

Motoko heard him clap his hands—a light sound, wasting no power or strength. At once, on cue, the screaming stopped. All helmets turned to Sensei.

A light, barely audible shuffle of feet that must have been the *godan*'s, the fifth-degree black belt.

Sensei muttered gravely, "*Saa.* There seems to be something missing here."

"Hai!"

"I think we need something extra. Something *special,* for speed and for endurance."

"Hai!"

"Today I think . . . I'm *sure* of it . . . Today you'll all run to Tokyo Station, and back, in no more than one hour!"

"Hai!"

The run could be done comfortably by one man, in one hour, one way—if it was other than rush hour. But twenty men, in full attire, making the round-trip at lunchtime?

Motoko gasped, astonished and dizzied by the prospect.

"Hajime!" the *godan* barked. Come on, let's get on with it!

"Hai!" the twenty cried as one.

And then in a thundering rush they were gone.

Sensei seated himself in a smooth, thoughtful move. He drummed his fingers on the desk, glancing at Motoko. From the lower right drawer he produced a black book. With a great "Five" on its cover.

"I assume," he said, "you've come for this."

"Gomen nasai." Forgive me.

"I was afraid you would someday. I warned you, child—"

"I had to."

"It won't help you. There are some things I can tell you that might. But first . . ." He slid his chair back; gave her a lingering, curious look; and rose slowly to his feet. "I've been wondering, for the longest time . . ."

Motoko's heart jumped. Please . . . Oh no . . .

". . . about your Special Exercise."

There were sixteen known ways to avoid saying—

"Come. We only have a little time."

"But, sir," she begged. "Oh, *dekinai!*"

"Of course you can. Come along."

Still Motoko did not move. "Please listen, believe me, I haven't had time—"

"Watashi wa dare deshō ka, ne?" Who *am* I, Sensei asked her.

"Itsumo Sensei desu." You are my teacher, always.

"You *deny* me?"

"Iie!"

"Come!"

Motoko padded slowly after Sensei to the dojo. She waited, helplessly, hands at her sides, while he fetched a practice sword off one wall. He set the sword squarely, still in its scabbard, on a mat between them. He took three good steps back from it.

Motoko said, "Oh, Sensei. Nothing has ever caused me more frustration or unhappiness."

"Sō desu ka?" Sensei answered. "Then it must be working."

"It is useless!"

"We will talk of that."

"I beg you—"

"Hajime!"

Motoko shook her fingers loose; rotated her neck and her shoulders. She held her wrist before her eyes and willed the strength back into it.

Sensei muttered, *"Chotto."* Wait.

"*Iie!* It is *nothing.*"

Sensei took two more steps back.

"Then go for it."

Motoko did.

"By the gods!" he sputtered. "Let us have that little talk."

TWENTY-EIGHT

Ben couldn't see the spot that pinned him to her white living room wall.

Faces out there. Uniforms. One of them surely the Admiral's.

(Dad . . .)

Disgusted voices searching for a punishment fit for the crime.

(Oh, mom . . .)

(Chiori, kneeling by the bed, slipped the first nightmare, as slow as a dream, from one sleeve of her kimono. Boy Wonder, cuffed like a pig for the slaughter—when had she done it? Oh God, while he slept!—promptly losing his lunch at the sight of the thing: its handle, eighteen inches long, with gleaming talons at the end. *Daijōbu da . . . That's fine, good boy . . . Just give me the coordinates you picked up on your radio . . .* Her eyes so calmly searching his, as if their legs were joylocked still, her light silky downfall of cunt on his cock.)

The thundering silence of gavels in air.

The spotlight, dimmed, forgiving sun.

The Admiral's voice on the way with the news.

A full paternal pardon.

And—

Ben blinked, the moment gone, like that, as it was always leaving him. Alone again. And in the dark.

"Not the pain . . . You know me . . . Dad . . ."

It had not been his pain that had coaxed him to talk, but the mad hope of *still* having her.

(Was a stepmother really a mother?)

(And if she truly loved him, could she *really* be a spy?)

It was not *this,* the pain to come, that froze him at this very door—

(I'll bet it hurts like hell, eh, Mo? . . .)

—but the dread fear of losing the one thing he had.

Whereas . . . if the *two* of them . . . He and *it* together . . .

What sense if the thing took his memory?

The old man braced against the wall and relit the old candle, let it burn.

(Chiori—

Mommy!—

By the bed, lay the talons on the floor. Rivulets of blood still coursed from the tracks on both sides of his torso. *No one ever has to know . . . If you tell me, there will be no war . . . If you don't, then your father may die . . .* She took him once quickly, a deep-throated kiss, before disappearing, just out of his view. A light scratching sound below. The mild uprising of sulphur. And, in one smooth ceremonious move, she had the candle in her hand. Ben writhed and made frantic sounds as the tape stretched from his left ear to right. *It was fun,* she said, *but now . . . You must tell me everything . . .*

He watched, half-blind with shame and pain, as she screwed the base of the candle into the eye of his cock. In a minute, the wax started dripping. The worst, by far, was soon to come.)

Now all the mind's candles were blazing on high. And Ben welcomed their strong light because it was *his.*

Because it burned from him to Mo. Though she looked at him still like a stranger. And cried for the denims and picture he took. And seemed to forget, oh, the simplest things.

Candles roaring through the sky . . .

Rows and rows of flaming Pearls that fell on screaming bodies . . .

(Dad . . .)

I think I've got it right this time . . . I'm feeling good, I really am . . . The garden, Dad, it's good for me . . . I think I can stop her before it's too late . . .

He'd filled half a wall in his workshop with copies of keys to all locks that he'd sold: never dreaming, not at first; but thinking, always thinking; and waiting and working it out in his mind, while he tacked one key after the next to the wall. Waiting for the day *she* came.

He had his now . . .

She had hers . . .

We all needed keys to Pearl . . .

Ben picked up his pace to the bedroom, going over the keys one last time in his mind.

Pearl keys on the dresser . . . Key photos on the wall . . . The silk rainbow key that he'd left on the bed . . . The long, flowing key that he'd left for her hair . . .

He knew how she wanted, and burned, to forget. But it took two to remember. And now—

Ben stormed out the bedroom door, knowing that this time he'd go all the way.

He'd stop her this time.

Stop them all!

He stopped beside the security door.

"You down there?" he whispered.

No answer.

He gave the door a shaky knock. "What's the matter? You're not—"

(—scared?)

(What the—)

(—devil?)

Ben knelt and pressed two wetted fingers at the small crack underneath.

Nothing.

Nothi—

(Bloody—)

(—*hell!*)

Another eerie trickle of dank, disgusting air.

(. . . when an intricate chain of events had conspired . . .)

(. . . an atmosphere so *right* . . . Bad vibes . . .)

Ben scrambled to his feet, hands shaking uncontrollably. "I love it!" he cried. *"I just* love *it!"*

He slipped the two bolts.

Turned the key in the lock.

And shut the door behind him quick before he changed his mind.

He did not bother with the light.

The old steps creaked beneath his feet and every step was music.

"Come on, you're *here.* I *smell* you. The serious shit is now going to start."

Three steps from the bottom, he heard the first sound: high and compressed, like a hurricane spinning to life from a seed.

Ben ran on to meet it.

"Come on you horny devil, do *it! Take me in the mouth!"*

He never knew what hit him.

TWENTY-NINE

"Burrrrrrrrrrrrrrrrrrrrrpppppppppp!!!"

THIRTY

Sloan reeled, with a smug woozy smirk, at the door, skunkdrunk at four on Thursday. He eyeballed Mo intensely.

Another belch, this surpassing the first in resonance and duration.

"Excuse me?" she said. "Mr. Sloan?"

A glint of recognition.

"Keys."

He took the steps, almost one at a time, and came back, minutes later, in a huff of boozy air.

Her name had been typed on the envelope.

The seal had not been broken.

Sloan gave her the ghost of last Saturday's smile. "Mo Leigh," he said. "Mo *Lee* . . . That's great. It puts a whole new *slant* on things. And thank you for the hair, it—helps."

Before she could thank him, his phone started ringing.

He slammed the door shut and was gone.

* * *

Mo loved the *feel* of the deadbolt, with its cocksure "try me" gleam, the door now a mighty conundrum to which she alone had the key. She turned the knob; twisted; pushed; threw her weight against the door.

(The closest thing you'll ever know to absolute security . . .)

So much had happened, so soon and so fast. But she was home.

By the gods she was *home*.

Mo slung the family honor, discreet in its black leather casing, over her shoulder and picked up her bags. She shuffled to the living room, where she cried out as if she'd been cut with a knife—struck first by the side flash of color she'd glimpsed on the futon; then the closer, alien presences tacked to the living room walls.

She dropped the bags. The sword fell to the floor. She paced and turned, taking things in, letting her emotions fly.

Something new . . .

on the wing . . .

dark and strange and savage . . .

Her knuckles cracked. The left fist screamed.

She pacified it, happily, putting it clear through the wall.

"New York!"

A SUMMER'S END FORETOLD: III

JULY 1985

It was Ben, but *not* Ben.

His features were no longer human: shock-therapy hair standing nearly on end . . . blue eyes rimmed with flaming red . . . and a hard-on that reached to his chest . . .

He licked his lips and snorted twice. Brown dribble oozed from his lips down his chin, followed by a tongue as long as a full-grown adder. He snaked that tongue out obscenely, licking the shit off the hairs on his chest. His tongue reached to his nipples, and showed no signs of stopping. It stretched all the way to the crown of his cock, around which it made a tight circle. He gave her the latest in shiteating grins. And then he started *nodding*, slowly and deliberately, working the ring of his tongue up and down.

His labored breathing quickened. She thought of a mad bull or rhino in heat. And, though her situation was hopeless and unjust, she thanked the gods that this part she'd been spared.

Ben cried **ROAROOOOO!** and finished in a blur of frenzied nods. A torrential spray of shit drenched her from across the room.

She was ready to die, almost eager to go. She knew she could not hope to last another round of questions. Or hope to figure who it was he wanted her to be.

At length, he started toward her, in a lazy postcoital shuffle.

Seconds now.

No more.

Unless—

A look of bewilderment filled his red eyes. He stopped midway to study her, as if he had awakened from a nasty, unsettling dream.

She thought she saw a flash of *Ben.* A glint of recognition. A softening somewhere inside.

She wrestled with the shackles and tried to call out through the tape: *Ben! Ben! It's me—please!*

The old man cocked his head. He made a puzzled, grunting sound and took a few more of those shuffling steps.

Her heart shot into overdrive, racing so fast that it surely must stop.

The tape was too tight, but she cried out again, hopeful now for the first time in months. For the first time since he'd brought her here. *Ben! Ben! It's me, Chiori Sloan!*

The Ben-thing shuffled to her side and turned her face gently with huge devil hands. Dagger choppers clickclickclicked and pantings streaked the air she breathed.

Chiori gagged, but choked it back. She had a chance, a small one, but . . . The thing of it was, to be gentle and cool . . . She screamed in a low tone of voice through the tape: *Ben, you're there, I can see you! Oh, Ben!*

And he was there, if just for a moment.

"Chiori? Is that you, girl?"

Frantic nods. And *Yes! Ben, yes!*

His voice was queer, mechanical. As if he'd learned English, perhaps, with a tape. But he was talking, anyway! And he was talking to *her*, for a change!

"Chiori Sloan . . . Well, blow me down. Girl, this has all been a—tragic mistake."

No words in the world could have been half as welcome. She had a flash: herself at home . . . her past indiscretions forgotten . . . her and Cotter by the fire . . . herself forgiven for the calls that Ben had had her make . . . Cotter laughing, even, and telling her over and over again how he'd searched for her all over town . . . Ben somewhere—oh, not in jail—she didn't wish him that, even now—but somewhere safe and in good hands and receiving the treatment he needed—

Chiori heard the light crackle of bones as Ben began to twist her neck at a dire angle.

Ben, come on, you're there! It's me!

"Chiori . . . I'm really sorry. I swear it's nothing personal. There's just been a small mistake. You see, you're not my mother. Right house, but wrong apartment."

No!

She heard a crack, much louder, and thought that her neck might be broken. But still . . . She and Cotter could have it fixed . . . And, if not, and he did really love her—

Ben!

Those hands began to twist and pull. And the pain was too much for a human to bear.

"I think *it's* coming back now!"

Huh-uhhh! Huh-uhhh! Huh-uhhhhhhhh!

ROAROOOOO!

Chiori Sloan babbled and started to scream.

The *oni* tore her head off.

PART THREE

RECIDIVIST

THIRTY-ONE

Shot from the pages of brother's black book, stick-men sailing through Mo's brain. The whole world spinning, in reverse. And nothing, nothing, nothing, real, or quite as she remembered it. Americans slippery as eels and as quick to scoot in opposing directions. Mo holding on, though, and shooting out stickmen to hold down what corners she could of her world.

"Yuh wanna wahlkus troo wonz more?" Officer Davies scratched at the belly just starting a roll on her belt. "Dey didden taykno foinuhjuh . . . Dey didden taykno pigchuhs . . . Dey didden taykno Calbun Klynze . . . Whaddey did diz time was diz—dey didden tayke nuddin at all."

"Sal?" Nesbitt made a muted sound, half sigh and half groan. "Mr. Daez, you said Tuesday?"

"Right. I came by to put in the deadbolts at three and took a look around. You know, make sure everything was cool."

"This like this that afternoon?"

Daez looked at the hole in the living room wall. "Uhh—yeah, I did that last week. I was changing a bulb. The damn ladder. Haven't had time to fix it."

Nesbitt pointed upward, left. "What about the posters, sir?"

"Guess so. Yeah. Didn't think, new pictures on the wall."

The Bronx Babe called out from the bedroom. "Whadz diz, Wahkeekee or wad? Whair dey godt beahjes like dad?"

Nesbitt shuffled over, right pinkie clearing his ear. "Hard to say. The shot is old. Honolulu, Waikiki . . . Maybe Japan. Mrs. Leigh?"

Motoko nodded dismally, shooting stickmen everywhere in increasingly rapid succession. "Maybe," she said. "It's hard to say."

"These things all locked up like this?" Nesbitt asked Daez. His beefy paw jabbed at a window.

"All locked. And the bars were up. The perpetrator had a key."

"Poypuhtrayduh!" Davies sneered. "Whadduh hell dey poypuhtrayd?"

Mo, out of stickmen, dizzy, and tired, had wandered off to the dresser, where she fingered the small sack of beads. "New York," she said. "Okay . . . Okay . . ."

The policeman, who'd joined her, just stood there a moment, staring at the pearly sack. "I'm really sorry, Mrs. Leigh."

"No, no . . . New York . . ."

"Ma'am, I know it may *seem* that we're not . . . Well, there isn't that much we can—"

"Sure."

Nesbitt flipped back a page in his notebook. "Well . . . Let's see if I've got this right. You returned this afternoon at three, after a three-day sojourn in Japan, and got your keys from Mr. Sloan. In the living room your attention was caught by a couple of Japanese posters that hadn't been up when you left. In the bedroom you discovered a silk kimono on the bed—predominantly pink, with crimson, black, and turquoise. Estimated value: ten to fifteen thousand dollars. One small photo on the wall: black and white, from the forties or fifties. Possibly Hawaiian beach. On the dresser you found a small sack containing six pearls.

"Wonderful. Some lunatic breaks in to give you presents. Look." The policeman closed his pad. "How 'bout if I *talk* with your husband?"

"No!" Mo cried. "It couldn't be! Michael gave me money!"

"Nod zo fast," the Bronx Babe said. She'd just had a little talk with the lady's landlord.

Daez draped an arm on Mo's shoulder and gave her a fatherly squeeze. "We'll be back in a couple of minutes. Be good."

* * *

Cotter Sloan had not gone gently, but cuffed, with some fine stickwork that would be needing stitches. The melee had been awesome, the screaming beginning the second he opened his door. Daez first. Then Cotter Sloan. Then Officers Nesbitt and Davies. The carnage starting in the hall and flying halfway up the stairs, with Mo waiting down below, repeating "Me too" and "New York." Then glancing through the curtain—to meet, before the car door closed, the haunted eyes of Cotter Sloan.

"Mo?" Daez stood at the door, smiling at her sheepishly. He nodded his head toward the sofa. "Can we sit down for a couple of secs? I've got a confession to make."

"No!" Mo cried. "You didn't!"

"Please. I did—and I'm sorry."

Scan in a tailspin, blipblipping like crazy.

(You scumbunny bitch of a fishlicking—)

"But—"

(And *thank you* for the hair? . . . It *helps*? . . .)

"Why?" Daez said softly. "Well . . . I'll tell you I've done smarter things. Renting the downstairs apartment to you with Mrs. Sloan gone just a couple of months."

"Japanese."

"Chiori-san. Beautiful, beautiful lady." Daez drummed fingers lightly on the cushion near her neck. A sad, liquid look in his eyes. "What can I say, Mo? I thought it would help."

(You do have an astonishing—)

(Penthouse . . .)

(That landlord of yours was putting the blocks . . .)

". . . you know, maybe you and Cotter . . . Well, I see how wrong I was now."

Scan wheeling and careening through list after list, voice after voice going off in her mind.

"You okay, Mo?"

"Fine . . . New York . . ."

"Can I get you something?"

"No. Me too."

"Why don't I call—"

"Oh, no. Pr-please. This is New York City."

Daez slipped over a couple of inches, his thigh not quite yet touching hers. He gave her neck a little squeeze. Leaned over

(**Ooooo**—)

and kissed her cheek

(No!)

and purred like a storybook cat in her ear.

"Mo, these are *Medeco* deadbolts. The finest in the world. They cost—two thousand dollars *each*! They came straight from the factory. You have a key. I have a key. No one, I mean no one, has another copy."

Mo Leigh nodded and looked at the walls. The posters there were naturals. Kyoto and Tokyo. She wouldn't mind more posters if whoever it was came again.

"Mo, honey, listen to me." Maybe a hair now between their thighs. Another squeeze. That wasn't bad.

Daez said, "Hey, I'll tell you what."

He reached into his right jacket pocket. *Miami Vice* in black and white. Collar straight up and both sleeves on a roll. A jingle. A twinkle in those deep, sloe eyes as he slipped her new key off the ring. The only other copy.

"It's all yours." He took her hand, pressed the key to her palm. He did not move his hand from hers.

"And as for our friend, Mr. Sloan, he'll be out by the end of July. Goombye."

"I know. I do. I understand."

(. . . about what you really need . . .)

(You scumbunny bitch of a fishlicking—)

(Hi . . . My door is always . . .)

"Listen, kid. Remember what I told you—"

"Sure. I remember everything."

(I hate these birds . . . I swear to God, they gross me out . . .)

"Terrific. Then you remember this, hon. You can count on me."

"I know."

"Tomorrow I'll check out the basement again."

"It's okay. I know."

"I will. Hey, I just had a great idea. Why don't I pick up a nice bottle of wine—say, early Mogen David—and drop by tomorrow?"

"Fine."

"You know. Friendly thing."

"Me too."

Daez gave her hand a squeeze, stroking the Ace with his thumb. "Is that an invitation?"

('Course the trick now's not to ask any—)

(Hi . . .)

Mo thought about that as she studied his eyes. She smiled, vaguely happy, in a funky kind of way. "This is New York City." She slipped his key back in his pocket. "My door is there. You have the key."

The World's Greatest widened his eyes and said,

(**Ooooo**—)

"Mo-o-o. Does this mean what I think it means?"

Mo lowered her eyes like a schoolgirl.

"But your door," Daez said slyly, "it'll always be there. Am I right or am I wrong?"

"You are!" Mo said. "Oh yes, you *are.*"

The World's Greatest leaned over suggestively. She did not move. He kissed her.

Mo said, "I'm New Yorker now."

Henry got up slowly, not even thinking to cover the bulge that hung a few feet from her face. "Tomorrow night we'll both be."

"Fine."

"About the wall . . . Don't worry."

"Sure." Pretty posters on the wall.

"Tell me, though. Just tell me. It *was* your special—"

"Yes. Tee-hee."

"I'd sure like to see it. You sexy little devil."

"Fine."

"We're gonna have a *great* time—aren't we?"

Mo smiled at him sweetly. "Welrl . . ."

"I'll be here," he said.

"My door . . ."

"We're gonna have a *ball*!"

Stickmen on the wing again, sailing through the candlelight to join the shadows on the wall. Mo, stripped right down to the basics tonight, bra and panties folded in a neat stack on the rug. The shaggy crimson kiss on cunt, a direct connection.

Mo Leigh, neatly lotused, sat while Scan blipblipped and wheeled and sailed through a series of mad four-wheel drifts through its lists.

FUTURE FILE

Abundantly
Cultured pearls
Myew-tah-bee-lees
Yamataka?
Have a word with
The right thing to do
Early Mogen David

LOOK UP

Correg me
Poypuhtrayduh
Poypuhtrayd
Goombye

PRACTICE

Hard to say
Bad vibes
Sexy little devil
Ball

More stickmen headed Scan off at the pass. Desperate flights for completion from the pages of brother's black book. Closed covers could not stop them now. Stickmen sailed everywhere in his tight hand . . . through Sensei's most urgent last echoes.

(*Eight years ago I told you all you need to know of this . . .*)

(*Yamada, Sensei, dōmo*. This is a difficult gift to repay . . .)

(*I tell you, the moment I saw you, I saw it in your eyes, your walk. You were born for kendo.*)

(I watched *onii-san,* that was all . . .)

(*You learned more by watching him—*)

(*Onii-san* was a genius!)

(*Your brother was a maniac . . . You do not want to know . . .*)

The stickmen sailing anyway. Scan blipblipping over the echoes to brake on favorite dimes. The last Subvariation flowed on through her in red waves.

When her forehead hit the rug, Mo Leigh really floored it: upright in a single bolt. She began the countdown, ghost pain throbbing in her wrist, Sensei buzzing in her ears.

Ten . . .

Nine . . .

Eight . . .

Seven . . .

Six . . .

Five . . .

Four . . .

Three . . .

(. . . *The mind is a river that leads you forever to the one . . .*)

Two . . .

(. . . *true Voice . . . One for me . . . and . . .*)

One . . .

(. . . *for you . . . Open yourself . . . Let the Voice lead you Home . . .*)

Light, the purest, whitest light, washed under the doorway in wave upon wave, over and under her feet. An angel's voice cried, "*Aka-chan!*" My darling little girl. Mo turned the knob and ran into the room, where grandfather and grandmother and *oya-san* were waiting. She heard the door close behind her. The voices started up again. "*Onna no kuse ni!* Repeat after me, my unfortunate dunce." "Because I am only a woman!"

(*Then again, as you well know, these things take a little time . . .*)

One A.M. She squeezed the ball, staring at the journal with exhausted eyes.

"I know," she said, "I know . . . Me too . . ." —And set about her business, armed in black and crimson sweats.

She lit six candles. Cut the lights. Ran a last check on the locks and the bolts. Squared off before the security door.

"I don't wear kimono. This is how I have my hair."

A hum of tires, nothing more, passing by her windows.

"And I will not be crazy!"

Echoes of ghost echoes speeding off in the night.

She finished the last Variation at two thirty-seven.

The night belonged to brother now.

Mo set the family honor, neatly centered, on the knotty pine. She took two steps back and then bowed to the waist, without taking her eyes for an instant from the security door.

Special Exercise: the Pure State: total concentration . . .

No Sensei . . . No Michael . . . No Henry . . . No Cotter . . . No garden . . . No mouse ears . . . No bars and no Ben . . .

No Bryant . . . No blue jeans . . . No tampons . . . No English . . .

November, 1970 . . .

Tokyo U . . . Brother's room . . .

His stylus bleeding *kanji* on the first page of the journal dedicated "To the Ages—and to Sister, Number Six."

Mo shivered, re-turning the page, and followed *onii-san* again from the start.

> So! Mishima has had the last laugh after all! He did what he set out to do: sailed off for the Void with his name in the stars and

his head neatly under his arm. While grandpa counts samurai sheep before sleep . . . grandmother drools in her soup . . . *aka-chan,* poor *aka-chan,* has her work cut out for her—sweeping, mopping, dusting, bowing in that wreck, the Grand Hotel . . . in this, the New Japan . . .

Our demons have grown so pathetically small.

The old ones drove Mishima.

Passed on now to Number Five.

What we need at this point is something new and special—a spectacular Technique!

Mo took another half-step back and set the journal on the floor. *Onii-san* had been taller, yes, but her legs were longer.

She looked at her wrist and said, "Quiet."

If she could follow Matsuo, step by step, page by page, then maybe she could put him, finally, to rest . . .

She took a breath.

(A piece of cake . . .)

Recleared her mind.

(The same mistakes . . .)

Quick-stepped and performed

a front flip to perfection over the family honor.

Mo crumbled into a heap of despair.

All these years—and no control!

Her body performing by rote the move she'd perfected through eight years of practice.

How thoroughly depressing!

(*No mistake: the same mistakes:* or failure was for certain!)

At length, Mo returned to the notebook. She studied his stickmen again and again.

Phase One: Day One: Try One.

And when she thought she had them right—that is, wrong precisely—she cleared her mind.

And took a breath.

And let the stickmen fly again.

(The old ones that once drove Mishima . . .)

(Kindly passed on now to . . .)

THIRTY-TWO

"You-u-u-u . . ."

The third new bulb had just gone dead and rewiring would cost mom a fortune. Daez had a good feeling about that.

Tonight at eight he had a date with sexy Mo on her futon. The World's Greatest felt good, very good, about that.

His pockets were lined with a sweet-pussy loan skimmed from arrears he'd collected in cash. And he always felt good when he hit the old bitch.

And the thought of himself in Miami with Mo . . . sucking Power from her pores . . . She'd go with him, she had to go . . .

It was possible, Daez supposed, that—with a slight shift of perspective—he might, just might, even feel good about being down in the cellar again. The promise, kept. The white hat, earned. Mo's silken pussy waiting . . .

(Ooooo—)

Daez cocked his ear. He'd heard nothing, but—

Nothing . . .

He catwalked, coiled and ready, though God only knew it was only a rat or—

A minishuffle to the left.

Daez wheeled, sweating mightily. He could not be certain—but in a single, and shadowy, flash he thought he saw the first box—

PING!

The World's Greatest wheeled to the bottles, iron fists now open-palmed in the classic Windmill, right foot loaded and ready for—

(**Ooooo**—)

PING! PING!

Impossible! Two empty bottles sailed from the shelf, hardily toasted each other and—

CRASH!

—shattered in a fine sharp spray that shredded his designer shirt and half of his beautiful face.

The World's Greatest whirled, on red alert, enraged and wholly wild.

He saw the first box coming.

And the second.

And the third.

One awesomely efficient triple snap kick floored them all.

He heard the fourth box drag its heels from the shadows surrounding the boiler.

Shuffle . . . Shuffle . . . Oooffff . . . Oooffff . . . A hundred pounds of broken bricks, with little clouds of dust arising through the tattered sides.

The box came to a dead stop before him, about eight feet away. Stunned by the idiotic dream he was in, the World's Greatest lowered his guard.

That instant was all the thing needed. It might have been shot by bazooka.

The World's Greatest screamed and threw up his left arm. The impact smashed his fist into his mouth, with whammy enough to propel him another six feet to the door.

The cardboard gave, all sides at once. He landed in a bloody heap within a cloud of rising dust.

(Well, well . . .)

Daez coughed and tongued a whole row of loose teeth and thought, Wait . . .

I really heard that . . .

(Ooooo . . .)

One of the pearly incisors slipped as if it had been sprung. And lay like a cracked figurine on his tongue. Daez removed it gingerly, the saddest thing in all the world, and could not take his eyes off it. His mother would kill him. And Mo, what of her? Did he really expect her to kiss him like *this*? With his shirt ripped to shit! And his face—Christ, his—

(Ooooo . . .)

Daez tilted his head, just a little, in an earnest attempt to refigure the boxes. He felt his mind slip, like a smooth cake of ice, over the edge of the earth.

I should make a note of that . . . The earth is flat . . . She'll want to know . . . I have a small concuss— No, wait . . .

Phone Channel Five . . . Dispatch a crew . . . Be on the news at six so Mo—

(Ooooo . . .)

And make sure they bring a good sound team . . . We're talking Sony here . . . San—

(Hennnnnnnnnn—
reeeeeeeeeeee!)

There you have it . . . You hear *that*? . . . We're talking flying boxes . . . fucking voodoo bottles . . . We're talking here about—

(Knock!
Knock!)

I say, we're talking here—

(Come here!)

Come on, we're talking megabucks! . . . Voices in the boiler, but they're *not,* they're in my *head* and—

(Ooooo . . .)

Come on, get up, it's time to split . . .

We're talking Saturday-morning cartoons in fifty different languages . . . We're talking rubber dolls for kids . . . if you can just hang tough . . . Get up . . . and pull yourself togeth—

(Hennnnnnnnnn—
reeeeeeeeeeee!)

Daez clambered to his feet, rising from the rubble, eyes dead on the boiler through a fading scrim of smoke.

(You have a small—)

(. . . a small—)

(. . . a small—)

The World's Greatest silenced the voices, the Power burning in his—

(Ooooo . . .)

Mild wafting of decay. Almost undetectable, yet totally inviting. Something rotting slowly and dangerously sweetly.

The promise, kept . . . The white hat, his . . .

Daez felt sleek and lithe and quick, muscles rippling underneath his shredded white and red silk shirt. Another step . . .

(A sudden stop . . .
And then two sniffs, one short, one long . . .)

"Come on, shithead, who smells *who*?"

Another step . . . Another . . .

Then . . .

Six feet from the boiler, the icy rush assailed him—

(Ooooo . . .)

and he started to shiver like crazy—

(That's cool!)

when the low-down shuffleshuffle brought the old man, grinning, out into the light.

Daez felt his voice buckle once at the start; but he marched the words out, little soldiers.

"Ben?" he cried. "Hey, what the *fuck*?"

Short angry jabs in the air with his right; his left arm fat and heavy from the elbow to the fist.

The old man seemed not to notice, though, and slow-shuffled in with a wolfhappy grin.

The light was dim, but good enough. Daez figured Ben was on crack, maybe speed, or some new designer combo that had souped up his engine and crossed a few wires. With electrical shock to account for the hair, a Don King Sunday special.

Instinctively, Daez stepped back. The sudden movement jerked his head. The earth tilted. The sun turned. He began to see things in a different light.

Not Ben?

(You have a small—)

(. . . a small—)

(**Hennnnnnnnnn—**
reeeeeeeeeeee!)

(We're talking fucking Disney—)

(**Huhhhhhhhh!**)

The low-pitched chuckle bubbled from Ben's mouth like a fart under water.

He slow-shuffled forward, twenty years younger. And solid and squat. A mighty trunk of oak on feet.

Daez rooted his toes in the rubble, curled steeled fingers into fists that could not think to fail him now.

"Ben, I swear to Christ, I'm hot! Whatever shit you're on tonight—"

PINGPINGCRASHCRASHSHU FFFFFFLLLLLE-OOOOOOOOOOOOO!

The World's Greatest ducked, fast enough for

the bottles. A nail from the crate sliced off half of one ear and he screamed in surprise and frustration.

(You have a small—)

(. . . a small—)

(Come on!)

The old man watching devil-eyed, with those hands at his sides like two big hairy hams.

(**Watch this!**) old Ben told him. He opened his mouth, wide as a saucer, and shot his fangs out into small daggerettes. He snapped them shut and blue sparks flew.

(The white hat—now . . . The promise, kept . . .)

The World's Greatest felt a great quickening, a sudden surge of light and force. The white hat his beyond all doubt . . .

He feinted and Ben made a pitiful sound, pushing both hands up to cover his face.

The World's Greatest couldn't resist. The gut, wide open, was broad as a barn. And the tip of his boot was as sharp as a knife. He high-powered it into a roundhouse that could have doubled Mo's hole in the wall. Shock waves rippled up his leg. He felt the impact, then a sickening squish. And he knew he'd kicked too hard, too hard, his boot had gone *clear through*—

(**Roarrrrroooooo!**)

—when suddenly Ben winked and started to laugh like the devil.

(**Huh-uh! Huh-uh! Huh-uhhhhh huh! Huh-uhhhhhhhh huhhhhhhhhh huhhhhhhhh!**)

Ben wriggled his nose like a rabbit and sucked Daez in almost straight to the knee.

(Where was he *putting* it?)

(You are in . . .)

(. . . shock . . .)

Ben studied his catch with a low-cunning look. Then yawned and clickclickclicked his teeth.

Daez began, discreetly, crabwalking backward to work his leg free of the impossible trap.

(He's got my leg in his damned *stomach*!!!)

"Hey, Ben, you're fucking great, babe! I've never seen anything like this."

Four inches . . . Five . . . He was on his way home . . .

(**Where you off to, Hennnnn-reeeee?**)

He heel-toed back, almost free to mid-calf, and reassured Ben urgently. "Hey, babe, not going anywhere. Just trying to get comfortable."

(**Sure thing, Hennnnn-reeeee!**) Ben fed him his leg to the ankle in a peristaltic gross-out, gut slime bubbling through the fabric of his new custom-made trousers.

Daez wriggled his toes, gauging the force of the suction that still held his foot in. The force redoubled. The World's Greatest pictured monstrous intestines like stainless-steel gums—

(**You want your foot back, Hennnnn-reeeee?**)

—closing ever so slowly. First he heard, then felt, the almost plaintive ripple of crunches spreading from his ankle down.

The noise alone was more than Daez's mind could stomach, though nothing had been broken yet that could not be fixed.

Ben drew him slowly back up to the knee with a series of gross and gooey sucks that left no room for any doubt. He was going to die. In great pain. By the inch.

The steel gums started on his knee, stopping just this side of shatter.

(**Huh-uh! Huh-uh! Huh-uhhhhh huh! Come on, Hennnnn-reeeee, feed my ears!**)

A first ripple of crunches on the eggshell-thin circumference . . . Another . . . Then another . . .

Daez heaved, but would not scream, for nothing else was left him.

(Huhhhhh! Huhhhhh! Huh-uhhhhh huhhhhh!)

Ben made a terrible face, his breath so bad it streaked the air, a thin stream of shit bubbling over one corner of his mouth. He licked it up and scrunched over a little. With a twist of his torso, he shattered Daez's kneecap and wrenched the hip out of its socket.

(Screammmmm!)

Daez was trying to. He tried and tried and nothing came.

(What's the matter, Hennnnn-reeeee?) Blue sparks from the snapping fangs.

"Aa . . . Aa . . . A
a
a
a
a . . ."

(Awwww . . . Snapsnapsnapsnapsnap! . . . I can almost taste those pearly whites . . . I'll bet they're really crunchy . . . Yummm!)

"Cha— . . . Cha— . . ."

SNAP!

"Cha—
a—
a—
a . . ."

(Hmmmmmmm?)

He was going to die, by the inch, in great pain. But first he wanted one small—

"Cha-a-a-a-n-n-n-n-ce . . ."

(Want your leg back, Hennnnn-reeeee?)

Daez nodded painfully, a pilot light of consciousness still flickering, but barely, the world slipping out of his eyes and his ears. He no longer trusted either. He thought he heard planes in the distance . . . In the corner, through the bloodred haze, a soft voice moaning, "Darling boy . . ."

Ben straightened and took a deep breath, relaxing the muscles below.

And The World's Greatest felt what was left of his leg slide out, then drop with a thump by his side. The pain had long since left his knee and spread through the rest of his body. He felt it in his corneas, his sinuses and tonsils. His tongue was made of kneecaps and all of them were shattered.

(Huhhhhhhhhh!)

"Ki- . . . Ki—I . . ."

(I'll bet you will!)

Old Ben, all red-eyed and long in the tooth, his voice a good twenty feet under the earth and coming from everywhere except his mouth.

(Tell you what.)

Ben shuffled closer, red eyes almost smiling, hairy hams behind his back. The dagger teeth shrank back to vampire size. And a minor spark of warmth informed the wolfish grin.

(Come on, Henry, put 'er there. Knock me down—hell, blow me down!—before I finish counting. I won't lift a finger.)

"N-o-o . . . tr-i-i- . . ."

(Me? Tricks? Come on, Henry, go for it! One good shot and you're home free!)

Not-Ben closed his eyes, his mouth.

Began the countdown.

(Ten . . . Nine . . .)

The World's Greatest took one long look at the stairs, but knew they had forsaken him. He focused, through the throbbing haze, on the unmitigated arrogance of that extended chin.

(. . . Six . . .)

The old man appeared to be dreaming. And whatever other tricks he had, surely the jaw would be glass for Daez, who felt the Power coming back . . . one last mighty

(. . . **Four . . . Three . . .**)

surge of the Real Thing. The anger roaring on down through his arm . . . his tooth in his pocket . . . his ear on the floor . . . yesterday's lunch in the seat of his pants—

(. . . **Two . . .**)

A direct connection . . .

Now!

The fist took off like a feathered charge of blasting dynamite and flew—

(Huh-uh! Huh-uh! Huh-uhhhhh huhhhhh!)

The shock was too vast to be painful.

Ben had Daez's fist to the wrist in his mouth, an exquisite hors d'oeuvre which he rolled on his teeth.

(Well, well, blow me down! I sure am getting hungry. Yummmmm . . .)

Daez heard a creaking sound, gross and eerie and painfully slow. And he wished he could have closed his eyes, but the sight was too spectacular. Ben moaned ecstatically as his fangs stretched out to dagger length, each of the blades almost three inches long, his mouth stretching out now on all sides at once, wide enough to devour a football . . . all without breaking the skin of the wrist . . .

(Huhhhhhh! Huhhhhh! Huh-uhhhhhhhh!)

"Be-n-n-n . . . Do-n-n-n-t . . . Pl-e-e . . ."

(Screammmmm!)

Daez, no longer proud, was looking for the sound within—when Ben rolled his eyes to the ceiling and *snapped,* with one mighty crunch, through the wrist.

The World's Greatest felt a great torrent of blood—and opened his mouth for the World's Loudest Scream.

But by then the *oni* had eaten his arm to the elbow.

THIRTY-THREE

January 15, 1971

I'd have given my arm to Mishima from the day that I signed on. What hopes I had then for the Tatenokai—"the world's least armed, most spiritual army." How smart, the spanking uniforms! How splendidly sculpted, our leader's physique! How brave and high-sounding his patter!

"Take their arrows in your foreheads, men, but never in your backs." Yes, sir!

"The focused mind can pierce through stone." *Dōmo*, Sensei, thanks a lot!

"If your sword is broken, then strike with your fists . . . If your hands are cut off, then attack with your shoulders . . . If your shoulders are gone, bite away with your teeth" . . . We will, sir, you can count on us!

The meetings were grand, if infrequent. What were we there for? Did anyone know?

Mishima, when questioned, could go on at length—his answers all vaguely autistic: the Jietai* had become a mere toy . . . They were not constitutional† . . . Modern Japan had no center, no spiritual foundation . . .

And so on and so on and so forth.

It half sounded like tripe to our ears even then. Why we were there? Because—who could resist?

No one pumped up like Mishima. He would lead us through drills, sometimes stripped to the waist, muscles bulging everywhere, that crazyman look in his eyes. His confidence, outrageous. His energy, so awesome. Buzz words straight from heaven falling on our willing ears: *Glory,* he promised . . . *Adventure . . . Our day will come, be ready . . .*

And since we were a secret, subterranean fraternity, Mishima Sensei had his little mantras for each one of us—to keep us in line, draw us into the web.

"Wooden swords for wooden men," he told me the first time we met—and I thought somehow he had seen through my soul. I asked him what he meant. He winked and said, "Follow me. I'll lead you to the Emperor."

July now in Manhattan. Dawn. The ghost of a merciful breeze slipping through the bars on the bedroom windows. Mo Leigh, deeply lotused, set the squeeze-ball by her knee and focused loosely on the page while drifting further back in time.

---

*The Japanese National Guard.

†Per the terms of the alliance after WWII.

Onii-san had written a number of times about the great man's "wooden swords." The day after meeting Mishima, in October 1969, he had written a long playful letter mocking the novelist's long "wooden books."

He'd seemed securely settled into his first year at Tokyo U, though he regretted frequently the lack of time for kendo. His grades were good. He had made friends. His spirits had sounded consistently high.

Time and again, Mo would reach the same point and lose the thread entirely. She'd read the journal, front to back, seven times since June, staring at the stickmen till they vanished from the page, her mind a vast white plain of iced incomprehension. And her tenuous union with brother would break, and she would be here alone, trying still to understand how a healthy man—as loved as he—could ever think of—

No!

(Surprise!!!)

Mo shook her head to clear it and

(Make no mistake: the *same* mistakes . . .)

tilted her pelvis a little till her forehead cleared her knees . . . pressed her arches hard to pine . . . and in a single fluid move stretched her feet high to the ceiling. And

(Ten . . .)

again the strong red waves began

(Nine . . . Eight . . . Seven . . . Six . . .)

to flow from the soles of her feet all the way to the

(. . . Two . . . One . . .)

crown of her head and the light flowing under the door drew her in

to a layer of home never dreamed of till now.

An unexpected progression of light through the pages of brother's black book.

Her safe cool detachment melting away till she stood here with

You-u-u-u . . .

I see you now more closely. My mind perceives more clearly how you moved from there to here. From grandfather's Bushido boy to grandma's gold-star student to—the enigma I now find before me.

You arrived at your station in Tokyo U, cut out for a glorious future. But before you had been here two months, another madman changed your life, with a cruel passing remark.

Small seeds had been planted, of darkness and doubt. And without your even knowing it, they sprouted, took root, and pushed out to the sun.

You met him again in December. This time in the city. You do not record the details. But you were a star, and a beautiful boy, and Mishima of course—was Mishima. The flowers bloomed. Your feelings changed.

You do not record the details, no. But I can hear the change in tone. He touched you in your place of dreams. A promise was made. A vision was passed. Your place was assured in the Army. The Real Thing, passed on straight to you from Mishima . . . Mishima . . . the Emperor's Man . . .

In the weeks that followed, your thoughts were almost of Mishima alone. And your glorious role in the Army.

Your first bitter taste of the truth came with your first parade.

> How can I forget their laughter from the square below? We stood on the rooftop, in a light gray drizzle, facing the palace across the great moat. We had concluded maneuvers, a rather impressive display, and were prepared to wait all day for the

Emperor to show. For Mishima Sensei had told us He would.

Our uniforms were soaked clear through. The polish from our boots began to puddle at our feet. Our hands shook. Our lips turned blue. The crowd below us jeered and mocked. A rock struck the boy on my right in the face. I heard a crack. He did not move. We waited for the Emperor . . .

We waited for an hour. Two. And the crowd beneath us waited too, growing in number and volume, as our situation grew more hopeless and absurd. We waited for the Emperor . . .

From time to time Mishima spoke; his voice was low and urgent. *Soon,* he'd say . . . *I felt it . . . The Emperor is coming* . . .

Something struck me in the knee. I did not look. I did not move. I waited for the Emperor . . .

Three hours passed . . . Then four . . . Then five . . .

The boy beside me fainted. I rolled him over with my boot to get his face out of the water. I did not move. I did not faint. I waited for the Emperor to wave and recognize us.

I was not aware of Mishima until he screamed "Attention!" He clicked his heels with a great splash that raised the fainter at my feet. Mishima's mad eyes twinkled. He had just divined the punch line to some crazy, cosmic joke—and decided the laugh was on them, not us. "Huh! Huh! Huh huh huh!" he shrieked. The maniacal sound was contagious. A group of tired, sopping fools, stood up by the Emperor—and having the time of their lives!

Mishima said, "I think it's time we made a date with Fuji-san*. June fifteenth, my pretties! From that day on, no laughter! Huh!"

Mishima whirled and clicked his heels, raising one hand to the palace. *"Tenno heika banzai!"*

At that moment we would have followed him gladly clear to the ends of the earth.

And so, we marched off, splashingly, to the hoots and the roars from below.

No one approached you about it, of course. But rumor spread throughout the dorm of your absurd adventure.

You began avoiding classes.

Your absences at first were rare and inconspicuous. In the weeks to come they grew in frequency and fervor. You raged against the Grand Hotel and wooden swords and wooden schools, and waited in your wooden void for a real taste of Sun and Steel.

Meetings were held at a high fever pitch. Mishima Sensei drummed the corps to a lather of hysterics, but remained vague about actual plans. On Friday nights you met the boys in selected city bars. The growing sense of comradeship began to overwhelm you. Your eyes met theirs. You raised your stein. And saw one night, as if in a dream, Mishima walk in around midnight. He put his arm around you and said, "Sooner than you think" . . .

I thought—my God, we all thought—I

---

*The affectionate name for Mount Fuji.

mean, we just *assumed* that some great plan, unknown to us, informed his every movement. Did he seem vague? Then, willfully! Abstracted? Perhaps, but specifically so! All would be revealed . . . explained . . . on June 15 . . . on Fuji-san . . .

Well, none of us needed the papers to tell us exactly how foolish we'd looked. Mishima's buffoons had been at it again! Keystone Kops on Fuji's slopes! Thunderflashes thrown from trees at imagined targets! Smoke bombs fizzing in the snow! Blank guns shot with fearsome cries of "Ack-ack-ack-ack-ack!"

The newsmen jeered and whistled. Mishima shrieked with laughter, rolling in the snow with some escaping POW.

My face was barely visible in the picture on page 3—but I felt as if it had appeared, in close-up, on the sky.

I could not bear to face the world. I scarcely left my room to eat. I had waited for the Emperor . . . waited then for Fuji-san . . . I waited now for my great shame to pass. But it seemed to grow worse by the hour, the day.

In April, a message arrived, hand-delivered, and bearing the red Army seal. I opened the message inside, as instructed. And found more of Mishima's mad clowning.

> Are you ready to go *all the way*? Are you ready to be one of Four*?
>
> If so, you will receive a second message from Morita.

---

*Mishima first recruited three Tatenokai members to assist in his ill-fated "coup." The chosen fourth refused, in fact, and was in turn replaced.

If not, return this message and forget about this visit.

M.

I crushed the paper in my fist, unable to think or to see through the haze. It seemed to me like the end of the world—one joke too many, and everything lost. I opened the door and I started to scream, my fist aimed at Morita's mouth. I saw the terror in his eyes . . . the chain of doors opening on down the hall . . . I shoved the message in his hand. And slammed the door. And heard him go.

You hid in your room.

You withdrew from all classes and shredded the warnings they sent you.

You went for walks. You agonized.

You drank beer and brooded and drifted for months and then one fateful winter day you learned that he hadn't been kidding.

And you returned to kendo.

(*Your brother was a maniac . . .*)

(. . . *a maniac* . . .)

(. . . *a maniac* . . .)

(*The moment he entered my dojo I sensed the wild horses in his heart. But none of my students was faster or fiercer or quicker to learn my techniques. And I swear that I never suspected, not until the very end, what he was really up to.*)

Mo tumble-rolled lightly back onto her feet, high from the blood that had flooded her brain. She paced a bit to level out, swinging her arms and rotating her neck.

This wasn't New York . . . and it wasn't July, the heat a hard bitch before noon . . . and she hadn't been fired because of her hair . . . and Henry hadn't been gone for a month . . . and the cops

hadn't come back with more questions . . . and
(**Ooooo** . . .)
there were no sounds in the cellar . . . no traces of drafts from the door . . .

Just here . . . Now . . .

Phase . . .

Three . . .

Mo flipped the page with her toes before shimmying into her sweatpants.

Stickmen flew and landed hard in brother's latest impassioned attempt.

(*I've given you the best of him,* Sensei said imploringly. *An Exercise to last your life. Child, you don't need the rest.*)

Wrong, she thought . . . *Chigaimasu* . . . I need to know *precisely* how *onii-san* reached the grotto . . . I have to feel it in my bones . . .

Mo slipped on into the sweatshirt, enjoying the big easy stretch of small breasts, nipples nestling into cloth.

She proceeded to the living room, where she centered the family honor on the freshly polished pine.

Brother had not used a mat. And the next false move would cost her if she failed to get it wrong—just right.

She took one last look at the stickmen before setting the notebook aside.

She had labored for years on this difficult phase, believing that it was the End in itself,

(*Techniques may come, techniques may go, but I gave you an Exercise.*)

while brother's vision had been all along—

Mo took a step back, then a quarter step in. A sip of air. Another.

She clenched her fingers; flexed her wrist, now an Easter-egg yellowish-purple.

Tokyo U . . . *Onii-san*'s room . . . Her mind-set

set precisely . . . on how, when fully expecting success, she must fail to the exact degree . . . Like brother . . . Just like brother . . .

(Make no mistake: the *same* mistakes . . .)

She cleared the sword in a fine graceful arc, grabbing it just at the apex, and pulling it out of the sheath as she flipped. Easy does it, no big deal.

Brother's mind was confident, the sword halfway clear of the scabbard, no sweat. His legs circled over, guided by past crews of stickmen.

Suddenly, he'd realized the degree of his miscalculation. A Shirata, he was short-armed; and, though he was used to the weight of the sword, the strenuous efforts to clear it had spun him to the right.

So far, so bad . . . Mo Leigh followed the stickmen, countering as brother had, with a twist to the left in the air.

Too hard! She felt herself diverging from the stickmen on the page. Brother's stumbling forward, off-centered and out of control.

Mo's landing, unbelievably, almost to perfection. Her chest opened wide, her arms stretched to the max, despite her avowal to fail.

Mo resheathed the family honor. She walked circles around it while catching her breath, as if casting a spell on the sword. She stood for a moment, her hands on her hips, eyeing the door to the cellar. Then she walked over, expecting the worst, almost hoping for it.

She knocked lightly a couple of times.

No reply.

She knelt, and pressed her fingers to the crack beneath the door.

Okay . . .

"You down there?" Mo Leigh whispered. "*Sō* . . . How is New York City, eh?"

She rose in a smooth cautious move to her feet and touched her fingers to the wood, as if attempting to feel for a pulse.

"It's okay," she said. "Me too."

On her fourth attempt, Mo recaptured *onii-san*'s mistake, with a shock landing that carried her forward just so. She abandoned herself to the loss of control and shot straight in a nosedive that ended on the cellar door. The blood from her nose splattered freely. She rolled onto her butt, swung around to the door, and let the blood drop where it might.

"Hajime," she murmured.

Yes . . . Yes . . . It was only the start . . .

She stroked the door with the sole of one foot and started to croak-giggle.

"This is New York City . . . We're gonna have a ball!"

Mo was well into the sequel mistake—sword cutting the hell out of old knotty pine—when the doorbell sounded.

She moved the red rug from the bedroom, covered the much damaged pine, and let in the first of her students.

THIRTY-FOUR

"Howdy."

"How-dee."

"Very good."

Bryant waited in the hall, the canvas case slung over his shoulder with no explanation in sight.

('Course, the trick now's not to ask any—)

(*Sō* . . .)

She stepped back, still torn between the need for caution and the obviating fact: that, until a week ago, Bryant had not even known where she lived.

Mo gestured with an open palm, the fingers pointing out, not in, while Scan blipblipped and raced for words.

But Bryant headed her off at the pass, stroking the lavender streak in his hair. "Well, this *is* Funky 101. Supposin' I just go and step right on in."

Mo checked a bow and said "Why not?" and closed the door.

One down.

The suggestion had first come from Bryant, in a call the week after her firing. Apparently, Kazumi-san, whose brains were truly in her tits, had snitched to the class that Mo hadn't resigned. And so Mo found herself in a fine spot, with Bryant feeling guilty now for having done the styling.

Her savings, with stretching, might last her three months. And she had no immediate prospects. But there hadn't been hours enough in the day for the mission she had with the stickmen.

(Yamada Sensei . . .)

(*Hai. Nani?*)

(Do you believe in—*onis*?)

(That rich baritone laugh. Sensei tickled his nose. *Does a bear shit in the woods?* he replied.)

Mo had left her apartment to shop a few times, begrudging the time from her labors. She ate sparsely, in accordance with brother's red-lettered dictum:

> RAW! RAW! RAW! RAW! RAW! RAW! RAW!
>
> When I think of the garbage the youths of today are shoveling into their gullets, my eyes fill with tears of frustration. By degrees I'd come to see the sinfulness of my own ways. I felt so soiled and ludicrous . . . so polluted and pumped full of poisons: from Mishima Sensei's treacle to grandfather's well-salted pabulum . . . to the steamed white rice and sugared teriyaki and boiled this and deep-fried that . . .
>
> I felt the need for purity. Simplicity. And

> valor. I purged my system with a fast. And I began to fill myself with vegetables and fruit, all raw, and seeds and nuts and water. I felt myself grow holy. My mind grew sharp, my spirit pure. My hair acquired a marvelous sheen. And children smiled at my eyes.

She worked out daily till she dropped . . . winded, and yet feeling lighter than air. The arm she could not lift, a cloud. Her leaden feet, balloons. And then she would flip through the stickmen again, from page 1 to present, going over and over and over again the progression of brother's mistakes.

The buoyancy somehow transcended the general strangeness around her: the midnight road along which Scan blipblipped and roared in overdrive.

The World's Greatest's mysterious no-show . . .

The notice hand-delivered by the bullish Mrs. Daez—relieving her son of his duties.

Her five-hundred-dollar reward for info leading to his lockup.

Henry, Ben, and Cotter gone . . . and not a word from Michael . . . But if the second break-in was connected to the first . . . the silk kimono, wig, and pearls, to the stolen blue jeans . . . then . . . clearly the thing of it was *Japanese* . . .

And if a waiting *oni* had now found his passport in . . . then maybe the form that the demon had taken . . .

Michael . . . It was possible . . .

Henry . . . Possible . . .

Mo replayed scenarios with shifting center pieces until her head began to spin.

And then there was Scan, there would always be Scan, still zooming at the speed of fright and screeching on those random dimes—

(You scumbunny bitch . . .)
(We're gonna have . . .)
(Hell, *I* need more Japanese women . . .)
even when the phone had rung with Bryant's ingenious proposal.

"You've lost some weight."
"I've *lost some weight*."
Not lose weight—but lose *some* weight . . . *Imi*, meaning, lose a *bit* . . .
They were seated on the sofa—the sole furnishing now in Mo's Workshop besides the secondhand table and lamp. Their voices echoed off the walls, in this, the first of her classes. Bryant kicked back easily, one foot propped up like a hand on his lap, one arm on the back of the sofa. He gave Mo a casual lopsided grin with those jumbo lips of his. Loose as a goose. A real Yank at his ease. With no transmissions whatsoever from the Grand Hotel. Mo wishing her own tootsies, eager to please, hadn't carboned and jumped into place. Her hands, first folded and then un-, two lost little fluttering birds.
"O-kayyyyy. What you want to do," he said, "in any situation, is *get down* and blend right in. And yet keep your distance. What we've got between us, if we're feeling Funky, 's an imaginary line. We're connected. But we're not."
"I see!"
"That's cool. So's 'Sure' . . . 'Uh-huh' . . ."
O-kayyyyy! . . .
"The place to start with English, Mo—I mean, if you're Funky—isn't with the words themselves. You start with your own *attitude*. Whose apartment is this?"
Mo thought about that for a moment, while Scan wheeled and skidded through several false

starts. "Hmm . . . Welrl . . . It's hard to say . . . I used to pay off Henry . . . But—"

Bryant chuckled drolly and gave a light tug at the stud in one ear.

"Easy, Mo, think for a minute. Forget about the words themselves. Forget about *Nihongo.* Where are you?"

"N.Y.C."

"All right!" He leaned in just a little. "Now forget about textbooks and critics and crap. Your attitude—your *Attitude*—babe, that's where it's at. Now . . . Whose apartment is this?"

"Welrl . . ."

"Don't cop out. Just say it."

"Mine?"

"So, how come you're sitting like the couch belongs to me? Repeat after me: I will bop till I drop."

Mo mimicked with a giggle, and tucked her feet easily under her butt, wrists adangle from her knees.

"O-kayyyyy." Bryant positioned his watch on the table, the dial turned away from Mo. "Now, then. Here's the picture. I'm an artist from Chicago, say. We had a little thing a while back. But I went my way, you went yours. I spy you on the subway and say, 'Girl, you're lookin' fine!'"

Mo shrugged and gave her fingers a sassy little snap.

"Oh, welrl, real-ly—what the heyyy!"

Baby-chick chirps issued from the Seiko in quick little beeps. The ten-minute rap had tired Mo out more than an hour of Technique. Her mouth was dry and a hammer was pounding a pillow somewhere in her skull.

For the next ten minutes, Bryant line-by-line

critiqued the more serious slangular howlers. Beginning with the first and worst—heard, she swore, the night before on a late-night movie.

"That's the problem," Bryant said. "It sounds too *antiscripto. Easy Rider* kaka. Dig? No attitude. No *Mo*, y'know? You wanna be Funky, you gotta be *you* like no one else's business. Now . . . I'm afraid it's my turn."

Before leaving, he slipped her a small sheet of paper, along with two ten-dollar bills.

"*Iie.* No, I can't!" she cried. "This was a—how do you . . . —Steven-exchange?"

"*Ima made, sō ja nai, boku to omoimasu.*" Not so far it's not, I think.

"Use *watashi,* please. Not *boku* yet. It still sounds too rough for you."

Mo pressed the money back into his hand and he set it right back on the table.

"Look," he insisted, "you're to charge twenty an hour. The names on the list have agreed. And—*'Oh, well, really, what the heyyy!'*—they can all afford it. Especially Wojciechowski."

The senior clerk at Blue Collar Temps.

"Oh, no," she moaned, "the dumb-dumb?"

"Yep. Mr. Tight-ass wants to loosen up."

There were nine other names from the class on the list. The last, Frankie Motta (with three question marks, parenthesized), was the only stranger.

"Who is—*Iie—who's* this?"

"That's a young guy who lives in my building. He's got a cute pen pal who doesn't speak English. I dunno, he's pretty broke. But maybe he can pay in trade."

"*Wakaranai,*" she told him. I don't know what you mean.

"He's a handyman, a carpenter. If you've got

any little odd jobs you need done. He's hell on wheels with a hammer."

Mo's eyes lit up. She nodded and asked him how soon this Frankie could start.

"I'll ask."

"And Bill, could you please check for me . . . Do you know candlemaker, too? Cheap, fast candlemaker?"

"You mean like one or two or—"

"No." Mo told him how many she wanted.

Bryant slung his case over his shoulder and gave her a curious look.

THIRTY-FIVE

A new dawn at midnight.

Piecing the letters together with the English still left in its gut, it had found the sign vaguely funny at first. Understanding, almost, in some misty intuitive way. But now it stood before the fridge, the red block letters winking at their increasingly alien joke.

YOU ARE
WHAT
YOU EAT!

The *oni* snorted and belched a brown streak and growled from the pit of its belly.

Although it had no appetite—and no actual feeding requirements—(indeed, it had gone centuries this time between contracts)—its hunger had grown steadily from the time it had first tasted blood.

(**Yummmmm!**)

Rat blood . . . spiced with poisons and the heavenly flavor of garbage . . . the frantic wag of the little tail fanning its lust for the feeding . . .

The blood of red-eyed rat bird . . . ooo, a serving for a king . . . with an *oni*-sized dollop of entrails spiked with (more, please!) chalky-flavored shit . . .

YOU ARE . . .

Dare wa? . . .

Who "YOU"? . . .

The *oni* felt annoyance. Its dreaded humor, bristled, piqued. It shuffled now before the sign, toes clicking on the tile, one hairy ham scratching its belly with retractable nails long as spikes.

YOU ARE . . .

What "WHAT"? . . .

Now, in Japanese—

But "you" was a you-man and "what" was a question and "eat," of course, was a command. The *oni* rescrambled the puzzle:

YOU ARE WHAT?

EAT, YOU!

It heard a buzz around its skull and it grew very silent.

These little flying buzzballs—a squish of red with tangy white—were snacks too sweet to be denied!

The *oni* stood straight as a doorjamb. It stilled the beating of its heart to an imperceptible tremor. The buzzball settled on its brow and started a light-footed tickly trek across the skin's Sahara.

The *oni* waited craftily . . . as it had waited long years for the girl . . . and licked its lips . . . and thought *Roaroooo* . . .

and gleefully whipped out its great stretch-a-tongue—twenty inches at the max—to flatten the fly to a micron. With long and serious scrapings of tongue it lifted the sweet from its forehead, and slurped the bits noisily down.

The *oni* smiled wolfishly back at the small Happy Face.

(WHAT ARE YOU?
EAT, YOU, TOO!
IF YOU CAN,
LITTLE MAN!)

Pleased, the *oni* laughed out loud. "Come on, you horny devil, do! Taking in the mouth!"

It could fill a stadium—simply by thinking a sound. It had no real need of its throat or its cords, and yet—as sometimes happened when it took on human form—it felt a perverse satisfaction in acting like a man.

Even with the limits of a body like the old one's.

The *oni* had ached in its bones for three days before it had started to fix things and *grow*. But there had been power too—fierce and unexpected—in the atoms of the old one's soul. For several days after possession, the *oni* had felt flashes that perplexed it mightily. Candles roaring across the sky . . . and thundering pearls from the heavens . . .

("Horny" . . . What mean?
Mouth of who?)

Flashes and feelings that couldn't be fathomed . . .

And staticlike tidbits of English . . .

(Mommy!)

(Daddy!)

(Darling boy . . .)

And the day it had eaten the Henry, a siege of English had shaken its soul. Words the *oni* had never encountered erupted as if in a trance. High-powered by some mighty—

WHAT!?

(Well, well, blow me down . . .)

(Come on, Hennnnn-reeee, feed my ears . . .)

After the feeding, the seizure had stopped. And by the completion of cleanup, the *oni* had felt as *regathered* within as the tableau all around it:

not a chip or brick or shard of glass or speck of blood in view. It had felt the atoms within slowly settle . . . as if the dish of the Henry had neutralized that of the Ben—leaving only a power within it, a sort of raw capacity for this curious, idiot tongue.

What "WHAT"!!!

And the *oni*, with a soft *Roarooo*, had known again what it was born for.

Motoko . . . Motoko . . .

The ultimate meal . . .

Seasoned now for fifteen years and sizzling hot on the spit.

By the gods, what dreams it had: the crunchings of her fingertips . . . the squishings of her baby blacks . . . the ripplops! of her beating heart . . .

The *oni* bowed to the small Happy Face and opened the door to the fridge. It sniff-sniffed, almost daintily, and then with quickened interest. The food balls of yellow and purple and red, the long fat sticks of orange, positively bloomed with health: liverlike circles and splotches of green. The odor, much stronger, was sweet and alive. And, though it could not chance this yet, the *oni* thought that—perhaps in a week—some might be safe for consumption.

Would it *take* a week, that was the question, for her.

The *oni*'s stomach rumbled and it stifled a *Roarooo.*

However long it took, it took.

Meanwhile, there remained, as ever, the intricate riddle of doors.

How to get from *here* to *her*?

The *oni* would use all the time it required as only an *oni* can use time.

For, it already had a plan.

And for the plan it would need a real voice.

And for the voice it would need words.

The old man's words.

The words *she* knew.

"Ben I am," the *oni* crooned, tickled again by the cords in its throat. Such a piddling sensation, and yet—

Was that *right,* though?

The *oni* concentrated, hard.

Or,

"Ben it is"?

Could *that* be it?

Chotto . . . Wait now . . . How about this?

"Ben I be—and . . . nice day have!"?

And,

YOU ARE

What "WHAT"?

WHAT!!!

YOU, EAT!

Halfway up the stairs, it stopped. This was where the creaks began and it wanted to stretch out the heavenly sounds. It proceeded with heavy, mock-menacing steps, thunder dreams dancing inside of its skull.

At the top it paused again, its reverie disrupted by a mild atomic rush.

A tug to the left from its favorite room, with the chair overlooking the small moonlit plot. The headstones, like notes in a heartwarming fugue. It could sit for hours there, drawing strength from the visions of men's painful deaths: from knives and heartaches and cancerous cells. With sobbings and curses and screams in the night.

But *shikata ga nai* now . . . It couldn't be helped . . . The atoms had stirred and the fine mood was shot and the *oni,* uncertain of where was its drift, found one foot leading the other.

With a series of somehow unsettling creaks.

To the door of—that *curious* room.

Vast were the regions the *oni* had haunted and various their atmospheres. From kingdom to cottage, from seashore to city, from fear at the nerve-ends to guilt at the core. It had seen old women pluck their eyes before its fearsome countenance. Heard grown men weep at the bones on its plate. Seen the lightning tell the thunder, Run dear, now the black rain falls.

The *oni* had created scenes that made the very walls run red and caused the gods themselves to turn away in pained disgust.

For gibbering terror and mind-blowing fright, the *oni* wrote the very book. And thought it knew the works by heart.

Yet the very first time it had glanced in this room—

(Mommy!)

(Daddy!)

(Darling boy . . .)

the *oni* had shut the door fiercely—

(Candles roaring 'cross the sky . . .)

(Pearls thundering down from the heavens in flames)—

and thought, *Roaroo.*

And, "He be here."

And, "Place no good for *oni* is."

As it shuffled past, the atoms stirred and it quickened its pace to the rear of the house, where it seemed somehow to have been called.

The demon stood at the window overlooking the darkening garden.

And thought, *Roarooo.*

And, How could it be?

This curious, *curious* fragrance of home.

THIRTY-SIX

March, 1971 (From *onii-san*'s journal)

Phase Three had just been perfected at six. And I was almost *there.* My spirit, by the hour, grew increasingly refined; my notions of salvation, more elegant and pure.

But last night something happened that changed my life completely.

Quite suddenly my nose kicked up! Before anything else, you see, there was the—smell. Of something rotten at the core though rosy enough on the surface. And then the vision came to me, like—I forget—on the road to—wherever. I saw my great future stretched out like a corpse: all dead meat and formaldehyde.

I'd still be Mishima's fool . . . scoring points with my *shinai* like some kid at pinball . . . with periodic demos of my glorious technique . . . as if it made any difference at all!

Life would remain a prison of complex and impenetrable Fives:

Father . . . Mother . . . Grandfather . . . Grandmother . . . and, all rolled in one now, Mishima . . .

I shook my head. But no release. The vision was unbearable and the smell of it sickened me right to the soul. No matter how quick or resourceful I was, there were Five points in kendo* . . . only *five* and never more . . . and all of them padded completely!

(*Wooden swords for wooden men* . . .)

And Mishima was laughing, high in the heavens, from the head still tucked under his arm—at the pride of my soul, my new Life in the Raw. I opened the fridge. And I reeled from the shock. For I knew he'd had me once again!

Vegetables . . . Fruit . . . Water . . . Nuts . . . Juice . . .

"Huhhh! Huhhh!" Mishima screamed.

1! . . . 2! . . . 3! . . . 4! . . .

5! . . . 5! . . . 5! . . . 5! . . .

He was laughing, as he'd always been and as he always would be. Mishima, Mishima, who'd gone *all the way.*

He and his glorious Four.

Five!

I walked that night—oh, how I walked!—all the way to Shinjuku.† Yankee sailors, rowdy and drunk, strutted, the

---

* *Men* points may be scored on either side of the helmet; *kote* points on either glove; *do* is a straight stabbing blow at the throat.

† The red-light district in Tokyo.

cocks of the walk. Whores not much older than Mo-chan called out from the doorways, their paws on their cunts.

I froze in the midst of the square. Shivering half from the cold. Half from the total aloneness I felt. I'd studied kendo for ten years, had a black belt in judo. Yet I'd never felt smaller in all my life. Near the bathhouse doors young Yakuza studs stood tough with tattoos and chopped fingers. And my nose screamed out a red alert: Danger! Run! The *Real* Real Thing!

(*Wooden swords for wooden men . . .*)

(1 . . . 2 . . . 3 . . . 4 . . .
5! . . . 5! . . . 5! . . . 5! . . .)

I froze there. I must have been staring. I must have been looking right at them. For suddenly a group of four began to move as one my way, and I scuttled off like a crab in the night to freeze at the opposite end of the square . . . while the crowd passed by me—and through me, it seemed—by the hundreds . . . the thousands . . . the millions! The world passed through me. Humanity. Life.

I stood in a blizzard of small snowflake people, whirling indistinctly, but all of them belonging to some larger picture of which I could not be a part. And all of them now passing through me. All of them going, *all,* all the way!

The sailors going to the whores . . . The whores to their Yakuza lovers . . . who in turn were on their way to still grander tattoos and chopped fingers . . .

They all passed through me in the night as I stood there shivering.

I may have stood there for hours, or

days. The smell was what finally moved me: dead meat and formaldehyde, a sickening scrim from my feet to my snout.

I picked up my collar and started home, my neck already tingling in anticipation. It seemed to me that in all the world there could be no grander sounds than the jerk of the noose, the snap of my neck. There could be no sweeter smell than the shit of my life in the seat of my pants—out of me once and forever.

("Huhhh!")

Never had I walked before with such a sense of purpose . . . not even the night I returned to kendo. I knew now that Mishima had sent me, cackling with glee at the hoax. I'd never before seen the man's humor as anything other than mad. But now it made such sense to me that I began to laugh myself. Oh, not your usual Japanese laugh—that constipated chuckle that can't stop bowing long enough to even clear the bowels. No, this was something grand and wild, savage in its sanity, outlandish in its freedom.

Mishima's famed laughter paled beside mine. I opened the floodgates and screamed to the night:

"Huh-uhh! Huh-uhhh! Huh-uhhhhh! Huhhhhh! Huhhhhh!"

I wished Mo-chan could have heard me. She'd always loved my stories, but said they'd grown too—serious.

How right she was. I knew it now. I knew it and I laughed out loud. I howled all the way from Shinjuku. People scurried from my path, which made me laugh all the harder. I watched two drunken

Yakuzas step back in stunned amazement, the butts just fallen from their lips sizzling in the snow.

"1! . . . 2! . . . 3! . . ." I screamed.

"3! . . . 4! . . . 5!

"HUH-UHHHHHHHH!"

At midnight I finally came to the dorm, my voice grown hoarse from laughing, as if the cords were sanded raw. But down the hall I heard the clicks of slowly opened doors. And I knew that they knew that my moment had come. From here on there would be no more laughter, save mine. I was one of the heroes now, one of the saints. And there could be no question I was going *all the way*.

Midnight. The witching hour. Brother's journal cast a spell that flowed from the soles of her

(Ten . . .

Nine . . .)

all the way to her

(Eight . . .)

and her

(Seven . . .

(Six . . .)

Elbows crossbarred to her head, toes pointed straight to the ceiling, she read from the inverted stand constructed by Frankie Motta. (Though the slowest of students, with pudding for brains and an accent that tortured her ears, the Hispanic asked no questions. If she wanted to read on her head—what the heyyy? Here you go, teach. Teach me now, how do I tell her she, like, wigs me out?)

The flames of the first fifty candles from Chuck—Bryant-san's friend, who worked fast if not cheap—flickered in their crimson shells and washed the room in bloodred waves that had set Mo back two hundred dollars. This place was her cathedral now. Confessional. Connection. And understanding, also, flowed through her now in crimson waves, each building somehow on the last. The closer she came to his end. And her Source.

(Four . . .
Three . . .
Two . . .
Ten . . .)

Scan took in the pages, constructed the scenes, started floods of red mood from her—

(Nine . . .)

You closed the door behind you. Saa . . . You had their full attention now. Your own laughter grew quiet within you at last. Silent and deep as the ocean at night. And yet you were laughing—oh yes, Number Five—laughing as you'd never laughed and never would again. Laughing at the rage you felt for Mishima and grandpa and grandma and father. Laughing at the love for me you'd never admitted, not once, to yourself . . . and would take with you now, all the way to the Void . . . to the

(Four . . .
Three . . .
(Two . . .)
one true
(Three . . .)
for-
gone conclusion of your life . . .
(Five . . . Five . . . Five . . . Five! . . .)

Mo tumblerolled onto the balls of her feet. Full-headed with the flow of blood and the last rush of thoughts in his mind. She slipped into her sweats. Felt brother's penis straining through the silk recesses of her cunt. Her stiffened nipples now were *his*. The ultimate turn-on. The hard-on for Death.

She took hold of the family honor and the coil of rope with the noose at the end. And then stood at the window a moment, letting the waves flow through, up and down, while she rested her eyes on the small moonlit plot. Hypnotic rows of headstones called. Mishima's and grandpa's and grandma's and mother's. Father's and brother's and now, at last, hers. Death to the old ways. Death to the new. Death to frustration and longing and hope. Death to futility. Death to success. Death to the pride at the heart of all humblings, the curse at the root of all prayers. Peace now. Sleep. Detachment. Rest. Death to all nations in this, the high country, where there are no strangers.

Yes . . .

Clopclopclopclop! Clopclopclopclop! Clopclopclop! Clop-

Oooooof! Oooooof!

A crescendo of furious footsteps was approaching hard and fast from the right. A midnight runner, by the sound, hell-bent on a record. Mo stepped back beyond the frame and lowered the shade in a smooth, subtle glide.

CLOPCLOPCLOPCLOP! CLOPCLOPCLOPCLOP! CLOPCLOPCLOPCLOP! CLOP-

(*ROARRRRROOOOO???*)

Mo lifted the edge of the shade a half inch. Saw a hooded figure go barreling past—

switching, without breaking stride,

to reverse???

She shook her head, then looked again. The runner was already well out of view, ghost echoes of footsteps half lost in the night. She'd slept too little. Worked too hard. And eaten one salad too many.

(Blue sparks???)

But she felt on the very verge at last of understanding brother.

And so she marched out to the Workshop. The room in which they would now die.

You left the lights on in your room. You did not flinch. Strong soul. Brave boy. No uniform for you tonight, you needed no man's army. No note. No speech. No cries. No prayers. No subconscious clues for the neighbors you heard straining their ears at their doors.

You went about your business now, as always with makoto, *as if this were the final Phase of your Life's Technique. Soon, when this brief task was over, you'd laugh for all eternity. Louder than Mishima. High as a kite, in the minds of the gods, on the glory you'd gone out with. For no one had ever died quite as you planned. Your death would be spectacular and wild and unique. A nightsong for the ages that ennobled the heart while it curdled the blood.*

Your song began in silence . . . and then with the cool chilling whacks of a hammer and chisel on the old wood floor . . .

Mo removed the measured wedge of pine cut loose by Motta. (Heyyy, you want holes in the floor? Say how big and how many! I'll dig all the way to Japan, if you like. But Teach', she's coming soon, real soon. And what do you call a girl's—well, like, you know . . .) Mrs. Daez would never forgive her, Mo knew, but the cut had been done to perfection. And in her heart, more than anything else, she felt *communion* as she worked the family honor in half to the hilt. She packed all the edges, as brother had done, with shavings and chips from the pine. And, when she was done, the blade rose from the floor like a gleaming, unshakable gift from the gods. She tugged hard at the tip and released it, thrilled to the depths of her being by the fixed and mighty *twang*.

The hammer song began again. You took apart an old wood chair and fortified the chandelier . . .

Mo's living room, regrettably, had lacked any

overhead fixtures. But what Motta-san lacked in a talent for tongues, he made up for—with flamboyant skill—in mechanical improvisation. (You wanna swing from the ceiling? Then, by Jesus Christ, you will! Heyyy, who am I to wonder why? But—Teach', if you don't mind my asking—how do I tell her it smells like a rose?) The oak ceiling joist would support a small swing seating a baby gorilla. It had been centered precisely above the brace they had dug in the floor.

Mo Roy Rogersed the noose in an underhand toss that sailed through the seven-inch opening and dropped, its shadow swinging on the wall.

She stepped back, another step; and then a half; a quarter. For long seconds she measured the distance from the noose to the tip of the blade. Then she stepped back another inch and—carefully regauging—thought, *Chōdo ii!* That's it—just right! She softshoed the slack, one slow step at a time, to the security door. Then fixed the end around the knob in a thick Gordian knot.

Mo circled the room, reappraising her work, the distance between her and brother as thin as the edge of the sharp, gleaming blade.

Onii-san, I mistook you. Forgive me now, I beg of you, and take me with you to that country where there are no numbers.

(Five . . .)

And where the laughter of the gods is

one

(Two . . .)

with the ache in your heart.

Mo squared off the first of two chairs she'd procured—painstakingly tested for hardness and height—on the left of the family honor. Then set the second on the right in a mirror image. Back to back, exact-ly, with two feet in between them.

You crossed the room. You had it now. And

through your body red waves of desire washed through, head to toe, for me . . . The ultimate turn-on . . . The hard-on for

You-u-u . . .

I mounted the two chairs with four easy steps, like an acrobat climbing the stairs to *sorei.*

The gods had preordained this death and given it to me alone. And so I sailed with confidence through all of the particulars. I slung the noose around my neck and pulled it snug. Just so . . . Just so! . . . I gazed down between my legs. Saw everything was as it should be. I would not be cheated. There would be no failure. No, this death was mine and . . .

Ours alone.

Propped on top of the back of the chairs, Mo slung the noose around her neck. She tightened it . . . Just so . . . Just so! . . . The closeness to brother crossed through her and through. And the point of her own sad existence awaited, feet below, between her legs, the first and last direct connection she would ever know.

Balance, oh yes, was the heart of it now. Balance and unflagging courage.

You did not deign to tie your hands or even cross your arms. Not you. You laced your fingers on your hara, *as if you were ready to take a long nap. The gods themselves had brought you here and they would see you through the pain. A pain like no other, not even Mishima's. Agony was what you craved—an exquisite and ultimate test of your self, your power to square to the nth degree the*

(Five . . .)

that had ruined you

(Four . . .)
ever more . . .
(Three . . .
Two . . .)
The last washed through: a wave of such ferocious strength she lost herself completely. Now there was no line at all between Matsuo and herself; his life, her life; either's death. Everything was.

"One!"

at last. And she began to call out loud, in crisp, decisive numbers.

"Two!"

One last look between my legs. I see the point, precisely placed, a soaring penetration.

"Three!"

One last check of the rope on my neck. All of life's strangleholds rolled into—

"Four!"

The vision flashes through my mind: two feather movements of my legs. A clean, straight drop. An awful snap. And three feet of shining honor coming up fast through my ass to my—

"Five!"

Mo froze, in brother's body; riveted, as he had been, by the cries from behind the left wall.

The students' mocking, jeering:

"Six!"

It fell, as music, on her ears. *Onii-san* loosened the noose through her fingers. Then stepped down, through her, from the chairs, muttering, "Of course! Of course!" And walked out through her, smiling, on the high road to rebirth.

Mo followed him into the kitchen.

Before her lay a twelve-ounce steak, so raw it might have just been torn from the side of a still-living steer. Beside it, in a glass stained red, the juices of livers and entrails. The moment of union had left her. And her courage was dwindling fast.

Dekinai, she thought. I can't . . .

With feverish motions she traced brother's *kanji*—all of them written, it seemed, with her blood. Yet still beyond comprehension. Or acceptance. Or belief.

By the time I arrived in Shinjuku, at two A.M., I felt filled with wonder at the beauty of it all. I hadn't been wrong, after all, only blind. Only blind as a human can be. And the gods, in their infinite mercy, had only been cruel to be kind. They'd been there. They'd been there by my side all along. Stretching me out on the end of my rope and then perching me there on the brink of my world.

To show me the difference a *number* can make.

Oh, my Six—my beautiful Six—my precious and lifesaving, singular Six!

In the square of Shinjuku the fat crowd was thinning, except for some muscular clusters of whores and Yankees and Yakuza thugs. Several of the latter, wearing stubs for pinkies, shifted their stances, their lips drawn like swords.

How pathetic they looked now, and puny! For, I'd grown on the way to Shinjuku. Grown to the height I had been all along—held back only by my fear, my lack of faith and vision.

I gave them a laugh like the old one and cried:

"1! . . . 2! . . . 3! . . . 4! . . .
5! . . . 5! . . . 5! . . . 5! . . ."

One of the Yakuzas stepped up and barked, *"Urusei, kono bakayarō!*"*

"Well, well, well," I thought. Here we were now, at the Gate. And the price of admission: a small test of faith.

Till now, my progress had been like a child's: a dogged procession of painful mistakes, with the errors scored in black and blue on my arms and legs.

But life had changed and I had grown and I knew that the gods were inside me. As I stood there looking at that leering face before me, I felt Phase Four *completed* . . . Phase Five already *accomplished* . . . My mind raced through pages of stickmen, absorbing them into my muscles and bones. And I knew I could take him right where he stood. Go all the way, if I wanted.

Tonight, though, my feeling was playful.

When I removed my jacket and gestured to the Yakuza a buzz of excitement spread through the crowd. From the bathhouse windows whores prodded each other and huddled to view, while six sailors stopped to watch, teetering from too much *sake.*

I shifted position a couple of times to feel the powder with my feet, while assessing the size of the man and his rage.

His anger was not hard to fathom. He

---

*Unlike English, Japanese is not an epithetic tongue. In this subtlest of languages, insult itself is a ritualized art. Here, the literal translation is absurd to coarsened ears: "What a noisy one is this fool!" But *urusei* is in street-level form—a brutal lack of etiquette—with *kono* ("this one") singling out the poor *bakayarō* from the crowd. The equivalent impact in English would be: "Shut up, you crazy fucker, or I'll kick your ugly ass!"

snarled and spat a great gob on my shoe, flanked by five nail-chewing cronies.

From the Yankees a bald-headed giant advanced, with blazing red eyes and a mouthful of stubs.

"Don't you worry, Jappo. Your side's just hit seven."

Footsteps scurried through the snow all around the lines we'd made. Six against six now, howling for action, with me in the middle between them.

If I did not act . . . and soon . . .

"Come on, you damn fool Jappo!"

I drew a broad arc with my hands, smiling sweetly.

"One and one is *true,*" I said. "Let our friends make a circle around us."

"You die!"

"Come on, Jappo!"

"Bakayarō!"

But, slowly, they encircled us and I focused my sight on the center.

"One and one . . ." I said again.

My opponent tore off his long leather coat and tossed it to an outstretched arm. Despite the cold—I had started to shiver—he ripped off his shirt, popping half of the buttons, and threw it to the wind. It sailed. The Yakuza was in a trance. And—hard to tell in the white powderfall—I thought he might be drooling. His torso was covered with scars and tattoos. But this had not caught our attention.

"Fucking Charles Atlas!"

"Christ!"

The Yakuza was truly alarmingly proportioned. For a small man, Mishima was powerfully built. And I myself had been no slouch in muscular development. But this man outweighed me by some thirty pounds and not an ounce that I could see was anything but muscle. He bulged and rippled awesomely, then threw shadow punches that shattered snowflakes in the air. And for a second I half wondered what the gods were up to . . .

"Uhh, Jappo . . . If you need some help . . ."

I lowered my center, half hunched like a cripple. And, with one hand raised in a palm-flash of Peace, I bent over and drew a straight line in the snow.

This, I told him, was my sword, using, alternately, honorific Japanese and what English I had for the Yankees. The circle around us softened slightly in stunned disbelief.

"Aww, Jappo, Jappo, Jappo . . ."

My opponent, however, would have none of this. He kicked the sword into a fine spray of powder and screamed at me to come die like a man.

"Yakuza-sama," I begged him. "*Mochiron.* I surely will. And be happy to die at your honorable hands. But first . . ."

The move caught his attention. I slipped my watch off my left wrist. The Seiko, a present from grandpa, had cost 100,000 yen. The gold band caught a flash of light and gleamed commandingly. I tossed grandpa's gift to the Yakuza, who snatched it and glared with suspicion, contempt.

"*Anata no desu,*" I said. It was his. The only thing I wanted was one minute of his time. One minute and one second, with the same allotted time for him. Time for myself, a poor mathematician, to demonstrate the beauties of the Higher Mathematics. Time for him to kill me.

"Kichigai!" he snarled.

"Yes. Oh yes, I am quite mad. I only ask you let me talk and do not interfere. For the *full one minute,* I swear on the graves of my mother and father to only talk and demonstrate. I shall not use my hands or feet."

The Yakuza chuckled and leered at the watch. "*E, to,* when your time is up?"

"I swear, on the graves of my mother and father, not to lift a finger, no matter what you do."

"Saa . . . Amerikajin wa?"

"One and one is true," I said. "All of the men in the circle around us must swear, on their honor, they won't interfere. Not during and *not after.*"

Consternation all around. The brute conferred with the rest of his gang while I pidgin-briefed the sailors. I don't believe I've ever heard such sounds of frustration and anger.

But presently the oaths were sworn, and the circle begrudgingly tightened.

I called for the time. It was 2:22. I asked that the time be called out, loud and clear. In ten-second intervals. Using my favorite numbers.

I retraced the line in the snow with my shoe, then stepped back, repeating: My sword was there. And I was here. And for the *full one minute . . .*

"What the hell's he up to?"

"Shhhh!"

At 2:23 the bald giant cried, "Now!" And from here they all counted together as one.

"I am here to teach," I cried, "the Higher Mathematics. These great numbers from the gods are what I have lived and may die for."

"ONE!"

(Ten seconds down now . . . and thirty to go . . .)

"One is surely a wonderful number," I said. "There's one of me and one of you . . . And one hope in my heart as I lead you to—"

"TWO!"

(Twenty down and halfway there . . . I straightened imperceptibly and started moving the pieces in place . . .)

"Two is every bit its equal in arcane fascination. I have two eyes . . . Two ears . . . Two lips . . . Two nostrils . . . Two hands . . . And two—"

"THREE!"

(The Yakuzas were laughing now, which suited my purposes fine. Thirty down and ten to go. They'd shaken their hands as I'd shaken mine and bounced up and down on their toes. But in their increasingly jovial mood, they'd failed to notice something. My legs were scissored now, not flush. I directed their attention to my three uplifted fingers.)

"Three is a number possessing the utmost significance in the Higher Math. For One and Two are Three, you see . . . and Three can only lead to—"

"FOUR!"

(Stickmen exploded in my soul. All of my life had been lived for this night. And even the snow powder sped me along, as if placed, by the gods, just for me. My limbs moved by rote, as if *I* were a stickman perfectly scribed by the gods in the air.

The Yakuza screamed in anger, and bucked. But he had been forsworn, of course: I had not used my hands or feet. I helped myself up with steel cords in my *hara* and resumed the lesson.)

"Four is a difficult number," I said. "You may not have noticed, but my sword has cleared the scabbard . . . which brings us now, at last, to—"

"FIVE!"

(The Yakuza gawked in amazement as I curled up and swung my right hand in a blow which I pulled at his neck. I held his stunned eyes while, locked to his torso, I concluded the small demonstration.)

"Five, I thought, was everything. But it

was only make-believe. So, since I have one second—"

"SIX!"

(I cocked my hand and delivered a chop that all but broke his neck. His tongue shot out, a purple slug. He gargled "Augg-ghhh!" And lost his head. And then our two bodies fell to the snow.)

"That, my friend, was a Five-and-a-Half."

If the leader was breathing, it wasn't by much. But rules were rules. I scrambled up and jabbed my finger at his men.

"*Hajime!* Start counting!"

The sailors were still laughing when I slipped away into the night.

At the end of the square I turned left up an alley—to the back door of a *soba* shop once haunted by Tatenokai.

For some time I stood in the shadows and watched while the owner made trips with the garbage. At length, I whispered, "*Chotto* . . . Please . . ."

The old man reeled, with one hand on his heart. *"E? Aa? O!"* he cried. "*Aa,* it's you, Shirata-san. By the gods, boy, you gave me a start!"

"Sumimasen," I said. "Daiku-san. I need a little favor."

"*Sō?* What is it you need?"

I told him what I wanted in no uncertain Japanese and the look in his eyes was quite frantic at first. But I wiggled my fingers and gave him a smile and pulled out a purse filled with thousands of yen.

When I left him, my hands were not empty.

I proceeded to another darkened section of the square. And, unable to wait any longer, I sank my teeth into the warm bloody beef . . . and then toasted the night with the drink of the gods.

(Your brother was a maniac . . .)
(. . . a maniac . . .)
(. . . a maniac . . .)
(My child, trust your Exercise . . . From here on, the way leads to madness and death . . .)

Mo shook her head to clear it of Sensei's impossible pleas. There was no way to stop, not now, when she'd stood with *onii-san* astride those two chairs . . . and known she would do it, yes, *go all the way* . . .

She took the steak between her hands, a giant bloody Eucharist, and raised it to her lips.

(Wild horses in his heart . . . I'd known from the beginning . . .

But when your brother returned to my school, he seemed no longer human. His always fierce demeanor had become absolutely ferocious. And the look in his eyes—like a beast set to kill. He shattered one shinai *that night, and then three more in the following two. I should have expelled him, I know that—I know! But he had moves I'd never seen, and yes, that was a part of it. But, truly, what kept me so helpless was the sense of the difference between us. Kendo was, for me, an art, a sport, a path to knowledge. Whereas your brother acted now as if his life—his soul itself—depended on his every move.*

"What's the matter, Sensei? Is kendo becoming too real?" he cried. "No longer like one of your movies?"

There were injuries—I cautioned him. Com-

plaints—I warned him outright. And yet I watched and waited. Knowing in my very bones that he was up to something.

And dying to know what it was.

Which, of course, suited your brother just fine.

For Matsuo was planning to kill me.)

Mo left the table, dizzy and queasy, picking gristle from her lips. And yet she felt, undeniably, a raw and vital charge.

She bounced a few times on the balls of her feet to equalize the energy.

Then wandered, almost aimlessly, to the Workshop and around the chairs. Back and forth. Around the chairs. Until, the pressure grown too much, she crumbled to her knees . . . then dropped . . . and lay back, knees spread, in a funk . . . as shaking fingers slid under her sweats . . . and under the band of red panties . . . to meet in a frantic and brutal massage the flaming red lips of her vulva.

She found release in seconds and cried out, in love and despair, "*Onii-san! Onii-san!* I love you!"

Minutes later, she found herself standing before the security door. She stroked the locks, and then the wood, while caressing one cheek with the lip of the glass.

"You down there?" she murmured. "Come, give me a sign."

A wave of silence from the cellar rose up in reply.

"I know," she said. "Me too. New York."

Mo held the glass before her eyes, gazing almost lovingly upon the small red waves.

When the contents had settled, she chugged the brew down and wiped the blood off with the back of her hand.

"Soon, I'm thinking. Pretty—"

THIRTY-SEVEN

(Soon . . .)

In the room overlooking the graveyard, the *oni* was having the time of its life. Small bones of a dozen odd mongrels and cats, collected on its midnight runs, made crunching sounds beneath its feet.

Saa . . . Dogs were good. And cats were fine (their supple spines were fun to eat). And, oh, the flying buzzballs were treats too sweet to be denied. But

(Soon . . .)

the *oni* had twice tasted *flesh*, his and hers—that curious, *curious* woman's—

(Ben!)

and nothing, but nothing, on earth could compare with the glorious texture and bloodjuicy taste of—

(Ben—
it's
me—

it's
Mrs.—)
(Ee?)

The *oni* crunchstepped through the bones and hairs and bits of eaten things. It paced back and forth, and around and about, at home most in darkness, yet drawn to the light.

The white light specked with speaking shadows in the front right corner.

The first week the box had been silent and dark behind its mask—a sheet of glass topped with long, thin silver ears. But then one night the *oni* had tripped on the tail that stretched out three feet from the back. Enraged, it had first thought to shatter the box or pitch it through the window.

But somewhere, very deep inside, a wave of ghost atoms rustled and stirred. The *oni* circled the curious box, running the tail through its huge hairy hams . . . poking those skinny, ridiculous ears . . . jabbing and twisting the round little bumps lined up in a row near the glass . . .

The mask stared back, impervious.

The *oni* commanded it.

More silence still.

Befuddled, the *oni* dismissed it, settled into the house and this favorite room.

It spent long hours at the window, dreaming its own moonlit plots for the girl.

It spent more hours, longer still, attempting to get its face right in the mirror. (The eyes, it was sure, were the old one's. Almost. The mouth was too hard, but it might do in passing in a darkened doorway on a vaguely moonlit night. The hair, as it had from the first, stood on end. And the teeth were wrong, all wrong—why, even an *oni* could see that—and yet . . . There was something, above and beyond it all,

missing.

The *oni* ran and caught things in the night and paced the whole house for long hours on end—avoiding, of course, that one troubling room—perfecting the use of the cords in its throat. Too loud at first . . . Too firm . . . Too—*too*—

"Ben, I am."

Well, there, *that* was more like it!

And—

"Have nice day!"

Ah, yes—go, *oni,* go!

"Taking into mouth of—"

(**WHO!!!!!**)

The *oni* tore oak chairs apart, using its hands sometimes, sometimes its teeth.

It adjusted its heartbeat.

Compacted its frame.

Built itself up in the shoulders and arms, and the thighs of those old spindly legs.

All these things it did, and more, without a glance at the cursed, useless box.

Until, that is, last evening—when, pacing around it, the *oni* had stopped. And felt the ghost rustle of atoms within. And then felt a *clicking* sensation—not in its own mind, its *hara,* but in that vague somewhere, close to the eyes, that had been home to the old one.

The tail . . .

The *oni* kicked it with one foot. The tail scarcely troubled to quiver.

And yet there was something about it that held the *oni*'s old one's eyes.

Something to do with the tail and the—

Click.

Something to do with the—

Click.

Click.

The *oni* closed its eyes and drew the last of the fading click-echoes

down . . .
to where they could be dealt with:
low,
and grounded in the *hara.*
Click.

The *oni* formed a picture in the center of its belly. Saw the tail running straight from the *idiot* box. Straight into the wall.

Click!

The *oni* knelt beside the tail; noted the sharp golden teeth at the end.

It wondered, *Ee?* What beast was this that ate with its ass through a wall?

But the picture remained, vividly etched, within the demon's *hara.* So it jabbed with the teeth at the plaster, attempting to translate the scene, until one tooth was bent in half.

Oh, maddening, maddening, *idiot*—

Click!

The old one's eyes lowered and focused.
On a glossy square.
Framing a twin pair of circles.
Mouths with holes where teeth had been.
Or—where teeth might possibly . . . ?
Click . . .
Click . . .
The *oni* jabbed and poked and—
Click!
—regarded the teeth and the holes in the wall.
"Ben I am. And have nice day."

With slow and deliberate movements—almost as if remembering—the *oni* straightened the crooked gold tooth and slipped the plug home in the socket.

And jumped back in amazement, with an uncontrolled
"ROARRRRROOOOO!"
For the long-silent box had just sprung into life.

"If you need me," it said, "you just whistle. You know how to whistle, don't you? You just pucker your lips and—"

Click.

Ghost atoms rustled and stirred once again. Little people in the box, moving just behind the glass, in costumes the *oni* had not seen before. Looking good enough to eat.

You just pucker your lips and you—

PHWEEEEEEEEE-PHWEEEEEEEWWWWWW!

The *oni* whistled, again and again, delighted by the sound of it and the rush of air over its lips.

But then a strange thing happened. The whistle-she-thing vanished. Replaced by the harsh "Arf! Arf!" of a dog chasing a long tooting something on wheels across the broad floor of a room.

The *oni* gave the box a whack. The case cracked in the upper right corner.

It poked the top knob and, when nothing happened, twisted it. The screen turned black. The *oni* grunted, twisting right, and the pooch reappeared in a blinding white light. The *oni* twisted a bit to the left. The scene was picture-perfect.

Saa!

It gave the next knob a turn to the right. The picture subdivided in a field of darkened lines. The *oni* turned it to the left until the picture was centered again.

On a roll, it worked the third knob and thus learned to manage the sound.

But none of its maneuverings could bring the whistle-she-thing back. And the *oni* was still wondering fiercely where the small creature had gone when it noticed the large numbered circle.

And turned it.

And saw the box's real magic.

Seven men on horses thundered across the

sands, with music, out of nowhere, swelling all around them.

Click . . .

The *oni* twisted the circle and—

Click.

A creature in a flowing cape gazed at the demon with unearthly eyes.

"Listen to the music of the chillldren of the night!"

The *oni* was staring intently, hypnotized completely—

The creature was replaced by a man with a stick and a map.

"High tomorrow of ninety-seven, lows in the high eighties. Increasing cloudiness and chance of thundershowers in the west. All this and more on the Late Nite News!"

Click.

Picture of a ringing something on a tiny table. A hand reached out. The picture changed. From ring-thing to a bald man's face, with a stick in its mouth.

"Yeah, yeah, talk to me. Come on, who loves ya, baby?"

Click!

The creatures came and went, in tales the *oni* could not fathom—forever trading places with babies and poochies . . . and Ko-teksu and Koo-keesu (*Saa* . . . which of the two did they put in their mouths?) The *oni* saw steel birds that flew, with—apparently—creatures inside them; carriages that raced along, drawn by invisible horses.

Impossible!

Ridiculous!

And yet . . . And yet . . .

The atoms stirred.

The atoms stirred and rustled.

And all of this day it had listened and paced, while the curious words came home.

"What's a dame like you doing in a place like this?"

And—

"Pa, don't you know me? Pa! It's your son, Pa—Horse!"

And—

"I coulda been a contender."

And—

The atoms stirred. The atoms gathered. And they were still gathering when the *oni* stepped to the window and saw a familiar figure passing.

The *oni* stared.

The atoms stirred.

The *oni* turned.

Then turned again.

From the sight of the vanishing he-thing.

To the door of that not-for-the-*oni*, closed room.

Which somehow seemed, remarkably, rather more—*inviting*.

With the feeding-room door just beyond it.

And the window overlooking—

Aa!—

the *curious* rush of the garden below.

The atoms stirred and rustled.

And, no longer questioning, the *oni* surrendered and drew them down.

Until, more and more, they were all one: the hunger that raged in its *hara* . . . the voices that came from the box . . . and the echoes that rose from the atoms themselves . . .

(*Mommy!*)

(*Daddy!*)

(*Darling boy* . . .)

The *oni* brooded and listened and paced and turned, on an impulse, the large numbered knob.

A woman—(*pret-ty* she-thing!)—cocked her head and murmured,

"You'd better fasten your seat belts. It's gonna be a long, stormy night."

The *oni* laughed and cried, "ROARRRRO-OOOO!"

THIRTY-EIGHT

Till now I had been practicing with a truly pathetic device: a modified coat rack I'd padded for bulk and weighted and nailed to the floor.

The day after Shinjuku, on an aimless and casual stroll, I chanced on a kimono shop I'd passed a dozen times before. I watched the two women, solemn as church mice, fitting measured lengths of silk on a wooden frame.

A dozen times I'd passed without stopping! I glued my face to the window, stickmen tingling in my toes.

I was smiling, certainly. Even laughing, it may be. But I lowered my shoulders and thought solemn thoughts and walked through their door with a deep, humble bow.

"Ladies," I said. "Please forgive me. But I have a small request to make."

My voice had never been so soft. But in my heart—

(Roarrrrrooooo?)

Mo rubbed her eyes and looked around. She'd worked too long and much too hard. The last time, like brother, she'd cracked her skull hard—and, aside from the bells, she was now hearing—

things.

Mo set down notebook and squeeze-ball and padded toward the kitchen.

No . . .

If the sound had been real, it had come from the front. Or maybe from the side.

She was halfway through the Workshop when three knocks stopped her in her tracks.

"Remember me?"

Mo did, but—

Ee?

How could it be?

Could it possibly be?

The hair . . . The face . . . The eyes themselves . . .

Everything was different.

"I know it's late," he told her.

"It's—midnight," Mo stammered. "And I was just—"

"Yeah." He lowered his eyes to one sneaker, still faded and tattered and loose at the lip. A last reminder of the past.

Mo's own eyes fluttered, flights of birds, attempting to take in the changes—the freshly washed jeans . . . the neatly pressed shirt . . .

"My door—" she started, stepping back.

The figure smiled ruefully and shook his massive head.

"Girl," he said, "I'm begging you. I'm different. Trust me. Please."

(Bow, you ninny!)

('Course, the trick's—)

(Mother, I'm coming to join you!)

Mo swallowed softly and looked in his eyes.

"Forgive me," she said. "Prease—come in."

THIRTY-NINE

"I'll only stay a few minutes," Sloan said.

Mo nodded happily at him.

His face, clean-shaven, looked twenty years younger. And his eyes had turned a stunning shade of Mediterranean blue. His whole body seemed relaxed; when he walked, he was floating on air.

"One down," she whispered.

"Sorry?"

"Prease."

Sloan stepped around the new dressmaker's doll; took in the slashes and chips on the door; settled his eyes on the sword.

"I see you're keeping busy."

"Yes."

"Care to talk about it?"

"Welrl . . ."

Sloan joined her on the sofa, crossing his hands on his lap.

Mo said, "Maybe someday."
"Fine."
"If you will tell me—"
(*Sumimasen!*)
"—what happened, Sloan-san, to your face."
Cotter held his hands up, palms quite dry and paralleled. And steady as two floating rocks. "Not a drop since that last night."
"Can you do?" Mo asked him.
"Yes. Been going to some meetings. Seen some guys there a lot worse than me. And what they've been saying—it makes lots of sense."
"Tatoeba?" she asked. "Like what?"
"Like how we can't undo the past: How what I did, I did, it's done. Like how we do, though, have to pay. You know, what we owe, all that."
"Are you low on dough? I can—"
Sloan cocked an eyebrow but thanked her for that. "Money's the least of my problems right now. Girl, I owe you something. I owe you an explanation."
"Sloan-san—"
"Cotter."
"Very welrl. Come over here, Cotter, and sit next to me."

Cotter Sloan took a deep breath and began.
"Well, I suppose, to begin with . . . My wife is dead—no, not like *that.* Hell, that girl—Chiori—she's a born survivor. Probably having the time of her life. What I mean is, she finally died in my *heart.*
"And, you know, the night she died there—about a week after I took my last drink—I found myself thinking about you. I'd be walking along, feeling proud as you please, seven, eight days without booze. And suddenly I'd get a flash. And remember some horrible thing that I said—just

because you reminded me of her. Because I hurt so much inside I had to hurt *somebody* back. Because I knew how wrong it was and felt so goddamn guilty. Because you were so sweet, so shy, so helpless with that *man* of yours. What could I do except hurt you some more? Before I got starting to like you too much. And forgot how I needed to hate her."

"I know." Mo touched his hand and repeated, "I know."

"You know, I think you *do*," he said.

"I do. We all have our ghost stories. Prease."

When he finished, a full hour later, she had been through worlds of pain that left her limp and humbled.

The beginning was classic *onii-san.*

Two lovers on a shady knoll, lost in some tune from the sixties . . . Helicopters, suddenly, over the slow, steady beat . . . with bombs now dividing the measures and a rolling crescendo of shots . . .

A sudden clash of *symbols* . . .

Cotter Sloan in fatigues, with a gun, bleeding from his eyes and ears . . . while, nailed to a cross, the boy he had been hung there forever in blue jeans . . .

And Cotter was laughing, and still wanting more, when suddenly more came straight at him: in the form of a woman, hiding a baby and wielding a great, heavy cleaver.

Mo followed Sloan home. Through support groups and taverns. Then to Japan, where he paid for his sins by not screwing pure girls from the farmlands.

She lived with him in Tokyo through long nights spent in glitter bars, trapped by the almighty cunning of the young Japanese bar girls. He was not certain, even now, if they'd understood two words. But he drank and talked and paid and filled their glasses with "champagne" at 20,000 yen a pop. Feeling emptied of pain and *forgiven*, somehow.

She followed him on to the Ginza, where he first met Chiori-san.

Who was all of the others rolled up into one, but with an incredible difference. From the first night, she bought *him* drinks. And seemed to like him for himself. Her English, sometimes comical, was often surprisingly subtle. She asked him questions, answered his with little circumspection. She rationed his beers, served him coffee and soda. She begged him not to smoke so much. And she listened, *listened* to the smallest details of his life.

The third night Sloan started closing the bar. The sixth, they went out for coffee and walked, hand in hand, to the Emperor's Palace, parking on an empty bench to talk for long hours of nothing at all. That afternoon a dozen roses came to Cotter's room. That same night the two became lovers. And Chiori, who had left him ragdolled and wearing an idiot grin, said: Please . . . Let's go slow, be careful, *ne?* . . . There are no third second chances . . . Sloan moved in the following week. In six months they were married.

Mo flew home with Cotter Sloan to wait for his darling Chiori: his loving, accepting, obedient wife.

Chiori arrived three months later.

Sloan had six weeks of happiness, the closest thing to total bliss that he had ever known. Chiori cooked and rubbed his back and crooned about their apartment.

Until one day an envelope with "Do Not Forward" on it arrived.

Chiori had gotten her green card.

* * *

"Do you know what it's like—" Sloan cried. "Well, hell, there's no way you *could* know. We'd be getting it on and she'd snap, 'Not like that—higher—harder—more to the left!' She'd tell me I was useless, she had more fun with her own finger. Left-right-left-right! Come on, damn it, harder! I was living with a maniac and there was no way to control her. 'Cause no matter what happened, I couldn't forget the incredible act she'd put on in Japan. Or, God help me, the wife in the rice field . . ."

"Sō . . ."

"But there was something else, you see. Chiori simply didn't *care.* Nothing I did had the slightest effect. I belted her once and she laughed in my face. I don't think she cared if I killed her. She'd call me a loser and scumbag and bum. She took a cleaver to the couch, threw the TV in the trash. Within two months she was coming home late, pig-eyed and leering and looking well fucked. I think she was sleeping with Henry Daez."

Sloan bolted up, looking ready to rip. Instead he leaned back once again on the arm and refolded his hands with great care.

Mo held his gaze and shook her head. "She was not. Berieve me."

"She must've been."

"A woman *knows.* Maybe others, but not him."

"You really think so?"

"Trust me. Yes."

"One thing I can't understand, though. I mean, why did it take her so damned long to *go?* And why did she keep up those phone calls?"

Mo answered softly, "*Giri**. She wanted to re-

*The intricate Japanese concept of debt—whereby all obligations must be met *exactly*. Anything under would mean losing face. And anything over would cause a new debt.

pay you. First, to make *you* throw *her* out. And then, when you didn't, to pay you with hope. Chiori-san was many things. And many of those things were bad. But she was also Japanese and there is no escaping that. A Japanese must always pay. And pay quite precisely."

"Well . . . I hope, wherever she is, she feels she's paid enough. It's late."

At the door Sloan shuffled in place.

Mo waited and smiled and said nothing.

"Maybe I don't have to say this," he said, "but it wasn't me, I swear to you. Not the first time, not the second."

"I know," Mo said. "I'm certain now."

"What I said to you about your hair—when I thanked you, remember, and said that it helped? You know, that was the only thing I told you that I really meant. Suddenly you didn't even vaguely resemble Chiori. Now there were no more excuses."

Sloan extended his hand. Mo ignored it, stepping in to draw him in the circle of her arms.

"This is what we call a hug in this here part of the world," she said. "We say hi with a hug. We say bye with a hug. And we welrlcome new friends to our lives."

Sloan stepped back, those Mitchum eyes opening into Newman's. "You are a remarkable woman."

"No. No, I'm not. Just me."

"Well, in case nobody's told you—it's certainly more than enough."

"I hope you're light," Mo said. "We'll see."

"By the way, I'll be staying upstairs a few nights. Old Lady Daez said a week would be cool if I then dropped off the face of the planet."

"I hope you will not go so far. Everybody's leaving now. Henry . . . Ben . . ."

"Yeah, I heard about Henry. Can't say I'm surprised."

"New York."

"Don't blame the city for Henry. But Ben?"

Mo nodded sadly. "Nowhere."

"Have you called?"

"Once or twice."

"Well, he's got family someplace, I'm sure. I thought he said Hawaii once. Lord knows, he can afford the trip with that crazy lock shop."

"What?"

"Oh yeah. You didn't know that? The shop's just out on Steinway. Henry gets all of his locks from Pops Shacklette. Same as sixty percent of the landlords in town."

"Is that right. I didn't know."

"Well, you've got to admit it's convenient."

"It *is.*"

"Mo—can I call you sometime? Please."

"My life is on the air right now. But yes," Mo said, "my door—you know . . . If you will tell me one more thing. You said my name put—"

"A new slant?" Cotter started fidgeting. "That was the old me again. You know, *slant:* a certain way of seeing things. It also means—well . . ."

"Slanty eyes?"

Cotter nodded, miserable. "And Mo Leigh—you know, Mo *Lee?*—well, there you were thinking the name's so New York. And it sounds like a damn Chinese hooker."

"Cotter Sloan. You're wicked."

"Yeah. And now that I've put all my feet in my mouth, I think I'd better run."

Mo closed the door behind him.

And when his door shut, said, "Me too."

FORTY

And so you started running, brother. Not from yourself, though—oh never, not you! Not from grandpa or grandma or father or me. You were building up speed for the stickmen. And feeding the wolf in your heart.

Mo opened stride at the third block of seven that sided Astoria Park. The air at 2 A.M. was cool and would have been pleasant to stroll in. But brother had worked up a passionate sweat in the dead of the Tokyo winter. And Mo was determined to match him. Drop for drop. Stride for stride.

(Like how we can't undo the past . . .)

(Not tonight, Sloan . . . Not tonight . . . You are right, but *later* . . .)

She measured her breathing and held sips of air, Reeboks raining pit-a-pats on the open runway. A mongrel snapped gingerly twice at her heels. But backed off, astonished, when she whirled on it, running a block—in reverse.

At Ditmars, she was halfway home and soaked clear through. Mo jacked the speed to red alert.

A drunk saw her coming and dove for the shrubs with a wheezing and panicky howl.

She took the next curve onto Boulevard Shore, much too wide, much too fast, barely avoiding the breakwall and a spread-eagle dive in the river.

Onna no kuse ni, ne? . . . Onna no kuse ni . . . Brother breaking clean away, miles and miles ahead of her now, and repeating it over and over: *Onna no kuse ni . . .* Because she is only a woman . . .

No!

Mo Leigh pushed off, with a cry, from the wall, one of the barbs pushing clean through her palm and plowing a fine stretch of lifeline. No time for the blood, she was off now and running—

Go!

—knees even higher than brother's and—

Run!

—the Reeboks were really two puddles of sweat and—

(*Onna no kuse ni!*)

(No!)

—she was closing in fast on the wolf in his heart and nothing but nothing could stop her.

Except:

The red Jaguar parked at the end of the stretch, its cracked windshield covered with tickets. The hubcaps, stripped. The tires, slashed. And a great empty hole where the engine had been.

"Hen—" Mo started.

And again.

Not enough breath in her lungs for the sound.

And not enough strength to decide what to do: cry or whimper or scream out her rage. And so she did all three at once, though most of the sound ended stuck in her throat.

"Hen-ry!"

Why didn't you go down to Florida, *ne?*

Why didn't you run from me?

Henry . . .

The thing is to run, Henry . . . Run, Henry . . . Run . . .

Her legs were moving on their own, her arms almost flapping like wings at her sides, as she flew between a cab and truck, against the light on Twenty-first, past six sleeping houses to the safety of her home.

To shut the door behind her.

And check the locks.

And check the bars.

And recheck the sliding bolts.

And tumble, winded, to the floor.

Running.

And running.

And running.

Away.

FORTY-ONE

"You've been hiding from us."

"Bill."

"Yehhhhhp. Your friendly stylist. Making house calls to touch up your hair."

Bryant, resplendent in lavender jeans and a fuchsia jersey, held up his small styling bag and pursed those jumbo lips. Green eyes on a merry roll beneath the turquoise running strip. "You don't mind if I come in, eh? Quick!"

(Yes I do not? Or I—)

"No."

Had, once again, by this maddening tongue.

Bryant stepped around her with a happy, self-satisfied grin, slipping the queer canvas case off his shoulder to prop it against the first wall.

"You see what happens to you when you go a whole week without Funky? The strangest creatures, like old friends, come calling at your door."

Mo shut the door behind her and followed him dejectedly, awaiting his reaction.

He was midway into telling her how badly her students missed her . . . how everyone was asking *when*—

when suddenly he stopped, more stunned than Cotter Sloan had been.

"My God!"

"Bill," Mo said, "I real-ly think—"

But Bryant was touching the seeds on the wall and the scattered stains of pink.

"Listen, Bill, I like you, but—"

But now he was circling the dressmaker's doll, cloaked in the rainbow kimono—with an oversized melon, capped with a wig, in a deep hole between the two shoulders.

"Bill, the reason I canceled my classes was . . . Bill—"

Bryant stepped back and eyed the *katana* centered before the great doll.

"I real-ly and trury believe you should—"

(*Go* . . . While there still is time for you . . .)

But his eyes were too quick for her and they kept moving.

To the nicks in the door . . . and the slashes through pine . . . and the bloody Ace bandage that circled her palm . . . and—

"*Prease!* You mustn't."

But he did. He knelt by the notebook and studied the figure she'd drawn just before he arrived. *Onii-san*'s Six. Accomplished.

"It's not what you think, Bill—you can't understand."

He just knelt there and studied the picture, as if he could, somehow, see the emptiness inside her. Now that she'd *done* it—and knew in her heart that it would never be enough.

"Yeah. Yeah," he said, "you're right. You're right. It's all too much for *me*." He looked around the room again, then looked at her with hurt green eyes, as he made his way up from his knees. "I don't get the doll . . . the wig . . . or the Samurai Sam sword there on the floor. I can't figure the candles you've got in your room—you must have a hundred, and all of them red. For the life of me, I swear to God, I am thrown for a loop by the *smells*. Take one whiff—it's roses. Another whiff—*raw meat?* Well, what the heyyy, you know me, I'm a funky kind of guy. I can handle being lost. But you know what really wigs me out?"

Mo shook her head, half swooning from the sudden rush of

Roses . . .

(What's been planted coming up . . . Don't let the names mislead you, dear . . .)

Bryant shifted the styling bag from his left hand to the right, looking defiantly crushed. "The thing that really just blows me away—"

(Well, well, blow me down . . . I reckon it's been about forty-odd years . . .)

"—is how you could *be* in such trouble—"

(Just follow the line of the garden . . .)

"—and not call for help from a big hunk like me."

(Myew-tah-bee-lees . . . Myew-tah-bee-lees . . . That's the ticket, eh, Mo? . . . *Change* . . .)

Bryant flexed a muscle the size of a fully grown olive. But, seeing the sad humor wasted, he said, "I'll just let myself out."

Mo threw her arms around him in a wild and abandoned hug. "Prease don't go. I nee— I mean . . ."

"Well, if you put it that way."

"Don't laugh at me. I'm serious."

"Me too. Oh boy, I think I *am.*"

"I want to show you something. Prease?"

Bryant glanced nervously once at the doll. "I gotta tell you something first. I'm a macho guy and all of that—but this stuff really spooks me out."

"Tee-hee," Mo croaked. "Oh no, not that. Hang it on, I'll be right back."

Bryant cleared his throat and said, "I really wish you wouldn't."

Mo sat beside him, closer than he seemed to have the heart for, with the cutting board squared on her knees.

He said, *"Mo?"*

But the smile she gave him just blew him away.

"It's okay," she said. "Just watch."

The cleaver starting moving: light and easy chops at first, almost in slow motion—with each blow delivered, though, so cleanly and precisely a mere touch could have cut through a bone.

Mo outstretched a finger. And proceeded to rain down a flurry of chops, none more than a hairsbreadth away.

Bryant smiled vaguely. Too funky to stop her, too frightened to move. When she finally set down the cleaver, he leaned back with an anguished sigh.

"Bill," she said. "Prease look at me." She could have made love to him there on the couch, he looked so downright lost right now.

"Don't be frightened, Bill," she said. "I have no one to show that. My whole life, from there to here, has been about mistaking. Never, never being wrong. Because people might laugh. Or shut me out. Or point at me and whisper, maybe, *'Onna no kuse ni'*—because she is only a woman. Or a sister. Or a wife."

"You mean that you've been doing this—"

"Oh no," she said. "Prease understand. A knife is only one small way. To make my tongue learn English, *ne?* So I say 'please' instead of 'prease.' So I don't say 'rearry.'"

"Mo."

"I know. I do. I see it's wrong. But how can I stop, when it's only one way? In Japan there are so many ways to keep us from relaxing. To make things go correctly. There are smiles and bows and kimonos and rules, and every situation has a certain way of doing. There are levels and levels of language. And the pressure is forever to be *chōdo ii*—just right. So no one can know you are wrong in your heart."

Mo regarded the cleaver and shrugged, sadly,

setting it down on the floor by the board. "I even had an Exercise. A very Special Exercise. It was simple, rearry. And probably totally useless. But I *believed* my teacher when he told me if I mastered it . . . if I could do *chōdo ii* . . . then I could do anything. For years I believed him. I started inventing hundreds, then thousands of small variations. But it was all just one more way of running from mistakes."

"This exercise," Bryant said. He nodded at the doll.

"Oh no. That is my *ultimate failure.* One day I learned that my Exercise was only the beginning. For somebody else, you see. And I felt my whole life had been—one big mistake. I turned from it. I closed my eyes and followed him through his mistakes. He dreamed of Glory; he thought it could save him. I dreamed of Perfection; the end is the same. All it is, is just mistakes. And stiffness and fear in the heart."

Bryant sidled over, close. About as close as a body could get. He was loose as a goose from the Mohawk on down, totally there and yet out of his skin.

He shook her gently by the shoulders. "Loosen up," he said.

"I can't."

He tweaked her ears; jiggled her cheeks; turned his own lips inside out and cracked her up completely.

"Bill," she cried, "don't do that thing!"

"Heyyy, that's what it's all about. Attitude—remember that? The way we *feel* about mistakes. This country was *discovered* by a guy who couldn't read a map. 'Whoops,' he thought. 'Well, this ain't bad. So, who the hell needs *India?*' Rock 'n' roll got *made* by dudes who thought they were singing like blacks. Mistakes. The best books ever written were whopping and crazy mistakes. Guys who didn't know the rules . . . or wanted to follow but couldn't . . . did the only thing they could—they just opened their hearts up and made their mistakes. But they made 'em like nobody else could. You see?"

"I do," Mo said. "And yet I can't. Too many knives and kimonos and dolls. My attitude—"

"A big mistake. And that's a good beginning, doll, if you can just accept it."

"Dōshite?" she cried. "How, though?"

"Just a minute. Let me think. This is really serious."

"Dōmo," she said. "Thanks a lot."

Bryant regarded her deeply. Then stuck one finger up his nose and wiggled it obscenely.

Mo blinked and gasped and dropped her jaw, fascinated totally.

"Sorry," he said. "Helps me think." He stuck another in one ear. And, with a grave expression, started flapping the rest of his fingers. "Ahhh . . . I *love* to concentrate. Today's kids don't know what they're missing. —Wait! By God, I think I've got it!"

"What?"

"Let's blow this joint and boogie!"

"Oh, that's a great mistake!" she cried.

"It is, if I do say so. Traveling by subway at this time of night. But first we have to fix your hair. It's starting to fade. It looks—*normal.*"

"Prease!"

"I think we'll do it crimson with a little twist of lime. They'll all be *green* with envy!"

Before they left, Mo asked him again, screwing up her courage, "Bill, what thing *is* in that case?"

"Oh, that—I guess that's *my* ultimate failure. Come on, it's Friday night, let's go!"

FORTY-TWO

The City is made for forgetting, at night. All the rest is daydream: the Yuppies in suspenders in their Temples along Wall Street . . . the limousines . . . the liquid lunches shared by smiling sharks. The foxes in their thousand-dollar Valentino casuals . . . the commerce, the hustle, the glitter, the ads . . .

By day, the City dreams of dreamers dreaming big dreams about Big City Life.

At night, the City's fantasies are its own entirely.

New York at night is New Year's Eve, with no white flags and no restraints.

New York is the hooker who gives the great blowjob, then blows you away with a few lines of Rilke . . . New York is the thug who lays open your skull and goes home then to take care of mother . . . New York is the splicing together, by a demented editor, of one hundred thousand films, in no apparent order—from "The Honeymooners" to *Friday the Thirteenth* . . .

New York is the dream you can't dream of escaping . . . though the gold rush excitement's a toss and a turn from your death in some alley, a shiv in your heart . . .

There is nothing but nothing quite like it.

"Well, how do you like it?" he asked her.

"*Sō* . . . This is New York City."

"Yeah!"

Sirens in the distance.

Screams.

Scrapers reeled against the sky, high on the rush of the blizzard below.

A black boy streaked past like a cheetah, grinning and swinging the purse he had snatched.

And seven cabbies hit their horns.

And sixteen buses answered.

And the scramble of voices came on to the Night, rubbing themselves on her long stockinged legs.

"Hey, honey, want some pussy?"

"Listen, all you sinners! Earthquake's coming! Earthquake soon! New York first, then Frisco!"

"Come on, you guys, let's get some—"

"You in the Pinto, pull over! Police!"

"Hey, honey, *have* some pussy!"

"Pete? Pete? Where *are* you, Pete?"

"Bill," Mo said, "I'm feeling drunk."

Bryant drawled, "I love cheap dates. Three beers and she's plastered."

"Welrl . . . Michael did not let me drink."

"Your ex sounds like lots of fun."

"No, just lots of money. —*Bill!*"

Bryant, who had seen Mo doze in the Village's funkiest club, followed her eyes over there.

He looked again. Then asked her, "What?"

"Dance-breaking! Come on, Bill! Come!"

* * *

Mo elbowed forward, forgetting herself, losing Bryant in the crowd. At length, she found a good front-line position and guarded the spot with her life.

Just as she came, the troupe ended a set and a kid with a hat started working the crowd. Mo fished in her handbag without even looking. For the six dancers, even in stillness, were poetry to watch: heads bobbing, shoulders rolling, fingers snapping to the beat.

They wore T-shirts and sweatpants and caps in reverse. They had faces of muggers and thieves on the prowl and her husband had warned her about them.

Seven black boys in the night, flashing their big pearly choppers.

Something tugging at her knees. Mo swatted absently, staring ahead. Another tug. A small, shrill voice.

"Come on, honey, give me ten

"And you can slap mah hand again!"

A dark cherub standing on tiptoe, collection hat in one small paw.

"Sumimasen," she said. "Sorry!"

She bowed.

Jingle-jingle went the cap.

"Fork it over, babe, come clean!

"We got moves you *never* seen!"

"Yes. That's what I need tonight! I need something Special." She dropped the bill in and fumbled for more.

"Uh-uh, baby, ten is nice.

"Ain't no need to pay us twice.

"You've seen all the others,

"Now you're lookin' at the brother

"Who can set your feet to tappin'

"With his crazy kind of rappin'!

"And. In. No. Time.

"It. Be. Show. Time!"

The boy lugged the booty-filled cap to the troupe.

One of the brothers looked over and down from a height of umpteen feet. He followed the imp's pointing finger to Mo. Flashed ten wiggling fingers: Yes? And dropped with astonishing speed to the ground, one long leg stretching halfway to Queens, the other out to Jersey. The awesome splits spread down the line. And seven black boys started *riding* the asphalt like broncos. And then, as one, on the crash of a beat, they all sprang up, impossibly—in seven *reverse* splits.

And then:

Low-down shuffles. Bugaloos. Cool moves that took your breath away. All of them fluid and shot from the hip, the city at night working through them. Taxi horns and drunken hookers and overhead choppers all found their way in. An imperfect flip circled into another, gleefully, and played for laughs—then into a hobble dance that made the whole crowd howl for more.

The tallest spun, a human top, across the open square. And finished with six back flips that brought him within feet of Mo.

"Come on, sweet thing, join me!"

He raised his hands and beckoned once, then he was off and spinning.

More voices echoed.

"Do it!"

"Go!"

And, to her astonishment, Mo felt her body *moving*. Very shyly. Japanese. Tentative movements in place. She tried to stop them. Couldn't. Shoulders rolling. Feet atapping. Fingers snapping. Crazy beat!

From behind, a voice she knew.

"Come on, Mo. Get out there. Go."

Bill's voice, maybe . . . Mother's, maybe . . . Maybe brother's in the night, weary of stickmen and urging her on . . .

(*Your brother was a maniac . . .*)

(*. . . a maniac . . .*)

(*. . . a maniac . . .*)

(*In the end, he showed up in my* dojo *with a wolf-hungry look in his eyes. He asked me to spar. I obliged him. He was swinging with murderous fury when our* shinais *collided, square. To my surprise, he dropped his, looking more pleased than dismayed. When it fell, I heard something. The faint clang of steel under wood. And I knew what your brother was up to, with a blade buried in his* shinai. *I had no choice but to stop him. By letting him go all the way. I stepped back. He circled, smiling, getting himself into position. I lowered my guard and said,* "Dōzo," *nodding once at his* shinai. *Your brother flew into motion, for a perfect and near-certain Six. But I was not a wooden doll. I pivoted and swung. He shrieked, landing squarely on his arm. The bone, of course, was set that night. But, believe me, your brother died there, on the spot.*)

"Come on, live it up, Mo—fly!"

Someone pushed her. Grandpa . . . Sensei . . . Henry, maybe . . . Cotter Sloan . . .

But there she was. Out There. With Them. And suddenly feeling so funky she couldn't decide what to do.

"Come on!"

So—*shikata ga nai*—welrl, it couldn't be helped—Mo turned the past loose and just let herself

"Go!"

Still gingerly.

Then not so.

Yeah. Shoulders rearry on a rolrl. Head, a funky pigeon's, bobbing inches off her neck.

"Eeeee-Hahhhhh!"

Feet, those crazy tootsies—

"Wheeeeee!"

moonwalking smooth across satin.

"I love you!"

Mo as Little Egypt next, hands snaking like asps at her shoulders.

With seven black boys in the night clapping and rolling their eyes at the sight.

Mo lickety-splitted as smooth as the troupe, then started riding on the ground, waving at the tall one.

Come . . .

The boy triple back-flipped and then started spinning four times faster than before.

Mo measured the distance and rode up and down, eyes on the top's crazy spinning.

This could be a Big Mistake.

She watched him and timed him and then gave that up, simply feeling the flow of the music.

When the time was right, she *knew*. For, nothing so far had been wasted.

Subvariation 6003: she sprang from the split, a high-powered reverse that carried her back to the balls of her feet.

And, in the move continued, she flipped herself into an absolute Four: legs locked tight around his arms, her torso stretched out like a flag in the night.

The boy's eyes popped. He looked at her with fear and admiration.

Mo pulled herself up—to the screams of the crowd—with steel cords in her *hara*.

"I am not a wooden doll," she said.

And gave him a quick nervous hug.

FORTY-THREE

It was good to be back, his heart told him, high in the sky in the Rolls near Mo's door.

For weeks he had stumbled and blundered along till it seemed he was starting to crumble.

Visions floated through him at all hours of the night. Pictures of his sailing days: waves and waves of Michaels on the seas of inner bliss.

Withdrawal pains.

He knew that.

He was not a stupid man.

He countered with conflicting slides: putting her things in a large plastic bag . . . flushing the snow candy out of his life . . .

He canceled more meetings and tore up more memos and sat in his office for hours on end, refusing to think about snow.

At the board's suggestion, he took a little time off.

A week to start.

Then two more.

And then the rest of the summer. He needed more time to not think about things, and not think of not thinking about them.

He could not remember now the night of the Great Insight. But he still remembered the electrifying jolt.

July perhaps—it had been, yes—for this was August, more or less . . . July and the walls had been sweating. You know what it's like when your underwear rots and your socks start to slip off your feet. And you're wilting in your penthouse, the air conditioner on the blink, with no way to get a repairman because your phone has just died from the heat. But you're keeping your cool, with your job gone to shit and your life itself going to blazes—

when suddenly you realize . . .

Wasn't it *just like a woman* to leave a man cold on a scorcher like this—and deny him the pure, simple comfort of *snow!*

Thank God he'd kept one small hit, just in case. For the day he returned to his senses.

Shaky hands. An anguished blast. And then Michael, on deck, was a Captain again. Sailing on high seas of peace, waves lapping with sounds of Forever. Far from kimonos and Mos in the night and the shores of his own beached mistakes.

He'd ordered more snow. And it came. It was good. He sailed on in his luxury liner. He never left. He never docked. He never set one foot on shore.

He'd stand at the window, the bridge of the ship, letting the snow fill the melting controls.

For the point of it—

(The point . . . The *point* . . .)

—was to go with the flow and just follow the tides.

Into the kitchen . . . The Captain must eat . . .

Chop some goodies with her knife . . . The Captain a snowman, at peace with his soul . . . Sailing . . . He was sailing . . .

Home.

Michael looked at his watch. It was half-past Forever. He'd let down his anchor three hours ago, the Rolls a dark ship in the night.

He measured time by cigarettes because his watch kept melting.

The waiting lasted seven more.

Then suddenly they crossed the sea on quiet waves of laughter.

FORTY-FOUR

Mo was still laughing when Bryant agreed *not* to get naked and boogie. He'd ogled her in the hallway and leered. Then followed her in, with his hands on her hips, making chug-a-chug sounds in his throat. He promised her three minutes of non-stop excitement and funky mistakes. Mo pleaded exhaustion: he said wrong was right. But her body was *sore,* she protested: those green eyes started glowing. Finally, catching on, she threw her arms around him. "Yes, come on, let's do it—the time is rearry perfect!" He shuffled off, demoralized—turning at the door though with one uplifted finger: "Wait! I *understand,* I really do—and that's a *big* mistake!"

Bill . . .

From the window she watched him go moon-walking off. An odd man who turned her on in his own strange way.

In her own way she hadn't been lying. The time

tonight *would* have been perfect. She felt horny as blazes and yearned for release. For that brief, crazy flight in the city had left her hungry for more.

She needed time to think, though.

Scan was acting up again, triggered by something she couldn't detect.

She took the tiny sack of pearls she'd come to call her worry beads, and clicked them as she paced the room.

She stopped before the photograph.

(Wadz dad, Wha-kee-kee or wad . . .)

Easy . . . Walk . . . Don't force a thing . . . Get those shoulders moving . . . Good . . . Just keep walking, keep your cool, and let Scan do the work for you . . .

(. . . sixty percent of the landlords in town . . .)

So Ben was a locksmith . . . Well, fine, what of that?

(Well, you've got to admit, it's convenient . . .)

(It *is* . . .)

Ben had *requested* the locks, though.

(That's the ticket, eh, Mo? . . . *Change* . . .)

And Ben had phoned Michael to warn him to stop.

(Here's the magic number . . . Now, you be sure to keep it . . .)

Ee?

By the gods, she was tired, too tired to think!

Dreaming of *onis* and eating raw meat—and now thinking of *telephone numbers*?

Click.

Henry left in a hurry, forgetting his car.

And Ben was in—

Hawaii?

Mo gave the sack a final click and packed in these thoughts for the night.

She was drawing the bath for a two-hour soak when she heard the three knocks on the door.

Bill! she thought. Thank God for Bill.

This was a night for grand passion, not thought.

So she opened her heart, all the way, with the door.

To see Michael before her.

The great knife in hand.

(Falling for the same trick twice . . .)

Surprise he'd expected.

Uncertainty, yes.

But the look in her eyes was so alien, it spooked him out completely.

And he'd sailed here with such mighty hopes.

Reaching out—the *only* way . . .

Mo stepped back, regarding her husband: the wasted eyes and ruined nose, snot and powder on his lip.

The knife shook uncontrollably. He reached out and kept reaching, as if he might stab her from three feet away, too stoned to step forward and use it.

She felt her fingers start to curl, Times Square coming back for more.

Michael . . . It *hadn't* been Michael . . . And yet . . .

(Just follow the line of the garden . . . I know you'll get the hang of it . . .)

She took another step and said—

Careful?

Sweet Jesus, the woman was frightened!

Michael looked at the knife and he wanted to cry. Could she *possibly* think he could hurt her? He loved her so much!

He said, "Mo!"
And said—

Yours?

Michael was trying to *hand* her the knife?

His words came out, weepy sludge, impossible to figure.

"Foryou . . . For youuuuu . . . Makelovetome . . . orrrrr . . . Jesussssssstopthesnowwwwww . . ."

She felt her heart begin to break in unexpected places.

"Put the knife down, Michael." She pointed at the door and said—

Put the knife down. Now. My door is there and here I am.

The knife floated out of his hand to the floor.

The clatter alarmed him and scrambled his brain.

He couldn't think. Or think to think. The hero's way now on bright pine. And nothing to reach with. Nothing to do except stand there and hear her torpedo his craft with a *No. Go,* she would tell him. And he surely would.

But—

"You'd better come in," she said softly.

She slid the knife to the wall with her foot, leading him in by the hand like a child.

He needed her. It was karma tonight.

"Michael," she said. "You are here. It's okay." She wiped off the snot with the cuff of one sleeve. "Hold me. You can hold me."

Her husband did, a stoned embrace, eyes glazed and runny.

Mo led him into the bedroom, where she lit a couple of candles.

When she turned, he was standing there, looking so lost she had to ask him outright—

Is this what you really need?

The anchor dropped. The sky was blue. And the snow was an ocean behind him. The Captain stood upon the bridge, gazing at this port of call.

An American chick now with rainbowy hair, sweatshirt, and black Reeboks.

Yes, he thought. Yes . . . Oh yes . . . I was right the first time . . .

"Michael?" she whispered.

He smiled and said—

"I'm gonna fuck you up the ass. You wanna stop me, get the knife!"

Mo was half thrown to the mattress. She took the fall lightly and lay there, just breathing, waiting for him to begin.

"You won't be smiling long," he said. He loosened his belt, dropped his pants to the floor.

"I'm not smiling, Michael. Come." She patted the mattress, beside her.

His erection vaulted through his shorts and he brandished the thing in his hand like a club.

Mo sat up. She said, "It's fine."

She tugged off her sweatshirt and gave it a toss, undoing her jeans as it landed.

"Michael," she said, "it's okay. Come on—"

Come on, let's get naked and boogie?

The Captain jumped her, a cry in his heart. He rolled her over, yanking her up. Then he homed in with a murderous stroke that brought the cry from his heart to his lips.

Cotter smiled, hearing them.

Admitting and accepting . . .

There *were* second chances, yes, he'd learned this at the meetings. But with whom, and in what form, not even an addict could say. Freedom meant accepting things for what they were, no regrets. From President to wino, they kept saying it over and over each night.

Admitting and accepting . . .

Chiori gone . . . His whole life in boxes . . . Himself on the street in the morning . . . No job . . .

These were the facts, Jack. And of his own making.

Admit them and accept them.

And carry on, full steam ahead.

From below came a great rush of love screams and shouts.

Admitting and accepting . . .

Admitting, accepting—and blessing . . .

He dreamed of second chances, oh, and wished that it had been with her.

Admit it and accept it, though.

And bless her on her lucky night.

Cotter Sloan was listening, admitting and accepting, when he heard the soft knocks on his own door. He ignored them a while, too contented to move, until the buzzer sounded.

Well . . . He butted out the cigarette (pal, you're hooked—accept that too!) and slowly descended the stairs.

"Ben?"

It really seemed impossible! Though he'd gone through some changes himself, he well knew, the sight that the old man presented almost defied belief.

The lighting, perhaps: the bulb crackled and dimmed . . . The hour, perhaps: at twenty past two, Sloan was half dead on his feet . . . The crazy getup, maybe that: Ben Shacklette—in August!—was in a greatcoat, with a toque that seemed ready to fly off his head . . . All of these, perhaps, combined to account for the vaguely skewed image.

But something was *wrong* with the eyes. And the mouth.

The old man muttered, "Boy—", then stopped.

And Cotter Sloan thanked God he did. For the horrible stench that had come from his mouth almost knocked Sloan on his ear.

Jesus, the man must be terribly sick!

"Good Lord," he cried. "What is it, man?"

Pops Shacklette cradled a huge, hairy ham—it must have been trampled to swell to such size. He looked at Sloan with those weird eyes and said, in a voice not quite—*something,* "They got me, Pa—they got me good!"

Sloan went rigid. "Who did?"

Old Ben nodded toward the door, looking faint now and ready to drop.

"They went that-a-way!" he stammered. Then, "Prithee, couldst thou fetch me a glass of cool spring water? Man, I just can't hack the pain."

Sloan feared that the old man had taken some licks and probably had a concussion. Sounded like three movies going on at the same time.

"Come on, old-timer. Come on up."

Old Ben smiled, a toothy smile—

(What the devil's with those *teeth?*)

and said, "Well, ah don't mind if ah do."

"Come on, I'll get us—I'll get *you* a beer."

"I need a Certs Encounter."

Sloan readily agreed with that. But, what the hell, life was short, and caring for friends was a part of the cure.

Admitting and accepting . . .

"Come on, Pops, you follow me."

"You bet your bippie."

"You're too much! Just shut the door behind you."

Sloan took the steps, the old man on his heels, breathing that horrible shit on his neck.

Sloan wondered how to ask Pops, politely, if he'd mind—

Wrong . . .

Admitting and accepting—

that something was terribly *wrong* . . .

"Huh-uhhhhhh!"

Sloan started whirling, ready for action.

The old man grabbed him by the throat and jerked him up two feet straight off the floor. And the grip was so tight . . . and the smell was so rank . . . and the look in those eyes was so mad and so *bad* . . . that he just hung there, crazy for some notion of what he might do.

The old man squeezed. Sloan heard a crack and guessed that his neck might be broken. Too bad. But that was the least of his worries.

Admitting and accepting . . .

that the worst was now to come.

The creature winked at him and said, "Hey . . . Guess Who's Coming to Dinner?"

Then he opened his mouth—impossibly wide—wide enough to devour a six-pack. So wide that Sloan could see, between the rows of dagger teeth, an evil-looking, hairy snout poking on up through the gullet. And then the little razored claws as the rat scratched its way from Ben's throat to his mouth, staring and screaming at Cotter.

The old man squeezed, then squeezed again, until Sloan's own mouth opened wide, silently screaming for air.

The rat leapt out, across, and in.

And then the real screaming began.

* * *

"Oh!" *"Ee!"*

"Oh!" *"Ee!"*

Mo was timing her cries to her husband's, determined to give him, for once, what he needed. This was his night and her body was his.

He'd taken her twice in a row, back and front, and was ripping on now to a tortured release—

when they heard a screech upstairs.

Then a thundering crash to the floor.

And a frenzied batch of flops and screams that froze them both mid-stroke.

"Michael—"

"You be quiet." He slipped out abruptly and looked at the ceiling.

The screams and thumps went on and on.

Mo covered her ears and cried, "No . . . Prease!"

Silence, then.

Then footsteps, heavy and slow down the stairs.

"Michael!" she cried. "You can't go! You don't know—"

But her husband had already slipped on his pants, a nasty glint in his dark eyes.

"I'm gonna teach that son of a bitch a lesson he'll never forget."

Mo snatched at his trousers, but Michael was gone. He stormed down the hallway to pick up the knife, and charged out as the other door opened.

The screams that came next were inhumanly high, launched from a whole new dimension in pain.

Hating herself, Mo froze on the bed—till the door slammed hard against the wall and footsteps ran off in the night.

The hallway seemed longer than she had recalled.

It took her a minute to get there, naked and feeling pathetically small.

When she got there she wished it had taken her years.

The front door was still quivering from the slam against the wall. She caught it on the backswing and heard, before she saw, the heavy dripping of blood on the floor. Followed by a slimy *plop.*

Slowly, slowly—*shikata ga nai*—she eased the door open full circle. And *saw.*

Michael was hanging three feet off the ground, slit from crotch to belly, and nailed with the knife through his chest to the door.

His hands made feeble efforts to hold in the rest of his *hara.* He seemed embarrassed, mortally, that she'd happened to see him this way.

He coughed. The blood all but covered her face.

"Mo—" he started. Cough. Cough.

She leaned in to hear him. *"Hai?"*

"Wasn't that—oh God!—the best . . ."

The Grand Hotel came to them both on a last wave of mercy.

She took his hand and kissed it. And said, just before Michael died, "Oh yes!"

Yes, it really *wasn't.*

PART FOUR

NEW YORKER

FORTY-FIVE

Alone again.

They'd left at six: flummoxed by the improbable facts; stymied by the rat droppings; and maddened by her silence, her refusal to leave the apartment. ("Don't leave town," the sergeant said. "We're gonna have more questions. *Lots.*" "It's okay . . . I know . . . Me too . . ." And so will Mrs. Daez. *Saa!*)

Dawn in its full glory now. Another day filled with new stunning reversals. But not before the flickering glow of a dozen candles led Scan through one final run.

(Blow me down, I reckon it's been . . .)

(. . . about forty years . . .)

Mo back in her favorite position, elbows crossbarred to her head, letting the waves flow on down . . .

down . . .

from

'85 . . .
to
'45 . . .
'4 . . .
'3 . . .
'2 . . .
to the *one* that had been there, of course, all along.
(It's the magic number . . .)

712-1941

7–12 . . . You fooled me out . . . In Japan the month, not the day, would come first . . . And the day, in Japan, was one sooner—because of the difference in time . . .

December 6
1941

(Wadz dadt, Wah-kee-kee or wad?)
No, that's a photograph—of a tiny sack of

Pearls . . .

Mo's pulse began to quicken. She tried to still her breathing. When Scan was *on* and in good form she must not interfere with it.

(That's the ticket, eh, Mo? . . . *Change* . . .)

Dawn looking in through the window to cast a rosy spell on crimson.

Mo tumblerolled onto the balls of her feet. She blew out the candles; slipped into her sweats; took a chair from the kitchen; and walked out the back.

Standing on tiptoe, she just cleared the cedar. The morning sun had a long way to climb, but the light that it did throw was more than enough.

(Don't let the names mislead you, dear . . . Just follow the line of . . . the line of . . .

the line . . .)

Except for the emerald square of the yard, the garden had turned almost totally red. All of the blossoms remaining—once lily-white, shell-pink or yellow—had darkened to rich shades of crimson. Where the petals had fallen, profusions of berries glistened, bloodred, over leaves.

(I just know you'll get it . . .)

What?

Seven black boys in the night dancing in absolute stillness . . .

Mo followed the line of the garden, walking her eyes through with Ben once again, forgetting the cedar, forgetting the names, taking it in step by step.

From the san-to-lee-nas . . . to the lovely myew-tah-bee-lees . . .

(Tomorrow the flower we're looking at now . . .)

past Frow Dagg-marr Hard-tops and Mrs. Will's Son's Roses . . . and

on to the maple, as dark a crimson as Michael's lost blood on the floor . . .

She teetered on the chair, dizzy from the rush itself—that curious fragrance of home—and Scan's burn-rubber four-wheel drifts. So close and yet so far away!

(What's been planted . . . coming up . . .)

All right: *Wakatta:* Red: Blood . . .

But—the garden was planted before I arrived . . . And how could the warning connect with the *line* . . .

Over and over Scan stopped on that dime, and yet she could not figure it.

Or begin to understand the powerful persistence of the vague, familiar scents.

Mo steadied herself, shaky-handed on cedar, and lifted her eyes to the window on top.

Where a shadow looked down through the curtains and waved.

Mo nodded and gave him an answering palm, though even her lips were now shaking.

So . . .

You want to play.

Okay.

FORTY-SIX

The midtown librarians had little time for puzzles. By eleven, the crew—looking harried and beat—clearly dreaded the sight of her presence in line. They took turns ducking out to smoke or to help some old coot, lost for years, in the aisles.

Dogged, though, and in no mood to quit, she kept showing up with questions.

How to *figure* the line of the garden . . . How to *figure* the curious fragrance of home . . .

By noon she had amassed a stack of tomes that made her head spin. Huge paragraphs of tortured prose came at her in thick, inky waves, murky and swimming with alien words: *mendocinensis* . . . *reticulata* . . . *thyrsiflorus* . . . *mezereum* . . . *willmattianum* . . .

Mo threw up her hands, wondering where to begin. The names she had written stared back at her coolly, defying her to find them.

"Honey, you look *buffaloed.*"

The small man, in his fifties, peered over the top of a stack to his chin.

"It's nothing," Mo said. "Just a puzzle."

"Oh?"

He almost jumped to join her.

"You just said the magic word." The face was a Cabbage Patch Buddha's. But the eyes were shrewd, alert, behind his thick ridiculenses. "George Bartola," he told her. "And you?"

"I am Mo—Shirata now. But you must not waste your time, sir. Prease."

Across the room an angry whisper told them both to shut their corks.

The Buddha quivered with anger and whirled. "Whey-*uhhhhh* did that sound came from? Which of you damned cretins made it? Confess!"

Astonished looks. But no replies. Satisfied, he turned to Mo. "Noo Yawk," he said.

"Oh, yes. I know."

"Went up North a few years back and thought I'd left it all behind. Off to the Peaceable Kingdom, you know. The start of the Orderly Life. Respected Scholar. Grand Old Man. But I'll tell you something, Mo. You never, ever leave Noo Yawk. Not if you've been here for even a day."

"Is that right?"

"Oh yes, it is. It most soytenly is. Five years I'm vegetating at the U. of T., writing drivel on Sanskrit and Whitman. One day an old friend comes to me—now they-uhhhhh was a guy with a puzzle!* A nutcracking, Noo Yawk–style twister. I was back here like a shot. Looking for something to top it, you see. Come on and show me what you've got."

---

*See the author's first novel, *The Suiting* (New York: Tor Books, 1988).

* * *

The Cabbage Patch Buddha had filled the first sheet of a canary legal pad with notes. He tap-tapped his pencil, then smoked the eraser, lost for a moment in thought.

"Naowww, you're absolutely *soyten* it has nothing to do with the names?"

Mo nodded, staring at his notes while the Buddha looked over her list.

"And you're *shuwahhhh* these are the names you heard."

Mo nodded again and said, "Yes, prease forgive me. But, you see, I have—a pornographic memory."

The Buddha blinked. "Well, good for you! We could've had some fun, though, if it had been phonetics."

"Phonetics," Mo said. "Then my spelling—"

"Oh, shu-wahhh. But your ear is remarkably good. Now, I don't know beans about gardening, dear, but I know a few things about language. You've got some Latin, German, French . . . Here's how they look when you spell 'em all out."

The Buddha matched his list to hers.

"Naowww, tell me again what he said to you, Mosie. I want his words exactly."

"'Don't let the names mislead you, dear. Just follow the line of the garden.'"

The Buddha levitated to fold his legs beneath him.

On the second sheet he drew three lines.

"Naowww, this was the shape of the garden, correct? And you started—left to right?"

He grunted and numbered the lines.

"So-o-o. We're reasonably soyten it *isn't* the *names*. We *know* it has something to do with the *line*—the changing of the garden from light colors into red. 'Come back in a month and see'?"

"Yes," Mo said. "He was smiling."

"Uh-huh. But the garden was planted *before* you arrived. So, the puzzle can't *just* be the colors . . ." The Buddha squinted at her. "If you'll forgive my language, hon, he sounds like an arrogant fucker."

"Tee-hee."

"But, you know what? We'll take him down. He's up against New Yorkers now."

He sketched three more lines—clean and straight—and started adding the names from the list.

"Let's just *break up* the line of the garden and see.

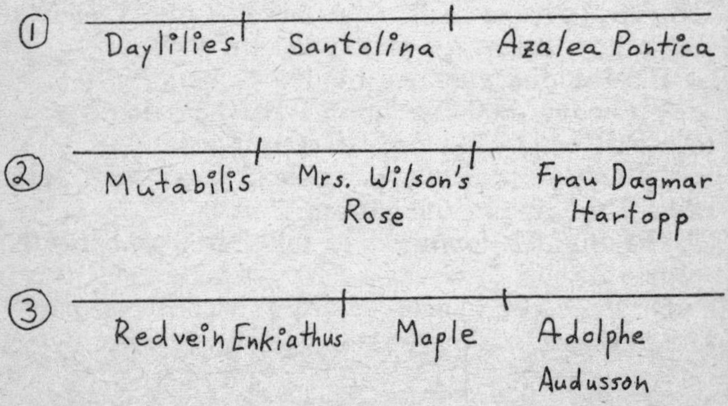

"Just follow the line of the garden, eh? One, two, three . . . One, two—"

"*Chotto!* I remember . . . This may onry be too small—"

"Hon, it's always the tiniest, tiniest piece that gives you the most trouble."

"Welrl . . . I never had timing for flowers, you see, and I cannot tell one from the others. But the maple tree is called an *osakazuki.* In Japan it is so common, everybody has one, I didn't even think."

The Buddha printed under "Maple":

OSAKAZUKI

"Anything else?"

"Welrl . . ."

"Fork it up."

"It seems to me . . . in line three . . . maybe already there had been some red."

"Redvein enkianthus . . ."

"*So.* And also here: Adolphe Audusson? If I remember—yes, inside . . ."

The Buddha bracketed the line and printed just beside it:

RED?

He smoked the eraser a moment, cackling softly to himself.

"Goddammit, this is wonderful! I tell you, that man is a real circus clown! Naowwww . . . Let's see these books of yours.

"No . . . No . . . Wrong, all wrong . . . Is this stuff what they gave you? Gawwwd. Hang on, Mosie, be right back."

Ten minutes later the Buddha returned, looking enormously pleased with himself, a single book tucked in one arm.

"The first thing to do with a twister, Mosie, is

whittle away all the extras. There's nothin' that we have to know—except for whatever it is that we do. If one of the lines was already red, then it can't be the change of the colors per se. It's gotta be just what he told you, the line."

He refolded his legs underneath him; rolled up the sleeves of his ratty gray sweater; and lay the book flat on the table: *Everyman's Companion to the Wonder World of Shrubs: A Dictionary for Green Thumbs.*

"You know what I think, Mosie?"

"No. *Oshiete,* Georgie."

"I think we're gonna *start* . . . with the one thing he said didn't matter—the names."

"I don't understand," she said.

"Well, all he really said was 'Don't let the names mislead you.' But he gave you the names and I'm wondering why."

For some time they toyed with acrostics—English first, then Japanese. Letter one, word one; letter two, word two; and so on, down the line. But the message lay buried as deep as the roots.

The Buddha seemed, if anything, even more intrigued.

"Mosie, I'm starting to pick up his vibes. I think the whole thing may be simple, like that damned *osakazuki.* So simple he knew he could slip it right by your pretty little nose. I think that was half the fun for him—slipping it *right by* your nose!"

"Georgie . . ." Mo said.

(. . . by the nose . . .)

The Buddha said, "Umm?" and opened the book.

"Nothing," she said. "Maybe . . ."

"Naowwww . . . What if we follow the names down the line—and break each part up into pieces? What *kinds* of flowers are they?"

The Buddha flipped through the volume, mumbling as he tagged the names.

"Daylilies—lilies, of course—nothing there . . . Santolinas—lavender cottons . . . Azalea pontica—rhododendrons . . . Mutabilis—roses, now . . . From lilies to roses . . . Just follow the line . . ."

(. . . by the nose . . .)

(. . . by the *nose* . . .)

(That curious, *curious* fragrance of—)

"Georrr-gie!"

"Wait, now—just a second—I'm getting *warm*, I know I am! From lilies to roses—"

"You've done it!"

"I *have*?"

The Buddha inadvertently bit off the rubber eraser.

"Just follow the line," Mo repeated. "Follow the line—by the *nose!*"

"Mosie, I dunno . . ." The Buddha started inhaling his thumb. "I mean, whey-uhhhh we gonna find an effing lexicon of *smells?*"

Mo Shirata touched her nose. "Right here. We are New Yorkers, yes?"

"You wanna *go* to the garden?"

"Not necessary, Georgie. My nose is not yet pornographic, but . . . Can this little bookie tell us—where the flowers come from?"

The Buddha grunted. "Yeah. I guess. And if it can't, there's one that will."

Mo leaned back, quite calm now. "Prease."

"Oh boy," the Buddha said. "Oh boy-y-y-y. Noo Yawk City, heahhh we come!"

His excitement carried him through the first two lines.

"Daylilies—not in here . . . Santolinas: Southern France . . . Azalea pontica: Holland and Wales . . . Okay, now the roses . . . Mutabilis:

'China Rose' . . . Mrs. Wilson's: England . . . Frau Dagmar Hartopp: Germany . . .

"We're getting nowhey-uhhhhh fast," he said.

Mo Shirata smiled serenely. "Georgie, we're New Yorkers now. *Makoto,* prease. Go all the way."

The Buddha continued, smoking his thumb almost to the webbing.

"Redvein enkianthus—hmm, nothing under 'Redvein' . . . Look under 'Enkianth'— Hell-ooooo . . ."

"Put it down, Georgie, prease, on the page."

The Buddha wrote:

JAPAN

Then again beneath "Osakazuki."

"But right here we lose the progression—Adolphe Audusson's about as French as you can get."

"Georgie . . . Prease look in the pages."

The Buddha, flummoxed, flipped and flipped. "Adolphe . . . Adolphe . . . Nothing . . . Audusson—'See "Camellias"' . . . Camellias . . . Cam— Oh, my Gawwwd: Japan it is."

(Oh, I just know you'll get it, Mo . . . To me, it's as plain as the nose on your face . . .)

The Buddha started babbling in his agitated state. "One, two, three . . . One, two, three . . . The third line was *already* red . . . Follow the line, just follow the line . . . And the garden was planted *before* you arrived . . ."

"Ex-act-ly," Mo told him. "Exactry. This isn't a square, it's a circle. And it starts at number three."

"But why, though, what's the point of that?"

"First blood," Mo said slowly. "What's been planted, coming up . . ."

"What's gone around, coming around once again?"

And the garden was planted *before* I arrived.

(It has something to do with another man's wife . . .)

Quite suddenly Scan came to an unexpected, screeching stop and Mo nearly flew from her chair.

(The world needs more Japanese women . . . Hell, *I* need more Japanese women . . .)

More!

"Mosie, whey-uhhhhh you goin', girl? We're just getting started!"

Mo slung her handbag over her shoulder and grabbed him by one tattered sleeve.

"Hurry, Georgie, time is short! Old newspapers now, all light?"

The Buddha followed her, huffing and puffing, huge eyes twinkling under glass.

"I can't believe it! I just can't believe it! I'm gay—and in love with a *woman!* Noo Yawk!"

Five minutes before closing time, they found what she was looking for.

FORTY-SEVEN

The atoms stirred and rustled.

From down the hall—in its favorite room—tiny, tinny voices drifted out of the idiot box.

The *oni* kicked back in the black leather swivel, taking in the voices *there,*

(Come on, Scottie, beam us up!)

taking in the voices *here,*

(You must tell me everything . . .)

in this curious, *curious* room.

Little pictures on the wall of bird-things soaring . . . ships in flames . . .

Led on by the stirrings and rustlings within, the *oni* swiveled side to side, surprised to feel the teardrops falling from the old one's eyes.

Curious . . .

How curious . . .

The hours passed like seconds. The atoms stirred and rustled, as new voices came from the box.

(Come on, punk! You feel lucky? *Do* you?)
(And now—*Heeeeeeeere's Johnny!*)
The *oni* swung, back and forth, taking it in, taking all of it in, as it sat there and waited. And waited.
At length, when it heard the faint ringing below, the *oni* smiled and thought *roarrrroooo* and started slowly down the stairs.

"Hello?" the tiny voice said. "Ben?"
The atoms stirred and rustled. The *oni* placed the ring-thing's hat against one hairy ear. Upside down, then right side up.
"Hello? Hello? Ben, are you there?"
Down, down the atoms went, with all of the voices that came from the box.
"Yeah," it said. "Yeah, talk to me. Come on, who loves ya, baby?"

Ben?
For one terrible moment she thought she was wrong. The voice sounded almost just like his. And the whole thing was so crazy. And—
Mo clicked the tiny sack of pearls.
Thought of her husband impaled on the door.
Remembered the terrified look in Sloan's eyes.
"It's—been a long time, Ben," she said.

The *oni* cradled the hat to its ear, the atoms now deep in its *hara*. Soon now, very soon, after one last little game.
"It has, doll. Yes." The atoms clicked. "Hell, I ain't seen you in a coon's age."
"Welrl . . . You know, the weather, *ne?*"
"High today of ninety-seven, lows in the high eighties."
"*Saa* . . . Tell me—how is *business,* Ben?"
The *oni* yawned and stretched its toes. "Closing

Dow Jones average: 2200, month of July. Taxpayer bailout of thrift industry looms. All this and more on the late-night news." The atoms rustled, stirred, and clicked. "But, hey, like I've been thinking, wow—it's time we got *next* to each other."

Click.

Mo gave the tiny sack a squeeze.

Michael hanging on the door.

Sloan with those *holes* in his *hara.*

Policemen sealing off his place. Nevermore to touch his hand. Or see his beautiful changes.

Mo smiled grimly and she said, "That would be nice, Ben. *Wouldn't* it?"

The atoms stirred. And crackled. The *oni* paused, thrown for a moment—

Yes? No? *Saa* . . . Which!

—then scratched its long nails on the floor, back in the saddle again.

"Hell *no,* sure it would!"

Gotcha, Mo thought.

Gotcha.

"Good. Shall we say tomorrow night?"

The *oni* stretched its lips back in a wolfish grin.

"You know how to whistle, don't you? You just pucker your lips and you blow."

Click.

Mo set down the receiver and started making the rest of her calls.

FORTY-EIGHT

The first candle's for you, Ben . . .

She lit it at midnight, precisely, hearing but not hearing the sounds beyond the door. Or the ghost-echo threats of eviction from the bullish Mrs. Daez.

Bill Bryant was working the wall with a ruler, ticking off places for hinges and nails along the penciled line.

Frankie Motta was cutting a slat for the wall—repeating, as he sawed away, Mo's latest, and Funkiest, lesson. ("Who's this? Teach'? What? Tonight? Well, yeah, I *could.* I guess I could. I mean, I got a whole shitload of wood. But Teach', you gotta tell me, 'cause Masami's comin' here next week. And, you know, in Japanese, have you got a word—for—well . . ." It was hard to explain it discreetly. And for a second the line was quite silent. But then Mo said excitedly, "Oh yes:

hamaguri! I berieve in English you say—snapping pussy?" "Around midnight you say, Teach'? You got it, I'm there!")

Chuck was fitting a reamed "candelabrum" onto one of the greased spikes he'd nailed through a slat. "Man," he said, "I am not *here.* I don't know nothin' about this. I make candles, that is all." But Motta was a genius and the fit, Mother Mary, was heaven itself, with the spike's wicked tip reaching just to the wick. "I don't know *nothin'* about this, you *hear!* Christ, just tell her to pay when she can, okay?"

Hyaku Monogatari. Night of a hundred demons. This is the way of my family, now passed on to me. I accept and start again with one hundred candles, like my father and brother before me. One candle for each demon who has found his way into my heart.

This first one is for you, Ben. For the pictures we found in the papers: of Admiral Ben Shacklette, who died on the ship *Arizona,* and your stepmother, Chiori-san—who disappeared, like you, that day.

It had something to do with another man's wife. A Japanese wife in Pearl Harbor. And that's another candle, *ne,* for surely she must need one: a Japanese woman in that place and time.

When did you first plant the garden, old friend? It must have been growing for years in your heart. And then one day, in your mind, a little seed was planted. Your own way of remembering the woman who betrayed you all.

I know that you helped her, you must have.

She must have hurt you terribly.

(For God's sake, put that candle out!)

At first, I believe, it was only a garden, planted to keep her alive in your heart. You grew to manhood, and grew old, and your life must remain a great mystery to me.

But then one day the garden grew . . .

Was it when the Sloans arrived? Did the simple name *Chiori-san* start the circle in your heart? When she cheated on Cotter with Henry Daez, did that set the old circle spinning? You took her from Cotter then, didn't you? You made her phone him every week—not to torture him, but her. You kept her alive, though, your plaything or pet, while the garden you'd planted kept coming around. And around and around in your heart.

For weeks, or months, that seemed enough. Until the day that I arrived and you felt the confusion and emptiness grow. "Chiori-san" was just a name. Your pet was a poor drunken bar girl, who'd been telling the truth all along when she begged you to please, please, please let her go, it was all a *big mistake.*

The first day you saw me, you knew it. The name was wrong this time around—but the face was *chōdo ii.* Just strip away a few minor confusions—my blue jeans, T-shirts, records, books, the picture of my mother—and then come back another day to give me what was "mine."

Georgie was right, Ben. You were a great clown. The garden was growing and coming around—and you wanted me to enjoy the great joke. You teased me and spoke Japanese. Extra poorly—winkwinkwink. (Soo-shee . . . Tair-ee-yah-kee . . . Yamataka Kiss-a-ten . . .) You wanted me to know you knew, but not to know how much.

I remember that day on the sidewalk, how you played the old cripple, your hand on your back. But now and then you'd straighten up, and stand there straight and tall and strong. You just couldn't help it—the garden was good. And the circle *was* making you younger inside.

The circle and all of your sly little jokes. You even got Henry to change all my locks before I bought new ones from somebody else. You must have laughed for days over that.

Laughed and kept getting stronger. I remember the day in the garden—how you looked a full twenty years younger!

You didn't need any *oni,* my friend. You'd been ready for me, in your heart, from the start. You just didn't know how to go all the way. Until you heard my story and the hunger went crazy inside you that day.

(But how, Mo—how exactly . . . Lord God Almighty, don't stop now!)

You were ready. You were willing. And the devil was ready and waiting for you.

And so, I light this candle. For the demons in your heart, which I call into mine.

Come to me. I need you. Thanks.

"Whoaaa!" Bryant opened the deep, heavy box in the corner. "Where the hell'd you get these *springs?*"

"Aaa, the biggies I already had in the shop. But, get this, on the way over I spot this fuckin' red Jag near the park. It's all cleaned out and beat to shit. Man, even the ashtray was gone. But the seats?" Motta tapped one temple. "I'm a fuckin' conceptual artist!"

"*Aa, sō.* I'll get the rope."

Mo lit the second candle.

This was for the Grand Hotel and the ghost stories still trapped within it.

Onna no kuse ni . . . Because I am only a woman . . . A belly borrowed to bear sons . . . A daughter . . . A sister . . . A maid . . . A Good Wife . . .

Grandfather put in new toilets for women—so, when they peed, jingles played and they didn't embarrass their husbands. It was one of our finest attractions. But it never held a candle to the things that he put in my head.

I light this candle now for him and for all of the prisoners who stayed there.

Come to me. I need you now. I need one hundred candles.

Come.

Three A.M. A trial run.

Bryant tightened the hinge of the first slat while Motta adjusted the last of the springs.

"Chuck, stand over here," Bill said. He pointed to a chalked *X* on the floor, a few steps forward from the back and just left of center.

"Man, I wasn't *here,*" Chuck said. "I was home all night long making candles."

Still, he assumed the position and watched with morbid fascination as Bryant walked the slat out from the hinge. The three slats above almost ran the length of the wall: each laid flat on brackets, with fifty votives set on each. Motta's inspiration, this, was six feet long, two inches wide and half again as thick. With twelve "candelabras" fixed upon the outstretched spikes.

Bryant walked slowly until one candle aligned with Chuck's chin.

"Naaa, you're a little shorter than what Mo seems to have in mind. But I think we get the picture."

The candlemaker touched his throat. "I was not here. I *was not here.* I'd better . . . cut the candles, though."

"*Cut* 'em?"

"Cut 'em on the sides. You want 'em to shatter on impact. Correct?"

Frankie Motta whistled. "Fuckin' *hamaguri*, Chuck. Come on, bring that baby to papa."

The slat strained against the springs. It took both of them to hold it down while Motta slipped the rope's end through the hole. He knotted it, then stretched the rope to the ring on the wall. One double knot. A snip. A sigh.

"You understand," Chuck said, "I mean, you guys *do* understand—"

"Yeah, yeah," Frankie said. "Hey, Chuckie, get back over there."

"No way!"

"Oh well . . . *Banzai!*"

The two men hit the floor as the Hispanic cut the rope.

Mo heard a fearsome *thwack*ing sound and then an endless quivering.

She smiled and lit the tenth candle.

Sensei. For you, this most special of votives. Because in your wisdom you knew all along: we all need something Special. We each must have our Exercise. A compass to steer by. A light in the storm. Some small thing we can "perfect" and grow to understand.

You gave me one to start with. And it was neither wrong nor right, except in the way that I saw it. I was wrong, of course, to think that it could be my everything. But that was right as well as wrong, for how could this candle ever have burned if not for the darkness before it?

Seven black boys in the night, dancing in absolute stillness . . .

I thank you for them. And I thank you for this bright candle burning on the wall.

I practice now by fasting. By sitting in stillness, accepting the flow of my own blood through my own heart.

Dōmo. Thank you, Sensei, for this difficult gift to repay. Accept this one small candle, please, and come to me now in my hour of need.

At dawn, the workroom looked half like a chapel—its thousand-plus candles all over the walls—and half, a cat's cradle of crisscrossing ropes.

Chuck stopped short at the door before leaving to point one last quivering finger.

"Relax," Bill said. "You *were not here.*"

Motta cackled, "Fuck, Chuck who?" and shut the door behind him.

"So, what do you think?" Bryant asked him. "You heard the news."

"I *heard* the news. Fuckin' *Friday the Thirteenth.*" The Hispanic circled the room, giving each rope a good snap for the *twang.* "I think this is all *hamaguri,* all right." He gave his shadow goatee a long rub. "But I'll tell you somethin' else. I think Teach' still needs an edge."

"My sentiments exactly."

"I'll tell you somethin' else I think. I think you're lookin' kinda tense."

"Yeah, welrl, what the helrl. You know what they say in *Nihongo:* The present's the best tense of all."

FORTY-NINE

Since nightfall they've been parked near the corner beside the small graveyard. Bryant opens his window a little to let out a bit of the smoke.

"*Saneko,* man." Motta sighs. "The ole little man in a boat. And *deepu surōto*—that's—"

"I know. Goddamn it, cemeteries always spook me out."

"I dunno. It's kinda cute. Guy up there sure thinks so."

"Where?"

Motta rolls down his window to cough up some phlegm; quick rolls it back up, not to lose any smoke.

"Upstairs window next to Mo's. Dude's been up there for over an hour."

A shadow, really, glimpsed through gauze, in a room that is almost as dark as the night, except for a tiny and eerie white glow.

"You think he's made us?"

Motta laughs. "Look at the fucker, he don't even move. He's trippin' on somethin' or zonked on the moon."

Bryant squirms a little. "Yeah." He asks for the time. "I don't like this. It's late."

The Hispanic gives Bill's sleeve a tug. "Teach'," he says, and jerks his chin.

Bryant follows the line to the shadow show behind Mo's chintzy shade: Teach' with her sweatshirt over her head, those funky little breasts of hers—

"Jesus," Motta says. "Some Teach'." Then, quickly, "Sorry, buddy."

"Sure . . ."

Motta kicks the seat back to give his spider legs some room. He gets a Camel going, takes in a lungful, and blows it in rings.

"Okay, Billy. Now we wait."

Bryant fingers the long canvas case at his side. "Yeah," he says. "That's—cool. What time—"

Motta gives him the latest in low-cunning looks. "Uh, Billy, by the way," he drawls. "You *do* know how to use that thing?"

"You *crazy?*" Bryant cries. "That's why I'm *goin'* to Japan!"

"*Hamaguri*, Billy."

"What time you got?"

"What time I got." Motta spits out the window and rolls it back up, the smoke in the car now a heavy blue haze. "It's two minutes after the last time you asked. And the shadow doll's still makin' eyes at the moon."

"Goddamn cemeteries . . ."

"Heyyy, watch your mouth. It's cute."

"I just hope Masami can handle the funky *Nihongo*. Been savin' it up, if you know what I mean. Playin' it real nice and easy and shy. None of the Hot Latin Lover stuff, dig? See, I bet she's never done it, 'cept with a horny ole *sankoki han.** So I kick back till she gets here. Start off slow. Make love long. Then show her I know how to talk to a girl. You know what it means when they yell out *'Ii wa!'?* Means 'Come on, sock it to me!' Yeah!"

"You know, I don't think . . . Uh-uh. Could never live across from one."

"Billy, if it bothers— Whoops! Hi! Hello there! How are *you?*"

Bryant looks over and sees Motta grinning and waving at the shadow doll, whose eyes are clearly on them now. The doll waves back, then returns to the moon.

"Now, *that,*" Motta tells him, "is the kind of fuckin' weirdo you don't wanna be livin' across from."

"You ever hurt somebody—bad?"

The Hispanic looks at Bryant with almost wounded eyes. "What the hell kinda question is that?"

"I mean—you ever *do* it?"

Motta chews on the question a second. Lights up a Camel. Shows Bill his watch. "It's ten to twelve. Okay?"

"I don't like this."

"Will. You. Wait."

"What time is it?"

"I just gave you the time!"

Bryant asks for a Camel, his first smoke in years. The first blast roars right through him like a runaway Mack truck. The second blast is lighter. The third, a warm smoky dream. "Thanks," he says, "I needed that."

---

*Three-and-a-half-stroke man; quick shooter.

"There's a word for what *you* need. Well, lookee there, it's Teach' again. What's she doin', anyway?"

Almost imperceptibly, the bedroom has started to dim.

"She's blowing out the candles, man."

After the last is extinguished, Mo cuts the living room light. Before their eyes, the distant light transforms to a flickering glow.

Then darkness, as she shuts the door.

Motta zips his jacket, pulls the black shitkicker's toque to his ears. Then he slips his piece out of his pocket to double-check the action. "Now," he says, "we fuckin' *wait.*"

"What time is it?"

"You've got the watch!"

Motta fumbles and looks, unaccountably spooked. "I don't like—"

"What *time* is it!"

"Twelve-oh-five."

"Midnight. She started at midnight last night . . ."

"I say— Wait a minute . . ."

"What?"

"Shadow doll ain't at the window."

"The back!"

Spider Legs and Funky Boy leave the car shaking behind them, taking the pavement in long frenzied strides up the alley between the two houses.

Stopping at this window first to gaze through bars and scant sliver of drapes upon an astonishing sight:

Mo, pale in the glow of the candles, hair cascading to her waist over a rainbow kimono.

Standing there, just standing there, looking small and helpless, tiny hands lost somewhere under the silk. She seems to be looking right through them under lids of sleeping eyes.

Footsteps somewhere in the night.

Echoes of somebody calling her name through a window that seems to be miles away.

An achingly familiar voice.

But there are just so many now, all of them calling and coming back home.

A hundred candles in her soul.

And seven black boys in the night, dancing in absolute stillness.

Re-laxxxxx . . .

Footsteps pacing. Voices calling. Someone raging at the bars somewhere in the Grand Hotel.

Come out of the darkness and into the light.

Heavy shuffling sounds below. Low dirge of black midnight crossings come home.

Come to me. Come to me.

Stair creakings under incredible weight, now making its way to the light.

Come home . . .

"I don't *like* this," Motta says. "She's out of it. She's out to lunch. Come on, come on! Around the back!"

The Hispanic has half cleared the alley when the absence of footsteps behind catches up.

Bryant is bleating pathetically, "Mo! Wake up, Mo, it's Bill!"

"You fuckin' comin' or goin' or what?"

"The goddamn door is *locked!*" Bill screams.

Motta spits and shakes his head. And then he's off and running, the Saturday night special in hand. "You dumb prick!"

Footsteps racing in the night. Wild shouts.

Be still now.

It's okay . . . My door is there . . . And here you are and so am I . . . And here it comes now . . . Hear it? . . .

Footsteps almost at the door.

Heavy breathing.

It's okay . . .

Nails raking the door top to bottom.

Come home . . . Come home . . .

"Come in," she says.

Funky Boy crying and tearing the zipper and dropping the case, like a clown, to his feet.

Sobbing madly, "Should've gone!"

And tearing the bow from its casing.

"Seven days a week," he wails, "and I can't shoot worth a *shit!*"

Spider Legs keeping his cool at the door, checking the scene before making his play. 'Cause the inside looks quiet and warm as a church. And Teach', as they all know, is funky as hell. And a shot in the night over nothing would—

BOOM!!!

Seven black boys in the night . . .

Mo is rolling her shoulders and letting them in, all of the footsteps and voices and candles, into the light of her *hara,* when she hears the great crash of the door.

And feels the dark presence behind her.

She turns.

Oni home come. Sweetness now. Inside cozy place to step. Naked and savage, unstoppable now. She-thing standing, little girl, wide-eyed and looking for mercy. But none. Long darkness before now. Long darkness to come. *Oishi.i.* Delicious girl. Bright interlude. Your candle-

light . . .

(*For God's sake—*

put that—)

Rustlestir.

Oni roaring light too bright!

(*Daddy!*)

(*Mommy!*)

(*Darling—*)

"Ben?"

She-thing in kimono crazy she-thing calling someone crazy he-thing pounding at—

ROARRRRRRRROOOOO!

Motta smashes the glass and is drawing a bead when suddenly the monster turns and spews out an ocean of foul-smelling shit. The door shudders. Panes shatter. And Motta tumbles down the stairs, retching and howling with anger.

He barely makes it to his knees when another great crash lands him back on his butt.

The back door, he discovers, has been doubled by the first.

"You cocksucker!" he screams. "Nobody shits on me! No-bo-dy!"

And, still screaming, he flies down the stairs to the cellar.

Funky Boy's fingers are bleeding from his efforts to string the long bow. He hears the screaming in the back. And then Mo's cry. And then his own as another blast comes at his window. Oh, shit . . .

The third wave half covers one wall. Easy now . . . Relax . . . Re-laxxx . . .

Mo cradles the *katana,* holding it close to her *hara* under the rainbow of silk.

"Ben," she croons. "Oh Ben, it's you."

The *oni* rages at the light with rows on rows of snapping teeth, monster muscles ripping through the seams of old Ben's shirt.

"*Omoimasen ka?* Remember? It's me."

The *oni* roars and snaps and spews. And Mo is covered, head to toe, reeling from the smell of it and from the unspeakable insult.

Seven black boys . . .

Easy, girl . . .

Hundreds of candles have sputtered and died, abominably dripping.

Hundreds still remain, though. And the time is almost—*chōdo ii.* So she shifts her position a little, a child's step to the left and back, calling the *oni* out to her.

And it looks like it's ready to take the small step. Into range of one lethal overhead slat, dripping, dripping, on the pine,

when—

Motta thunders up the stairs, shrieking "Mother—Jesus!"

His eyes had been blazing. The fire goes out. The gun slips right out of his fingers. He is looking at Conan, with choppers like knives and eyes to give Lucifer nightmares. Just then, the demon swings one arm, very fast, very clean, with nails that weigh in at four inches, two pounds. And as he falls, Motta knows that he really is going to pieces. Body tumbling down the stairs, thumpity-thumpity-thumpitythump, while here *he* is rolling like some bloody ball. Blinded with the shame and pain and the last and worst thought of them all: Masami would never forgive him.

* * *

Bryant hears the screams inside, Mo's and Motta's and *its*—**ROARRRRRROOOOO!**—and is smashing the glass with the tip of the bow, screaming himself as he tears at the curtains. And screaming again at the sight of the *haze* that hangs there where they've fallen. A thick brown fog that blinds him to everything beyond it. And blows him over when he breathes.

"Oh, Jesus Christ, I should've *gone!*"

But he slips on an arrow and tries not to breathe, zeroing in on those cool funky Zenmen shooting their arrows out straight from the Void. Blindfolded bull's-eyes at midnight.

Mo screams and spins. And, in a Three as fast as any dreamed of, flips. Midway, she unsheathes the *katana*. And, landing, cuts one of the ropes.

ROARRRRRROOOOO!

Mo sheds the kimono beside the lost wig. There's no time to look, but the flash is so gleeful—so bloody-outrageously good!—

the *oni,* rocketed right off the ground by the force of the blow and the great jolt of pain, one candle spike nailing its shoulder, another homing just under its throat.

A bright current of hope charges through her. And she knows there is nothing beyond her tonight.

You like that Three?

Well, here's another!

I'll give you three Threes in a row!

She eyes the slat that is aimed for the groin.

Then she's airborne and smiling and nothing can stop her—

Funky Boy aiming and thinking, Don't aim, 'cause it doesn't make any damn difference at all, the bull's-eye comes out of the *hara,* the Void, you point your finger, not the bow, and that's okay for starters, boy, but when you've gotta lose them too, no fingers or legs in the Void, boy, only bull's-eye and blindfolded Zenmen.

Come on, do it, Funky Boy.

And God help him he does it, he does, really does, he feels the shot leaving the heart of the Void, drawn on to the bull's-eye **ROARRRR-ROOOOO**, and the joy in his heart is too much for one man—

But how can it be that she's screaming like that?

The arrow enters her left side at a dire angle: just under the ribs and narrowly missing the gallbladder and colon.

Her body feels jerked, by molten barbed wire, from the smooth arc she had set on.

Crazy arms scrambling for balance.

That's wrong . . .

Legs akimbo.

Wrong, all wrong . . .

Torso twisted.

Big mistake.

But

(Rock 'n' roll got *made* by dudes who thought they were singing like black guys!)

somehow—though she can't see through the red—seven black boys in the night bring her to the ground.

For a moment she lies there, aware she is stunned, yet thinking how dreadfully sharp the point of her life has become. All that talk of *haras*, when the point of it all was right here in her side.

She feels it with her fingers first.

Then lifts her head to see the point redwinking in the candlelight, along with three inches of shaft.

She sees the *oni* grinning then. As it takes a deep breath. Tears out the spikes. And shatters the slat on its knee.

"Mo!"

Funky Boy loading another, but lost. The screaming has stopped. There are no more *roarrrrroooooos.* He should've gone. He should've! As long as he lives he will know this, unless—

(*Come on, come on! Around the back!*)

He falters. Babbles. Hates his voice.

(*You dumb prick!*)

"The fuck I am!"

Funky Boy standing there, holding his ground, willing the fingers right off his hands, and then the hands off at the wristbones. And finally he disappears, must be like some cool funky Zenman. Only the bow now. Only the arrow—awaiting the bull's-eye to strike.

Good time now to *oni* come. She-thing broken bleeding good. Good be blood. Good be pain. Good be she-thing lying there. Rustlestir. Rustlestir. Feeling fading rustlestir. Old one lost in body pain. Body pain be *oni* strong. (*For God's sake, put that—*) Rustlestir. Darkness filling *oni* heart. All black making candles be. Rustlestir. Rustlestir. Feeling fading deeply good. Long time coming. Long time gone. *Oni* only time be

Now . . .

Closing now be old one eyes.

Looking now be *oni* eyes.

Oni light be now to see darkness in this she-thing soul.

Oni now play she-thing game.

"*Aka-chan?* Darling girl . . ."

Mo comes to with a gasp of pain, but not from

the shaft that's still piercing her side. It is the light, the blinding light, and the sound of lost heavenly music. *Sorei.* Here there are no candles or need for anything like light. For in *sorei* the clouds are of such purity and beauty that everything they touch turns white.

She feels her body rising on a magical billow of clouds. No need to walk. They carry you. In *sorei* there is only surrender.

Floating. She is floating. Wonderstruck, it seems, through eyes. An illusion, she knows this, for surely she's died. And in *sorei*, where all are one, surely a spirit has no need of eyes. But, what the heyyy, she thanks the gods and savors the image before her.

Mother, it is mother, alive in cherry blossom silk and as young as the day Mo was born.

"*Aka-chan* . . . My baby . . . Come . . ."

And Mo is whispering, "Yes, mother, yes," as the wonder-clouds carry her closer to home.

Funky Boy blinks. He hears music inside. Music and a voice that sounds like a heavenly choir of one. And the sadness, the beautiful sadness, wells in his heart and pours out of his eyes. He lowers the bow and just listens and weeps.

"*Aka-chan* . . . Oh, darling girl . . ."

Mother is smiling the sweetest of smiles.

Mo reaches out to touch that hair, the blackest, most beautiful hair in *sorei.* But her fingers are no longer fingers, of course, and the pleasure of touch was a thing of the earth.

Mother's flowing and beautiful hair feels oddly—coarse and lifeless.

Saa . . .

Mother takes Mo's hand in hers, the smallest and daintiest hands ever seen.

But—why do the hands feel so hairy and huge?

And why is the point, vaguely, still in her side?

"*Aka-chan*—I need you!"

"*Hai.*"

Mother raises Mo's hands to her strawberry lips.

But—how, in *sorei,* can Mo feel the *hot* breath?

"Darling, darling, little girl." Mother kisses Mo's dream of a pinkie and croons, "I've been so lonely.

"And empty.

"And—*hungry.*"

Suddenly the music stops. And Funky Boy, swooning, comes to with the slap of the piercing and terrible cry.

There is no time.

The time is now.

"Mo!" he screams. "Get down! Get down!"

He draws on the power of ten thousand Zenmen and feels himself fading fast in the night: first the head; then the feet; with the arms and the legs on their heels. But the fingers—he can't shake them! Fingers, fingers on the bow! And he's *aiming,* he can't help himself, at a bull's-eye just over her head.

How astonishing that in *sorei* you could lose bits and pieces of things you have lost.

She is thinking, or dreaming she's thinking, this thought as mother encircles her finger.

Slowly and exquisitely.

And snapsevers it at the first knuckle.

Mo hears the cry and thinks it's hers and thinks there are more cries behind her. But how can there be, this is *sorei,* and Mother looks so—

Twannnnnnnnnngggggggggggg!

Swoooooooooossssssssshhhhhhh!

Thwack!

Quivvvvvvvvverrrrrrrrrrr!

You're such a silly—

Billy?

There aren't any arrows in heaven, you know!

Even *oka-san* looks over her shoulder, smiling at the sight of it. Lost in the clouds far above us, way over there on the—

wall?

Mother smiles, licking her lips with a tongue that looks like it goes on for miles. Loving eyes, now raging eyes. Snowteeth, sprung to dagger size.

But—

Seven black boys in the night . . .

Easy now . . . Easy, Mo . . .

Silly Billy's little arrow still quivering there in the clouds, on the

Wall.

Silly arrow, off by a mile, but wearing a chunk of the

Rope

on its nose.

Twine stretching.

Strands snapping.

Slat creaking overhead.

Candles burning to be sprung.

But the foot to the left is a mile to go.

Seven black boys in the night . . .

Come to me . . . I need you now . . .

Long tongue lapping final spurts from the stub of finger.

(Come on, baby, give me ten and you can slap mah hand again!)

"Okā-san," she murmurs. "It's cold here. Please let us go to the light."

Mo taking inch-sized steps, leading the *oni* with love in her eyes.

All the way . . . *Makoto* now . . .

Finally, they're standing there, hot wax dripping from above.

Twine stretching.

Strands snapping.

Slat straining and creaking like crazy.

Mo extends the bloody stub, the price of a few seconds' time.

"Prease, mother, you must have more. I want you to have *all* of me."

Shikata ga nai, no, it cannot be helped!

The *oni* stretches back its lips and slowly encircles the stub to the root. It rolls its eyes and is ready to snap.

When something snaps inside Mo first.

(*Attitude . . .*)

(*Wrong is right . . .*)

"*Chotto!* Just a minute!"

Creeeeeaaaaakkkkk.

"Prease, this helps me—*concentrate . . .*"

She twists one finger up her nose, wagging the rest of her fingers.

"*Aa,*" she says, "that feels so good." She unscrews her finger—(not this—*dekinai!*)—and holds it up straight as an arrow. A tiny green catch on the tip.

The *oni*'s eyes open as wide as its jaw as she licks up the snot with a flicker of tongue.

"*Oishikatta!* Very good! Here . . . This is for you—*Ben!*"

The finger just floats there a moment—

CREEEEEAAAAAKKKKK!

—then homes with deadly speed into the center of one eye.

(Seven black boys . . .)

(Make that eight . . .)

Mo licketysplits to the floor, beneath the slash of razor claws.

ROARRRRROOOOO!

The next scream comes from hell itself as the nine-foot overhead springs free.

Mo screaming, "Now, Billy! Now, Billy, now!" while backrolling over and off to one side, and hoping to heaven his aim has improved.

NowBillynowBillynowBillynow!

Ten thousand Zenmen—and none worth a shit!

Funky Boy, finished and emptied of hope, stands there raging at the night.

He feels cheated and useless, and knows it's all lies, the fool dreams of Zenmen and magical Voids. All there is is here and now, a funky, thick-lipped, heartstruck boy losing the woman he loves.

He wails, "Shit!"

And he closes his eyes.

And he just lets go.

Mo's thinking this may be a fine way to die, just standing here watching the *oni*'s crazed spin. Unable for the life of it to begin to think where to begin. With the spike through its skull, or the pair through its spine, or the ripsnorting fourth up the anus. Or, perhaps . . . with the last arrow straight through its maw.

Candles, candles on the wall, begging her to set them free. With a flick of her wrist, the mere kiss of the blade.

That too would be wonderful.

But she is fading, fading fast and knows there is a better way.

For once in her life now to—go all the way.

Makoto . . . Makoto . . .

Makoto!

"Mo!"

She hears the cry behind her. And she answers, faintly, "No."

"Now?"

"*Iie,* Billy! Close your eyes . . . Close and, slowly, count to four . . ."

Mo drops the *katana* and gives it a kick.

The angle is funky.

But— Welrl, wrong is right . . .

"One!"

This is surely a wonderful number . . . There's— one of me and . . . one of you . . . and one hope in my heart . . . as I lead you to—

"Two!"

Every bit its equal . . . in arcane fascination . . . I have two eyes . . . two ears . . . two lips . . . two nostrils . . . two hands and two—

"Three!"

A number, in the Higher Math, of the utmost significance. For One and Two are Three, you see . . . And Three can only lead to—

"Four!"

The *oni* wheels to face her, now working the spikes from its spine. But the stickmen have come home to her, with seven black boys in Times Square. All of her life has been lived for this night. And even the slip on her blood on the pine speeds her along, as if placed by the gods.

She twists, midair, as she snatches the sword. Twist-reverses for the Four. And deadbolts the *oni* supremely with iron squeeze of scissored legs.

There is no pause.

There is no Five.

There is no break in the arc of the Six.

The *oni* roars and bucks, then screams, as its head bounds off in a geyser of shit that douses three candles above it. And the fountain, like Fuji, continues to spew.

The body spins and thrashes in its frenzied, final dance. She locks her legs and rides it, rides, determined to go all the way. And Mo is laughing in her heart as she feels herself fall to the Void.

EPILOGUE

This rare night in September.

Mo has taken a small studio on one corner of Washington Square. Home in the heart of the Village at last. Nights, the hallway rubadubs play doorman for a dollar. Mornings, she takes gingerly steps over their comatose bodies. The faucets drip. The walls have cracks. And mice too cagey for the traps party all night in the pantry. But none of this makes any difference to Mo, who can stand at the window for hours on end watching the great flow of life in the Square.

Or reading last month's headlines in the September sky:

JAP BEAUTY LOSES FINGER, QUEENS MONSTER LOSES HEAD!
2 HEADLESS TORSOS FOUND—IN 200 LBS. OF . . . YECH!
NEW YORK'S FAVORITE LADY RELEASED FROM HOSPITAL!
CRIMINAL CHARGES STILL PENDING? COME ON!!!
KENDO CUTIE BOUNCED AND SUED BY MONSTER LADY LANDLORD!

Oh, welrl . . . Life goes on as always—completely on the air . . .

Her new room is a happy suspension of the atoms in her soul. *Bonsais* on the windowsill, beneath a snow-white lantern . . . Brilliant posters on the wall, of the Boss, Kyoto, Madonna, Mount Fuji—and Mr. July, neatly framed and well hung . . .

Two Muppet dolls from Georgie protect the pair of folding screens setting off the futon in the corner.

Upon the crimson sheets they lie.

Funky Girl and Funky Boy.

One small candle's burning now and even that seems much too bright, their eyes are so helplessly open.

"Oh boy," she says. "Oh Billy. I never knew that thing before."

"Say what?"

"I mean, I never went."

"You *came?*"

*"Hai, ikimashita**."

Funky Boy taking her hand now, the left.

She flinches.

He says, "Easy, Mo," and draws it gently to his lips to kiss the sewed stub of her finger.

She whispers, "That's *makoto,* Billy. That means your heart goes all the way."

He touches the scar on her belly and says, "Maybe I'll take up the flute."

"Shh . . . I need to *go* again."

"Japanese."

"English." Mo winks and smiles craftily, climbing back on board. "It *rearry* saved my *rife.*"

---

*I went. (The Japanese do, indeed, "go" when Americans "come." The timing can get tricky, but the contrast is exquisite.)